Praise for *A Letter from Lancaster County*

"*A Letter from Lancaster County* is a touching story that explores the way relationships intertwine and the varying ways people interpret the same truths. This book drew me in from the beginning, kept me guessing, and touched my heart—everything I want in a book. Highly recommended."

Beth Wiseman, bestselling author of the
Daughters of the Promise series

"Two sisters, one man, and a Mennonite farm are at the heart of Kate Lloyd's new novel about family ties. When Angela and Rose, sisters who are opposite in every way, return to their mother's childhood home, they come to grips with issues long neglected...and emerge from the visit transformed. Lloyd's fine storytelling in *A Letter from Lancaster County* will captivate and delight fans."

Suzanne Woods Fisher, bestselling author of *The Quieting*

"Kate Lloyd's *A Letter from Lancaster County* is a wonderful read. I was wrapped up in Angela and Rose's story from the first page and couldn't read it fast enough. Kate has a way of writing that feels fresh and new. It was descriptive, meaningful, at times humorous, and always gripping. Anyone who picks up a novel by Kate Lloyd is in for a treat."

Shelley Shephard Gray, *New York Times* and
USA Today bestselling author

"From the first page, I was drawn into this lovely story and felt as if I were walking with the characters through the plain and simple community in Lancaster County. This book will touch your heart."

Vannetta Chapman, author of *Anna's Healing*

"Fans of Kate Lloyd will adore this new women's fiction set in Amish country. Dynamic protagonists and an increasingly tense narrative set the scene for a heart-wrenching and engaging story."

Laura V. Hilton, author of *The Amish Wanderer*

"Kate Lloyd's newest novel offers an insightful look into the lives and loves of two very different sisters. While dealing sensitively with the very real issues of temptation, brokenness, and unforgiveness, Lloyd manages to avoid pat answers while still offering the hope of redemption. *A Letter from Lancaster County* is a thoroughly engaging read."

Ann Tatlock, award-winning author of *Once Beyond a Time*

"In *A Letter from Lancaster County*, Kate Lloyd tells a thoughtful and compelling story of two sisters and their life-changing journey. Kate's sense of setting (lovely!) and her depiction of realistic characters quickly draws readers into the drama. As the story unfolds, themes of reconciliation and redemption are explored in a heartfelt and gracious manner."

Leslie Gould, bestselling and Christy Award–winning author

"Beautifully written, *A Letter from Lancaster County* is a truly mesmerizing tale."

Patrick Craig, author of the Apple Creek Dreams series

A Letter from Lancaster County

Kate Lloyd

HARVEST HOUSE PUBLISHERS
EUGENE, OREGON

Cover by Garborg Design Works

The author is represented by MacGregor Literary, Inc.

This is a work of fiction. Names, characters, places, and incidents are products of the author's imagination or are used fictitiously. Any resemblance to actual persons, living or dead, is entirely coincidental.

A LETTER FROM LANCASTER COUNTY
Copyright © 2017 by Kate Lloyd
Published by Harvest House Publishers
Eugene, Oregon 97402
www.harvesthousepublishers.com

ISBN 978-0-7369-7021-1 (pbk.)
ISBN 978-0-7369-7022-8 (eBook)

Library of Congress Cataloging-in-Publication Data

Names: Lloyd, Kate (Novelist)
Title: A letter from Lancaster county / Kate Lloyd.
Description: Eugene, Oregon : Harvest House Publishers, [2017]
Identifiers: LCCN 2017002904 (print) | LCCN 2017007079 (ebook) | ISBN 9780736970211 (paperback) | ISBN 9780736970228 (ebook)
Subjects: LCSH: Amish--Fiction. | Lancaster County (Pa.)--Fiction. | Domestic fiction. | BISAC: FICTION / Christian / Romance. | GSAFD: Christian fiction.
Classification: LCC PS3612.L58 L48 2017 (print) | LCC PS3612.L58 (ebook) | DDC 813/.6--dc23
LC record available at https://lccn.loc.gov/2017002904

Printed in the United States of America

17 18 19 20 21 22 23 24 25 / LB-SK / 10 9 8 7 6 5 4 3 2 1

PROLOGUE

*S*ilvia Donato's hand shook as she put her pen's tip to the stationery. She hesitated, but then prodded herself no matter how much her fingers ached. This was her last chance to repair much of what had gone wrong. Before it was too late.

> *Dearest Angela and Rose,*
>
> *Please visit me. This invitation may sound crazy. After so many years, I wouldn't blame you if you couldn't care less about your aunt. But I'm getting older, and how I regret not asking you sooner, as well as the tension between your mother and me that separated us for so long.*
>
> *How can I entice you to travel clear across the country? For one thing, I still live in your grandparents' house where your mother grew up. You might wish to take a memento home with you. Anything you like. Lancaster County is truly magnificent. To my way of thinking, autumn is its finest season. Please come.*
>
> *Fondly,*
> *Aunt Silvia*

ONE

Angela

My younger sister and I trailed our cousin Phyllis across the slate path toward Aunt Silvia's house. I inhaled Lancaster County's earthy farmland aromas and a trace of smoke wafting through a wooded area, up from the valley below. Horses clip-clopping in the distance sounded like muted steeple bells from another century.

A kaleidoscope of expectations swirled through my chest. I felt as if I were a little girl opening a present, discovering Santa had delivered exactly what I'd asked for.

But then I glanced over my shoulder and saw Rose lugging her duffel bag like the hunchback of Notre Dame—acting like a five-year-old, when in fact she was thirty-six. Was she limping? This morning, she'd made a last-minute trip to a restroom near our gate and then sprinted onto the plane and lobbed her bag into an overhead bin just before the flight attendant closed the door. I had nearly hastened back down the jet bridge, convinced she wouldn't make it and I'd be on my own.

A temporary lapse in judgment, she'd labeled it—her excuse for all her wild stunts. Like finding her boyfriends in bars. They could be serial killers, for all she knew. Not that I didn't have my own foibles. But asking her to come on this trip could have been a mistake.

Several yards from the front door, Phyllis brought our lopsided trio to an abrupt halt to dig through her purse for a key, giving Rose time to catch up. She dropped her bag and lifted her chin to survey the two-story red structure, once our grandparents' residence. Her dark bangs slanted across one eye. "Was the house always this color?"

"Yes." Elation rang in my voice because I was jazzed to be here. Finally. "Remember Mom's photo?" When she was still alive, our mother kept that photo in her desk drawer, out of Dad's sight.

Rose squinted at the clapboard siding. "It reminds me of a caboose. You'd never see a house that bright in Seattle."

Heat surged up my neck. "Rose, where are your manners?" Her scowl told me I sounded like Mom, her former nemesis.

She glanced at Phyllis. "Sorry, cuz, I didn't mean to be disrespectful." Rose and I hadn't set eyes on Phyllis for twenty years, and my sister was already calling her a pet name.

Phyllis spoke in run-on sentences. "Not a problem, if I had my way Ma would sell this dinosaur and move into assisted living. Sorry she's not here I told Ma what time I was picking you up at the airport." Her mousy brown hair hung limply around her small face, and her pinched features hinted of frustration as she mounted the one step.

When Phyllis jiggled the key into the lock, an ocean of throaty barking erupted. She tugged the door open and a black mongrel the size of a Saint Bernard barged out.

Rose, usually brave—reckless was a better description—dropped her bag and tucked her hands under her chin. "Does it bite?"

"Only an occasional FedEx driver. Pay no attention to Rex, he's all show although the postal carrier refuses to set foot on the property. If Ma's mail won't fit in the box down by the road it doesn't get delivered." She kneed the massive dog out of her way and entered the house.

With hackles raised, Rex sniffed my pant leg. I hoped he really was a pussycat behind his bravado. I took a chance and extended a palm to the dog's graying muzzle. He gave my fingers a cursory sniff before trotting into the house, clearing an avenue for me to follow Phyllis.

For the first time in two decades I crossed the threshold of the family home. Aunt Silvia, Mom's younger sister, had kept our grandparents' well-worn furniture exactly as it was. The same oval, braided rug spread across the hardwood floor to the rock fireplace. The low-beamed ceiling hung above paned windows framed by walnut-stained timber, and the couch dissected the room, creating a dining area on the other side.

I sniffed the air. "Something smells good. Baking squash?"

"Good Lord, Ma left the oven on?" Phyllis loped past the dining table and into the kitchen, with Rex scrambling after her, barking. "Hush!" she yelled at the dog, and he fell silent.

Through the doorway I saw Phyllis yank open the oven, peer at something inside, and then slam the oven door before turning a knob. She raised her hands above her head and shook them, as if imploring the Almighty. Then her arms flopped to her sides and she returned to the living area.

"Sorry 'bout that I swear Ma's going to burn this house down." She expelled a lengthy breath. "Well, guess we should get you two settled."

"I know where I want to sleep." I guided my wheeled suitcase through the living area and down the hall to the back bedroom, as if drawn by a magnet. There was the canopy bed Mom used as a girl, and where Rose and I slept on our few childhood visits with Mom. My mind hadn't exaggerated how high the four-poster stood. I needed to stretch on tiptoes to sit on the patchwork quilt, and when I did the mattress squished down comfortably like a feather pillow.

Rose poked her head in. "Where should I go?"

I knew from experience, when Rose was miserable the whole world suffered. I said, "You can have this room, if you want it." But I sent her mental images of luxuriating in another bedroom; I didn't want to give up my Shangri-La.

"Nope, you get first dibs. Coming to Pennsylvania is your gig."

Hoping to release the tension building in my temples, I yanked my shoulder-length hair out of the scrunchie. "Don't say that, Rosie. We're in this boat together."

She didn't reply, as if our dinghy had already sunk.

Phyllis appeared at Rose's elbow. "Ma uses the bedroom across the hall for sewing and ironing, but there's another one right above this."

"I remember. The itty-bitty one." Rose's face turned glum, but she never looked bad. Her black brows and Venus de Milo mouth gave her the appearance of a young, brown-eyed Elizabeth Taylor. My opposite in every way.

While she and Phyllis climbed the wooden staircase, I kicked off my loafers, dangled my feet over the side of the bed, and admired the wallpaper—lilac blossoms floating against creamy beige—Mom might have picked out as a girl. At my feet spread the hooked rug—a floral motif—where she must have played with dolls.

If she liked dolls. I knew little about her childhood; she rarely spoke about it. I had countless questions, one reason I'd come to see Aunt Silvia. Although my husband, Frederick, a master at cross-examining witnesses, had warned me I might not like what I found. Before hiring a private detective to shadow a client's spouse, he often cautioned them, "If you can't live with the worst-case scenario, sometimes it's better to let sleeping dogs lie."

Overhead, floorboards creaked and complained. Hearing Rose's muffled voice sent a thud of sadness through my chest. My only sibling had disliked me since we were teenagers. Boom, one day my sweet giggly little sister metamorphosed into an ogre. An onset of raging hormones? Or had she been snubbed at school by the queen bee? And I didn't think she had a boyfriend to break her heart until at least college. In any case, I would have done anything to repair our tug-of-war relationship, including making this trip together.

Minutes later, Rose plodded into the room and landed on the

rocking chair by the lace-curtained window. She was wearing skinny jeans, riding low on her hips, and she'd changed from her turtleneck into a V-neck sweater, a provocative look I thought was inappropriate here in the land of the Amish.

"My bedroom's cozy," she said, which I assumed meant cramped.

"You'd better sleep here, Rosie." I slid off the bed and gave it a pat. "I insist. I was acting selfishly. You deserve to enjoy yourself too."

"Nah, that's okay. I'll get used to it. The bed upstairs is too small for you."

I clenched my teeth, flattened my lips.

"I don't mean you're big, sis. Just four inches taller than I am."

I let Rose's comment go. If I agreed or disagreed, she'd be all over me like a hornet.

She rocked back and forth, the toes of her suede boots tapping the floor. "Really, the whole room is made for a shrimp like me." She was trying to gloss over her innuendo that I'd grown porky. But she was right. I'd gained over twenty pounds since giving birth years ago: ten per child, and several more consoling myself with food after Frederick informed me he was getting a vasectomy, as if he were going to do nothing more life-shattering than remove an inconvenient mole.

"Pay no attention to me" she said, breaking into my reflections. "I'm acting cranky."

Phyllis leaned through the doorway. She was my age, thirty-nine; the skin at the corners of her eyes was accumulating the same pesky crow's feet as mine. "I've got to get back to work." She frowned at her wristwatch. "Where could Ma be?"

"We can entertain ourselves," I said. "She's so nice to have us."

"Rose sprang to her feet with agility. "Yeah, nice." In her heeled boots she stood almost my height.

"In her letter, Aunt Silvia seemed determined that we visit." I hoped our aunt hadn't been overly gracious when she'd written us. I couldn't really remember what she was like, but Dad said Aunt

Silvia and Mom hadn't gotten along. Rose thought their dispute had to do with a man, her answer to everything.

"Yep, Ma's the best," Phyllis said without conviction. "But call me if anything unusual arises, okay? My number's by the phone."

Rose and I followed her out the front door. Afternoon salmon-colored sunlight stippled the amber and russet-colored leaves in the wooded hillside above the home. I was relieved when Rex trotted around the side of the house—in case the mailman had pegged the dog right.

"Sorry gotta run," Phyllis said. "Let's get together before you leave." She bustled to her SUV as if she couldn't wait to make her exit. A moment later, her vehicle lurched over the gravel driveway, stopped at the road to allow a horse and buggy to pass, and then sped away.

I was tempted to dash down to the road to grab a look at the buggy, but it was too late. As we were chauffeured here from the Philadelphia Airport, I'd seen many horse and buggies, but Phyllis kept her SUV aimed straight ahead, skimming by them without interest.

Meandering back to the house, I inhaled to my fullest. The late-autumn breeze—a potpourri of moist soil, drying corn husks, and fallen leaves—was as fragrant as ripening grapes at a vineyard.

An automobile approached from the other direction. Then an aged, beige-metallic Buick ground into the drive and stopped in front of the weathered two-car garage that looked as though it hadn't been opened for years. My feet skipped across the path when I spied Aunt Silvia's face through the Buick's window. She didn't resemble our mother, who'd been fair-skinned and blonde like me. Silvia's salt-and-pepper hair, once espresso-brown like Rose's and long enough to wear in a bun, was lopped to about three inches.

"Hello, dear ones." Silvia got out. "I'm sorry. I meant to be home earlier." Standing several inches shorter than I did, she clasped me in a tight embrace; I felt more bones than flesh. As she hugged Rose, Silvia's eyes moistened behind her tortoiseshell glasses. She patted under them with her fingertips. "Finally, I'll get to know Juliana's daughters, all grown up."

When I heard Mom's name, my breath froze in my throat. After a year, I thought my mourning period was over, but a familiar aching tightened my chest like goliath hands gripping my ribs. Her death remained a mystery, a slow decline that had lasted a couple of decades. Each specialist gave a different perspective: arthritis, MS, lupus, fibromyalgia. Then heart failure.

Silvia reached into the car to retrieve a small paper bag and tucked it in her purse, out of sight. "I had several errands…"

"That's okay," I said. "We're just happy to be here." At least, I was.

Her mid-calf skirt swaying, Silvia moved around the car and opened the trunk to reveal two full grocery bags. Rose—always a step ahead of me—scooped up the larger one and I took the other.

Halfway to the house, Silvia slowed us to a stop to watch five swallows gliding in flamboyant arcs, then land on the sloped roof. Warmth from the lingering sun radiated off the shingles and transformed the house's siding to rusty-orange. Fortunately, Rose made no snide comments.

"This old place sat empty for over a year after my mother, your Grandma Luisa, passed away," Silvia said.

"I remember." I rearranged the bag in my arms. "When no one wanted it, Mom toyed with the idea of using it as a vacation home."

Rose sneered. "Nah. Father would have nixed that idea in a split second."

"He never had much use for this house," Silvia agreed.

"He calls it a claustrophobic rat's nest," Rose said, and Silvia's beautifully creased face broke into a smile.

"I don't doubt it. He called my mother—your Grandma Luisa—Loose Wheel."

Rose chuckled, and I couldn't help joining in. "I'm glad you moved here," I said. "That it didn't leave the family forever."

"It seemed natural when I became single again." Silvia was a widow, but Mom told us Silvia and her husband, Frank, had been separated when he died. Apparently he was a womanizer who'd propositioned Mom at his own wedding.

Rex bounded out of the woods, panting and flagging his tail. "Where have you been?" Silvia asked him. "In the neighbor's chicken coop again?" As though they'd had this one-sided conversation before. Then she led us around the side of the house and opened the glass-paned kitchen door. Rose and I placed the bags on a yellow Formica table in the center of the room.

With the dog milling at her feet, Silvia pulled out cheeses and meats wrapped in white paper and a loaf of hard-crusted bread. She tugged an apron over her head and cinched the strings around her slender waist. I could tell she'd been digging in the garden, doing chores that had chipped her blunt nails and left a slight discoloration on her fingertips—unlike our mother, who'd insisted on weekly manicures and a housekeeper who kept the family home looking like a page from *House Beautiful*. Not that I blamed Mom; she always seemed fatigued, on the verge of a yawn.

"How was your flight, girls?"

"It took forever," Rose said.

I felt pent-up ire lifting my shoulders. "It wasn't so bad. My frequent-flyer miles upgraded us to first class." I bet it was the only time Rose had sat in the first cabin. "We got a nice chance to chat in the Red Carpet Room in Chicago."

"If you say so."

Had I talked too much during the layover and flight? I chattered on like a parrot sometimes, especially when nervous, which Rose made me because she analyzed every word, storing them away for future ammunition.

"Hey, Aunt Silvia," Rose said. "Want me to set the table?"

"Yes, please." Silvia pointed to a wall cabinet crammed with mismatched china. "Use whatever plates you like. The cutlery's in that drawer and the napkins are in the sideboard in the dining area."

Using methodical movements, Silvia heated oil and butter in the skillet before unwrapping boneless chicken breasts and dredging them through salted flour. As she spoke of her parents—what accomplished chefs they'd been thanks to their Italian roots—I let my vision drift around the room and was transported back to my childhood visits, times of contentment. The same brass light fixture that shined on Grandma Luisa Moretti's shoulders as her plump belly pressed against the sink cast a golden glow. Copper and stainless steel pans and a collection of ladles hung from the rack above the chipped white enamel stove. The air was thick and touchable. The aroma of sweet garlic and basil filled my nostrils. On a wall a framed embroidery proclaimed *Dopo il bruto viene il bello*. Years ago, Mom told me it had something to do with the weather turning beautiful after a storm in Italian.

Thirty minutes later, Silvia poured boiling pasta into a strainer. A cloud of steam burst up, floating to the windowpanes.

"This kitchen smells divine," I said, my mouth watering.

She drizzled olive oil and balsamic vinegar over lettuce leaves, basil, and diced tomatoes and then handed the wooden bowl to me. "Go have a seat, girls," she said, handing me the salad. "I'm almost finished."

I set the bowl on the oval table in the dining area and then straightened the flatware Rose had placed on either side of three blue-and-white plates. The knives faced out—I flipped them over. And the water glasses stood on the wrong side—I repositioned them. Had she forgotten everything Mom taught us?

Rose noticed me; her eyes bulged. "Are we getting compulsively neat in our old age?" Any chance to remind me I was older than she was, and that I fussed too much.

I eased down onto the chair facing the living area. To keep my hands busy, I rotated my wedding band in the white groove on my ring finger. How startling: I hadn't thought about Tiffany, my fourteen-year-old daughter, or my eleven-year-old son, Daniel, for hours. They usually flashed like neon lights in the electrical current streaming through my brain. And Frederick? I must have been more tired than I realized. I could barely visualize what he looked like.

"I guess I should call home," I said. "No, never mind, my cell phone battery's dead. I was so worried about leaving reminder notes for the kids this morning, I forgot my charger." I scanned the room for a telephone and spotted a black model out of the fifties on a side table by the fireplace. "I could use Silvia's."

"Don't bother." Rose parked herself on the chair across from me. "It's three hours earlier in Seattle. Stop worrying. They're fine."

What did she know about raising a family? She was childless and doted over her Cairn terrier as though it were a baby; she was paying a dog sitter forty dollars a day to come to her house to feed and coddle it.

I checked the carriage clock resting on the mantel. "Six p.m. Three in Seattle. I guess you're right, Rosie. The kids are getting out of school and going to their friends' houses. I wonder what Frederick's up to."

"While the cat's away?" Rose raised her sculpted brows as if she knew the inside scoop on Frederick's supposed clandestine activities.

"Don't make insinuations without proper evidence," I said, quoting my husband. "He's on the phone or with clients. Sitting at Daddy's old desk." But his office, once our father's, with its new, plush carpet, cushy leather couch, and gas fireplace, would be a cozy nest for a rendezvous. Only last week, when entering Frederick's office unannounced, I'd found his new paralegal, Stephanie, a voluptuous twentysomething, reading his computer screen over his shoulder. But when she noticed me she straightened her spine. Spouting legal jargon, she'd fled the room.

"You wouldn't want to mess with Freddie Strick," Rose told Silvia as our aunt carried a platter of browned and succulent chicken to the table. "He's a pit bull in the courtroom. Famous for winning humongous divorce settlements." Rose bopped into the kitchen for the bowl of squash and then sat down again.

"Frederick," I said. "He hates to be called Freddie. And you make him sound awful." Not that he didn't enjoy pinning his opponent's shoulder to the mat. A favorable verdict seemed to satisfy him more than helicopter skiing in the Rockies, scuba diving the Great Barrier Reef, or even making love.

"I doubt he'd mind being called aggressive." Rose reached for the water pitcher and filled her glass. "The truth is, I'd hire him myself if I had someone to sue." She gulped a mouthful and found a chunk of ice to crunch into. "That's one advantage of staying single."

"You're trying to convince us you're unmarried by choice?"

"I'd rather be single than stuck in a dead-end marriage."

My hands clenched. Every molecule within me wanted to unleash my tongue and hurl caustic words, but I figured Rose probably wished to be married as much as any woman her age. I should show her compassion.

Thank goodness Silvia paid no heed to our banter. She served the meal, passing Rose and me plates mounded with chicken, noodles, and squash. Rex wandered into the room, plopped down at Silvia's feet, and bellowed out a moan.

My mouth salivated. "That's way too much." I unfolded my napkin, flattened it on my lap atop my black Chico's knit travel slacks. "I'm sort of on a diet."

"Which one this time?" Rose asked.

"Low carbs." I slathered butter over my squash. "I'll start again tomorrow."

She snickered. "I've heard that one before."

"So? We're not all size six petite like you."

"Girls, shall we thank the Lord before we eat?" Silvia bowed her head.

"Oops, sorry." I glanced over to Rose, who wore the expression of a woman sentenced to life imprisonment. Figuring she'd be watching me, I clamped my eyes shut. It wouldn't hurt Rose to pray, not that I attended church other than Easter and Christmas, and mostly because I liked the music. When you hum along with Handel's *Messiah* you feel inspired. But Sundays I was busy orchestrating breakfast, reading the paper, and carpooling Daniel to soccer practice. And it was Frederick's only time to unwind when not away on business or on the golf course.

"Dear heavenly Father, thank you for this meal, for Rose and Angela's safe trip, and for our lives." Silvia's voice cracked with emotion. Then she finished with, "Each day is precious. Amen."

"Amen," Rose mumbled. She sliced off a morsel of chicken, plunked it between her lips, and swallowed. "Aunt Silvia, this is scrumptious."

I sampled the chicken. "Yes, it tastes like a dish Mom made."

Silvia said, "Thank you," but her features lay passively, and she stared straight ahead at nothing in particular. Maybe out the window at the darkening sky?

Rose shot me a quirky glance, and I shrugged back.

I swallowed a mouthful of pasta. "Everything okay?" I touched Silvia's speckled hand, startling her. "You're not eating."

The corners of her mouth lifted, but her eyes remained flat. She jabbed at a lettuce leaf and then set her fork aside. "Suddenly I'm all tuckered out. Would you mind if I napped for a little while?"

"Of course not. I'm worn out from the trip myself." Tired of Rose was more like it.

Silvia used her hands to push herself to a standing position. Her napkin floated to the floor next to Rex, who sniffed it.

"Don't you two girls do a thing. I'll clean the kitchen in the morning." Silvia padded out of the room on bare feet. She'd slipped off her shoes and left them under the table.

"Weird," Rose muttered. For the first time in months I agreed with her.

Two

Rose

Crows cawing outside my bedroom window sounding like arguing old men woke me. Trussed like a mummy, my legs were tangled in sheets and my nightgown was twisted around my waist. Good grief, this lumpy mattress should have been replaced fifty years ago.

I hadn't slept worth a hoot. All last night the crickets outside had resounded like trumpets blaring. Not to mention the clippity-clopping of horses' hooves down on the road. I'd closed the window, which amplified the clicking of the wind-up clock on the dresser. And around midnight I heard an animal scratching on the roof. Attempting to dig through the shingles and into my room? An ill omen, warning me to pack my bags and flee while I still could. How's that for creepy?

A whiff of coffee drifted up the staircase and under my door. I cracked my eyes open to see sunlight glaring through the ivy-patterned curtains. The clock declared it was seven o'clock. Only 4:00 a.m. at home. But I'd never get back to sleep.

I didn't like being a morning person. The early hours were the stillest of the day, when my mind took liberty to retrace the past I couldn't erase from my memory. Always revisiting that hideous night God deserted me.

No, I wouldn't dwell on Dirk Dunnagan another moment.

Rolling onto my side, a muscle spasm zinged from my shoulder up my neck. I stretched to my feet, made a quick trip to the bathroom, and then tugged on jeans and a knit shirt. As I reached for the doorknob, the floorboards under my feet produced a high-pitched creak that made me shudder. I hoped I hadn't awakened Angela. I wasn't ready to hear her cheery "Good morning, Rosie."

I reminded myself I was here to support my big sister. She'd begged me to accompany her on her quest to reunite the family in the land of the Amish. Of all oddball places. Eventually I'd caved in, because I loved her more than anyone. Even if she and I were opposites. I admit, I was prickly and intolerant. A thorny rose bush. But she was too wishy-washy. A weeping willow, swaying in the wind any which way.

I stepped into the hall and saw Silvia's door standing open. Her quilt lay folded back, exposing white sheets. On the nightstand sat a Bible that looked as though it had been read a zillion times, a half glass of water, and a prescription bottle tipped on its side. I hoped it contained benign pills like the blood pressure medication Dad took.

A small wadded-up paper bag crouched on a throw rug. Nothing escaped me. She'd tried to hide her parcel.

At the bottom of the staircase, Rex dozed on his side, blocking my path. What was he? A black Lab and Newfoundland mix? I was a dog lover, but didn't trust this canine, and he knew it. Dogs are smarter than people think. They read body language and voice intonations.

Yesterday, he'd foraged through the kitchen begging while Silvia prepared dinner. She'd tossed him a noodle. Something I would never feed my darling Cairn terrier, Minnie. Human food wasn't good for dogs. In fact, most of it wasn't good for humans. I didn't want to give up the ghost like Mother. She'd had a sweet tooth and rarely consumed fruits and raw vegetables. Her doctors couldn't determine what caused her illness, but her fatigue, migrating pain, dizziness, and mental confusion didn't spontaneously arise out of nowhere. Although I'd wondered if her pitiful condition was psychosomatic.

I descended the stairs. "Good dog?" I said to alert him of my presence.

He responded with a growly moan that could mean either "Hi, babe" or "I'm going to rip your throat out if you come closer."

Assuring myself I could bluff my way through anything, I gathered my courage and stepped over him. He got up and shadowed me to the kitchen. I spotted Silvia dropping two slices of wheat bread into the toaster. She wore a longish skirt and a denim jacket with red embroidery on the pockets and cuffs.

"Hi, Aunt Silvia."

"Good morning. How'd you sleep?"

"Just great." Big lies, little lies. I was a master at deceit. No one would like me if I told the truth.

I pressed my palm across my yawning mouth. "Is Angie up?"

"She's still sleeping." Silvia brought an earthenware mug out of the cupboard. "Coffee?"

"No thanks. I'd better stick to herbal tea if you have it. When I gave up caffeine last year, my head throbbed for days. Not a good idea to go cold turkey, let me warn you. I don't want to suffer through withdrawal again when I get home."

"I have lemon-ginger tea bags." Her hand moved to the kettle. "I'll put on water."

"No, never mind. I need a jolt to wake me. One cup of coffee can't hurt."

She poured syrupy liquid into the mug. I lifted the brew to my nose to inhale the nutty aroma. A moment later, the java grabbed my taste buds, sending a bittersweet message across my tongue. I splashed in half-and-half and then returned to the urn to top off my mug. I got this strange notion that going off my eating regimen was tantamount to wading into quicksand. But I pushed it aside and enjoyed another sip.

Silvia's gaze grew intense. "I've been thinking of you as a little girl all these years. I see the same pretty brown eyes and wavy hair. When did you mature into an adult?"

"I got old, all right. I'm thirty-six. Thirty-seven next April Fools' Day. No joke. And I still hate my hair." I fluffed my curls and screwed up my mouth. "I've had a lifelong battle with this frizz. I've tried everything to make it long and straight, like Angela's. I even bleached it once. Let me tell you, with my olive complexion, I made an ugly blonde. I finally gave up and cut it short."

"Rose, dear, there isn't a woman alive who hasn't battled with her hair. It seems we all wish we looked like someone else."

I couldn't imagine anyone wanting to look like me. Short and nondescript.

"When you get to my stage in life, dear, you're glad to have any hair at all."

"You look great, Aunt Silvia." But I noticed her salt-and-pepper hair thinning in places. Poor thing.

"I gave up trying to change myself." But in truth I'd considered growing out my hair last week when my boyfriend, Brad, ogled a woman with a mane down to her waist. "Any man who wants me will have to take me the way I am."

"Good for you." She tilted her head the way Mother used to. "Is there someone special in your life?"

"Sort of." I felt Rex's moist nose on my hand and then his tongue bestowing a lick. I stroked his broad skull and felt satiny fur.

"I imagine a lovely young woman like you has many suitors."

I sputtered a laugh. "I wish." No husband. No children. Time ticking, almost too late.

"I'll bet the perfect man comes along one of these days, soon. In the meantime, there's plenty to keep a girl busy."

"Good luck convincing Angie. According to her, life's not complete without Mr. Right. Meaning someone exactly like Fred."

"Not your type?"

I felt a prick of guilt. Phooey. I hated it when Angela gossiped, and here I was running off at the mouth. "We have different tastes in men, is all."

"It's better that way." She let out a sigh. "When sisters love the same man, it leads to heartache."

As I waited for her to expound on this juicy topic, I tried to imagine Angela and me falling for the same guy—a calamity that would never occur. Although, I had to admit, Angela chose a good provider like Father. That wasn't a bad thing, even though I sometimes detested how Frederick treated her.

The toast popped up, snagging Silvia's attention. She offered me a slice.

"No, thanks. Too early."

"Never mind, we can eat breakfast later. I don't have much of an appetite either." Silvia left the toast on the counter. "I need to go out to the vegetable garden. Care to join me?"

"Sure. I could use the exercise. At home I do thirty minutes of cardio, and then I lift weights every day. Hope I don't turn into mush while I'm here."

"I can't imagine that will happen in such a short time, dear. Any woman would be envious of your figure."

She took a wicker basket from the window ledge and rattled open the kitchen door. Rex rushed out, sending a half-dozen crows fluttering into a mass. Cool air whooshed into the kitchen, reminding me to fetch my Nikes and a hoodie.

Outside, Silvia set the basket aside to spray our ankles and legs with two kinds of bug repellant, and then she instructed me to tuck my pant legs into my socks.

"Ticks carry Lyme disease." She described the head-of-a-pin-size insects that spread the serious condition and other co-infections I'd never heard of.

I got the willies, feeling itchy-crawly all over. "Maybe we should stay inside?"

"I think you'll be all right." She slipped her arm through the basket's curved handle. "But do be watchful. Tick bites cause some people to get a bull's-eye rash, but many don't notice they've been bitten. We'll check you over carefully when we get back to the house."

I followed her on the walkway heading away from the garage. A stand of maples, dogwoods, and oaks stood between us and the road. Amid the branches, sparrows, goldfinches, and juncos trilled a symphony. I heard the puttering of automobiles and horses' hooves. *People on their way to work*, I thought. Where I should be.

As I recalled, farms and fields extended down the hill. They'd come into view once the garnet and mustard-colored leaves dropped. And the fog lifted. I wouldn't be here that long. Fine by me.

"I remember when you were young, dear," Silvia said. "You wanted to be a veterinarian."

I didn't know why this fact embarrassed me. "Father talked me out of going to veterinary school." I lowered my voice and stabbed the air with my finger, the way he did when driving home a point. "He said, 'If I'm going to dish out that kind of money on your education, you should go to medical school. Who in their right mind would spend their days treating stupid animals?' In the end I didn't do either. I earned a BA in psychology."

"That sounds interesting."

"For some, maybe. My heart wasn't in it."

The path ended. We moved onto dewy grass and strolled toward the vegetable garden. All the while I hoped the bug repellant was doing its job.

To the left, on the hillside staggered in lush knee-high grass, stood half-a-dozen apple trees, their gnarled limbs still partially covered with fruit and foliage. I caught the honeyed scent of fallen apples, smelling like fresh juice. Behind the apple trees, the dense forested hill mushroomed. Looming and unwelcoming.

Ahead, behind a six-foot-high wire fence, lay raised rectangular planting beds.

"I haven't gotten around to harvesting this year, but much is still salvageable." With some maneuvering, Silvia unlatched the wrought iron gate. It opened at a tilt.

I strode inside the vegetable garden and spotted carrot tops, lettuce, cabbage, pumpkins and gourds. Stalks of corn at the far end.

Silvia proceeded to the nearest bed. "When you were young, you said you wanted to live in the country and raise horses."

I chortled to cover up more feelings of discomfort. "I haven't ridden since I was a preteen. I got bucked off after mounting a stallion by mistake. I swore to never get near another horse again."

I stepped back, almost tripping on the raised bed behind me. I regained my balance. "And that was before I discovered Nordstrom and Macy's. Now I can't imagine living more than a ten-minute drive from a department store." Although I couldn't remember the last time I set foot in one. Shopping was Angela's bag.

Silvia yanked several carrots from the black soil and arranged them in her basket. Then picked a head of romaine. "We move at a slower pace out here, but at my age I don't want my days flying by unnoticed and unappreciated."

I tugged up a carrot by its crinkly leaves and handed it to her. "That's how I like it," I said. When my mind was occupied with trivia, I forgot my troubles.

"Then we'll have to find ways to liven things up."

I jotted down the directions to a town Silvia recommended as an excellent hunting ground for antiques. I still hoped to squirm out of going with Angela. My sister could afford to fritter away her money and time. But I was the sole proprietor of a mail-order business. With Christmas only two months away, I should have been home. Boxing and sending out merchandise.

"If I had more energy, I'd go with you." Silvia handed me a key on a safety pin.

I held the key between us. "Sure you don't need your car?"

"Positive. I'll use the time to make phone calls." Her shoulders slumped. She looked fatigued from our walk in the garden.

Minutes later, Angela and I proceeded to the Buick. Rex traveled between us. Reminding us he was alpha male, his hips bumped our legs. Dogs do that. They're pack animals.

"I wish we could have kept our Springer spaniel puppy," Angela said, tentatively patting Rex's back. "But Frederick couldn't stand its toenails scarring the top of his shoes or the way it bounded up and down the stairs."

My hands grasped my hips. "Golly, don't you have any say?"

"Of course I do." She lengthened her stride. Her flats clacked. "Anyway, it was for the best. What do I know about dogs?"

"More than I know about kids and you said I'd make a good mother."

"Well, it's too late now."

The truth of her comment speared right into me. Deflated my lungs. Why would she make such a cruel statement?

She must have noticed my hunched shoulders and narrowed eyes because she added, "I'm referring to the dog, Rosie. You're still young enough to have children."

When we reached the car I thrust the key into the door, found it unlocked. I settled into the driver's seat. Angela galumphed around to the other side. Then I backed us down the drive and paused to watch for cars and buggies.

"We're okay." Angela leaned forward and blocked my view. "You can go now."

"Thanks. It's kind of hard to see through your head." I pulled onto the asphalt road.

The hazy sky drooped low. The crowns of the trees—flashes of canary-yellow, ruby, and ochre—melded into the fog. The car glided along like a water bug on a pond. I tightened my grip on the steering wheel. Silvia must have liked this floaty feeling. But if I wasn't careful we could drift into a field or crash into the next ditch.

Not that I'd lose control of the wheel. I was always alert. At the top of my game. Except for that one afternoon right after Mother died. I hadn't slept well for weeks. In my exhausted state, day-to-day living seemed too hard. Pointless. If only I could close my eyes and submerge into endless slumber I'd find peace, was all I could think. Rolling my car into my garage and lowering its door with the remote, I'd sat with the engine idling. Wondered how long it would take for the fumes to invade my lungs, asphyxiating me. Would my death even be noticed? Doubtful. I was a solitary uninhabited island that wouldn't be missed if a wave swept it away.

Then I remembered I hadn't made provisions for my beloved Minnie. She might starve to death. And even if my body were discovered soon, I couldn't trust Angela to find Minnie a good home. Frederick would take her to an animal shelter.

Now, a year later, I was glad I came to my senses for Minnie's sake. If nothing else. Snuffing myself would have been tantamount to admitting defeat. Giving Dirk his final victory.

Silvia's sedan cruised past a farm with a massive white barn, what must be a chicken coop, and a cluster of smaller outbuildings. A dozen bored-looking Holstein cows grazed in a grassy fenced enclosure. Behind them in a cornfield, a bearded Amish man wearing a straw hat harvested acres of corn using a team of humungous draft horses. The animals trudged forward in a precise straight line. I couldn't get my mind to accept the fact a man would choose to harvest without a tractor.

"He must be nuts," I said.

"Really? I think it's wonderful." Angela prattled on about how industrious the Amish were, living without electricity, the Internet, and phones in the house. Her words sounded like gibberish. I missed Seattle's steady grind. An ambulance siren, the neighbor's teenage son's booming muffler, or planes roaring over my house never bothered me. Give me the city any day. And give me solitude. Angela's constant blathering made me nuts. When in close proximity to her I felt like a time bomb ready to detonate.

"Look out!" she squealed.

I slammed on the brakes. The sedan skidded to a stop.

"What?" I glanced in the rearview mirror and was relieved to not see a semi's chrome bumper barreling up behind us. Then I noticed a horse pulling a gray rectangle-shaped buggy headed in our direction.

"Rose, could we stay here until it passes?"

"I guess. But they don't want us ogling them. Remember, Silvia said they can't have their picture taken. Not that I'd want to." I raised my window. "How do they stand that putrid stench of manure on the road?"

"I'm sure you get used to it. Ready-made fertilizer."

"I never would." My hand swiped my nose.

"I don't mind it in the slightest. When we were young, visiting Grandma, I wanted to ride in a buggy in the worst way, but Dad would never let me."

"All of a sudden my big sister's turned into a country gal?"

I allowed the car to creep forward, but had to admit I was curious to see who was in the buggy. Its driver was a woman about my age, wearing a white head covering. Two children wrestled in the backseat. As she neared us the woman turned her head to speak to them.

I pushed my foot on the gas pedal. The car's wheels spun.

Shaking its head and chomping its bit, the horse reared up on its back feet. I mouthed the word *Sorry* to the driver, but her attention was aimed at settling the mare.

Dread clutched me as I imagined the buggy overturning. Or a car smashing into it. "You wouldn't catch me in one of those flimsy things."

"Really? I'd adore riding in one, but I doubt I could ever learn to bridle a horse, let alone drive a buggy. But you could, Rosie."

"Yeah, right."

Minutes later, the Buick labored to the crest of a hill and then jutted down toward a valley I figured was the heart of Lancaster County. I turned off the car's fan, but dusty warmth radiated from the heating vents. Moisture accumulated under my armpits. Angela lowered her window a few inches. The air smelled like drying hay and newly turned soil. More pleasant than I'd expected. The pungent odor of manure didn't pucker my nose anymore.

I'd forgotten the area possessed so many pristine barns and fields, and also stretches of woodlands. I'd pictured the whole East Coast jam-packed with fast-talking people. But our aunt spoke in a measured cadence less hurried than my own. Unlike her Phyllis. She reminded me of a chipmunk.

"Can this be right?" Angela pored over the directions. "It looks like we're coming to a dead end. No, it goes all the way through. I guess all these roads connect up."

We found ourselves in a village. "Are we here?" I asked.

"Not yet. This is Quarryville. Keep going. And watch out for buggies."

"You think I'm going to ram into the back of one on purpose?"

An open buggy driven by a young man wearing a straw hat headed in our direction. I pulled to the right to give him ample room. As we passed him, I glanced at his cleanly shaven face. Angela waved and he waved back.

"Did you see that?" Angela craned her neck. "He waved at us. From what I've heard, they're not supposed to interact with outsiders."

"Too good for us?"

"Apparently the Bible instructs them to remain separate from the world."

"If you say so."

We finally entered the town of Strasburg. I had to admit it was quaint. The wide main street was dotted with restaurants and shops, some located in old houses. And a smattering of people. Using one foot, a young Amish woman propelled herself on a scooter with bicycle-sized wheels but no pedals. Huh?

"This is it," Angela announced. I pulled up to a curb and set the brake. She seemed happy enough to dance a jig. Like the first pilgrim landing on Plymouth Rock. "Silvia said stores get crowded with tourists on the weekends." She opened her door. "It's only Tuesday, so we'll get first pick."

Angela shepherded me down the sidewalk and into a quasi-antique store situated in what I figured was a former warehouse. We entered a cavernous room. A sea of tables and cases laden with knickknacks left little space for walking. The air smelled of must and mold. I felt an oncoming sneeze that refused to bloom.

My sister moved at half my speed, looking like she was searching for a pearl in an unpretentious oyster. She handled and scrutinized every piece of flatware, salt and pepper shakers, you name it. Nothing I'd ever buy. Excruciating to watch. As she browsed I did a neck roll, but my shoulders remained blocks of cement.

"These are cute." She picked up two faceless rag dolls dressed like a miniature Amish couple. "Maybe I should start collecting them."

I found their blank faces unappealing, but I said, "Not bad," hoping she'd make a purchase so we could leave. On the way into town I'd noticed a gift shop where I could buy something for Brad, even though he'd come home from Mexico last month empty handed. Men were like that. Last birthday and Christmas, Father gave me a card and a hundred-dollar bill. Which of course I could always use. But it made me think. Now that Mother was gone I might as well forget about presents from anyone except Angela.

She sat the dolls back on the table. "They aren't too expensive. Back home, I've paid twice as much for things half as adorable." Then she moseyed to another table.

I was struck by the walloping sensation someone was staring

at me. I spun around and glanced up the wall to an oil painting of a girl, maybe six or seven years old, dressed in antiquated attire, holding on to a pony's bridle. Out of nowhere I was filled with the warmest sensation. Like I'd run into an old friend after years of separation.

If my child had been a girl, she might have looked like that. Small-boned, with chocolate-brown eyes and hair. I noticed the price tag—a hundred and fifty dollars. I could afford it if I didn't spend money on anything else while here. The frame was nothing special, its gold finish flaking at the joints. The painting's surface was cracked with age. But the urge to buy it to hang above my fireplace seized me. I might call the girl Emily, a name I always liked. On lonely evenings, Emmy and I could keep each other company.

I dipped into my shoulder bag and fished for my wallet.

No, stupid, I told myself, extracting my hand empty. A painting wouldn't fill the hole in my womb. If anything, it would serve as a reminder of what I'd lost.

Across the room, Angela picked up a snow globe the size of an orange and shook it. Opalescent flakes swirled through the glass sphere. She turned the orb over and wound a knob on the bottom. Classical music spilled out its song.

An older voice said, "Isn't that lovely?" A woman at least Silvia's age, who looked straight out of a Charles Dickens novel, perched behind a low desk. "I've never seen a snow globe like it before. Only twenty-nine dollars."

No doubt Angela was gullible enough to believe the woman's flimflam. Heading toward my sister, I cleared my throat in protest. Except for the painting, everything in this rabbit warren was commonplace and over-priced.

Angela returned the globe to the table and unfolded a patchwork quilt. "Maybe I have enough stuff," she stated as though she'd happened upon a major discovery. She refolded the quilt. "I don't know what I want to collect now, but it's going to be something totally different. Maybe nothing. Maybe I'll start getting rid of things."

As the two of us made our way toward the exit, I checked over my shoulder at the painting once more. The girl's eyes were following me.

"Goodbye, Emmy," I whispered.

THREE

Angela

By the time Rose and I straggled into a café, the small of my back was complaining and my feet felt as though they had expanded two sizes. We stood at the register reading the menu written on an overhead chalkboard. A pretty young Amish woman, her flaxen hair parted down the center and mostly concealed behind a heart-shaped cap, took Rose's order in a singsongy voice.

As Rose counted her change, I scanned a rack of bread—whole wheat, white, plastic bags of muffins and biscuits—and a glassed-in case displaying a plethora of cookies and baked goodies I'd kill for. My eyes honed in on chocolate whoopee pies I recalled from my youth, making my stomach squirm and my mouth water for a confectionery treat. But when it came my turn to order, I asked for vegetable-lentil soup and cornbread, just like skinny Rose. Maybe if I ate like her, I'd look like her too.

Waiting for my Visa card to be authorized, I searched the bottom of my purse to make sure I hadn't accidentally-on-purpose pilfered an irresistible item from the antique shop. In the past, my husband had bailed me out twice. "You're lucky I'm an attorney," he'd said with disdain. And once I started crying so hard the manager at Chico's told me to keep the thirty-nine dollar earrings as a gift because I was such a good customer, most of the time.

I made a vow to never shoplift again, especially this week. Why, if Rose saw me, she might turn me over to the police and bring up the incident for the rest of our lives.

Rose and I were the only patrons in the small eatery. I let my sister choose our spot among the six tables; she always preferred facing the door, as if a terrorist were going to sneak up on her. And she thought I was fussy?

We settled near a low counter lined on one side with several vinyl-topped swivel stools. It felt heavenly to take the weight off my feet. Elbows on the table, I rested my chin in my cupped hands and closed my eyes. Sometimes, even when I should be having fun, it felt as if a ball and chain encircled my neck, dragging me down.

What was wrong with me? I possessed everything a woman like Rose would want: a successful husband, two children, and a five-bedroom home. Yet I felt vacant inside, like the soufflé I'd made when Frederick's mother came over for dinner several weeks earlier. Right out of the oven, my poofy creation appeared exactly like Martha Stewart's, but by the time I served the dessert its crown had collapsed into the baking dish like a punctured balloon. His mother curled her lip and said she was too full to eat another bite.

I heard the café door breathe open and then heavy footsteps on the wood floor. I opened my lids to find myself gazing right into a man's hazel eyes, framed by thick brows and long brown bangs. He seemed to be looking into my very depths as if reading my thoughts. A tingle rushed from my chest to my throat and warmth fluttered in my abdomen. Realizing I was staring, I averted my eyes. As Mom would have said, one mustn't gawk at strangers.

I turned to Rose, who sat across the table removing her jacket. "Aunt Silvia is a dear woman," I said as though pondering the thought the whole time.

"Yeah, she's a sweetheart." Rose draped her jacket over the back of her chair. "But eccentric. Half the time she's off in another world.

I hope it's not the first signs of senile dementia." Leave it to Rose to come up with the worst-case scenario.

I lessened my volume; people here might know Silvia. "First of all, she's only in her midsixties, and she seems as sharp as anyone I know." Yet I'd also noticed her day-dreamy moments that I assumed were brought on because Rose and I reminded her of the good old days. And she yawned a lot, but so did I.

Rose unfolded a paper napkin and dropped it into her lap. "Father said many years ago Silvia considered joining the Amish church—a lifetime commitment. 'The stupidest idea I ever heard of.'" Rose mimicked Dad's gruff voice. " 'Thank God she came to her senses. But then she turned around and became a Mennonite, and now attends a church that includes a mishmash of Mennonites and ex-Amish.' When I asked him why, he rolled his eyes and said, 'Who knows? She refuses to own an air-conditioner, TV, or cell phone. Your aunt's always been a kook.'"

"I hope he's wrong." Once more, my vision meandered over to the man, now chatting with the young Amish woman at the register. He was a local guy, I surmised, who looked everyone over on weekdays assuming they were from around here.

As he sat at the counter behind Rose, his long legs were forced to one side of the stool. He was the opposite of my Frederick. Judging from this man's weathered denim jeans and the dried mud caking his boots, he was some sort of construction worker. His hands weren't the hands of a man who earned his living at a desk. I guessed his rugged face had seen forty summers in the sun.

He turned my way and again his eyes searched mine. I experienced another trance-like moment; my chest buzzed with a zany wave of excitement I hadn't experienced for years. Not since I married Frederick. I couldn't care less about other men, yet I felt oddly connected to this man—like a kite to a string.

"Do you mind?" He pointed to a folded newspaper on the corner of our table. I could see the words *Lancaster News*.

Rose tossed him a pretty smile. "No problem. It was here when we sat down." She languidly passed it to him.

"Thanks." He turned to the counter and perused the first page.

Someone else took over the register, and the young Amish woman he'd been talking to brought our food. I watched a pat of butter melt into my cornbread and then glanced at my left hand. My wedding band, one-point-five flawless carats mounted in platinum, was hard to miss. Surely this man had seen it. Besides, men didn't give chubby women second looks.

"Here ya go, Glenn," the waitress said to the man. *Glenn*, I repeated in my mind. His name fit him. Masculine and strong.

"*Denki.*"

"*Gem gschehne.*" In a playful manner, she tugged the newspaper out of his hands before placing a wedge of fruit-filled pie à la mode in front of him. Her face wore the expression of happy expectancy, as if her life hadn't yet tasted disappointment. "Don'tcha let the ice cream melt." She wore an azure-blue dress that echoed her eyes, a black apron affixed at the waist with long straight pins, and not a trace of makeup on her flawless skin. Her youthfulness made me feel over the hill, like a pair of old ratty socks.

She broke into what I assumed was Pennsylvania Dutch, because it resembled German but wasn't. Glenn answered with ease, as if entirely comfortable with this second language, striking me as odd.

I dipped my spoon into my bowl, blew across the glob of lentils to cool them, and then swallowed a mouthful. This lovely girl obviously had a crush on him, I thought, noticing her refilling Glenn's coffee cup. This pretty young woman was flirting with this fine-looking gentleman, and for a moment I had imagined he was admiring me. Luckily I wasn't the type who wanted or needed men fawning over me, since it rarely happened.

As Rose and I consumed our lunch, several customers entered, ordered, and seated themselves by the front window. Rose and I ate in silence.

Finally, after finishing his pie, Glenn refolded the paper and set it aside. He swiveled his stool and asked, "What are you two young ladies up to today?"

"We're on a treasure hunt." Rose's lips formed an enticing pout. She was being sarcastic; she found my collectables tacky.

"Sounds interesting. Any luck?"

Her face twisted into a mask of exasperation. "Not yet." I can't explain it, but her underlying message was *I'm available.*

"I hope you find what you're looking for." He extended his right hand. "My name's Glenn Yoder."

She shook his hand, almost double hers in size. "I'm Rose Webster, and this is my big sister, Angela Strick."

At the mention of my name—or was it the word *big?*—my pulse started racing and a jittery shyness engulfed me. I managed to utter, "Hi," but hid my hands under the table.

Rose lowered her chin and gazed up at him with doe eyes. "We don't look like sisters, do we?"

"I'm sure you have much in common," he said.

I wanted to join in the conversation, to confirm that indeed Rose and I did share personality traits, but my mind faltered; I couldn't think of a single example—probably because there weren't any. Oh well, it didn't matter. My sister was eligible and cute. I should keep quiet and watch the sparks ignite. But part of me wished she'd disappear so I could garner Glenn's full attention. Why should Rose have all the fun? Since my late teens, when I met Frederick and gave up the one thing I truly loved, it was always the same: me on the sidelines watching others bask in the limelight on center stage.

He got to his feet. "Nice to meet you." He moved past our table toward the exit. "*Denki*, Olivia," he called to the waitress.

"Don't be such a stranger." She twirled one of her white cap strings. "Don't ya like my cookin' anymore?"

"Yah, 'tis *appeditich*—the tastiest in the county and you know it." A grin spread across her mouth.

Striding toward the door, he glanced back at our table.

"Bye-bye, Glenn." Rose waved with her fingertips. "My, he sure is tall," she added, sotto voce. Through the café's wide window, we watched him cross the street and enter a bookstore. "Not bad looking, either, even though he could use a better haircut. And apparently he reads."

"Rosie, you've been here one day and already met a good prospect."

"Him? Nah. Remember, Father said there were people born in this county who never left. Glenn looks like one of those local yokels."

"Don't be a snob. That kind of life sounds nice."

She finished off her cornbread and tidied her mouth with her napkin. "It would drive me insane. I'd die of boredom within a month."

Rose and I had grown up on Seattle's Queen Anne Hill on a street with sidewalks where everyone knew each other, but I barely recognized my current neighbors in Redmond, who lived in houses concealed behind fences or sitting inside circular driveways. I was lonely in my own home.

"Anyway," Rose said, "I already have a boyfriend."

"The one I met at your place last month?" I'd stopped by without an invitation, because I never received them. And she always found an excuse not to visit me.

"Yeah." She wadded her napkin and chucked it onto the table. "Brad Symington."

I recalled his curly blond hair and smooth skin. He appeared five years younger than Rose. "He's good looking enough," I said. "Nicely dressed, but he didn't even get off the couch to shake my hand." The whole time I was there he'd watched TV and savored his Heineken beer, as if counting the minutes until I left. "He didn't seem like good marriage material."

"Who says I want to get hitched?" Her voice took on a crisp edge. "I'm perfectly content the way I am."

I'd wager she'd be thrilled if Brad asked for her hand, but didn't dare mention it. Anyway, he was the last man I wanted for a brother-in-law.

I lay three quarters on the table as a tip, even though this place was mostly self-serve. Rose tossed two one-dollar bills on top of my money. Why must everything be a competition? You'd think we were teenagers again.

Minutes later, we were out on the sidewalk where Silvia's car waited at the curb.

"Hey, sis, you didn't buy anything today," Rose said with a wry smile. "Are you all right?" She was taunting me, her brand of humor, but at least she was in a jovial mood.

"You're right." I felt my forehead with drama. "I can't remember the last time I came home empty handed, but I think I'm going to live." If only running to the drugstore to refill a prescription, I usually spotted a new shade of lipstick or hand cream I wanted, occasionally stashing the loot in my pocket or handbag without paying. Wearing bulky clothes and carrying a sack purse had their advantages. Often, I'd berated myself when I got home. I had enough money. There was no excuse for my out of control behavior.

"The only thing that caught my eye other than the faceless dolls was the snow globe with the ballerina inside." It was too big to steal, but I dipped my hands into my jacket pockets to make sure they were empty. "It played a piece I like." The music had catapulted my thoughts to a long-lost era; the melody almost brought me to tears.

"You want to go back and get it?" she asked.

"I suppose I could—for Tiffany, my future prima ballerina. No, I don't have the oomph to walk that far. Anyway, Tiffany's threatened to give up dancing. That would be a crime. Imagine throwing all that talent away."

"Like you?"

"It's not the same. I didn't have half her ability."

"Sure you did." She unlocked my door, but stood on the sidewalk blocking my entry. "When we were kids, you were fabulous." She fingered the key. "I'll never forget how incredible you were in *Swan Lake.*" She was referring to my part in the Pacific Northwest Ballet School's annual end-of-year performance. Somehow, at age sixteen, I'd scored the lead part in Tchaikovsky's ballet.

"I was blown away when I realized the apparition in white feathers vaulting across the stage was my big sister." She swooped her arms and I chortled. It felt good having the tension eased.

"But I didn't have what it took to make the big time. You know, in New York or Chicago."

"How can you be sure? You never tried. Why did you give up dancing?"

"I wish I knew." When I was a girl, the stage lights shone so brightly I couldn't see the audience's faces, but I sensed their approval of my pas de deux and pirouettes. I'd relished their applause when I bowed. Why had I discarded what brought joy? As I had many times, I attempted to excavate the recesses in the back of my mind, but came up empty. "I guess I had other priorities, or maybe I was lazy."

"Nothing lazy about you." She leaned against the car with her arms and ankles crossed. I figured she was stalling.

"You were a straight-A student." Her glance swept across the bookstore's facade. "You earned money babysitting and volunteered at Children's Hospital. According to our parents, you did everything right."

"But you're the daughter Dad admires. I could use some of your spunk." Maybe a smidgeon would rub off on me during our trip. The image of my returning home gutsy and outspoken brought a smirk to my face until I recalled Frederick didn't like pushy women. So why did he hire Stephanie from Long Island? Why that secretary of his? They both seemed plenty pushy to me.

I glanced over the car's roof and canvassed the bookstore's front-age. I wondered what kind of books Glenn read. Biographies?

Mysteries? I'd brought a romance novel along for the trip, but could always use a spare. And I hoped to bump into Glenn again, for Rose's sake.

Before I could suggest we go in, Glenn sauntered out, carrying a book. Rose unfolded her arms. "That was quick."

"He must have had something on hold," I said.

As Glenn approached the curb, an Amish man in his twenties—his chin cleanly shaven—brought his buggy to a halt, blocking Glenn's path. The two men spoke for several minutes, the younger man's voice raised and ragged—not that I could comprehend a word. He finally slapped his reins, initiating a sudden departure.

Glenn stood staring at the buggy as it diminished from sight.

"I wonder what that was all about," Rose said. "That Amish guy looked like he was ready to punch Glenn's lights out."

"I doubt it. I read that Amish are nonresistant, a level beyond being a pacifist. Anyway, who'd pick a fight with a big man like Glenn?"

Glenn glanced across the street at Rose and me, and sent us the nicest smile.

"Check who's at the restaurant's window," Rose said. I looked over my shoulder and saw Olivia peering out. Had she seen the altercation? Was she spying on us? Or was Glenn the object of her attention? "I bet she has the hots for Glenn," Rose said.

Glenn waited for traffic to let up before climbing into an American-made pickup parked facing the opposite direction as Silvia's. Faded light blue, it must have been twenty or thirty years old, the kind of utility vehicle Frederick would consider beneath him. But I liked it.

Glenn fired the engine and his pickup rolled away from the curb.

Rose's spine straightened like a soldier's. "Let's go." She whipped around the back of Silvia's car to the driver's side and I hopped into the passenger seat. Then she gunned the engine, hung a U-turn, and sped out of town with Glenn's pickup ahead of us.

"You're following him?" I buckled my safety belt and gave it a tug.

"Don't be ridiculous. It's just a coincidence. We happen to be traveling in the same direction."

I couldn't wait to find out what would happen when we caught up with him at his house or place of employment. Would my indomitable sister finagle her way in?

A horse and open wagon pulled out of a side street in front of us, forcing Rose to jam her foot on the brakes. "Phooey." She tailgated the wagon for several minutes until it turned off at a Y in the road.

By then Glenn's pickup was nowhere in sight.

Four

Rose

Trying to find our way back to Aunt Silvia's, I piloted her car into unknown territory. "We're lost," I said. "We got off course—"

"When you followed Glenn's truck?" Angela cut in. "Don't deny it, Rosie, you were chasing him."

"No I wasn't. But if I were, it's nothing I haven't done before. I follow men until they catch me. My version of fishing, baiting my hook and trolling."

Angela sat primly, Silvia's directions in her lap. "You flirt with strange men and you're proud of your behavior?"

I gripped the steering wheel. "Don't worry, I have no interest in Glenn. I wouldn't waste energy on a backwoods hick." Not entirely true. I recalled his rugged features and broad shoulders. And he'd noticed me. Gave me the once-over. The man was a hunk even if he spoke Pennsylvania Dutch. What was that all about?

Too bad he didn't live in Seattle. How gratifying it would be to see Brad seethe with jealousy just once. Which made me wonder what kind of trouble that man of mine had gotten himself into in my absence. Not that he was mine. Only last week, he'd made it clear he wasn't ready to commit himself to one woman. At least, not this one.

A home resembling a box on a kid's train set whizzed by. Had

I seen that exact one earlier today? My memory was a mélange of images from childhood trips and our mother's photo album.

"We shouldn't have taken that right turn a few miles back." I wanted to hear her apologize for letting me.

"Oh, well, this is exciting, like a Lewis and Clark expedition." She sounded like a mommy trying to coax her child into eating lima beans.

My vision locked onto a dilapidated barn in the corner of a field. Its battered sides, silvered by the sun and eaten by decades of wind and rain, would make perfect lumber for the birdhouses I fabricated. The barn was falling down anyway. I bet I could pay the owner a nominal sum for the structure and hire someone to dismantle it. But how would I send the wood home to the other side of the country?

The car flew past several farms. One with an elaborate purple-martin birdhouse that could accommodate dozens. Then a store with quilts hanging from a clothesline.

"Oh, look at that darling place." Angela pressed her face against the window. "Maybe we should check it out."

I kept us barreling straight ahead, passing an open buggy driven by a bearded man. "Nah, we should get back. Silvia might need her car." And I needed to pee. I should have used the ladies' room at the café.

A moment later, we happened upon a village. "We'd better stop to ask for directions or we'll never find our way." I was being a drama queen. But enough of this crisscrossing the county. I noticed a hardware store that belonged in a Norman Rockwell painting. Along with trucks, several buggies and horse-drawn wagons waited at a hitching rail out front.

On a corner stood a drugstore housed in a low brick building. I parked next to it and got out. Shouldering the pharmacy's door open, I let my sister enter first.

"I hope they carry St. John's wort," Angela muttered in my ear. "I forgot mine."

"What's it for?"

"Depression."

I sucked my lips together. St. John's wort was better than Prozac, I told myself. At least she wasn't dependent on prescription medication. She didn't strike me as really depressed, even though I knew she'd taken our mother's death pretty hard. She just seemed her usual ditzy and bored self.

The front half of the pharmacy displayed Amish souvenirs—miniature windmills, postcards depicting Lancaster County, and other doodads. Toward the rear of the building, I spotted a pharmacist standing behind a counter—a balding man who looked beyond retirement age, wearing glasses, helping an Amish woman.

"Ask him if they carry it," I suggested as the Amish customer took her medication to the cashier by the front door. But Angela ignored me.

"I bet they do. I can find it." She rarely heeded my suggestions, while I was supposed to act upon her every snippet of advice. I tailed her up and down the aisles until she finally approached the pharmacist.

"We're expecting a shipment later today or tomorrow." He capped a pill bottle. "I could call you when it arrives."

"Do you know Aunt Silvia's telephone number?" Angela asked me.

"Nah, I've never called her. You handled all the details."

The pharmacist reached under the counter and produced a telephone book. "Want to look up the number?"

"Thanks." Angela opened the book to the D's. "We're staying with our aunt, Silvia Donato."

"Why, I've known Silvia all my life." With a smile he must save for regular patrons, he turned to his computer screen and tapped on his keyboard. "I have her number right here." Then his voice turned serious. "It's been a while since I've seen her." He pushed his glasses up on the bridge of his nose with his middle finger. "Are you Leo's children?"

"No, Leo's our uncle. Juliana was our mother."

His mouth hardened. "I see."

"She died a year ago," Angela said, solemnly.

"Sorry to hear that." But he didn't sound sorry in the least, and I wondered why. His hands moved to the keyboard and he began typing.

"Do you know where our aunt lives?" I asked. "Could you give us directions to her house?"

He tore a sheet of paper off a pad, ripping one corner, and then tossed it and a pen on the counter, and started rattling off instructions and street names. Did he think I was a professional stenographer? I wrote them down as best I could. All the while I wondered if we'd done something to insult him, other than being Juliana's daughters.

His phone rang. He grabbed the receiver and then pivoted to the wall to speak.

"Thanks for your help," I said to his back. He didn't respond.

Minutes later, after dodging into a donut shop to use the restroom, I drove Angela and me out of town on the two-lane road heading south.

"Did you notice anything strange about the pharmacist?" I asked.

She swallowed a bite of her newly purchased chocolate-glazed donut. "He was a bit stand-offish toward the end of our conversation."

"Humph. He was a regular Dr. Jekyll and Mr. Hyde. First, all concerned about Aunt Silvia. Then a blink later, treating us like trash once he knew whose daughters we are. What did Mother ever do to him? Leave the area? I can't wait to get back to the Northwest where people are friendlier." Although folks complained of the "Seattle freeze," a tendency to look right past others unless they first initiated a conversation.

"Glenn was friendly," she said.

"So I noticed."

The fuel gauge needle rested below the halfway mark. At the

outskirts of town, I saw a self-serve gas station. "I want to bring the car back with a full tank." I swerved off the road and pulled up to one of the two pumps.

She scarfed down the rest of her donut before fishing out her wallet. "I'll pay."

"Nah, I'll get it. Just because Fred rakes in tons of moola doesn't mean you have to treat me. But you're welcome to do the honors."

Her jaw slack, she looked at me without answering.

"Pump the gas," I said.

She fiddled with the wallet's clasp. "I've never pumped gas in my life."

I was amazed how little I knew about my own sister. "What do you do when your tank's empty?"

"I go to a place with an attendant or Frederick does it."

"That's ridiculous. Women should be able to take care of themselves." I opened my door, stuck my leg out. "Come on, I'll show you how."

Her hands in her lap, she stared at them. "Really, I don't want to know." She cast me a sidelong glance. "Can't we go to a gas station where they do everything for you?"

"There may not be a full-service station around here. If there is, the gas could cost twenty cents a gallon more. Never mind, I'll do it." I leapt out of the car, selected the mid-octane gas, and then jimmied the nozzle into the fuel portal. I squeezed the handle with all my might to make the gas flow faster. But it took its lazy old time, like everything else in Lancaster County.

The handle jerked, informing me the tank was full. As I removed the nozzle a long drip of gasoline spattered across my pant leg and sank into the fabric. When I slid back into the car, Angela's eyes appraised the dark spot on my jeans. Growing up, she was fastidious. At age six she made her bed every morning without being reminded. She wouldn't step outside the house unless her hair was neatly combed and her outfit matched. While I lived in messy chaos. A tomboy.

I sat for a moment waiting for her chastisement. Thankfully none came. Trying to ignore the gasoline fumes floating from my jeans, I lowered my window two inches and clicked on the fan. I tapped my fingers on the steering wheel as if my favorite song, something bluesy, heavy on the bass, were entertaining me. Following a horse-drawn wagon laden with hay, we rode in silence. Like two strangers on a Greyhound bus.

Finally, I began recognizing familiar landmarks. The gigantic red windmill, its blades spinning. The row of poplars protecting a pasture of grazing Holsteins. The field of dried corn husks lying helter-skelter on graying earth. So Angela wouldn't freak out about my driving, I cruised along with extra caution and came to a full stop at the next crossroad. The wagon turned right. I looked in both directions before pressing my foot on the gas pedal. The car sped forward, but in the center of the intersection the engine missed a beat. The world stood still. Visions of our being stranded by the side of the road streaked through my mind. I didn't have my cell phone with me. I should have brought it even if the reception back at the house was sketchy. Now that I thought about it, I hadn't seen many cell towers. How could people live like this?

The car sprang to life again and proceeded forward, down the dip and across a short bridge.

"Did you feel the engine stall?" I asked and got no response. I checked Angela and saw she was snoozing.

A half-mile further I turned into Silvia's driveway, and "Thank God" slipped out of my mouth. Not that I bought into that religious rigmarole. My Scripture-quoting mother would be disappointed to hear what I dared not tell her while she was living. When Angela and I were young, Mother insisted we attend Sunday school and youth groups ad nauseam. You wouldn't believe what some of those well-meaning Sunday school teachers force-fed trusting children. For instance, they claimed God knew the number of hairs on my head even though he was up to his eyeballs keeping the world spinning on its axis and taming natural disasters. Give me a break.

Once, as a girl, when visiting a friend's Catholic church's Christmas bazaar, I'd inched over to a statue of Christ and touched his marble foot. I'd averted my eyes, partly so no one would notice me. Also because I feared God might blaze to life and smite me. But he remained lifeless. No breathing spirit there. No love from a hard piece of stone.

Last year, in a desperate act, I gave prayer one final shot. I said, "Okay, God, if you can part the Red Sea and resurrect a dead man, how about saving my mother's life?" Know what happened? Her disease sank its teeth into her flesh with new vengeance like a pack of wolves closing in for the kill. She died two weeks later. Which proved we were born into this world alone and exited that way too. No use fighting the inescapable.

As I cut the engine I glanced off to my left, away from the house, at the stone-fortified embankment. Behind it, the forest tangled as densely as a jungle. A perfect place for Hansel and Gretel to get lost.

"We're here, sis."

Angela woke with a start. She turned to me, her cheek against the headrest. "Sorry you got stuck with all the driving. Next time you be the navigator and I'll drive."

"Uh, that's okay." I recalled my last ride with her. While initiating a lane change on the freeway, she'd neglected to check her blind spot, forcing a minivan to swerve and honk. "I don't mind. Even Brad likes it better when I drive."

"Really? Most men prefer sitting behind the wheel."

"Brad's not most men. And I'm an independent woman. That's why he likes me." I did wish he'd open the door for me and help me with my coat, but I wouldn't broadcast my complaints.

To end the conversation, I jumped out and strode purposefully to the house with Angela in tow. Silvia opened the front door before I knocked. Rex hustled out. He must have warned her of our arrival.

"I was beginning to worry," she said.

"We took the scenic route." I heard a bite to my voice I'd meant to suppress.

"But we made it," Angela said. As if arriving home safely with me at the wheel was a feat in itself.

Silvia stepped inside to let us enter. "Coming home empty handed?"

"I didn't buy a thing." Angela flipped her palms up. "But we met a man who'd be perfect for Rose. His name's Glenn." The way she savored his name in her mouth, extending the one syllable, made him sound like a celebrity. I tossed her a glare. She caught my displeasure and winced.

"I'll never see him again." I felt a feeble round of regret, much as I had last month when I'd misplaced my credit card and needed to request a new one.

"Not so quick," Silvia said. "I wonder if that was Glenn Yoder of Yoder's Nursery. Tall, nice looking with dark hair?"

"Nah, this county must be teeming with tall men." But only one had caught my fancy, temporarily. "Glenn's a common name."

"Not around here." Silvia pointed out the window at three bronze-leafed bushes. "He'll be by to move those photinias any day. He warned me not to plant them there. Said they'd never submit to my pruning, and sure enough they want to grow ten feet tall. No matter how much we try, some things are out of our control."

FIVE
Angela

First thing out of bed in the morning, I caught my reflection in the mirror affixed to the back of the bedroom door. Through my nightgown, my breasts drooped like half-full water balloons, my tummy paunched, and my expanded thighs made me look like a hippopotamus. Hard to believe I used to be as slim as Rose. I'd never wear shorts in front of Frederick and couldn't recall the last time I'd wriggled into a bathing suit. He seemed to avoid intimacy unless the lights were dimmed...and unless he'd downed at least one scotch.

I stepped closer to examine my uninspiring face. The fine lines on my forehead, merely wisps two years ago, had deepened into creases. Mom once told me my eyes sparkled like sapphires, but they'd turned blah. At their corners, crow's feet would soon spread like crevices.

Frederick hadn't mentioned my appearance in years. Compared to the women at his office, with their sleek hair-dos, skillfully applied makeup, and Barbie doll figures, I was Jumbo the Elephant with a bad hair day. I envisioned him packed in the elevator on his way to the twenty-first floor with a half-dozen beauties, their perfume tickling his nostrils. Surely he'd reached out to one of them. Many times I'd envisioned him—particularly when he came home late from a dinner meeting—with someone I imagined was female.

Behind my closed eyelids, I saw their tryst in vivid and sickening detail, right down to her lacy camisole. I'd even stooped to checking his collars for traces of lipstick and the shoulders of his suit jacket for stray hairs the next morning, and entered his home computer searching for incriminating emails. But he was either on the straight and narrow or hiding the evidence.

Did I care anymore?

And our two kids had become stubbornly independent—healthy according to the experts. It felt like rejection, as though they were yanking their affection away from me.

I slipped into my bathrobe and cinched the waist. There was no need to plaster on makeup in a house full of women. Not being on display felt liberating. I could be me—whoever that was. I ran a comb through my hair, but unruly frosted tufts sprang out on the side, telling me I'd spent the majority of the night in one position. I'd slept soundly. None of my typical 3:00 a.m. wake-ups when I lay in a cavern of worry, pondering problems that eluded me once fully awake.

Wandering into the kitchen after a stop in the bathroom, I noticed an aqua-colored vase brimming with long-stem red roses on the table in the center of the room. I'd always favored yellow roses, but these were the most beautiful roses I'd ever seen. The flowers, their petals tipped with burgundy, radiated an enchanting fragrance that insisted I draw near, close my eyes, and inhale to my fullest. The scent reminded me of Mom's perfume. When sorting through her belongings after her funeral, my nostrils had detected the delicate aroma lingering on her clothing as if a trace of her survived. I'd buried my face in her favorite mohair sweater and tried to relive the feeling of being unconditionally loved.

The kitchen door opened and a block of cool air replaced the warmth.

"Good morning, dear." Silvia was practically singing, she sounded so happy. I looked up to see her carrying a pair of clippers and a basket. Next to her stood the man Rose and I spoke to in the restaurant.

I felt topsy-turvy, a bottle of oil and vinegar shaken upside-down. My mouth dropped open in a most unladylike fashion.

"Do you remember Glenn Yoder?" Silvia asked.

"Uh...yes." I couldn't have looked worse. I wanted to sprint out of the room, but my muscles froze; I was a possum caught in the middle of the road. I straightened the front of my robe, made sure the belt was tied securely. Heat roiled up my neck. I fixed my eyes on Silvia, as if not focusing on Glenn would make me invisible.

"How are you today?" He smiled. Did he find me amusing? Laughable?

"Fine, thank you." I backed toward the door to the hallway. "I didn't know we had company. I was just admiring the roses."

"They're lovely, aren't they, dear?" Silvia placed the clippers and basket on the table next to the vase and then sniffed the flowers. "They're a hybrid Glenn developed a couple of years back and named after me, of all people. Silvia's Delight."

"I've never known anyone who's created his own flowers." I imagined Silvia's joy when he'd presented her with the first one. I finally looked at Glenn straight on and took in his features. Yes, it was the same guy. His hazel eyes reminded me of the woods up behind Silvia's house. Brownish-green flecked with gold—nothing special. But staring into them made me feel like a capricious teenager. "They're gorgeous," I said. He was gorgeous.

"They're no lovelier than the woman I named them after." Silvia put her hand up in protest. "I know beauty when I see it," he said.

Her cheeks flushed, she shook her head. "You can see Glenn likes teasing an old woman."

"You're not so old." I pictured Mom's symmetrical face. With her hair swept back to accentuate high cheekbones and a straight nose, she was a head-turner. She stood five feet eight inches, the opposite of Silvia in most respects. But Silvia's beauty radiated from the inside.

"I agree with Glenn." I grasped my bathrobe together at the neck. "You're beautiful."

"Enough of this flattery. You two are embarrassing me." She tugged open the drawer under the counter. "We came inside so Glenn could write down my bulb order."

He extracted a small notebook and pen from the breast pocket of his wool shirt. "I'm at your command."

"Next spring, my garden must be at its best." Her voice swelled with intensity. "Between the garage and the front door, and behind the house, I want the beds planted in red. A sea of red tulips. Do you think that's too garish?"

"Not at all," I said, as if my bedraggled appearance wasn't making me self-conscious. "It sounds festive, like a party."

"That's what I want. A celebration."

"Any idea which variety?" He rolled the pen with his fingertips. "I carry parrot, lily-flowered, and peacock tulip bulbs. One called Red Emperor."

"Several kinds." Silvia wiped the corner of her eye. "At least one that blooms early so I'll have color right after the snow melts."

He nodded, but his features turned sober. "And maybe a hint of lavender at their feet to accent them. Blue phlox would do nicely. You'd better stop by the nursery. If you don't find what you want, take a look through my catalogues. I'll contact my wholesaler in Holland and have the bulbs sent right away."

Silvia leaned her hip against the counter; her gaze lowered to the floor. "*The Farmers' Almanac* says we'll have an early spring next year." She glanced up at Glenn and they seemed to share a simultaneous thought. "I hope they're right."

"So do I." He slipped the notebook and pen back into his pocket. "But March and April can be fickle."

Silvia turned to me. "We never know. Sleet and ice one day, seventy degrees the next, and then two nights later the temperature can drop to freezing."

"We have early springs in Seattle," I said. "Come visit us. We have a guest room that's never been used."

Glenn looked my way. Did he think I'd included him in my invitation? I backstepped until my shoulder bumped against the doorjamb.

"That's sweet of you, but I'm not much of a traveler, dear. When you get dressed, come outside with us and make a bouquet for the dining table. Pick anything you like. It promotes new growth."

"Where's Rosie?" I receded toward the hall.

"Outside."

Returning to my room, I pulled a powder-pink turtleneck sweater over my head, and wriggled into the brown corduroy slacks that made me appear thinner than I really was. Then I hurriedly brushed my hair, dabbed on foundation, and applied mascara. Not that married women needed to doll themselves up. Still, I didn't want Glenn thinking I was frumpy—my being Silvia's niece and all.

By the time I returned to the kitchen, Silvia and Glenn were gone. Basket and clippers in hand, I stepped outside. The air was warmer than yesterday. Wisps of paper-thin clouds floated against the crisp blue sky. Evaporating dew on the grass shimmered as sunlight filtered through the row of chestnut trees. I heard a horse and buggy on the road, birds trilling. No sign of Glenn, Silvia, or Rose.

As I made my way through the garden I passed a stretch of chrysanthemums, some as tall as my shoulders. I decided to compose my arrangement of tangerine and gold, colors I never used at home. My own garden was planted in a benign combination of pink and white—how I'd wanted it until today. Was it possible to change my favorite color? My thoughts transferred to my walk-in closet, a vast space crammed with clothes, some still donning price tags. My wardrobe was comprised of black, white, and muted tones. And our living room, with its off-white walls, was decorated in beige and taupe, as was the master bedroom.

I lopped off several chrysanthemums and lay them in the basket. When I got home I might turn adventuresome and buy the paisley dress I'd seen at Chico's last week. Or wear it out of the store under my raincoat?

No, no! I reprimanded myself. Never again.

Cutting more stalks, I heard chattering above me and spotted a gray squirrel on a branch of the nearest oak tree. "Hush," I said, but it continued scolding, its tail held high as if I were trespassing on private property.

I noticed a vine of crimson leaves encircling the tree's thick base that would tie my floral arrangement together perfectly. They'd anchor my composition and add new definition and texture. I felt a swell of pride as I envisioned my future work of art. Maybe I should sign up for the flower arranging class I saw advertised several weeks ago at a community center.

I lay the clippers in the basket and reached my hand out to snap off a shoot.

Glenn's voice flooded my ears. "Hey!" He grabbed my upper arm so forcibly I dropped the basket, almost losing my balance. A gasp blew from my mouth. His other hand swung out to steady me at the waist. I was light-headed, the earth swaying beneath me. As I regained my footing, I breathed in the sweet aromas of aftershave and sweaty dirt radiating from his shirt.

We stood there for a moment longer than necessary. I didn't try to break free from his hold; if anything, I sank into it.

He finally loosened his grasp. "I guess you don't have poison ivy in Seattle."

I observed the leafy tendril and recognized it from childhood. Thank goodness I hadn't touched the noxious weed. I turned to him and said, "We only have nettles. And poison oak, but I've never seen it."

He stared right into my face as if expecting me to say more, something profound, making me self-conscious. So I clammed up. Back in high school, when the captain of the football team, Dirk, asked me to the prom (I think his girlfriend had ditched him at the last minute), I'd been so astonished I could barely tell him I already had plans with my steady boyfriend, Rusty. I was as speechless now.

"Sorry if I scared you," Glenn said.

I patted my hair. "That's okay. I'm fine." Then why was I flustered and my legs shaky, as if I'd just stepped off a roller coaster?

"I usually don't sneak up on people, but you looked deep in thought." His arms long and agile, he retrieved the basket and clippers. "A tussle with poison ivy can make you miserable for days." He scooped up most of the flowers and lay them in the basket.

"Thank you." I took the basket's handle and then busied myself straightening the stems. I flipped a flower over and it smiled up at me like a clown. I felt awkward, self-conscious.

"I'm a great admirer of your aunt." He was apparently oblivious to my confused state. Or was he trying to move us beyond this incident so we could both forget it ever happened? Maybe he already had. "I'm thankful you and your sister came. Silvia mentioned she had two nieces she particularly wanted to see."

"I'm glad too. My one regret is that we waited so long to visit her." I hesitated, wondering if I should mention it took Mom's death and Silvia's invitation to get us here, but I hardly knew Glenn. Why share personal history with him? Yet something made me want to tell him everything about myself. Except the parts that included Frederick.

"I'd better get back to work," he said.

"Then goodbye. And thanks for saving me." That came out wrong. Poison ivy wasn't life threatening, although I recalled as a child wandering into a patch; every inch of my skin and scalp had been assaulted with itchy blisters I couldn't resist scratching.

"Glad to help. Any friend of Silvia's..." His eyes questioned mine. Was he looking at me because he was as surprised to see me again as I was to see him? Then he turned and I watched his tall frame stride away, disappearing around the side of the house.

Above, the squirrel rebuked me again, its tail a waggling finger. I glanced around to see Rose and Silvia inspecting a fence over by the road. I was relieved they hadn't notice what just happened.

Not that anything happened.

Six

Rose

*T*his day had been veering off track ever since Glenn showed up. Talk about from out of left field. I'd never expected to see him again.

When he said, "Good morning, Rose," meaning he remembered my name, I morphed into a meek little mouse. I was usually witty around men. Charming and flirtatious. I couldn't help myself. But all I did was gawk up into his face and tell him I wished he lived in the Northwest so he could advise me on my own garden plantings. Dumb. I couldn't care less about flowers and shrubs.

Now that he was gone, I wished we'd invited him to stay for lunch. A man had to eat, after all.

At this moment, Angela, Silvia, and I sat dining at the wrought iron table on the lawn. Rex lounged at Silvia's feet. The sun lazed in the sky, but it was only in the midsixties. Not suntan weather. Ten minutes ago Silvia lamented, "This may be my last chance to eat outside." I supposed with autumn dwindling she was right. So we bundled up, sprayed our legs with insect repellant, and carried our luncheon to the spot she described as the location for many family meals. Mother might have sat here in this very chair. The metal kind that bounced when you rocked.

I remembered Mother staring vacantly out the picture window

of their home on the golf course greens. She'd sat on the couch or at her writing desk—the one piece of furniture she'd kept from our old house—while Father jabbered on the phone with retired business cronies or practiced putting.

As if Mother were here right now, I could see her withering away to a flesh-covered skeleton. But never speaking of her impending death or expressing despair. She was a private person. She kept her thoughts and feelings under wrap. The way I did. But that's where our similarities ended. She and Angela were clones, but I barely knew Mother. And she understood me even less.

A colossal hand wrapped around the bottom of my throat. Gagging me. But my eyes remained dry, as always. Mother had been dead for one year. When would my tears flow?

Had I used them up?

To keep from thinking about the morbid subject or ruminating about how Glenn's muscled strides could cover a mile in half my time, I'd concentrate on the lunch I'd prepared. Potato salad and tuna sandwiches with sweet-pickle relish on toasted bread.

Silvia sat staring at one wispy cloud in the pale blue sky.

"Don't you like lunch?" I asked her. Then wondered what Glenn ate for lunch, of all idiotic thoughts. What tantalizing meals would attentive Olivia prepare? Idle curiosity, I told myself. I was a woman on a safari, taking note of the local inhabitants' mundane customs.

"Rose, dear, everything's tasty. I don't have much of an appetite today." Or any day, apparently. Silvia had yet to ingest a substantial meal in my presence.

Angela speared a chunk of potato and stuffed it between her lips. "The potato salad's heavy on the mustard."

She was right. My salad verged on school bus yellow. "If you don't like it, don't eat it," I said with a snap.

"It's still good, Rosie. But I can feel the calories migrating to my hips."

"Your problem is you need more exercise." I noticed a healthy glow in her cheeks. "And eat smaller portions." She should follow Silvia's routine.

Angela directed her words to Silvia. "You wouldn't know it to look at me, but I used to be even thinner than Rose. I practically starved myself to please my ballet instructor."

"Angie was a promising ballerina. I remember the spotlight glinting off her hair like the sun's highlighting it right now. She seemed to defy gravity with her grace. While I was the duckling sitting in the third row. Mother always cried during performances."

Angela's eyes gathered moisture. "She never missed a show."

"I would have loved to see you dance, dear."

Angela reached for the sugar bowl and plunged her teaspoon in. "I'm afraid you missed your chance, unless you know a way to subtract twenty years from my age. My daughter, Tiffany, she's the one you should see."

I set my chair pumping as I recalled how Tiffany recently confided in me she wanted to quit dancing. She had complained her grueling rehearsals were a drag and she never had time to hang out with friends. She'd rather take up tae kwon do or learn rock climbing. Which I thought demonstrated moxie.

"Tiffany's auditioning for *The Nutcracker* again this year." Angela stirred the white crystals into her iced tea. Her spoon clanked against the glass. "She's nervous, but I know she'll be great."

My tongue took on a will of its own. "Get off her case and find a way to dance, yourself."

Angela frowned. "I'm way too old."

"Compared to me, you're still a young woman, dear. You both are." Silvia walked her chair away from the table and stood. "I'll be right back. I want to show you something." She slipped into the house. I spied her through the window, hesitating in front of the bookshelf by the fireplace. As if she were second-guessing her mission. She finally selected a volume.

Waiting for her return, I inhaled the fresh scent of mint. Then I

saw its familiar leaves growing near the stone retaining wall holding back the forested area above the house. The air was pleasing now
that I was used to it. I wished I could bottle the collage of drying
grasses, fallen leaves, and warming soil to take home. I hadn't seen
bottled air in my competitors' catalogues. Just kidding with myself.
Although I was on the prowl for new items.

Silvia returned carrying a photo album, its black jacket brittle
and peeling with age. "Here's Juliana at eighteen." She opened it in
the middle and placed it on the table for Angela and me to see.

Staring at the five-by-seven black-and-white photo, I couldn't
pick Mother out of the group of four, all in their late teens. I recognized Silvia, her foxlike eyes and arched eyebrows much the same.
And there was stocky Uncle Leo, a bachelor now living in Pasadena.
Since then, his bulbous nose had doubled in size. So had his waist
measurement. Which left a young man and a young woman. Was
Silvia suffering a memory lapse?

I swallowed a mouthful. "Mother isn't in this picture."

"In the center, dear." She pointed to the older teenager wearing
a mid-calf-length dress. Its stripes swirled from a slim waist and
flowed over curvaceous hips as if still in motion. Her thick dark hair,
brushed to the side, cascaded forward across one shoulder. Hey, her
hair looked my color. I thought Mother was a blond. Her playful
eyes flashed as if she were about to divulge the punch line to a joke.
Or some delicious secret. Between full lips, white teeth gleamed. I
couldn't remember her with long hair. I rarely saw her teeth. Her
lips were usually held softly together. But I recognized the bridge of
her nose and the set of her eyes.

"I can't imagine her dressed like that," was all I could think to say.

"Me neither." Angela gulped her tea.

Silvia scooted her chair in. "Juliana was always wearing something colorful or exotic. Usually an outfit she'd sewn herself. Your
mother was quite a seamstress. She used to whip things out of practically nothing."

"Like Scarlett O'Hara?" I recalled the curtains Scarlett had passed off as a sumptuous gown in *Gone with the Wind*. But when it came to beauty, movie star Vivien Leigh couldn't hold a candle to our mother in this photo.

"Mom's sewing machine hasn't been out of its case since we were kids." Angela sounded as confused as I felt.

"Yeah, she never made clothes for herself. Only tutus for Angela and an occasional Halloween costume for me." The leopard had been my favorite.

"Juliana adored fine clothing, but we couldn't afford to buy them off the rack. And she loved to go dancing." Silvia's voice rose to a crescendo. Speaking of Mother must fill her with an edgy emotion I couldn't decipher. "She often dragged me, her little sister, along, because Mama wouldn't let her go alone." Silvia glanced at the photo and gave her head a shake. "She'd refuse to head home until the joint closed down for the night."

"Mother swing dancing or doing the twist. Or whatever they did in her day?" My mind refused to wrap itself around this nonsensical information. I crossed my legs at the knee and jiggled my foot. I remembered Mother sitting in the corner of our parents' living room writing a thank-you note to one of Father's clients for a lovely dinner. *Lovely* was her favorite adjective.

"Mother always turned in early," I said. "She wasn't a night owl."

Angela pulled the album closer. "Who's the guy?" I was wondering the same thing.

"That's Chester." Silvia's words floated like the breeze fluttering across the yard.

"He looks Amish. That straw hat, goofy long bangs, suspenders." But handsome in a homespun fashion.

"Yes, but he was crazy about Juliana, ever since we'd been kids. He treated her like a princess. We all wondered if they'd eventually marry against his parents' disapproval."

"What?" Angela said. "They didn't like Mom?"

"Dear ones, Chet would have been forced to sever ties with the Amish community or Juliana would have had to join the Amish church—highly unlikely. Very few English, as they call us, successfully do. Poor Chet was devastated when she came home from college wearing an engagement ring from your father."

She removed her glasses and polished them with the hem of her skirt. "The next year, Chet got baptized and married an Amish girl from around here. They had a child. You know him. Glenn's their boy."

Angela's eyes met mine in silent surprise.

"Glenn?" My voice turned raspy. "The guy working on your yard? So he's Amish?"

"Yes and no. He was never baptized into the church. Although his parents are still pressuring him to find an Amish bride, live with them, and settle down."

"Meaning he'd drive a horse and buggy, and give up electricity?" Angela's words sounded muddled. She must have been as confused as I was.

"Yes, dear. I hear tell there's a young woman who's mighty sweet on him. But all the while she's dating a troublemaker." She slipped Rex a corner of her sandwich. He downed it in one gulp before scuttling off to sniff the garbage can stationed by the kitchen door.

I recalled the young woman in the bakery in her Amish attire. "How do you know all this?"

Silvia chuckled softly. "The Amish grapevine. No phones in the houses, but they have phone shanties and love to talk at social gatherings. Nothing mean-spirited, mind you."

"May I see that, sis?"

Angela passed the album to me. I breathed through my mouth as I examined the photograph. Chester's substantial arm draped behind Mother and his hand held her shoulder in a possessive manner. Looking at the camera, she leaned into him, her head inclining in his direction. He wore a straw hat. His shadowed face tipped down as he gazed at her, making it impossible to read his expression. But I guessed it would reveal affection.

What a dolt I was. Until now, it never occurred to me Mother might have loved someone before Father. The image of her kissing a strange man caused a ripple of uneasiness. Like swallowing an ice cube by mistake. I assured myself her relationship with Chester was innocent, even platonic. Unlike me, who'd lost her virginity at age fifteen, Mother had waited for her wedding night. She was prim and proper.

Feeling restless, I sat forward in my chair, shut the album, and nudged it toward Silvia.

"I'd hate it if Rose moved far away." Angela licked her fork. "Did you miss Mom?"

Silvia straightened her glasses. "Yes. Not that she and I were seeing eye to eye at the time. To tell the truth, dear, the day Juliana left I thought I might never see her again. Isn't that silly?" She paused to watch Rex sprint toward the vegetable garden. When she spoke again her voice sounded haggard, as if keeping up a cheery mood burdened her. "But in a way that did happen. She changed after she married your father."

If she was going to criticize him, then I could not—would not—tolerate it. But before I could defend him, she said, "I remember the first time she came back to visit," and my curiosity was piqued.

"I'll never forget how Juliana looked disembarking the plane." Silvia's smile seemed tight, her lips white. "Like a porcelain replica of my sister." She noticed my concerned stare. "Oh, dear," she stammered. "I don't mean to say there was anything wrong with your mother. She was still beautiful. And dressed in sophisticated new clothes. But her hair was lighter. And something else. She wasn't the Juliana I knew. And she still wasn't the few times she brought you girls to visit."

What on earth was she trying to tell us? There was a time I would have reveled digging up dirt on Mother, but now that she was buried, why perform an autopsy?

Silvia hugged the album to her breast. "I want you girls to have fun while you're here, not listen to me reminisce. What shall we do with the rest of the day? It's only one thirty, and I need groceries. If you come with me, I could show you where your grandparents lived when they moved up here from the city."

"Whatever you two decide. We could go antiquing if Angie wants to."

But Angela shook her head. "There's no need to rush off, is there?" The opposite of what I expected from her. I thought she'd be gnashing at the bit to stuff her suitcase with booty. "I should call Frederick." She sipped her tea. "I told him I'd report home every day. But he'll probably be at work, so I'll first have to talk to Jill, his uptight secretary who guards him like he's the president of the United States."

"Sis, I've been to Fred's office. Jill is actually pretty nice." Any woman who'd work for him for ten years deserved a Purple Heart.

Angela pulled her hair back and then let it splash forward, a habit since her teens. "Well, I'm sick of being polite to her when half the time she won't put me through to him."

"It may not be easy working for Fred. She's probably doing the best she can." I'd never much cared for my brother-in-law. In my opinion he didn't treat Angela well enough. And he wore an ostentatious diamond Rolex, Armani suits, and loud ties, telling me behind his smooth exterior dwelled an insecure man.

"She makes me feel like I'm an intruder at my own husband's office, and I don't like it." Angela munched her last cube of potato salad and then washed it down with a gulp of iced tea. "It used to be Daddy's practice before it was Frederick's. I have every right to be there. Then again, my husband's eyes scan his computer screen or his iPhone the whole time, so what's the point? And there's always an endless flow of incoming calls." She tapped her chin with her index finger. "Sorry, Aunt Silvia. I usually don't gripe this much."

"That's okay. Every so often, we all need to let off a little steam."

From half a mile away Rex started baying. I imagined he'd treed a squirrel or raccoon.

Angela got to her feet, and then she thudded back on her chair and started it bouncing. "I think I'll wait until tonight to call him, or maybe even tomorrow. Who knows, Frederick might miss me."

"Way to go. I didn't talk to Brad last night and it felt great." I opted not to mention he hadn't answered when I'd called or that I'd left a sultry message. "Let's have a week without men, okay?"

I cleared the table, stacking the plates, scooping up the silverware, and carrying them to the kitchen sink to find it was the right height for a shorty like me. As I fit a plate into the dishwasher, I imagined Mother standing in this room preparing a meal. For Chester? In my mind, I saw him watching her with hungry eyes.

I jammed in flatware. A fork's prongs gouged my palm. "Ouch." No, I wouldn't allow such thoughts to pollute my mind.

Angela entered the kitchen carrying the tray of glasses, and Silvia the almost-empty iced tea pitcher.

"After fixing that nice meal, let me take care of cleanup." Silvia urged Angela and me out of the room. "Please, dear ones, I insist."

As Angela made her way to her bedroom, I moved into the living area and noticed a partially completed jigsaw puzzle sprawling on the table by the window. I scouted around for the box top, but couldn't locate it. Most of the puzzle pieces lay heaped to one side. I hunted through the pile and found several edge pieces, bridged one side together, and then another. Minutes later, I'd connected the whole perimeter and experienced an unexpected rush of accomplishment.

I remembered a puzzle Angela and I completed as children. We'd sat across from each other for hours and hours fitting the fragments into place. I'd discovered I possessed a knack for detecting the needed colors and shapes. Being several years younger, I'd felt ecstatic pretending to be Angela's peer. When the puzzle lay completed, we'd admired the scene of Cinderella arriving at the ball.

"That's me," Angela had said, pointing to the blonde beauty in a wedding-cake gown.

"Then who am I?"

"You're one of the mice, Rosie. Remember, you love animals."

It still irked me how Angela always emerged victorious. Whether it was who got to select our Easter dress first—Angela adored pink, leaving me with lime green or baby-boy blue—or who would sit in the front seat with our mother, who favored Angela. When it was my turn to choose, somehow Angela manipulated me into making the wrong decision. "I'm sick of pink," she'd say with disgust. "Only sissies wear that color." Or, "Oh, goody, I get to sit in the backseat and play with my dolls." And I'd snap up the bait like a stupid little minnow.

I never felt Angela's equal. Wearing her hand-me-downs, walking in her footsteps, trying to fill shoes always one size too big. I'd been sure when I reached her height all that would change, but I stopped growing at five three. Four inches shorter than my older sister and feeling punier in every way.

SEVEN

Angela

T stood at the foot of the oak tree scrutinizing the poison ivy. Uncanny how such a pretty vine was so treacherous.

I remembered playing in the thicket on the other side of the vegetable garden as a child. That evening a fiery rash had raged across my arms, legs, and torso. Sobbing, I ran to Mom, who sponged my blistery skin with calamine lotion. But the horrific burning and itching persisted for days.

Thank goodness Glenn came to my rescue. My hero, as if in one of my romance novels.

In the past, I'd wondered what the protagonists in my books experienced when their mouths met the heroes', their lips softening into a glorious union. I'd lived vicariously through these fictitious women. I'd stopped reading innocent prairie romances long ago in favor of stories with more spice. More pizzazz.

The breeze tickled my face. I inhaled, trying to recapture the aroma of a man at work: rich and virile. I could almost feel Glenn's strong hands holding me. This time, in my muses, he turned me to face him and then he drew me closer.

What was I doing? I must not taste forbidden fruit. Reams of advice Mom and Dad had spouted when I was growing up jeered through my mind. "Don't put your hand near the flames. Don't talk to strangers." I was the obedient daughter, the compliant girl who didn't get crazy notions.

I glanced down around the base of the tree and spotted several of the chrysanthemums I'd picked earlier. Careful not to make contact with the poison ivy, I stooped to gather one. Its leaves had drooped; its head flopped like a rag doll.

I found myself musing about Glenn again. I bet he could repair the latch on our screen door at home. And he probably wouldn't mind carrying out the garbage, unlike Frederick, who refused to perform menial tasks. And Glenn didn't strike me as a man who'd spend his weekend on the golf course even though his wife wanted him to splurge on a romantic getaway with her.

Rose appeared wearing a T-shirt with the word *Fearless* scrolled across the chest, running tights, and Nikes. Her bangs lay pasted to her damp forehead. I scoped out her sleek legs, the way Glenn might. I hated her for looking so good. Not really. I loved her, even if she'd loathed me since we were teens.

"Out for a jog?" Her smirk told me I was asking the obvious. "Right after lunch? Isn't that bad for digestion?"

"Nah, I didn't go very far—only a mile or so." She panted like my son, Daniel, coming off the soccer field. "I don't want to turn flabby while I'm here." She wiped her forehead with the back of her hand, spiking her bangs, then noticed the limp flower in my hand. "What are you doing?"

"Thinking—about Frederick. I guess I miss him."

"Then call him."

"I tried, last night. The sitter said he was at a meeting." I'd asked to speak to Tiffany and Daniel, but she said they were enmeshed in a video game and didn't want to come to the phone. Maybe they were mad because I insisted Frederick refuse to let them stay home alone while I was so far away. For once he'd listened to me.

Or he was with another woman and didn't want to be bothered with the kids.

As I picked up another chrysanthemum, my hand skated dangerously close to the poison ivy. "I know you don't think much of my husband, but I love him and wish he were here." Or did I? He'd be bored stiff.

She gave her eyebrows a Groucho Marx wiggle. "Having him along would have its benefits, at night."

I tried to imagine Frederick and my snuggling together in the canopy bed, but could only hear his hog-like snoring. "The truth is, on the rare occasions we get together, he dozes off right after, leaving me—" I clamped my mouth shut, wishing I could retract my words.

"Keep going." She dried her hands on her T-shirt.

"Never mind." A fly circled my head; my hand swerved out to swat it away. "I should tell Frederick, not you."

"That's probably the best idea. But even when you spell things out for men, sometimes they can be so dense."

"You're right. Frederick doesn't have a clue."

"Are we talking about making love?" The words marched out of her mouth with such force they assaulted me. I'd never spoken of these personal matters with anyone. I felt like I did when Mom caught me as a seven-year-old paging through Dad's *Playboy* magazine he'd hidden under the cushion of his easy chair.

Mortified, I nodded.

"And you've never told Fred?"

"No."

She grimaced. "Don't you enjoy it at all?"

I lowered my gaze so she wouldn't see my humiliation. "In the beginning I did. But now I wonder. I had nothing to compare it with."

"You'd think he would have suspected something. Men can be so dimwitted. They really are from Mars."

"I don't want to be from a different planet." The fly spun around my head, hissing in my ears. I swiped at it with the flowers, but the insect hovered out of reach. "I'm tired of trying to second-guess

Frederick." I tossed the chrysanthemums back under the tree. "When has he ever taken the time to figure out what makes me happy?"

Rose looked like she had plenty to say, but she moved toward the road. "I need to keep walking until I cool down."

"I'll come with you." As I fell in next to her I noticed two birds landing on a bush near us. Warbling and tails bobbing, they darted off together. "I've heard some birds mate for life." A gust of wind ruffled the treetops, sending drying leaves skittering by. "They only worry about building a nest in the spring, feeding their young, and then making it through the winter until they repeat the cycle. Why do human's get so snarled up?"

"We think too much." Rose reached down and plucked a long blade of grass. She wound it around her finger and then let the green coil spring through the air, a trick Dad taught her when we were kids.

"If I ever get married, it'll be to someone who knows how to listen. And who's cute. And turns me on, of course." She was immature when it came to relationships; she'd failed to mention the most important qualities, like work ethic and honesty. Not that Fred didn't fudge the truth now and then. I'd recently overheard him on the phone bow out of a lunch date with his mother because he was tied up in court when in fact he planned to play golf with a client.

"Infatuation naturally fades after two people stay married." Was I trying to convince her or myself? "They sink into a comfortable rut, but that doesn't mean they don't have a satisfactory marriage."

"If you say so."

"There's more to marriage than a good love life." I picked up the pace. "Like mutual respect and shared interests. I admire Frederick." Some of the time, anyway. I doubted Frederick respected me. And we shared no interests.

"When the kids get older, he and I will probably spend more time together and start having fun." Was I trying to convince her or convince myself there was hope? "I'm thrilled to be a stay-at-home mom. I have no desire to do anything else." At least that was true.

We came to the road, about two hundred feet from Silvia's driveway. I heard a cow mooing in the distance. On the other side spread an embankment of deciduous trees Silvia said belonged to the Amish farm beyond. Most of the trees in the Northwest were evergreen: cedar, spruce, hemlock—forever dark and heavy—while these immense ash, maples, hickory, and oaks seemed weightless. As I recalled, a creek flowed nearby, meandering under the small bridge down the way and then between the two nearest hills.

We stepped out onto the narrow shoulder as a buggy headed toward us. My eyes strained to see who was driving. "I wonder who that Amish guy talking to Glenn outside the bookstore was."

She kicked a pebble. "Why would you care?"

"Idle curiosity. It sounded like a one-sided argument."

"Bet he's Olivia's boyfriend."

As the buggy passed, I tried to make eye contact with the bearded driver, but he jiggled the reins and increased his pace.

Rose and I headed toward the driveway in silence. A sporty roadster approached from the other direction, forcing me to fall in behind Rose. The driver, a man in his thirties, slowed to pass us. His head rotated and his gaze traced Rose's svelte figure, but she didn't seem to notice or realize how desirable she was.

There was a day when men found me attractive, but I couldn't remember the last time a man couldn't tear his gaze off me. Except for Glenn in the restaurant. But who knows, maybe I had food stuck between my front teeth—although Rose would have gleefully pointed it out. And later in Silvia's kitchen, it would have been impossible for Glenn not to stare at me in my bathrobe.

We arrived at Silvia's mailbox, then took a right onto her gravel driveway. As we reached the tangle of lavender and rosemary bushes growing on the side nearest the house, Rose came to a halt. "I need to stretch my quadriceps." As nimble as a flamingo, she balanced on one leg and then pulled her other heel back to touch her bottom.

The air smelled as fragrant as a candle shop. Wanting to bring some of the perfume back with me, I ran my fingers over the rosemary leaves. Through the branches I glimpsed a dark shape. An animal? I jumped back with a start, my heart pounding, proving once again I was a fraidycat. The breeze swayed the leaves and all the earth moved to its rhythm, but the object remained motionless. Using a long arm to spread back the foliage, I saw a bird lying on its side.

"Did you say something?" Rose asked.

"A dead starling." Its eye, a perfect black bead, stared at me without blinking. Its bill was like burnished steel and each speckled feather a masterpiece even Leonardo da Vinci couldn't have produced. "Should we bury it?"

"What for?" She switched legs.

"Isn't that what you do with dead things?"

"Nah, leave it alone. It'll be some other animal's dinner."

I let go of the branch and the leaves flipped back into place. Under all those bushes, I thought, a city of animals was busily fulfilling their destinies. "Daniel's science book illustrated the cycle of life. From dust to dust. Nothing is wasted."

"Every death has a purpose."

"What do you mean? You think Mom's death had a purpose?" My words bore teeth.

"Why do you have to take everything I say the wrong way? You're not the only one who misses her."

She was right; I was being insensitive, just what I accused her of. Not to her face, mind you. "I'm sorry," I said. "I'm sure you miss Mom. You have a different way of showing it."

"You think I should act all teary eyed and snuffly?" Her supporting leg wavered, but she recaptured her balance. "I'm like Father and always have been. You don't see him flaunting his emotions like a billboard."

"That's true. I have yet to see him shed a tear. But I assume he has, behind closed doors." I hoped so, anyway.

"That's because he's a private man. He keeps his feelings well hidden, which made him a top-notch attorney. 'Always keep them guessing,' he used to tell me. 'Never tip your hand.' And he was right. I wish I'd listened to him more."

"Funny, but that's the side of our father I've never cared for." When young I'd needed his attention, a compliment or hug now and then. He'd always admired Rose's impertinence, but seemed to find me insipid because I couldn't stand up to him. He probably still did.

She lowered her foot, distributed her weight on both feet. "I wonder if he'll remarry."

"He'd never do that. Would he?" I considered Mom's former friends. Three were single—two widows and a divorcee. They could be on the lookout for spouses. And now that I thought about it, the country club would be an ideal hangout for women prowling for husband number two or three. I hoped Dad wouldn't notice their come-ons. The thought of his embracing another woman made me cringe. Not that I'd seen him kiss Mom for years, except on the cheek or her forehead as she lay dying.

"A lot of men remarry within the first year," Rose said. Miss Know-It-All. "And sometimes their new honeys are much younger. The same age of the man's children. You and I could have a step-mother younger than we are, a gold digger who would turn him against us and tap into our inheritance."

I felt like plugging my ears. "Why are we talking about this? He loved Mom too much to ever look at another woman."

"I know plenty of men who've remarried," she said, in a mocking voice. Then she turned on her heel and trotted toward the house.

"You're wrong about Dad." But doubt was worming its way into my mind.

EIGHT

Rose

I paced outside the front door. "What's taking her so long?" I sounded like Father when Mother kept him waiting. Silvia was ready. My sister was the dawdler.

I stuck my head inside. "Let's go!"

"One second." Angela's voice emanated from the downstairs bathroom.

Thirty minutes earlier Silvia had mentioned she wanted to swing by Glenn's nursery on the way to town. It turned out he was the sole proprietor. Rather impressive, but it was probably a postage-stamp roadside setup. Teensy compared to Sky Nursery or Wells Medina back home.

Out of the blue Angela insisted on returning to freshen her makeup. "Why bother fixing yourself up to look at plants?" I'd asked, but Angela paid no attention.

Soaking in the afternoon sun, I strolled halfway to the car. The weather here was nicer than I'd expected. Warmth penetrated my damp hair. Not that I needed much of a shower after my run. I only covered a mile at most, not my usual twice around Green Lake's circumference, almost six miles. My shoes had felt heavier today than normal. I'd been sluggish ever since we arrived. Maybe too much rich food had sapped my energy. Or perhaps Newton's Law of Inertia was taking hold and slowing me down to Lancaster County's lethargic pace. And get this. I was so bored that our trip to a podunk nursery and seeing Glenn sounded exciting. I was beginning to scare myself.

I removed my jean jacket, draped it over my forearm, and started back toward the house just as Angela strode outside. With her lips stained cerise and her eyes shadowed a pale blue, echoing her irises, she looked as if she were on her way downtown. Except for her laced walking shoes.

Silvia coaxed Rex into the house with a doggy biscuit and locked him inside. Although I doubted anyone would dare enter with him standing guard. Soon, with Silvia manning the steering wheel, I perched on the squishy backseat. Just like when we were kids. But fine. Angela was the one who wanted to take in the sights and gawk at buggies.

"You're in for a treat." Silvia seemed alert and used both hands on the wheel. "Yoder's Nursery is somewhat of a tourist attraction. People come from all over to see it." Her tidbit of folklore was hard to believe, but I found her assessment sweet. She was sweet, really. Though we'd been here just two days, I'd grown fond of her.

She took a left and conveyed us past acres of harvested corn and emerald fields of low-growing plants I figured could be alfalfa. Her gaze caught mine in the rearview mirror, making me nervous. She should be watching the road.

"Rose, dear, do you enjoy gardening?"

"Nah, that's Angie's bag. She and Fred spend a bundle on their place. It makes my yard look pathetic."

I could tell by the way Angela stiffened that I'd said the wrong thing. "We have a big yard," she said. "It's too much for me to handle."

"You don't need to make excuses." I tried to soothe her fresh wound. "If I didn't have to watch every penny, I'd do the same thing."

"You just wait. Your business will take off one of these days and you'll be a millionaire. Silvia, you know Rosie owns her own mail-order business, don't you?"

"Yes, she mentioned it."

We merged with a two-lane highway, lined with humongous barns and bounteous fields, and then almost immediately zipped off onto a windy road.

Angela turned to speak to me over her shoulder. "You should send Silvia a catalogue. You should have brought some along, silly."

I was proud of my business, but receiving advice from a woman who'd never worked a real job, other than babysitting or doing odd filing in Father's office, made me grit my teeth.

Silvia's eyes found mine in the mirror again. "Rose, I'd love to see one."

"Okay, I'll put you on my mailing list." I realized she was waiting for me to expound. "I made the first birdhouse for fun." I leaned forward so she could hear me better and still watch the road. "To try out the jigsaw I bought for small home repairs. I can't afford to call a handy-man every time something needs fixing."

"The birdhouse was so darling." Pride buoyed Angela's voice, as if she were bragging on one of her kids. "I begged Rosie to make me one and then one for Mom for Mother's Day."

"It was also Angela's idea to start the mail-order business." I was in my sister's debt, but for some reason couldn't bear to thank her. "And to advertise in the back of *Sunset* magazine."

"That was four years ago. Rosie has sold more than five hundred since then."

With Mother gone and a father who'd never been effusive with praise, Angela was the only person who seemed to care about me, even if she irritated me no end. I had several girlfriends, but they focused on their marriages. And their children. Not that I blamed them.

The road took us through a pint-size village. A grocery store, post office, and some shops appeared relatively new. Several had been fabricated of brick and finished with white trim to complement other buildings that could date back to the 1800s for all I knew. In a blink we were out of town and traversing a knoll, then wending our way across flat pastureland. I was turned around. Even with written directions I'd never find my way back.

"Do you make the birdhouses yourself?" Silvia asked.

"Sometimes. But I got so swamped with paperwork, packaging, and mailing that Walter, my next-door neighbor, does most of the work now. He's a retired Boeing engineer." I remembered when the slow-moving gent first offered to help carry my three-quarter-inch-thick red cedar planks into my garage. He let slip he was handy at woodworking and that it would be a treat to make just one. Now he spent at least a couple of hours most afternoons fashioning the avian habitats for minimum wage, which I had to force him to accept. "He says he hasn't experienced as much enjoyment since he helped design the Boeing 747. A college student comes in on weekends to help me pack."

"She sells all sorts of things," Angela said.

"Two years ago, I added wind chimes, several yard ornaments, and a sundial with a Scottie dog. My own design that a metal shop makes exclusively for me."

"She sends her merchandise all over North America."

I swore I wasn't going to agonize about work while here, but Christmas lay around the corner. In the mail-order business, October was a critical period. My livelihood depended on my business now that I no longer worked at the Nordstrom customer service department part-time to supplement my income.

From way down the road I spied a sign with Yoder's Nursery inscribed in tall letters. A moment later Silvia motored into a dirt-and-gravel parking lot large enough to accommodate fifty cars, although only a half dozen were present today. A large van and a late-model pickup, both with Yoder's Nursery painted on their sides, were parked there too. Several horses and buggies were stationed at a railing. I canvassed a retail shop's exterior, four large-scale greenhouses, and behind them acres of deciduous and evergreen trees planted in neat rows. At the far end of the parking lot stood a three-story house painted a startling white, with black shutters framing the windows. Even under the grayish sky the structure's brightness made me stare. Next to the house an enormous maple tree spread elephant limbs.

"Is that Glenn's home?" Angela sounded as wowed as I felt.

"Sure is." Silvia drew near the greenhouses. "He's done a nice job restoring it."

Maybe Glenn didn't live alone, I considered. Silvia never said he was single, although he wasn't wearing a wedding band. But some men didn't. The other day at the café, he'd seemed awfully chummy for a married man, but he could have been making idle chitchat, as I did sometimes. Yesterday he'd been polite but seemed preoccupied. Maybe he'd found Silvia's plants more interesting than me. Not that I'd targeted him as a prospect, mind you. Heavens no.

"This place is spectacular." Angela practically sang. "I think I've seen it on TV."

"I wouldn't be surprised." Silvia brought the car to a stop. We got out and followed the flagstone path anchored by moss and lined with decorative containers displaying combinations of flowers I had to admit were original and attractive. We slowly strolled under a trellis cloaked with coral-pink climbing roses intertwined with a wine-colored vine I guessed was clematis.

A young Amish man wearing a straw hat passed us carrying a tray of disheveled succulents in need of repotting. Another followed him dragging a wagon, transporting a terra cotta urn, its contents spilling out to expose roots and dirt.

I assumed someone had been careless. "Silvia, aren't all Amish men farmers?"

"Not anymore, dear. As the population grows, farmland shrinks. Amish men own or work at businesses, from furniture-making to construction. And each year many families move to states with available farmland at a cheaper price."

"Their population is growing?" Angela caught up with us.

Silvia swiveled toward her. "My, yes."

I latched my arm through the crook in her elbow. "One last question. How can you tell if an Amish man's married?"

Angela huddled close to catch Silvia's answer. "Bearded men are married. No one wears a wedding band, man or woman. Jewelry is strictly *verboten*. Including wristwatches."

"Crazy." Although I often neglected to wear one myself.

We three walked past a spacious greenhouse ablaze with hanging baskets and tropical flowers. I had to admit, this place was incredible.

As we neared the retail shop a chocolate Lab bounded around the side of the greenhouse. The dog's belly hanging low, she announced our arrival with a friendly woof and a beating tail. A moment later Glenn appeared, accompanied by Olivia. Out in the sunlight, she was what Brad would call drop-dead gorgeous. And now that I looked Glenn over with a discerning eye, I saw he was extremely attractive and successful enough to land himself any woman. He wasn't Peter Pan, pretty-boy handsome. Just manly. Appealing.

He and Olivia were conversing intently, as if immersed in a serious discussion. I finally made out her words. "I don't believe 'tis John."

"But I hear he boasted about it."

"I'll speak to him."

"I doubt he'll listen. He's a bad seed, Liv."

"*Nee*, he's not."

Glenn finally noticed us. Both he and Olivia paused for a moment before continuing forward, gaining distance from each other with each step.

"Welcome." He gave Silvia a hug and then introduced Angela and me to Olivia Beiler.

I forced a smile. "Nice to meet you again." I saw myself through

Glenn's eyes and felt dowdy. I should have worn makeup, although Olivia's face looked freshly cleansed and her cheeks glowed. Tendrils of flaxen hair escaped her white heart-shaped cap, its strings hanging behind her back.

I was surprised by Angela's silence. Had she addressed Olivia when they shook hands? Angela's vision drifted like a trout in a current, not landing anywhere. Ordinarily, she found common ground with every woman she met. Not a terrible trait, just annoying when we were out together and I couldn't gain her full attention.

"I'd best help out." Olivia tilted her head toward a man replacing a pane of glass on the greenhouse.

"You work here?" I asked her.

"*Ya*, on my days off from the café."

"She's helping me plan a project." Glenn's gaze met hers and she batted her lashes in return. "Although she won't accept a penny for her time," he said.

She shot him a grin. "Just wait 'til we're in full swing." Then she sashayed over to the man repairing the greenhouse.

As Glenn and Silvia discussed compost and then shrubs, using their Latin names, I watched half a dozen birds descend on a feeder hanging from a nearby pole. They were having a dandy old time, chirping and picking out the shelled sunflower seeds. I was particularly taken with two scarlet birds with black throats and faces and a crest on their heads. They were singing the prettiest melody. I realized they were cardinals that I'd seen only in books. As I recalled, they were one of several birds that didn't nest in birdhouses, but rather chose trees. I'd have to look them up once I got home.

When starting out, I'd crafted my birdhouses to be decorative, until two wrens took up residence in the one I painted turquoise and affixed to the top of an old shovel where the handle once resided. The birds guarded their new abode, flitting in and out when they thought I wasn't watching. I began researching which species preferred what type of birdhouses. I had no idea the size of the house and the diameter of its hole and the height at which it was placed, as well as its proximity to other trees and bushes, held so much importance.

For instance, chickadees prefer dwellings eight to ten inches in height with a four-by-four-inch floor and an inch-and-one-eighth diameter entrance, placed at eye level and hung from limbs or secured to tree trunks. And who would have thought that perches below the entrances should never be added because they offered starlings and other predators a place to land? I still had a bundle to learn.

"Say, Glenn," Silvia said, "why don't you join us for dinner tonight? Phyllis and Hugh are coming."

"Sounds great. I'd never pass up a chance to eat a home-cooked meal, especially when you're the chef."

I was pleased, but said nothing. I didn't want him getting the wrong idea. I glanced to Angela, who stood with her arms crossed. I was used to her being the cordial, outgoing sister, but I stepped into her role and said, "See you tonight, Glenn. And by the way, I absolutely, positively adore your nursery." Gee, had I just professed such a smarmy sentiment?

Luckily, he smiled as if my ardent declaration were normal. Little did he know I rarely spoke in superlatives.

His name was announced over the PA system. He strode off to answer the phone. Why didn't he just use a cell phone?

"I'm going to have a look around." Angela wandered toward a greenhouse. Fine, I could use some time away from her.

"Okay, I'll go see what's in the shop. Come get me when you're done." I was on a reconnaissance mission, always hunting for new items to add to my catalogue. Why reinvent the wheel? And who knew, Glenn might be interested in selling my birdhouses here.

I entered the smallish structure made of gray stone. Inside, an Amish woman about ten years my senior stood at the register, ringing up bags of daffodil bulbs for a customer. One interior wall was bedecked with rakes, shovels, clippers, saws, and gloves. Hardly a square inch of space left. The opposite wall displayed rubber boots and clogs, hoses, and watering cans. And at the far end stood a collection of flowerpots: ceramic, metal, and cement crafted to look like stone. No birdhouses in sight, but Glenn might carry them in the spring and summer. I imagined his stock was low this time of year.

On a nearby table I spotted a sundial with a circumference larger than a pie tin and finished with a gray-green patina. I reached out to feel its cool metal surface. I couldn't resist flipping the object over to see it was manufactured in the USA at a foundry I'd never heard of. I made a mental note of the name and would jot the information down later.

"It's too big to fit in my suitcase," I told the saleswoman as she moved from behind the counter. I rarely revealed my business when out investigating.

"We'd be happy to mail it to you." She smoothed the front of her black apron. "Would ya like one of our catalogues?" She whisked one off the counter and handed it to me.

"Thank you." The weighty publication made mine look paltry and downright amateurish. A photo of Glenn's house graced the cover. Clumps of daisies crowded the foreground, a hammock hung beneath the maple tree, and a black cat posed on the railing of the wide front porch.

I encountered an unnerving wave of jealousy. Or was it longing?

NINE

Angela

"Glenn's nursery is rather outstanding," Rose said from the back-seat, approval and awe shaping her voice. "And his house isn't shabby either."

I assumed she was infatuated with the man who lived there, which I could understand. If I were single I'd be thrilled he was coming to dinner tonight. Well, I guess I was—for Rose's sake.

As Silvia took us the length of the parking lot Rose pressed her face to the window and ogled the three-story home. "It's even big-ger than yours, sis."

"But the opposite in style," I told Silvia, flatly. "Mine is modern: mostly glass and metal. Too many right angles, like an office build-ing. I would have preferred the Victorian in Wallingford—"

"My neighborhood," Rose interjected. "Aunt Silvia, I dwell in the slums according to Fred. He insisted they move to Redmond. He makes all the decisions."

"He does not." Or did he? I slouched against the car door as we cruised onto the road. "It's a beautiful neighborhood," I said.

"No argument there. But you should have insisted on a house like Glenn's." She let out an atypical sigh. "I can picture a gigan-tic Christmas tree standing in Glenn's bay window. Scads of people gathered around."

"It's not like you to conjure up sentimental scenes, Rosie. I thought you hated Christmas as much as Dad." I directed my words to Silvia. "Our father always insisted on an artificial tree because it didn't drop needles or bother his allergies, and he made Mom dismantle it and repack every trace of the holiday before December thirty-first."

"No New Year's Eve festivities at our house," Rose said. "In fact, our parents hardly ever had people over."

Silvia's foot eased off the accelerator as she neared a horse-drawn wagon. "That surprises me. Juliana led me to believe she entertained a lot."

"Lunches with her girlfriends at a nearby restaurant, if she felt good enough," I said. "But Dad didn't enjoy get-togethers unless they were business-related. Small-talk and the high-pitched voices of women and children annoyed him."

"We probably were annoying," Rose said, always defending our father. "When Angie and I were kids, sometimes we giggled so hard we cried. On bad days we argued like sirens going to a fire."

"I suppose we were hard to live with." I watched Amish toddlers frolicking in a yard around their mother as she hung laundry on a line, the clothing sorted by size and color. "But I adore the sound of children's voices."

"Aunt Silvia, did you find what you wanted at the nursery?" Rose asked, and I understood my sister wished to change the subject. You'd think she hated children. But I knew better.

"Yes, dear." Silvia picked up speed as the wagon turned into a lane I would have loved to explore. "Although what I want and need are not always the same thing." She took us past a splendid farm, freshly harvested fields, a flock of sheep. No electrical wires, I noticed, and yet an idle tractor stood in the barnyard. The many inconsistencies fascinated me.

"If I had a double lot like yours I might do the same thing," Rose said. I contained my immediate response. She hadn't even walked through the greenhouses. Now me, I'd explored Glenn's entire nursery, my eyes embracing every shape: pointed and round leaves—each uniquely ablaze or serenely variegated—old barky vines, and climbing roses spilling onto the walkways. My feet sank into a cushion of color; my legs brushed against the grasses—lovely when allowed to sprawl and wander. My own yard was without personality; gardeners tidied up every leaf as quickly as it floated to the earth.

An idea took shape in my mind. "When I get home I might try my hand at gardening. In the back, I'll let leaves accumulate into thick layers, like pages of history."

"That would be lovely." Silvia transported us past a farm with a windmill, its blades revolving lazily. "Call your nearest nursery and they'll get you started."

"I wonder if they have anyone like Glenn who'd deliver plants and give me advice."

"Exactly like Glenn?" Rose spoke in my ear.

"I meant a professional landscaper to hire." I tried to sound nonchalant, when in truth hearing Glenn's name titillated me, stirring my emotions. "It could be a woman. Yes, I'd prefer a woman." Yet I considered Glenn's arriving at my house, spending all day pruning, mowing, and edging and putting in bulbs. At lunchtime, it would be rude not to invite him in.

"What is it with Glenn, anyway?" Rose asked Silvia. "How come he speaks Pennsylvania Dutch, but doesn't dress Amish and drives a pickup?"

Silvia followed behind a buggy, allowing it to set her leisurely pace. "His parents are Old Order Amish and still live close by. He took off during *Rumspringa*—what the Amish call their running-around period starting at age sixteen, until they're ready to become baptized. Most stay in the area and live at home."

"But not Glenn?"

She slapped the turn indicator. "No."

"Why did he leave?"

"A number of reasons. For one, he wanted a higher education. The Amish only attend school through the eighth grade."

Rose chortled. "You've got to be kidding."

"Now, don't put them down," Silvia said. "Most graduate with at least as good an education as I did at the local high school. They read and are extremely industrious."

"So then he started the nursery?" Angela asked.

"Not right away." Silvia ran her tongue across her lower lip. "You can ask him yourself so I don't make myself into a gossip."

"Did he run off with a woman?" Rose asked.

When Silvia didn't answer, I couldn't help but say, "With Olivia?" I did the math in my head and knew I was way off.

Silvia gave her head a shake. "No, she was quite a bit younger back then. But she seems sweet on him now."

"To put it mildly." Angela's voice sounded terse.

"She has several suitors." Silvia slowed where the road intersected a larger one. "Olivia is not yet baptized Amish, which is a lifetime commitment to the church. Once baptized, she must marry a man also baptized Amish. That would put Glenn out of the running unless…"

Silvia pulled to the side of the road. She ground to a halt in front of an abandoned two-story clapboard building with peeling paint, boarded-up bay windows, and a Do Not Trespass sign guarding the front door. "This is the grocery store where my grandparents worked. They lived in the room upstairs. You wouldn't know to look at it, but *La Croce*—meaning the cross in Italian—was a popular place to shop and run into friends. A mixture of every ethnicity."

"Even Amish?" Rose asked.

"Yes, we all knew our Amish neighbors well." Silvia's voice grew somber. "Perhaps a little too well."

I wanted to hear more about Silvia's ambiguous remark, but Rose said, "What happened to this place? It looks haunted." The screen door, devoid of wire mesh, hung at a tilt, the two second-story windows were broken out—probably from rocks hurled through them—and the crooked chimney appeared ready to crumble.

"It passed hands several times after the original owners retired, and then it went out of business when a chain built a supermarket down the way and everyone started shopping there." She cut the engine and set the parking brake. "This whole area has changed. Every year someone builds a fancy new store that draws more shoppers onto the highway or down to the mall."

"Can we take a look around?" I hoped Silvia would remember something she needed to purchase at the nursery after all. Rose grumbled about being hungry, but I got out anyway and so did Silvia. I stepped around a cement platform that once housed gas pumps to reach the front door. A fading King Arthur Flour sign was affixed to the wall at shin level beneath one window and a Salada Tea sign under the other. The store name must have hung above the front door where a rectangular shape of darker paint remained.

As I craned my neck to view the second story, Rose exited the car. "They lived up there? It's tiny."

She was right; the second floor looked to be the size of our den at home. I tried to envision Frederick returning after a day's work and entering a one-room apartment to find me cooking—an impossible scene. Except to eat breakfast, he rarely set foot in our kitchen unless it was to pour himself a cup of coffee or a glass of wine.

"During the Depression, this was luxury." Silvia guided us around the side of the building over packed dirt and weeds. "Remember, people lost everything," she said. "Not that my grandparents had much to lose. They came to this country with practically nothing. Only the desire for a better life and a trust that God would provide."

"They were brave." I noticed a one-story house in equal disrepair hunkered in the over-grown field out back. "I can't imagine moving to a country where no one spoke my language. And I'd miss my family and friends." Yet the thought of stepping into the unknown tantalized me, tugging at the mortar of my foundation. I'd heard of women mysteriously running away from home, husband, and children—without warning. Did they even bother to pack? I had my purse with me and a few changes of clothes. Did I need more?

"I wonder why they moved out here, of all places." Rose eyed the rotting back steps leading to a door with no handle. Cigarette butts, broken glass, bottle caps, and a flattened garbage can lid lay scattered at our feet.

"At one time they intended to stay in the city, but 1929 and the early thirties were rough years." Silvia's eyes grew smaller. "It's impossible for someone even my age to imagine what the Depression was like. My grandparents had only been in this country a year. My grandpa lost his job, like most everyone. Bread lines congregated under their apartment window. Men in business suits, women with crying babies, most everyone brought down to the same hungry level." She raised a hand to her chest and patted it. "Those were bleak times. Fortunately Grandpa knew the owner of this store, who gave my grandparents jobs and a place to live. And the Amish helped with food. If you have Amish for neighbors you'll never starve."

She looked up to the second story at the remnants of a window box. "When your great-grandma got pregnant, your great-grandpa worked as a carpenter on the side to make ends meet. Then he started his own business. By the time he died, he owned the lumberyard." Her eyebrows lifted, opening her face to a grin. "'Only in America,' he used to say."

"We all have so much these days," Rose said. I presumed she was referring to me.

Silvia nodded. "And we take everything for granted, not aware of our abundance. 'Everyone should live through a Depression once,' my grandpa used to say. 'Otherwise you'll never appreciate what you have.' And he did. Every time he bit into a tomato out of his garden, he'd take a moment to savor the taste and smack his lips. 'Now that's a tomato,' he'd say, 'grown in our soil, the earth we own. Thank you, Lord, amen.'"

I envisioned a swarthy man, round at the belly, his craggy face changeable as the clouds in the sky. "Not a bad way to look at life," I said. "I wish we'd gotten to know him." I wondered what kernels of knowledge he might have imparted. "Your grandparents struggled for everything and weren't embarrassed to admit it."

"Yes, it made their victories sweeter. They were proud to have started from scratch."

How opposite was our father, who enjoyed name-dropping his alma mater, his tax bracket, how he legally avoided paying the IRS its due, and the fact he'd inherit a small fortune someday when his mother died.

"Rose and I never lacked for anything and now my children have even more. My kids are spoiled."

"That's for sure." Rose was slamming me. "I mean most kids are these days, Angie."

"But I don't want to deny them just to teach them to be grateful. Although Tiffany and Daniel rarely bother to thank me. I guess they do expect and get everything, but isn't that what our parents did for us?"

"Yeah, we were pampered." Rose swung out her foot and kicked an empty pop can, skidding it several yards, where it hit the bottom step. "And given way too much. Stuff, stuff, stuff. I've been seriously thinking of downsizing my life. Getting rid of things I don't use."

"Huh? Your living room is a white cubicle with a few prints on the walls, a minimalist couch, and a couple of straight-back chairs. If anything, you could use more in your house."

"What for? I don't like meaningless knickknacks gathering dust. Really, lately I've had the urge to give half my belongings away." She was sending me a message about my stockpiles of clothes, antiques, and books.

"You hang on to things as hard as I do." I laced my fingers. "You're doggedly independent and resistant to everything I suggest. That's holding on too."

She didn't respond, thankfully, but instead grasped her hands behind her back and dug her toe into a crack in the dirt. No doubt she was using Herculean energy to keep from verbally slashing me.

"I hear this place is going on the market." Silvia jiggled her keys. "A nice young Amish couple who work for Glenn have been asking about it. Why, if they purchased the place, their whole community would come help spruce it up like new."

"Really?" Rose said. "For free? You'd never see anything like that where we live."

My admiration for the Amish was skyrocketing. But I wouldn't say anything that might encourage Rose to move here. Bitter irony if she did; I was the sister who'd wanted to come here, not her.

Minutes later, we three piled into the car. Silvia backed us onto the road, causing an on-coming SUV to stop. In Seattle the other driver would have leaned on his horn, but people here seemed more tolerant of each other. Yes, I could get used to living in Lancaster County.

"Now you know why my house is crammed to the gills." Silvia moved us forward and gave the SUV's driver a thank-you wave. "Thinking left over from the Depression. The belief that all could disappear in the blink of an eye made my folks accumulate like pack-rats storing up for winter. I'm afraid I inherited their habit. 'Mama, you can't take it to heaven with you,' I would complain. Now Phyllis is saying the same thing to me."

"It'll be a long time before you have to worry about that," I said. But her general fatigue and slow-motion thinking reminded me of Mom.

"I bet you live to be a hundred years old." Rose reached forward to give Silvia's shoulder a pat.

"I don't know about that," Silvia said. "So far the family hasn't done well in the longevity department."

We came upon a railroad crossing. The car slowly joggled over the tracks. I glanced out the side window and spotted a locomotive

as tall as a house off in the distance. The signal lights at the crossing weren't flashing, nor had the bar come down to block our path,
meaning the train must be too far away to be hazardous. But still,
what if Silvia's car got stuck on the tracks? What if the train was
hurtling toward us at sixty miles per hour? It would smash us to
smithereens.

Frederick complained I worried too much and Rose echoed his
sentiment. I suppose they were right. I didn't start experiencing
episodes of anxiety until Tiffany and Daniel were born. No, that
isn't true. I remember, one Saturday, right after Frederick and I got
married, he went off skiing with his buddies and didn't return until
2:00 a.m. They'd stopped somewhere for drinks, but I was so fran-
tic for Frederick's safety I called several hospital emergency rooms.
Now when he was late—at least once a week—I took a Benadryl
to make me sleepy and turned the clock around so I couldn't see
the time.

"Scientists have figured ways to add years onto people's lives."
Rose seemed oblivious of the approaching train. Or maybe she saw
it and didn't care.

"True," Silvia said. "I know people who've lived far longer than
anyone predicted. They've endured terrible circumstances, even
come home from wars all in one piece when the odds were a thou-
sand to one. But ultimately, when it's our time, it's our time. God
makes the final decision."

"You mean God let Mom die at an early age on purpose?" Rose
asked. "Like some sort of punishment?"

"Punishment for what?" I felt indignant. "Mom never did anything wrong. She was near perfect."

Rose snorted a laugh. "Don't go overboard and canonize her
into a saint."

"I don't want to talk about Mom anymore." I rotated my head to
watch the scenery. "Or death."

"Oh, my." Silvia swatted on her blinker and turned at the next crossroad. "I was planning to drive you girls by the old cemetery where my folks are buried. But let's do something more entertaining."

"Maybe we could go there another day," I said. "We know so little about your side of the family. Mom rarely talked about her parents."

"Yeah," Rose said. "Except for those few visits here, it was like we only had one set of grandparents. Our father's."

"And Grandpa Webster died when we were in our teens."

"Father's mother, Grandma Webster, isn't exactly the warm, fuzzy type." Rose's volume increased. "I don't think she ever babysat us. Which is just as well."

"Yes, I've met her," Silvia said. And then she added, "I'm sure she has many fine qualities."

"Father claims she's loaded." Rose flopped back against her seat. "That was the reason Grandpa married her."

"She was beautiful when she was young." I thought of the photo on Dad's desk taken on his parents' wedding day. "Some people are that way once they've raised their own kids. They don't want to stay home and take care of children anymore."

"All I know is, she'd be a hard person to have for a parent." Rose shivered for effect, her hands shaking like a bird's wings. "A scary thought." Imitating Grandma Webster, she spoke through her nose. "She's never liked me. I'm a disappointment. She thought I should turn out to be a famous scientist or mathematician because I was the intelligent granddaughter."

I felt her stare piercing the back of my head.

"Angie was the beautiful one." Her voice turned syrupy. "Grandmother calls her Princess."

"I don't think we should talk about her." I frowned into the rearview mirror at Rose. "She's an old lady. She says what's on her mind."

"She's always been like that. You like her because she lavishes your kids with presents."

I heard sadness warping Rose's voice. "I'm sorry. Do you want me to say something to her?"

"Don't be ridiculous. She's eighty-eight. She's not going to change."

We drove in silence for several minutes. Glancing at me, Silvia said, "I think we've done enough sightseeing for one day, unless you want to find an antique store on the way to the market."

Our previous conversation had leached my stamina. Spending time with Rose wasn't drawing us closer—quite the contrary. "No thanks. I'd be just as happy to buy food and then go home."

"No way," Rose barked. "If we get back to Seattle and you haven't found all the junk you want, you'll never forgive me. I know how that works."

Suddenly, I'd endured enough of her stabbing remarks. I swiveled in my seat to face her. "You make me sound awful. When have I ever said anything like that?"

"It's not what you say. It's your cold-shoulder treatment."

"You mean the times I don't call you, hoping you'll call me first?" I tried to stare her down, but her defiant glare made me glance away. "Rosie, why must I always be the one to initiate the first move? If I didn't, I'd probably never see you again." The fact my sister couldn't stand me hurt so much I could have cried. But a show of emotion would only serve to distance her more.

The tiniest smirk lifted the corners of her mouth. "I'm sure Silvia doesn't want to hear us squabble." Her chilly tone filled me with shame.

I started to apologize to Silvia, but she smiled. "Don't worry about it, dear. When two sisters are in close proximity for a few days, there's bound to be a skirmish. Believe me, Juliana and I had our moments. But we never went to the next level and talked things out, which was a mistake." She rolled into the market's parking lot and positioned us near the front entrance. "It's better to put your grievances out on the table."

I wondered if she were correct—if someday I should provoke Rose until her dam burst and a blast of hostility came boiling forth—if we should verbally duke it out like a couple of alley cats, no holds barred. Spewing her stockpile of pent-up venom at me might deflate her hatred; maybe after, we'd find healing.

But was I brave enough to stand up to her? I imagined myself watching the locomotive barreling toward me. I saw myself tossed into a ditch, brutalized, snapped in half like a twig. Later, Rose, whose memory was a bank vault, would cling to my words and use them against me. I would find no resolution, only her increased animosity.

TEN

Rose

I sat across from Glenn at Aunt Silvia's crowded dinner table, hoping to mention my mail-order business. But the opportunity never presented itself. Through the main course, Cousin Phyllis and her husband, Hugh, described the family's thriving lumber and construction business. Then Glenn mentioned his intentions to build a new mini café in his nursery for shoppers and locals.

"An Amish man will act as contractor and Hugh will provide the materials," he told Angela.

"A young Amish woman, Olivia Beiler, did a fine job designing the interior space." Hugh forked into his lasagna. His face boyishly round, he appeared a good-natured and likable man, in his mid-forties. According to Silvia, a stockbroker when he and Phyllis met.

"She'll do the baking and manage it," Glenn added between bites.

I couldn't imagine why this information harpooned into me, making my stomach clench and my hunger dissipate. Was I jealous of someone I didn't even know?

"I hear the nursery suffered another act of vandalism." Hugh's short reddish hair popped up like bristles on a scrub brush. "Any leads?"

"Not yet." Glenn set his fork aside. "So far, nothing too serious, but it has me worried."

"We don't want anything slowing down your project." Hugh turned to Angela. "Next week my men will lay the foundation." His freckles danced as he spoke. "The structure will house a small café with an indoor fountain standing in a shallow koi-filled pool."

"A nice spot for Glenn's customers to relax with a latte or iced tea and a snack." Phyllis glanced to Silvia's dinner plate and her brows lowered. "When folks find out Olivia's baking, they'll come flocking."

"Sounds great," I said, but no one seemed to hear me. As far as I could tell, Glenn hadn't noticed my presence, even though I was wearing my black skinny jeans and a fuchsia V-neck sweater. I wasn't accustomed to being invisible.

"You're gorgeous," Brad declared the last time I saw him. Was I actually gorgeous? Brad tossed out glittering adjectives and clichés like pennies into a gumball machine. I still hadn't spoken to him yet. In my mind, his voice sounded high-pitched and insincere compared to Glenn's. I was expecting to miss Brad, but was aware how few times I'd thought about him. Didn't absence make the heart grow fonder?

Hugh swallowed a mouthful of lasagna. "Our goal is to lay the foundation and complete the outside before the first snow."

For five minutes I heard much speculation about whether an early frost, as predicted by *The Farmers' Almanac*, would spoil their plans.

Finally I decided to dive into the conversation whether invited or not. I chose Phyllis as my target. "So Glenn buys his lumber from Hugh, and Hugh and you purchase all your plants from Glenn?"

"We're a close-knit group, everyone knows everyone around here." Phyllis's words dovetailed together.

That much familiarity would feel like a stranglehold to me. As if reading my mind, Silvia said, "If you don't make peace with your neighbors, you may find the plumber living down the road doesn't show up when your pipes burst on the coldest day of the year."

Phyllis's nose wrinkled as she grinned. "It keeps us honest."

"You ladies make us sound like a vindictive lot," Hugh said.

Glenn rested his hands on the table. "Yes, I like to think we put out our welcome mat to strangers."

"You know what I meant." Phyllis raised her shoulders. "If I'm brusque with the cashier at the hardware store, I'm apt to run into him again at the lumberyard, only this time I'll be waiting on him."

"I hope I never see that crabby pharmacist again," I blurted out. "I'd rather lose business than speak to him." I found I'd gathered Glenn's and everyone else's attention. Five sets of eyes locked onto mine. I looked to Angela to confirm my statement, but she sliced into her lasagna. She'd apparently missed my hasty remark. Or maybe she wanted no part of my faux pas.

I scarfed down a mouthful of lasagna.

Silvia patted the corners of her mouth with her napkin. "Was there a problem?"

The pharmacist was apparently a long-time friend of Silvia's; he'd told us so. I didn't want to reopen the scar left by his unkind reaction to Mother's name, let alone her death. "It was no big deal. And I suppose it does pay to be polite to everyone. Look how Angie and I met Glenn."

Again I turned to Angela, who was maneuvering her food around on her plate. Eating even less than Silvia. My sister had been unusually quiet all evening. I wondered if anyone else noticed. Looking at Angela's docile face, you wouldn't know she was usually a chatterbox. Maybe she was coming down with the flu. After we left the nursery, she didn't even want to explore the thrift store Silvia pointed out as her favorite haunt for finding secondhand bargains. I was the one who led the way into the building and then emerged the owner of a heart-shaped wrought iron trivet that cost only three dollars. I bought it on impulse and would no doubt give it away when I got home. I didn't like other people's discards. But several other items had also caught my eye. A decades-old State of Pennsylvania tablecloth. Some monogrammed napkins. What would I do with a tablecloth when I ate most of my meals in front of the TV? And I stuck to paper napkins out of convenience.

While in the store I also found myself admiring a set of pink glass dessert dishes. Not my style either. My small home was bathed in restful colors. Cocoa and camel, melding together into tranquility. My own china—stoneware, really—was the plainest white and purchased from a restaurant supply outlet. I consumed organic mixed salad greens using heavy, modern flatware, its stark surface a brushed aluminum. Only Minnie ate from a yellow polka-dotted bowl sitting on a polka-dotted mat. One carefree statement at the corner of the kitchen by the back door where no one saw.

"Rose, dear." Silvia's voice broke into my thoughts. "Tell the others about your business."

"Yes, please." Phyllis begged me to send her a catalogue and Hugh asked a myriad of questions about the mail-order business. I guessed craving the limelight made me egotistical or needy. I enjoyed the attention, especially from Glenn. He didn't say much, but I could tell he viewed me at a new slant, as a person of interest.

"How about you, Angela?" Phyllis asked, during a lull in the conversation. "How do you spend your days?"

Angela seemed atypically paralyzed. I'd always watched my sister from the sidelines with envy. She was more capable than most people realized.

"Just a housewife." Her narrow smile might have fooled the others, but it looked phony to me.

"There's not a thing wrong with being a homemaker," Silvia said.

"Of course not. Until ten years ago I stayed home until our three were in school." Phyllis had mentioned earlier she adored spending her days at the lumberyard. She acted as bookkeeper, answered the phone, and wrote up orders during peak hours.

"I find ways to keep myself busy." Angela emitted a trifle of enthusiasm.

"I'm sure you do," Silvia said. "There's more to life than work and money."

I wondered why my sister hadn't depicted her usual Angie-in-Wonderland story. I'd often heard about her volunteer fund-raising. She'd chaired her children's school's phenomenally successful auction three years in a row. And she usually found a way to drop Fred's name into the conversation. How he'd aced a case with a lucrative settlement or was representing someone famous. In essence, how perfect her life was. I was tempted to describe it myself.

"I'll get the coffee urn." Angela jolted to her feet and collected Silvia's plate, empty for the first time since Angela and I had arrived. I'd noticed Silvia serving herself a small portion. And I also noticed Phyllis watching her consume every bite.

Phyllis cut the apple crisp she'd brought as Angela delivered the coffee urn, cups, and dessert plates. Phyllis pushed back her chair but Angela laid a hand on her shoulder. "Stay where you are. I'll clear the rest," Angela said. As she collected the other dishes her gaze remained downcast. She seemed to be holding back tears. Minutes later, through the door to the kitchen, I watched her standing at the low sink. It appeared as if she were allowing the hot water to flow over her hands. Not much else. Maybe she missed her children. I should be sympathetic. A woman would miss her kids. And, who knows, maybe she really did miss Fred.

Phyllis finished her coffee. "We should be on our way. My husband isn't supposed to rise with the Stock Exchange's opening bell anymore, but his early mornings haven't changed."

"Okay, I'm guilty. But it's a good kind of early. I rise when our Amish neighbors milk their cows and often go over and help." Hugh stood and pushed in his chair. "Silvia, as always, your cooking is the best. Except for my lovely wife's."

Phyllis got to her feet and kissed Silvia's cheek. "Ma, you look like you've lost more weight."

Silvia smiled up to Hugh. "Don't you and the kids give this girl of mine enough to worry about?"

"I do my best." He winked.

Phyllis gathered her purse and slid her arms into her jacket. "Ma, I can take tomorrow off and come pick up Angela and Rose. Eat lunch, shop, whatever."

"And leave me at home?" Silvia harrumphed.

"You feel up to it, Ma?"

"Sure do."

Phyllis and Hugh stuck their heads in the kitchen to say good night to Angela and then left. I was glad Glenn remained longer to savor the last bites of his dessert. It was nice having a man seated across the table.

"I'd better be on my way too." He folded his cloth napkin as if he planned to use it again. "Silvia, I just remembered I brought along that pruning book. It's out in my truck."

As he stood his hair brushed the edge of the brass chandelier. "I'll go fetch it and be right back."

"Rose, dear, would you run out there and get it? I don't want to ask too much of Glenn. He may decide this old lady is too much trouble."

"That won't ever happen," he said.

"Sure, I'll go with him." I shot to my feet. "It'll feel good to stretch my legs." As I pulled my jacket off the hook by the front door, I heard my sister gathering the dessert plates and then retreating into the kitchen again without saying goodbye to Glenn.

A smile curled my lips. "I'm all yours." I followed him outside.

One low-wattage bulb illuminated the darkened walkway to the garage. The moon rode low in the sky, just above the treetops. The half orb had shrunk a skosh, but emitted glowing radiance. Its craters and intricate texture were visible in a way I'd never seen in the city. I figured that without electricity the Amish must depend on its luminous light.

Coming to a halt midway to his old truck, I turned my eyes upward and saw first one flicker and then another, as the stars populated the sky. My gaze embraced the ever-illuminating heavens.

"Sorry for slowing you down." My eyes drank in the Milky Way. "I don't remember ever seeing as many stars. Not since I went to camp as a kid, anyway. I was lying in a sleeping bag counting shooting stars. I know now that they're not really stars, but I saw thirteen that night. I'll never forget it."

The stars blurred, melting into a creamy haze. Were my eyes tearing up? Struggling to blink them away, I ached to be held, enfolded in someone's arms, as if inside a flower, its petals reclosing back around itself. Warm, safe. To be loved, really loved, just because I was Rose. Didn't my parents first take me in their arms, only thinking about caring for me? Or did they always love Angela more? I recalled starting school and accepting other adults as my teachers, my guides. Then friends became all important. Is that when my parents stopped loving the real me instead of my achievements?

I glanced over to see Glenn's profile as he scanned the sky. The air stood starkly quiet. Not that crickets weren't humming. Or that I couldn't hear the well's pump thumping around the side of the house and horses' hooves in the distance. But without the city's sounds—busses, jets, and cars zooming past my house with their stereos thudding rap music—the air seemed vacuous. Unable to grasp something tangible, my ears searched the void until they found my own breath. Encouraging me to suck in more air and allow it to descend deep inside of me. I held my expanded lungs for a moment before returning the warm current to the cool atmosphere. I released a sigh he must have heard.

"The stillness is what I missed the most." His words became clearer as he rotated toward me. "When I turned seventeen I informed my parents I'd had enough of Lancaster County to last me a lifetime. I was done mucking out the barn and watching cars speed past my buggy, spooking my horse. I'd never come back. I thought if I didn't leave, I'd be smothered to death."

"That's understandable. I don't think I'd ever get used to living in the country." Hearing my somewhat rude reply, I added, "But it's beautiful. I'm just not used to everything being so slow. I mean, what do people do for entertainment?"

"Well, now, I used to ask the same question." He shifted his weight. "Late one night, when I was seventeen, my former girl-friend, Mary Ann—she was Amish too—and I snuck away together. We hopped on a bus and then another until we reached the Pacific Ocean, where we planned to play volleyball on the beach and bask in the sunshine."

He cleared his throat. "But once we were in Southern California, we needed jobs and soon found ourselves dashing off in a mad rush, either to work or back to our tiny apartment. My clock radio would go off, spitting out the morning traffic report, which ranged from bad to worse. I'd race to the freeway to sit in my car, shaver in hand, congratulating myself that I was making such good use of my time. Staring at the headrest of the guy in front of me, we'd both swerve off the exit, each of us trying to be the first to hit his air-conditioned office, as if that was some great accomplishment."

His voice turned melancholy as if he were filled with regret or loss. "Then one day Mary Ann told me she was tired of it all. 'I can't stand this rat race anymore,' she said. She'd decided to move to a remote spot in New Mexico. 'I'll come with you,' I said. 'I only live here to be with you.'"

His voice grew louder as he stepped closer. "But, of course, things are never that simple. A few days later, I found out about Phil—I mean Philip, as Mary Ann insisted on calling him."

Cool air traveling up my sleeves made me shiver. I struggled for a meaningful reply. I'd never run away from home and then been deserted. Yet I was the person my girlfriends often approached with their agonies, asking for counsel. I usually spewed my insights, calmly and mechanically, like a therapist, and then was thanked for my sage advice. But as I listened to Glenn I was overcome with a throbbing pain and unable to speak.

"It turned out for the best," he said. "Isn't that how we always make things right in our minds? Mary Ann and Philip are still together, and I wasn't cut out to live in New Mexico any more than in Southern California. This is where I'm supposed to be. It sure feels good when you finally figure that out. Now only a few decisions left…"

In the following moments, I tried to envision this man, who appeared a casual, simple sort, wearing business attire, his waves of brown hair severely slicked back. Movie stars were chameleons, I thought, able to peel one disguise for another as quickly as they moved from set to set. Was it possible Glenn clothed himself in a superficial masquerade, leaving his original identity to shrink until it no longer existed? Glenn Yoder, making ruthless deals, walking over his opponents as if they were convenient stepping-stones? Cursing at the car in front of him that didn't accelerate quickly enough when the light turned green, the way Father did?

In the dim light it was difficult to tell if I still held Glenn's attention. Did he want to end this conversation so he could give me the book and go home? Probably. But I didn't want to lose him. Not yet.

"Silvia said your parents live close by." I knew his father had. I'd been gripped by the photo of his arm around Mother's shoulder. Since closing the album, I'd clutched that image in my brain as if encountering the scene of an accident, determined to affix the details clearly in my mind's eye.

"They live five miles from here," he said. "I could never figure out why my pathetic parents stayed. I dreamed of going to a big high school. The kind where kids poured out of double-wide doors at the end of the day, wearing the latest clothes and talking about things more important than whether the Millers' barn had really been struck by lightning or if one of their sons had snuck out for a smoke and set it on fire."

"What made you change your mind and come back?"

"About ten years ago I found myself a single, lonely man. I decided to return and be a contented nobody."

"You're hardly a nobody."

"Not according to my parents and their bishop."

"An Amish bishop? Would you ever turn in your car keys and join the Amish church?" I expected him to chuckle. But his words remained somber.

"I think about it sometimes."

I heard a horse's hooves on the road and wondered if the sound served as his anchor. "But you've got that fabulous nursery," I said. "Could you still run it?"

"Owning a nursery wasn't what I had in mind when I started out. I was actually interested in the house." He was altering the trajectory of our conversation, avoiding my real question. "I didn't want anyone building right next to me, so I bought the land around it, with two greenhouses. Compared to California prices, they practically gave the property away."

"And now you're a plant specialist?" Not that I doubted his expertise.

"Okay, you found me out. I'm a fraud. I took the GED, got a scholarship to UC Berkeley, and earned a degree in business, a subject I wasn't particularly interested in but figured I needed in order to get rich—what I thought would make me happy."

His explanation sounded too easy-peasy. "Owning a successful nursery is a giant leap from that," I said.

He laughed in a relaxed manner. "If it makes you feel any better, when I was a kid I earned money doing yard work for neighbors. And I've become a Master Gardener, attended seminars, and read every horticulture book I could get my hands on. When I bought the nursery, it was about a quarter the size. I thought I could get away with hiring one person to run it for me."

I considered my birdhouses, my helpful neighbor, and the

lumber stacked between our houses waiting to be used. "That's sort of how my business got going. It started itself."

"Some of the best things in life force themselves upon us. All we have to do is ease up on the reins and let the good things flow."

"Sounds rather metaphysical."

"No, no. God's the one handing out the gifts."

Glenn believed in that hocus-pocus I outgrew at age fifteen? Since then I'd had no use for religion, yet knowing he believed in God made Glenn trustworthy. I was tired of men acting as though they were king of the world.

His gaze turned upward again. He was indeed handsome. Not that I cared what he looked like. When had appearances ever mattered? I recalled several of the good-looking men I'd dated. When we broke up, sometimes at my request, usually at theirs, all I saw were twisted, belligerent features. Then the backs of their heads as they made their final exits. Once a guy I liked got his nose bent out of joint over something minor and stormed off, leaving me at our restaurant booth with the unpaid bill. I could have died when I opened my wallet to discover I'd left my credit card at home and had only twenty dollars. Not that I didn't sometimes pick up the tab. Modern women were supposed to do those things. Although deep inside I hated it.

I inched toward Glenn. My chest swelled—there's no other way to describe it. I would have done anything to avoid appearing foolish, but decided to heed his advice, to let go of the reins I grasped so tightly. I could risk rejection and remorse. I had nothing to lose with a man I'd never see again.

I put my hand out to take his. I imagined his warm hand grasping mine, and then he'd take me in his arms.

"I'll get you that book," he said, making me start.

I snapped my hand back to my side. My heart started pumping enough blood to get me through a marathon. I reassured myself he hadn't known what I was planning. What had I been thinking?

He moved to his pickup and I followed. Reaching in through the open window, he extracted the book. "Here ya go. I'll walk you back to the house."

"No, that's okay, I'm fine." I took the book from him. As I turned to leave, a massive force rammed against my legs, almost knocking me over. I swung around and saw a menacing shape at my feet. Emitting a yelp, I dropped the book and spun back to Glenn for safety. His arm wrapped around my shoulder in a brotherly fashion.

"You city girls are skittish, aren't you?"

I made out Rex's shaggy outline. "I'm usually not such a wimp."

He picked up the book and handed it to me. "No, you seem like a woman who can handle anything that comes her way."

"I used to think so, but lately I'm beginning to wonder."

Eleven

Angela

I sat on the canopy bed reading a romance novel that captured only a quarter of my attention. When I was six, this mattress had seemed ten feet off the floor, a mountain I'd climbed straight up until I spotted three-year-old Rose, napping. I'd tickle her and then, like rambunctious kittens, she and I would giggle and wrestle on this same patchwork quilt, covering the same ivory-colored bedspread, its textured surface worn to a downy softness.

When had Rose and I ceased playing together? When did we stop confiding in each other? We'd shared a bedroom until I turned thirteen. On that auspicious day Mom gave up her sewing room and converted the space into a bedroom for me. When not at the dance studio I'd spent my free time fussing with my hair, wondering if the girls in the popular crowd liked me, or trying to conceal pimples erupting on my nose—I'd feign menstrual cramps to avoid going to school with even the slightest blemish. And then came boys. Or rather, the boy: Rusty Harris, my first love. Rose, on the other hand, had still been enamored with horses and hated boys; she was a late bloomer. But when she finally bloomed...look out, world.

Still, she and I had slept right across the hall from each other, sharing the white-tiled bathroom. Why did we become disconnected, like pulling an electrical cord out of a socket?

I heard someone running water upstairs and then snap it off, telling me it was Rose, who did everything in a hurry. Frederick labeled her Type A. But in spite of his negative appraisals—he said she was a bigmouth know-it-all who would never find a husband—he admired her gumption. And I knew he wished I were more like her.

The floorboards above me squeaked as she settled into bed. She'd certainly dallied outside with Glenn a long time. What did they talk about? Or do? Over dinner, he'd seemed captivated with her, as any man would be. And Phyllis and Hugh were impressed with her accomplishments. I shouldn't let Rose's abilities make me feel inadequate, but they did. I knew nothing about business; I was sure I couldn't even balance my checking account. I had never tried.

I clapped my book shut and set it on the bedside table. I should be tired, but reading for an hour hadn't induced sleepiness; in fact, it left me agitated. The novel's story was set in Saint-Germain-des-Prés, on Paris's Left Bank, but I'd read the basic plot so many times I already knew what was going to happen. The heroine, Amanda, an American student studying abroad, had met a handsome French stranger, Ramon, who claimed to be doing research at the Louvre but was actually involved in espionage. Because Amanda had been hurt in the past and didn't trust men, she resisted his advances, but found herself helplessly infatuated, tumbling into confusion and desire. She'd attempted to translate his motives: Were his intentions malicious? Or was he the one good man she'd waited all her life to love?

The man she'd waited to love, I repeated in my mind. The notion disturbed me. My head sank into the pillows propped against the headboard. Out of the millions of people on this spinning globe, did women really find their one perfect love? I supposed I had. Ironically, when I met Frederick in college, I'd barely noticed him; I didn't consider him good-looking, what with his pudgy nose and swaggering gait I later found endearing—most of the time. Even his name seemed comical until he reminded me he shared it with the king of Prussia. He'd told me he was studying law and had big plans for himself, and seemed most impressed when I spoke of my father and several of his clients.

Before I knew it, Frederick dominated my mind. I lost my appetite when I thought he was attracted by a sorority sister, and I slumped into depression when he didn't call me every day. Out of desperation I cleverly molded myself into the shape of his ideal woman so he'd love me in return. Although sometimes I wondered if he loved me or if I were merely a necessary appendage.

Had Mom acted the same way when she met Dad? I'd always assumed as a youth she was simply Mom in a younger version. But when Silvia showed us the photo of her with Glenn's father, I realized I barely knew our mother, jarring me. It was like rereading my favorite novel, *Gone with the Wind,* and finding Scarlett O'Hara loved someone before Ashley Wilkes. Like dominos falling, that plot twist would change the rest of the story.

Donning my robe, I wandered into the living area, turned on a lamp, and stood before the bookcase. My hand located the photo album. Flipping through the pages, I viewed sepia-colored portraits: ancestors frozen in time—several maintaining severe scowls on their faces—children in christening gowns, and my grandparents' wedding picture. I came across Mom as a baby and then as a youngster posing with her siblings. Finally I located the object of my search. When Silvia first showed us this photograph, I hadn't recognized my own mother. I could detect some family resemblance—the bridge of her nose, the slant of her eyes—but that's where it ended, because in this photo Mom's lips appeared full, dark, and sumptuous, her eyes flirtatious. Provocative, really. How unlike her usual unreadable Mona Lisa face.

Captured forever, Glenn's father supported her firmly. He looked like a younger Glenn: tall, broad shouldered, his jaw square, his brows bold. But wearing a brimmed hat, the shadow across his eyes made it impossible to read his expression. I tipped the album, trying to catch the light better. What was his father's name? Chester. If he were indeed Amish, we might have passed his buggy on the road.

The fact that Amish blood flowed through Glenn's veins enthralled me. He'd held me this very day. His name was etched in my mind like the reframe of a treasured song.

I wondered what his hands had felt. Was he appalled by my fleshy, round waist? Or did he long to pull me closer? There was a time when Frederick found me irresistible, but not anymore. He looked the other way when I stepped out of the shower, making me want to hide behind a towel. I longed to be appreciated by someone, even a near-stranger, to verify I was still a woman, not just an outdated mom and carpooler.

Flabbergasted by my runaway thoughts, I glanced at the photo again. Silvia said Glenn's parents were still living. At a secondhand store several months ago, I'd flipped through old framed photographs filed in a cardboard box. Scrutinizing the portraits, I'd been struck by the fact that most, if not all, of the people had passed away.

At Mom's burial I stood staring at her gravestone, wondering if she were really dead. A marble marker, pewter-gray like Mom's favorite St. John suit. Dad sent that suit to Goodwill, along with the rest of her clothes. "Why keep it?" he'd said. Mom's dresses, her purses, her scarves—why did he clear away all traces of her so quickly?

Of course Dad had been heartbroken when Mom died. Husbands missed their wives as much as their children did. She was his best friend, his confidante. After all, what did he and his golf cronies talk about? The latest news, the Stock Exchange index, the Seahawks and the Mariners? Nothing that mattered in the middle of the night.

Perhaps women shared too much and were too transparent, I considered. I'd revealed some of my disappointments to Rose and later felt embarrassed. I had far more wealth than she, and two children, so I was sure she thought I had no right to complain. She'd never understand that sometimes the responsibility of trying to keep Frederick and the kids happy all the time sucked the air out of me.

Don't be silly, I told myself, fitting the album back between two books. My life was a good one. Better than good. The morning paper and six o'clock news reminded me daily of the despair the rest of the world endured. Yet on TV sometimes those ravaged people seemed happier than I was. Last week, the children swarming around a newscaster radiated more energy than my kids, who often looked bored even when wolfing down a chocolate sundae. In spite of our blessings our family rarely experienced joy.

The clock on the mantel bonged eleven times—only 8:00 p.m. in Seattle. I reached for the phone and dialed my home number. Daniel answered, but after only a few words, he passed the receiver to Frederick, who didn't inquire about the trip or how Rose and I were getting along. To create conversation, I said, "We should bring the kids here next spring break. It's beautiful."

"Are you nuts? You'd choose Lancaster County over Maui? I want to go to Napili, like always."

I coiled the telephone cord around my index finger. "You might like it here." But my mind already questioned how my family members would occupy themselves without a golf course, swimming pool, or TV.

"Angela, Napili was voted one of the most beautiful beaches in the world. Why go anywhere else?"

"Then how about Christmas?" I imagined the four of us trudging through hip-high snow into the forest to uncover a noble fir. Frederick could chop it down—if he knew how to use an axe—and then we'd drag the tree back to the house to enjoy steamy hot chocolate.

"Please forget about this," he said. "What's gotten into you?" He lowered his voice to a loud whisper. "You going menopausal or something?"

I reminded myself he didn't like change unless he initiated it. And he was rarely without cases demanding his supervision. Even in

Hawaii he spent hours on his cell phone making client calls. Sometimes when he noticed I was listening he'd cloister himself in the bathroom and lock the door.

"Well," he said—my cue he was done speaking to me.

"Goodbye, Fredrick." The words sounded final, resolute, like I'd never see him again. So I added, "I love you."

"I love you too." He didn't utter that phrase often so I'd cherish the words. Yet I felt oddly detached.

"Talk to you later, Angela." His voice faded before a click—and then silence. He was probably watching a TV show and the ad just ended. Fair enough. The whole world didn't come to a halt because I happened to call.

I stepped into the center of the living area, pressing the ball of my foot across the rug as I moved. Until my late teens, I'd glided through the air with grace and fluidity, riding the crest of the music. I'd been a fairy princess, a swan, whatever I desired, leaving the rest of mankind behind in their seats. The stage became the real world and the melody my lifeline, the spotlight following me. I'd worn my hair in a tight bun, no doubt giving me a wide-eyed expression.

"Tell me you're kidding," Frederick once said when I asked him if he only defended people he thought deserved his representation, people innocent of any wrongdoing. I wasn't naive, but at this moment a sliver of shame cut through my chest again. I was not his equal, this I knew, but I had perfected a blasé mask to wear on my adult face, just like Mom had. When she'd returned from eighteen holes, her lips formed a placid half-smile as she stowed Dad's gear, then mixed him a martini. She'd listen to him relive the game, as if she hadn't been there herself, as if it were the most spellbinding topic on earth, when I doubt she even liked golf.

As I strolled aimlessly around the room I remembered when my folks moved to gated Broadmoor; the golf clubs took up residence in the closet by the front door. The course itself was beautiful, like an emerald-green velvet dress with a bit of ruffled eyelet tucked here and there to snag the elusive white balls, raising the scores of the men who completed the circuit daily. Mom's illness had been like going back and having another swing at a game where no one hit a par. Same greens, same sand traps, same old players, same old slice.

Their new home was smaller than the house Rose and I grew up in. One of the few pieces of furniture Mom brought with them was her small writing desk, now residing in the corner of Dad's living room with stacks of magazines covering its austere surface. My father preferred grandiose, heavy furniture. "So you don't feel like you're going to topple over," was his theory. He'd complained about the two Amish-made pine chairs Mom brought to the dinner table when entertaining guests.

I turned my vision to the dining area and realized they were identical to Silvia's chairs. I felt compelled to move to where Glenn had sat earlier, and then I stared at my spot, trying to picture what he'd seen when he glanced my way over dinner. At home, I was a mere blip on Frederick's radar screen; he rarely looked into my face the way Glenn had. Even when Frederick related a brilliant closing statement in the courtroom or how he'd bumped elbows with a senator, or even when complaining that I'd over-cooked the lamb, his gaze didn't rest on mine. In court, he certainly must hold eye contact with the judge and members of the jury. Maybe I wasn't important enough.

I got to my feet and moved to the living area. Rocking my head back and forth, I relaxed my taut shoulders. An imaginary string lifted my sternum, helping me stand erect; I was taller and my arms longer. I elevated my right arm, arcing my hand and fingers. At the dance studio, an ancient sandy-haired gentleman—I realized he was not much older than I was now—had produced rippling notes on a stand-up piano. Closing my eyes, I heard him change tempo. I sensed his fingertips stroking the keys as the melody quickened. Time for a pirouette and then a leap.

I raised my other arm and commenced a turn, but stubbed my

toe on the corner of the couch. The clock clucked on the mantel and Rex rustled in the front hall. I scanned the room to confirm I was alone, thank goodness.

My foot throbbing, I hobbled into the kitchen for a glass of milk to induce sleep, and noticed two items I'd neglected to put in the dishwasher. I rinsed a dessert fork and a coffee cup. Were they Glenn's? When I'd cleared his plate my forearm brushed against his, sending my pulse racing. He'd turned his head enough to meet my lowered gaze. He was an attractive man; it was only natural to be drawn toward such a compelling force.

I closed the dishwasher before reaching into the refrigerator and extracting the carton of milk. I poured the white liquid into a glass too quickly. Some of it cascaded over the rim onto the counter.

As I swabbed my mess with a sponge that should have been thrown away ages ago, I told myself I hoped Glenn liked Rose. The two of them spent the longest time fetching that gardening book, and then I heard Rose humming when she returned. She seemed brighter, even talking to Silvia about the garden and asking when Glenn would return to do more work. Silvia said this was the slow time at the nursery so he was available to help the old folks in the neighborhood.

The thought of Glenn's truck crunching up the driveway filled me with giddiness.

Yes, it would be perfect if Rose fell head over heels for him. Watching their love affair from afar would be heavenly.

Twelve

Rose

I heard a man's whistle, sending a flutter of anticipation from my ears to my chest.

Glenn?

My eyes popped open to see early morning sunlight slanting through the curtains. I lay motionless in my bed, not allowing the sheets to slide against my legs or the bedsprings to whine.

The five-note melody repeated itself. Only a bird. Some variety we didn't have in the Northwest. Another joined in and the two volleyed their calls back and forth.

Stupid birds.

Gee whiz, I'd come close to acting like a Loony Tune last night. Would I have swooned into Glenn's arms if he'd tried something? No. My desire for him was a silly, momentary quirk. Although in the past I'd recklessly plummeted into pseudo relationships without doing my homework first.

Staring up at the crack in the plaster ceiling, I pushed the back of my head into the pillow and gave it a shake. There was nothing to be afraid of now. I'd once read that the fear of heights was actually a person's dread of impetuously, uncontrollably jumping off a cliff. I'd never been tempted in the slightest to leap out a window of a high building. I wouldn't have acted rashly with Glenn either.

Would I?

Closing my eyes, I recalled his face. He wasn't like Brad, whom I considered one of the most exquisite-looking men I knew. Where Brad's nose was finely chiseled, Glenn's could almost be considered coarse. Brad's boyish, pale blue eyes sparkled, while Glenn's eyes were deep pools needing to be examined closely to discover his true nature.

Maybe he wasn't handsome, after all. But in the dreamy night, what might have transpired if I'd reached out to him and he'd taken my hand before sweeping me into a powerful embrace? In my bizarre mood—vulnerable and weak—I might have returned the kiss with abandon. Who knows how far things might have gone? Yikes. Today I'd be cowering with the embarrassment and regret I'd known too many times. After breaking up with a boyfriend, I always hoped upon hope I wouldn't pass the fellow on the street. Or, worse, meet up with him at a friend's home or the grocery store where I'd be forced to act as if he and I had barely spoken before. At least here in Lancaster County I could avoid seeing Glenn again.

Yet as I assured myself of this fact, I felt a heavy emptiness. My mind's eye surveyed his splendid nursery, and then I watched his animated face as he'd described his new building. Constructing an indoor fountain with a fish pond and lily pads. How many men who grew up Amish would include aesthetic touches like that? Or was the design all Olivia's, even though she had grown up in the Amish community as well?

After Glenn left, my attempt to contact Brad was fruitless. "Are you being a good boy, Bradley?" I'd purred into his voice mail. Why hadn't he answered? He never turned off his iPhone. Where was he? I hadn't asked him to stay home every night waiting for my call. In fact, I'd joked he should party with the guys every night of the week and I wouldn't care. An absurd statement.

With three hours' difference, it was way too early to call him now. *Don't come unglued, Rosie, old gal*, I told myself. He was flopped in bed with one of his cute hairy legs out of the covers.

But was he alone?

This disturbing thought roused me to a full-conscious state. I couldn't fall asleep again if I tried. I must have already adapted to East Coast time. My return home would be a bear.

I couldn't smell Silvia's coffee yet or hear Rex stirring downstairs, but I stretched to my feet. I was clad in pajamas. I hadn't thought to bring a bathrobe, and my clothes hung in the closet on the other side of the room. I wasn't a neatnik like Angela. She sorted her socks by color and folded her underwear neater than Nordstrom's lingerie department. She even entered her kids' rooms while they were at school to make beds and straighten. Her house reminded me of a furniture showroom. I subsisted on the other end of the spectrum. My dirty clothes ended up strewn in layers on the chair in my bedroom until I washed and dried a gigantic load. I mean, who cared if sweat pants got wrinkled? But here, with my hostess sleeping across the hall, I was forced to improve my slovenly ways.

I pulled the closet door open. Half the space was filled with aged drapes folded on hangers and encased in plastic bags. As I removed my cotton shirt it slipped off its hanger and collapsed to the floor. Reaching for it, I noticed a smaller door in the back of the closet. As far as I knew, there wasn't another bedroom on the other side. It must lead to a storage area. My hand pushed it. The door yawned open as if it were lonely and wanted me to come in for a visit. Stale air smelling of cedar, dust, and mothballs floated out. Inhaling, I was flung back to childhood. Angela and I had played dress-up with Grandma's clothes in a room smelling like this. I recalled an embroidered dress with billowy sleeves and a hunter-green skirt with sequins sewn at the hem. There'd been a jewelry box made of myrtlewood laden with costume jewelry Angela and I coveted. And fans, silk and woolen scarves, and a fur stole we took turns modeling in front of a mirror.

The doorway was low, even for me. I bent my neck to step into the darkness. Only a sketchy web of light peeked in from a small window behind what must be the fireplace chimney. As I entered another couple of feet I saw a string hanging from the ceiling. I took each step slowly, but the floorboards emitted a groan each time I shifted my weight. I hoped Rex wouldn't start barking.

I pulled the string. A bare lightbulb cast an eerie glow across the tops of several large steamer chests and more than a dozen cardboard boxes. A Christmas wreath made of silk poinsettias hung on a nail next to a painting of a beagle in a broken frame. A lamp, its fringed shade at eye level, stood next to a birdcage and a coffee table missing a leg.

As I moved toward the axis of the house my eyes grew accustomed to the light. I was standing in a space the size of the living area below. At the far end was another door that must have led to Silvia's bedroom. A shoe rack crouched on the floor near it, and a pair of leather boots leaned against each other like old friends. On a hook hung what appeared to be a homemade Amish dress and a black apron. Weird.

At the other side of the door, I assumed, our aunt still slept. Unless I'd woken her.

Turning to leave, I smacked my knee. I stifled an "Ouch." My hand lowered to soothe my aching joint before swinging out to feel the source of my pain, a trunk's metal lock. I couldn't help but notice the latch wasn't fastened, inviting me to explore. I wondered if Grandma's embroidered dress was stored in the trunk. According to Silvia, nothing had been given away. I might even come across Grandma's moth-eaten fur stole. Not that I'd wear such a ghastly thing. Still, it would be fun to see again.

As I raised the trunk's heavy lid, the Greek mythical story of Pandora's Box streamed through my mind. Would evil spirits spew from its depths and take over my world? I had to snicker at my melodramatic thoughts. Father called me levelheaded. I liked to think I was. But lately, since coming here, my imagination had carried me onto shaky ground, as evidenced by translating a simple bird's whistle into a man.

I continued lifting the lid until it fell back against the wall. My hands dove in like a child playing in a sandbox, touching woolens and then sliding across satin, heavy and supple. I removed the slippery fabric to view a striped dress, royal blue and ivory. The skirt's panels were sewn on the bias so the hem splashed to my ankles. It swayed when I swished my hips like a hula dancer. Recognizing it from the photo of my mother, I pulled the garment to my breast and hugged it. I would do anything to feel Mother's arms around me, even though I'd shrugged off her embraces. Why had I pushed her away?

Clasping the dress to my body, making it a part of me, I remembered Mother waiting for Angela and me in the kitchen every day after school. As the two of us trounced through the door, she'd inquire about our days. Unlike Angela, who shared her private contents with Mother like they were best buddies, I never gave her a straight answer. But my evasiveness didn't stop Mother from asking. It had sounded like nagging to me.

I was a willful child and then a surly teenager. I had every right to be. For instance, Cynthia, my playmate since kindergarten, had pledged to remain my best friend forever. But she discarded me like rotten hamburger when we entered middle school, a blow that sent me skulking to the nerdy crowd, who didn't mind my acne or frizzy hair. Two years later, I'd hoped stepping into high school would broaden my social possibilities. I remembered dressing and primping for the first school dance. That night in the gymnasium, after leaning against the wall watching the others socialize for an hour, I felt a tap on my shoulder and looked up to see a hulk of a boy, Dirk Dunnagan, the studly football player. He asked me to dance. I was flattered and imagined every girl in the room jealously watching me receive his attention.

When the song ended he told me he needed something from his van. Judging from his acidic breath, I assumed it was more booze. But I went with him anyway because I wanted him to think I was older and sophisticated. Getting into the back of his van two blocks away, he opened a can of Budweiser and offered it to me. When I shook my head, he took a chug, then gave me my very first kiss. Initially I enjoyed it, but his lips latched onto my mouth with such force I couldn't breathe. His hand grappled with the top button of my blouse, and then with one jerk he ripped it open. I struggled. But he weighed twice as much as I did. I couldn't get free or even cry out. Not that anyone would have heard me.

After, I walked home. Over three miles. I crept into the kitchen and upstairs to shower. I couldn't tell my parents. They would have been furious. They'd warned me never to get in a car with a stranger. I'd disobeyed. Worse yet, they might have called Dirk's parents. It would have been his word against mine. He might have retaliated by telling everyone I'd come on to him. I would have been the laughing stock of the whole school. I wore long-sleeved sweaters for weeks to cover the bruises on my arms.

Thinking about Dirk still made me want to wretch or scream or break something. I was cheapened. Dirtied. Defiled. Still today, if I weren't afraid of guns, I might have bought one. I'd pull the trigger and watch the blood spurt from his ruptured face. I still despised him that much. And I hated myself for not fighting harder, for not reporting him to the police. And for being a coward—what Father despised more than anything.

Dirk was probably a family man now, leading a fat-cat life in the suburbs, the coach of his son's Little League team. I doubted he remembered me. Nor did he know he got me pregnant.

I refolded the dress and slid it under several layers of clothing until my fingers touched something hard. I felt what seemed like brittle envelopes held together by a ribbon. A stack of letters? My hand groped the papers' surface. My heart raced as if I'd discovered a vein of gold. I couldn't wait to look at them.

As I pulled the parcel up, careful not to disturb other items in the trunk, I heard a low clonking sound downstairs. I felt like a thief.

Caught. I stuffed the envelopes back down into the center of the chest. Someone was running water in the kitchen. Silvia, no doubt. I closed the lid quietly and then reached over to the string to give a quick tug. The twine flew up out of my hand. In darkness, I inched my way back to my room. Stepping through the closet, I redistributed my clothes and the curtains across the rack. I grabbed the shirt I'd originally sought and got dressed.

Descending to the first floor, I smelled oatmeal cooking and the aroma of freshly ground coffee beans. Rex, sacked out at the foot of the stairs, glared up at me as I stepped over him. His tipped-back ears and serious expression informed me he knew I was poking around where I didn't belong.

"Dear, how are you this morning?" Silvia asked as I entered the kitchen. A pan sat on the front burner, steam gently lifting its lid.

"Uh, fine." I tried to sound casual, but heat traveled up my neck. "Say, I hope you don't mind. Somehow I ended up in the storage area in the back of my closet."

"Not a problem. I'd planned to sort through those boxes next month." Using a hot pad, she removed the lid and stirred the contents. Creamy oatmeal stuck to the wooden spoon. "But while you're here, you and Angela might have a look and select some mementos."

I wondered if Silvia knew about the letters. They could have been to our grandparents from the old country, written in Italian. Or maybe they were love letters from our father to our mother. I had a hankering to find out.

"That would be fun." I dribbled half-and-half into my coffee and stirred. For sure, I didn't miss herbal tea. "And I'd like to poke through Glenn Yoder's shop again if we're in the area. I'm always hunting for new ideas for my own business." Again I attempted to speak with indifference. "When I saw Glenn's catalogue, I realized mine needs spicing up."

Only part of my motivation for going there. Mostly I wanted to see Glenn.

THIRTEEN

Angela

Exploring Bird-in-Hand had been one of the reasons I'd wanted to come to Lancaster County. I'd seen photos of its farmers market and shops, so unlike the airless malls back home. But as I cupped my coffee mug in my hands, I felt content to lounge at Silvia's dining table and wait. For what? The only person we were expecting was Phyllis, who would join us on our excursion this morning.

I hoped Glenn would swing by to see Rose. She was already showered, dressed, and had sculpted her hair to one side in a new fashion. She looked especially pretty, and the sullen expression often darkening her features had lifted. "Hurry up," she'd teased me over breakfast. "I thought you wanted to hit every store in Lancaster County."

I almost mentioned something about her going out on a date with Glenn while she was here. I felt sure Silvia and Phyllis would agree; Rose and Glenn were a perfect match—since I couldn't have him. But it never paid to give Rose advice. She'd do the opposite just to have her way, like refusing to sing "Happy Birthday" at family functions after I'd raved about her soprano voice, and buying a tiny Cairn terrier right after Frederick suggested she get a Rottweiler for protection. Her life could be so much fuller if she'd listen to other people more.

Rex barked at the front door. Someone rapped twice, and then Phyllis let herself in. She said hello before marching past us and locating Silvia in the kitchen.

"Ma, are you sure you're up for this today?" she asked in a hushed voice.

"Phyllis, I'm fine."

"Why don't you let me take them? You stay here and rest."

Silvia came out of the kitchen with Phyllis tagging behind her.

"My daughter's going to be our chauffeur today."

"Okay, I'll get ready." I downed my remaining oatmeal, took a brisk shower, and got dressed.

When I returned to the living area, Silvia thrust her fists through the arms of her jacket, its shoulders sagging halfway down her upper arms. "I don't think my daughter has confidence in my driving anymore."

"Now, Ma, that's not what I said."

We loaded into Phyllis's SUV—Silvia suggested Rose sit up front with Phyllis, who insisted we buckle in before she'd move an inch. Then in a burst she took off like the Big Thunder Mountain Railroad ride at Disneyland.

"My daughter's a snappy driver," Silvia said, and Phyllis accelerated to pass a buggy, making me wonder if her erratic driving was for Silvia's benefit.

"Are you sure this is the best route?" Silvia asked as we cut off the main road and descended a bumpy hill.

"Yes, I always go this way. It's faster."

We passed expansive farms, men harvesting with mules or draft horses, lovely well-kempt homes, laundry hanging on lines affixed to pulleys stretching up into lofty trees.

Ten minutes later, the sign for the village of Bird-in-Hand appeared. The area was saturated with horses and buggies galore. I craned my neck to see each one. We passed a medley of shops. Phyllis pulled into a parking lot and up to, according to its sign, the

Bird-in-Hand Market. As we entered the spacious building, alive with activity and color, I inhaled the aromas of sugar and cooking dough. But I wasn't in the mood to explore. I couldn't remember the last time I hadn't been drawn to sweets, even with cases of chocolates and cookies beckoning me.

Rose wandered over to watch a young Amish woman fashion pretzels. "I wish I could cook better," Rose said.

"I'd be happy to give you lessons," said Silvia.

Rose guffawed. "I don't have the patience. I've never been good in the kitchen."

"Rosie, you're good at everything." I spoke so Silvia and Phyllis could hear. "How many women own their own successful business?" I'd been frightened for her when she'd quit her real job, scared she'd starve to death. But she'd triumphed over every obstacle.

Rose turned to me. "I should be at work right now."

I felt the weight of guilt being placed on my shoulders like a lead blanket. "Everyone deserves a vacation."

"Sis, you've never had to support yourself, so you don't know what you're talking about. This is my busy time of the year."

Rose could make me cry, but I'd always held in the tears when her searing tongue cut into me—as if balancing on a tightrope every time we spoke.

Surprising me, she purchased a pretzel and chomped into it.

"We should get you a snack," Phyllis told Silvia.

"Maybe later."

"Are you tired? Do you need to go home?"

"Not yet. I'm enjoying myself." She moved toward a wall displaying canned vegetables: beets, baby corn, pickles, and a relish called chow chow.

"You look pale," Phyllis said.

I pretended not to notice the friction between them. If Phyllis only knew how lucky she was to have her mother still alive. She reminded me of Rose, who used to give Mom rations of guff. I assumed it hurt our mother's feelings more than she let on. She practically begged Rose for tidbits of information and offered to drive her most anywhere, much like she groveled after Dad and was never appreciated.

It also used to infuriate me the way he'd demean her in front of Rose and me. Quips about her cooking that an outsider might not pick up on. Just once I wish she'd stood up to him. But who was I to throw stones? I could barely maintain eye contact with my own father. He goaded me, badgering me about my kids' manners and making snide comments about the way Frederick managed the office. I wondered if Dad would like me better if I told him to drop dead.

But I couldn't.

A periwinkle-blue and white quilt hanging on the wall caught my attention. I guessed I could afford any article in this store, but I wasn't sure. The accountant at Frederick's office paid our bills every month; she knew more about our finances than I did. I signed our IRS tax statement each April without inspecting it. "Can we afford this?" I'd ask Frederick, and he'd either nod or shake his head. I did sometimes wonder how much money we really had, but Frederick resented being asked, which must mean he thought I was questioning his ability to support us. I didn't want to hurt his feelings. Or start a spat.

I moved closer to the quilt. The triangle pieces seemed to undulate like waves in the sun. This was a quilt to snuggle up with in front of the fireplace on a winter's night. In this vision I couldn't see whom I was with. Last night I'd dreamt I wasn't even married to Frederick. I was lounging in an unfamiliar living room and felt the weight of a man's arm around my shoulders. I turned my head toward him but didn't recognize his features.

Pressure had been building within me this last year. Like a genie corked in a bottle, would my contents gush out given the chance? There had been instances recently when I'd felt like acting recklessly, propelled by a force bigger than rationality. A month ago, I told my hairdresser I wanted to be a va-va-voom redhead, but at the last instant, just before she applied the first glob of color, I changed my mind, apologizing profusely. Then I signed up for a belly dancing class at the University of Washington Experimental College, but called back the next day and lied that I couldn't take it because I'd sprained my ankle. I was glad I'd come to my senses before Frederick found out and had me committed to a mental institution.

"Angie," Rose said, "we're leaving." I checked my pockets and purse to make sure I hadn't stolen anything. I didn't trust myself. Last week I got home from Bartell Drug Store with a hairclip I don't even remember admiring, let alone pinching.

We four piled into the car and drove to Bird-in-Hand Family Restaurant and Smorgasbord. Inside, we each gathered food, and then Rose, Phyllis, and I congregated at a table while Silvia found the ladies' room.

Phyllis placed Silvia's plate on the table next to her own and then added some of her turkey, mashed potatoes, and vegetables. I wondered if Phyllis expected Silvia to consume more than Phyllis originally had served herself.

"How's Ma?" She sat and cupped her chin in her hands.

I said, "Fine," without thinking. An automatic response.

Phyllis stole a glance in the direction of the restroom. "She says she's taking her medication…"

Rose sliced into her turkey and swallowed a mouthful. "What's the medicine for?"

Phyllis's lips parted and then flattened together.

"It's none of our business, Rosie." I was curious too, but glad Phyllis respected her mother's privacy. Two years younger than Mom, Silvia's eyes radiated vitality, even if her movements seemed labored.

"Hugh and I are thinking about leaving town for a few days," Phyllis said. "We hardly ever get away and wanted to take the kids to see Hugh's folks in Virginia. Since you two are here, we thought you could keep an eye on Ma." Her gaze shot over to Silvia, who was returning and slipping in between Phyllis and me.

"You look awfully serious." Silvia scooted in her chair. "What were you talking about?"

Rose poked her fork into a green bean. "Phyllis was mentioning a trip she and Hugh might take."

"Oh?" She must have noticed the excess of food on her plate but didn't complain.

"It's in the planning stage," Phyllis said. "Do let us know if you're ready to go home."

"Home? We haven't even eaten." Silvia opened her napkin. "I'm getting my second wind." She sampled sweet potatoes and then set her fork aside.

A waitress arrived with coffee and hot water for tea. Silvia sipped her tea while the rest of us ate. I scolded myself for gobbling too much gravy-covered mashed potatoes. Oh, well. I didn't want it to be tossed away with the garbage.

After a few minutes, Phyllis said, "Ma, you've hardly touched your food. How about a nice slice of pumpkin pie?"

"Okay, that sounds good."

"I'll get you a piece with whipped cream."

"Thanks, darling."

"Anyone else?"

"I'm stuffed," Rose said, patting her tummy.

"Me too," I said, in spite of my wanting dessert.

Minutes later, Phyllis returned with Silvia's pie.

It was plain to see Phyllis was one of those overly protective children who wouldn't allow her aging parent breathing space. I bet my kids viewed me in the same light.

"I'm having such a nice time." Not reacting to her daughter's hurried movements, Silvia sipped her tea. She looked at me and then Rose. "Being with you two reminds me of Juliana. It seems impossible she's really gone."

"Ma, must you?"

I noticed yesterday's arrangement of wilting flowers sitting on another table. Mom had faded the same way, giving up without a fight, resigned to death.

"I wish we'd had a memorial service here where she grew up," Silvia said.

"Me too," I said, "but Dad insisted we have a small, private funeral." Like unfinished business, her ashes lay hidden under her gravestone with few witnesses.

"You two may think I'm batty, but I still catch myself picking up the phone to call her."

Phyllis's eyeballs enlarged.

"Poor Phyllis is sick of hearing me talk about my sister. She hardly knew Juliana, and I regret that." Silvia grinned like a child confessing she'd eaten the last cookie. "Your father was never terribly fond of me, but I should have visited anyway. I could have stayed at a hotel."

I'd heard Dad complain about our mother's nutty sister, Silvia: eccentric and she talked too much. He wouldn't care for the conversation we were having right now, to put it mildly. He would have gotten up and left the premises as he did when displeased. End of discussion, always giving him the final word.

Thirty minutes later, we four poked through Amish novels on display near the cash register, then trundled outside to Phyllis's SUV again. But we'd fizzled and decided to go home.

"Thanks for looking after Ma," were Phyllis's parting words as she discreetly passed me her cell phone number and the contact information where she and Hugh would be staying.

Again, I was disturbed by Phyllis's attitude toward Silvia, who was not a little girl, after all. Why all the secrecy?

Then I got a panicky feeling in the back of my throat, like something was terribly wrong.

❦

I lay the Amish fiction paperback I'd purchased for Tiffany on the bed. My headstrong daughter would probably never read it. I didn't think I was being paranoid when I concluded she was like her Auntie Rose, resistant to everything I did and said. Was that why Tiffany had insisted on attending soccer goalie camp over the summer, even though a sports injury would knock her out of dancing for months? Or why she was priming for basketball season, asking her brother to play defense? The girl possessed such agility and dancing talent, even if she were growing lanky. From her first day on earth, I'd envisioned her on stage, the lights spraying through her tutu as she took her final bow. I wanted her to experience what I'd missed.

Rose stepped into the room and eyed the book. "You going to start reading that tonight?"

I scanned the Amish lass on the novel's cover. "It's for Tiffany, not me."

"Hate to rain on your parade, but the last book I saw your daughter reading was fantasy with a gargoyle on the front."

Leave it to Rose to spoil my fun. "Why didn't you say something at the store?"

"You didn't ask." She perched on the rocking chair.

Now that I thought about it, Tiffany had turned up her nose at sweet romances years ago. "She might become interested in the Amish."

"I would have gone to one of those outlet stores and bought her a warm-up suit," she inserted like the final nail.

I hated when Rose acted as if she knew my daughter better than I did. Well, maybe I was out of touch with all my family members. I could practically guarantee they didn't know my favorite anything. The other day, on one of the rare occasions Frederick poured me coffee—only because he and I were both standing by the coffeemaker in his office—he'd asked me if I took cream. Imagine, a man married for sixteen years not knowing his wife drank her coffee black.

I believe his secretary bought my birthday and Christmas presents, because I saw her wearing the exact same charm bracelet once. Or had Frederick bought both of us the same gift?

"Rosie, we should have stopped somewhere so you could have gotten yourself a new outfit as a souvenir." I wanted to transfer the focus to her.

"You mean an Amish getup? Wouldn't that be a hoot? I'd skewer myself with those humongous straight pins. I bet it would make me look like a blimp."

"Impossible. I've always been jealous of your figure."

"Nah, I've always been envious of you." She raked her fingers through her locks. "I've spent a lifetime wanting straight blond hair."

"I love your natural waves." I'd permed my hair for years and finally gave up trying to coerce my limp mop into holding a curl.

"You've always had it made, sis." She situated herself on the rocker. "You haven't lived until you've followed in my big sister's footsteps."

"I hope you're kidding." After admiring the enchanting young woman on the cover, I slipped the Amish novel into my empty suitcase. "You're witty, smart, and beautiful. And skinny."

"I hate being called skinny."

"I'd be thrilled if someone called me that. Fat chance, no pun intended. Rosie, I envy anyone who looks good in shorts."

"So how come I'm still single? You landed the rich guy who adores you the way you are, right?"

The idea that Frederick adored me made me smile and then frown. He might have at one time, but not anymore. My marriage cup had drained to half-empty. But I mustn't complain about Frederick to Rose. She'd turn it around and gripe about how hard it was to find anyone decent.

"And you have two kids." She tapped the chair into motion.

"My life isn't perfect."

"That's okay, sis. You don't need to feel guilty." She jammed her heels into the rug and the rocker jerked to a stop. "The truth is it doesn't seem I'll ever have a child. Maybe I should have adopted, or let myself get pregnant and never told the guy."

Her admission hit me like a meteor falling out of the sky. Rose had professed she didn't want children. She coochie-cooed over Minnie and had often said dogs were better than kids because you could stick them out in the backyard for the day without paying a babysitter. And they didn't demand an allowance.

"Would you and Brad ever get married?" I asked.

"Nah, he's a lost cause." She started up her rocking again. "I can't even get him to commit to making plans more than a week in advance. Anyway, he told me he doesn't want kids."

I wanted to offer her comfort. My sister was opening up to me and mourning her childlessness.

"Rosie, my kids adore you. When you visit, Tiffany drops everything and comes running. All you have to do is sit and listen, and she pours herself out. You'd make a wonderful mom."

The corners of her mouth dragged down. "I've waited so long that I may be too old. Menopause is lurking around the corner. Women only have so many viable eggs. And I'd be risking a Down syndrome child, although they have tests these days so you can tell ahead of time."

"What good would that do? You wouldn't terminate the pregnancy, would you?"

The rocker slowed to a standstill. "No, I wouldn't."

"Good."

Her face wan, Rose stared at a threadbare spot in the rug. "But raising a kid with special needs requires more patience than I have."

"All parenting requires patience." What I considered one of my best attributes. But recently waiting around for others had aggravated me. A few weeks ago, with both my children out for the evening and not knowing if Frederick would show up, I snacked on cheese and crackers, and purposely didn't prepare him dinner, to teach him a lesson—a trivial act of defiance.

But at six thirty guilt set in; I exhumed frozen spaghetti sauce and defrosted it in the microwave oven—all for nothing. He didn't come home until ten o'clock, and then he insisted he'd told me he had an office meeting over a meal at Daniel's Broiler on Lake Union. To make matters worse, his colleague and wife had joined them. But I didn't make a big deal out of it. There was no use starting an argument with my husband because I always ended up apologizing. I let him win.

I regrouped my thoughts. "I'm sure you have the stamina to take care of a baby."

"Nah. I'm getting cantankerous in my old age." She lugged herself to her feet and moved toward the doorway with lethargic steps. "There's no use spending time worrying about something that won't ever happen."

I'd told myself the same thing, that I should be content with my marriage and stop trying to maneuver Frederick into cherishing me above all else, but hearing the defeat in her voice made me want to adjust her attitude.

"Maybe it's time you and I both make some radical changes," I said.

She looked at me like I'd turned bonkers, as she'd put it. Maybe I had.

Fourteen

Rose

I heard a man's whistle. A real one this time! After scrambling to get dressed, I scurried outside into the chill morning air. Glenn stood at the end of the lane, filling in dirt around the base of a three-foot-tall bush.

As I approached him, he didn't notice. I wished I'd checked the mirror before leaving the house. "How many plants are you putting in?" I asked without saying hello first. My typical foot-in-mouth disease.

He smiled back, apparently not offended by my uncouth manners. "After these bulbs are in the ground, I'll be done for the year." He dug a lump of soil, filled in an indented area, and then stabbed the shovel into the dirt. "I hope Silvia holds on long enough to see them bloom."

"What do you mean?" I expected he'd tell me that her impatience to see the look-at-me red tulips would make it difficult for her to wait out the long winter.

He dislodged the shovel and stomped around the bush, compacting the soil with the thick soles of his boots. "I thought you knew." His eyes squinted as though the morning light was blinding. "There's no easy way to say this. Silvia has a serious heart condition her doctor thinks was caused by Lyme disease. She may not last more than a few more months."

"From a tick bite?"

"Apparently, although she never saw the actual culprit or had the telltale bull's-eye rash that sometimes follows. And her blood tests came back negative, although that isn't uncommon. She remembers getting what she thought was the flu fifteen or so years ago, and then other symptoms started appearing, like stiff joints and achy muscles and dizziness, which the rheumatologist pronounced to be arthritis. For a while her doctor thought she had lupus or Parkinson's disease. Then heart blockage."

The words hit my eardrums like a shotgun blast. All the soldiers—Phyllis's anxiety and protectiveness, Silvia's fatigue and lack of appetite, and her desire for early blooms—trooped into place to form a battalion.

"There's no cure?"

"Yes. If treated right away, antibiotics can eradicate Lyme infestation in a couple of months. And I've heard of chronic Lyme sufferers recovering. But Silvia isn't doing well. The medications make her sick to her stomach and more fatigued, piled on top of the pain she carries around every day."

The lump in my throat blocked my vocal cords. I stared past Glenn into the sun-tipped trees that looked serene, like an Impressionist painting. Why hadn't Silvia told Angela and me? Why would she even invite us here? How could she act as if she didn't have a care in the world? She'd warned us about the ticks. I was glad I'd taken heed and applied the bug repellant liberally. But she should have informed us they carried a debilitating illness. My sadness coagulated with fear.

He looked at me straight-on, no doubt assessing my reaction. But I'd learned to wear a poker face as if nothing fazed me, when in fact my chest was caving in. It took all my willpower to not collapse to the ground, bring my knees to my chest into a fetal position, and howl.

"I hope I didn't overstep myself by saying anything," he said.

"No, I'm glad you told me." Not true. I preferred ignorance to the ripping pain seizing my torso. "Phyllis hinted around, and I saw a pill bottle by Silvia's bed. But I assumed all older people took some kind of medication."

Allowing me a moment of silence, Glenn gave the soil a final smoothing. "Want to walk down by the creek?" He must have understood I was too shaken to return to the house. How would I muster up a smile the next time I saw Silvia?

"Sure."

He drove the shovel into the ground and left it standing. Then he shepherded me around the vegetable garden on a grassy lane. Ahead, off to one side under a towering chestnut tree, sat a cherry-red Adirondack chair, brilliant against its gold-and-green backdrop. So far from the house, it seemed an odd spot to place it. But at this moment everything stretched beyond my understanding.

We continued, passing under a canopy of trees, our shoes scuffing the fallen leaves. I figured I was safe. Despite my hurry to catch up with Glenn, I'd applied bug repellant to ward off the ticks, stuffed my light-colored pant-legs in my white socks, and stretched rubber bands around my cuffs.

"Your aunt has been good to me." Glenn slowed his pace so we could walk side by side. "When I showed up nine years ago, she practically adopted me. I'm guessing because she knew my father so well, but most likely because she's a generous woman. She could tell I was lonely. When I started the nursery, she was my first and best client. Word of mouth is everything around here. She encouraged everyone in the county to come in."

I heard the laughter of water rippling up ahead. As the path narrowed, I fell in behind my guide. In a minute we were standing at the edge of a stream, no wider than twelve feet. It flowed transparently over mossy stones, and there were spots where a person could easily ford it and only get her ankles wet. As if Glenn had been here many times, he lowered himself onto a rock the size and shape of an overturned wheelbarrow. "Have a seat." He motioned me to a flat slab next to it.

"This creek winds down past my folks' house, five miles away, as the crow flies." His gaze was glued to its satin-smooth surface. "I've spent many an hour mesmerized, watching the water. There are fish in here, but I seldom bring a pole."

I stared into the moving liquid. Every drop zipping away by the time my eyes grasped it. Every instant of time disappearing forever. I thought about Mother's final days, how I'd sat by her hospital bed and waited for the inevitable. I'd never said, "I love you," even when the hospice nurse told me Mother might still be able to hear me though her eyes were shut and her breathing was shallow. How I regretted the gulf of distance separating us. Was that why the news of Silvia's illness crushed me?

"Silvia told me your mother passed away last year," Glenn said. "I'm sorry."

"Thanks." Did he know his father once loved her? According to Silvia, Chester wanted to marry Mother, but there was no way to ask Glenn without making this conversation more awkward.

An idea found its shape and took root in my mind. *I must speak to Chester.* "I'd like to meet your father. I mean, your parents, if that's okay."

"Sure. Why not?"

A male purple finch landed by the branch near us. For a moment I held my breath, not moving a muscle. I watched the bird from the corner of my eye until it sprang away. The air was coolish. My hands nestled in the felt pockets of my fleece vest. I listened to the water gurgling in a deeper pool downstream. A dog in the distance barked. Horseshoes clopped on the road. More birds in conversation. All melting into a hum. Two miles an hour instead of the city's frenzied beat.

I figured Glenn could tell I was deep in thought. Maybe he was, too, but he wasn't reflecting on me other than considering how stunned I was by the news. Something in the way he invited me here announced he had no romantic motives. Another woman encompassed his thoughts. Olivia or some other beauty. Which annoyed me.

Why did I care? I didn't know how much my attraction to him—yes, I found him attractive—had to do with my being away from home. I was reminded of a weekend in San Diego five years back. Down to attend an old college friend's wedding, I was staying at a nearby hotel. That July, the air had sizzled and recorded conga music played around the hotel's swimming pool. He and I met at the deep end, which struck me as ironic. I was in over my head. By that evening, we were locked in each other's arms in a movie-set embrace. Fortunately, the cell phone in his pocket chirped. He turned away from me and cupped his mouth so I couldn't hear him speak. Once the call was over, he admitted it had been his wife. He came up with a phony story about being separated and weeks away from a divorce. I'd almost believed him until I inspected the white groove on his left hand where his wedding band usually resided. How moronic was that?

Glenn was so near, but he would never hold me, except briefly in his glance, which might see a lackluster woman with no physical appeal. There was nothing remarkable about me to make him wish to learn more, to move closer than arm's length.

"Come on." He got to his feet and proffered me a hand. As I rose, he pulled me enough to ease my burden. I was grateful for that small gift.

I followed him down the path toward the house. Entering the clearing, I spotted Silvia praying on her knees by the red chair, right there in the damp grass. Her hands steepled, her head bent. A beautiful scene, like a mural on a convent wall.

Glenn and I stopped in our tracks and watched her. Taking in the tableau, I felt as if scales had been removed from my eyes. I viewed Silvia differently, no longer seeing her robust vitality but instead a frail older woman who insisted on wearing a false cloak of cheerfulness and strength while her mind and body decayed. According to Glenn, Lyme disease invaded a person subtly, an invisible nemesis moving through the blood vessels and organs with masterful precision.

This could be Silvia's last autumn, I told myself. *Her heart was so damaged she'll be lucky to make it through winter.*

Silvia said in a clear voice, "Thank you, Lord."

I couldn't imagine why she was thanking God. What favors had he done for her lately? Maybe she was resigned to passing into oblivion without a whimper, like Mother did. But if I had Lyme disease from a stupid little tick, I'd be fighting mad. I'd be shaking my fist at the sky and cursing.

Pressing both hands on her thigh for balance, she stood. I half expected her to cross herself, but remembered Father telling me she'd joined the Mennonite church.

Silvia's loose jeans wore wet spots on the knees. She gave them a swipe, and then she noticed us. "I was looking for you two."

Moments later, as we all strolled toward the house, Glenn explained where we'd been. I stared straight ahead so I wouldn't have to look her in the face. But I needed to get my act together before we reached the kitchen door. Within yards of it, my nose caught the scent of browning dough.

"Something smells delish." It took all my strength to produce my upbeat remark.

"Oh no!" Silvia charged into the kitchen. Her hands dove into hot mitts. She swung open the oven's door and pulled out a muffin pan. "I hope they aren't burnt. I got distracted."

She overturned the pan onto a wire cooling rack. The muffins tumbled out, their bottoms caramel-brown. "Looks like I got lucky. Go have a seat, you two." She handed us plates, flatware, strawberry jam, butter, and honey, and then she sent us into the dining area where Angela was already seated.

I didn't confide in Angela very often. If you have a problem, who can stand reams of un-asked-for advice from your big sister when all you need is a listening ear or a nod every once in a while? But after what I'd just learned, I was going to burst if I didn't talk to someone. I'd wait until Glenn left and then speak to Angela alone.

However, as I removed my vest and hung it over the back of my chair, I wondered if Angela had known about Silvia's bad health from the get-go. Silvia might have confided in Angela, the older sister, last month when she'd arranged this trip. Angela could have come up with some lamebrain excuse for not telling me. That would be her style. I was tempted to say nothing to her at all.

She flipped through a magazine. "This is *The Connection*, an Amish magazine." She glanced my way. "I'll have to subscribe to it when I get home. Where were you just now?"

I'd intended to sneak back to the brook for solitude, to fill my ears with nature's melody. Alone. But I said, "Glenn and I walked to a little creek." I couldn't fib in front of Glenn. I cared what he thought of me.

I sank down in the seat across from my big sister, and Glenn sat by me. Silvia entered the room carrying a basket of muffins and set it in the center of the table. Then she sat down next to Angela. Glenn and I grabbed for one simultaneously. Our knuckles softly collided. His warm skin grazed mine. The corners of his mouth raised a skosh, a reaction I couldn't interpret.

"Ladies first." He allowed me to procure a muffin, and then he passed me the butter. I sliced into it. The creamy yellow slab soon melted, slipping, soaking into the dough's steamy surface.

As I savored the taste, I listened to Glenn describe the early blooms expected from the bulbs he'd just planted. "As soon as the snow melts," he promised Silvia.

How would I spend my days if I were in Silvia's place? I didn't have a clue. Yet I could be snuffed out today, our car crashing into a truck while passing a buggy. This could in fact be my last meal. The frieze of the Last Supper hanging behind the pulpit at the church I'd attended as a child came to mind. Knowing he would die, Christ elected to surround himself with friends. Were these three people sitting here—my aunt, whom I'd really just met a few days ago, Glenn, a near-stranger, and my sister—the people I held closest? This thought filled me with a warmth that threatened to overflow through my eyes and form words in my mouth like *I love you* and *Cherish this moment*. But I wouldn't let myself turn sappy and embarrass us all.

Silvia covered her yawning mouth. "We've got nothing planned for today. Glenn, will you help entertain these two gals for me while I take a nap?"

"I'm sure he's a busy man," Angela said. Leave it to my sister to foil my plans.

"I've got plenty of time." His right hand rested on the table. "Things are winding down at the nursery."

"You're good to me." Silvia reached across the table. Her fingertips touched Glenn's. "When I was your age, I would have been bored silly catering to a senior citizen."

"You'll always be young in my eyes." Was he memorizing her features and thinking he'd recall her as she looked today?

When Angela and I left Pennsylvania, we'd say goodbye to Silvia for the last time. How did I want to remember her? I wished I'd brought my camera. But my iPhone would do the trick. I glanced around the room and decided I wanted to inherit a keepsake from this house. Something with Silvia's stamp on it, like her favorite chair or footstool. To help fill the empty cavity her death would leave in my heart.

I sat in the middle of the wide bench seat of Glenn's truck he'd informed me was a Ford. When I'd asked him if it was a Chevy his brows had lifted and he gave me an "Are you kidding?" look.

My knees leaned toward Angela's. We jostled down the valley, heading north and west. Glenn shifted gears and his arm brushed against mine in a commanding way. When I got home I would insist Brad do the driving. Should I ever see him again. If he was cruising bars trolling for women every night, then good riddance. Or would his bad-boy behavior set his hook deeper into me?

Glenn downshifted as we rounded a corner. Again his arm touched mine. I wished he and I were by ourselves. When he'd invited us to visit his parents, I'd hoped Angela would politely bow out. What interest could she have in meeting them? Couldn't she tell she was the third wheel?

We pulled into a lane leading to a white two-story house with a smaller home attached to one corner. Flowerbeds surrounded the wraparound front porch and a tidy vegetable garden nestled behind a fence. A sizable barn stood in the background. Several horses grazed in a pasture next to a vast field of drying cornstalks.

No cars. Maybe no one was home. Then I noticed a light-gray buggy.

Confusion surrounded me. I reminded myself Glenn had been brought up Amish. This was an Amish farm. Not an electrical line in sight.

Glenn gave his horn a tap as he drove into the barnyard and to the back steps. We three exited the pickup as a bearded man in his late sixties with a funky haircut came around the other side of the house. He wore loose black trousers held up by suspenders, and work boots. Even with his straw hat and scruffy beard, I recognized Glenn's father, Chester, from Silvia's photo.

He was still a fine-looking man, erect and square-shouldered. I could see why Mother had been attracted to him. I wondered why she'd lost interest. Because he was Amish, no doubt. Could I imagine Mother living on a farm? Heavens no. But I'd recently found appearances could be misleading. When I'd met Glenn, I was way off base.

"Hullo, *sohn*." Chester removed his gloves.

"Hi, *Dat*. This is Angela and Rose."

"Pleased ta meetcha." Chester shook Angela's hand and then mine. His fingers were callused, his knuckles gnarled. Except for Walter next door, none of the men in my life were what you'd call handy. I was beginning to think handiness was a good quality in a man. I'd grown weary of being Miss Fix-it. I even replaced Brad's stovetop element last month. Not difficult to accomplish once you read the directions. He could have done it himself.

"What are you up to?" Glenn asked.

Chester gave him a sheepish grin. He led us around the side of the house to a heap of wood lopped into eighteen-inch lengths. A splitting maul lay on the ground next to a stump, its flat surface marred. The air hung with the fruity aroma of green wood.

"They were supposed to split and stack it." Glenn gathered up several wedges of split wood and placed them atop others assembled against the house.

"That costs an extra forty. I told them to leave it like this. *Alles ist ganz gut.*" Chester, his back bending at the waist, picked up a slab of wood and added it to the stack. His hand moved to his hip, then the small of his back. Glenn shook his head as if they'd had this go-round before.

"Exercise is *gut*." Chester slapped his hat against his thigh. "And I've got an appointment with the chiropractor tomorrow. He'll fix me up. He always does."

I tried to imagine Mother living on this farm. I wondered if she'd have been happier here than spending her days at our parents' new home. She'd seemed to tread water all day waiting for nightfall and the comfort of sleep. In the old house, where Angela and I grew up, Mother had tended a rose garden of a dozen bushes. Not to mention the climbing yellow roses scaling the trellis against the side of the house. Then Father hired a team of gardeners. In the old house, she'd spent hours in the basement laundry room folding and ironing. But once they moved, she'd sent most everything to the dry cleaner. And in the old house, she made Pres-to-Log fires in the kitchen fireplace as soon as the weather dropped below fifty. She'd rarely lit their new house's gas fireplace.

Father had insisted they move. He said in his old age he didn't want to deal with the yard or climb stairs. But if Mother had remained responsible for handling the household maintenance and keeping up the garden, she might have clung to life with more tenacity.

An Amish woman appearing several years Chester's senior exited the back door. Or maybe she just hadn't aged well, what with the cobweb of lines on her cheeks and crevices around her lips. No laugh lines there. Clad in a black apron over an elephant-gray, mid-calf dress, she descended the steps.

At the bottom, she bestowed a peck on Glenn's cheek. She stood taller than Angela. Maybe five ten. Her wispy eyebrows lowered as she gave Angela and me a perfunctory glance. She said something in Pennsylvania Dutch to Glenn that didn't sound like a warm welcome.

"*Mamm*, I'd like you to meet Angela and Rose." He turned to us. "This is my mother, Lilly."

The corners of her mouth drew back into a contrived smile. Rather than shaking our hands, she polished one thumbnail with her other thumb. Maybe she was worried about catching a virus. I supposed some older people were like that.

"*Kumm rei*, Glenn. You should have warned me. I'd have made ya something special ta eat. My goodness, what do we have?"

"Don't fix anything," Glenn said. "Silvia's been stuffing us."

"*Himmel*, you should stop here first." Her rasping voice made me think she considered Silvia a rival for her son's affection.

"I was working for her."

She straightened her prayer cap. "But we need work done around here too. Look at this farm goin' ta waste." My gaze canvassed the stately white barn. It appeared freshly painted.

"Now, Lilly." Chester scuffed the soles of his boots on a metal boot-scrape. "Shouldn't we invite these young ladies inside?"

Her thin lips revealed tension. "*Yah*, but I sure hope Bishop Lapp don't pay us a visit."

"He swings by the nursery at least once a month, *Mamm*," Glenn said. "He and I get along just fine."

"Maybe on the surface, but he probably thinks you're *ab im Kopp*."

"He doesn't think I'm crazy, *Mamm*. And remember, I live in a different district."

"So? When you move home, Timothy Lapp will be your bishop again."

"*Mamm*, can we discuss this another time?"

"*Yah*, if you'd come by more often." She glanced my way without actually making eye contact. "Please come in. Excuse the mess. If I'd known ahead of time…"

We mounted the back steps and trailed her through a lantern-lit room housing a wringer washer, plastic tubs, a deep sink, counters, and cupboards. The odor of bleach invaded my nostrils. A moment later, we entered a kitchen the same era as Silvia's, but the opposite in nature. Smaller windows, knotty-pine cupboards, and a skimpy overhead light fixture gave the space a cold atmosphere. Could be pleasant in summer, but depressing during the winter. The counters, hosting glass canisters containing what looked like flour, sugar, and tea, were spotless. Gleaming pots hung from a rack, and hand towels perched on the oven's handle in a precise row. Was this her idea of messy?

Chester and Glenn removed their shoes.

"Should I take mine off?" I asked as Chester hung his hat on a peg on the nearest wall.

Lilly scowled at my shoes. "*Nee*, they look clean enough, and ya won't be staying long."

"*Mamm*, please," Glenn said before slipping into Pennsylvania Dutch. Chester threw in a remark as well, and then she lowered her chin in a compliant manner.

"*Ya*, I suppose I should be happy anytime you stop by," Lilly said to Glenn.

"How are you and your new refrigerator getting along?" he asked her.

"Fine. So modern. And a freezer." Her hand reached out to stroke its white surface. "So modern, but Bishop Lapp said it's okay."

"It's powered by gas," Glenn told Angela and me. "As are the stove and lights."

"We thank you, *sohn*." Chester tugged on his beard. "Would ya like to make yourself comfortable in the sitting room?"

We followed him past a table hemmed with four chairs and into a living room. Its walls were bare except for a calendar with a deer and two fawns gracing its cover. Partially closed forest-green shades hung at the windows. A crocheted throw draped over the back of a serviceable couch, sitting perpendicular to a love seat. On the fireplace mantel I expected to see Glenn's portrait or something personal. But nothing except for a kerosene lamp and a clock.

In one corner of the room resided a child-size rocker Glenn must have used when a youngster. I imagined his hands grasping the chair's arms and his legs so short they barely reached the oak floor. I felt a tug of fondness for him. But I still couldn't wrap my mind around the fact he'd be wearing Amish clothing with his bangs cut long. The Amish boys we'd passed looked like someone had placed a bowl over their heads and snipped.

"Are you two from around here?" Lilly asked as Angela and I got situated. I'd ended up landing between her and Chester on the couch. Angela nested with Glenn on the love seat.

"We're from Seattle," Angela said. She and Glenn couldn't have been sitting closer to each other. The way her hands were folded primly in her lap, the tilt of her head . . . If I hadn't known better I'd have thought she was tickled pink to have him to herself.

"We're Silvia's nieces, Juliana's kids." I hoped to start us talking about her.

Chester's posture, relaxed when we arrived, stiffened.

Lilly crossed her legs at the knee. "How long are ya here?"

"A little over a week," Angela said. "We arrived Monday."

"Our time is halfway spent." I should be elated, but I wasn't. When Angela and I first arrived the hours had snailed by. But now time sped too quickly. I wasn't ready to go home.

"I've never been to Seattle." Glenn leaned forward to get a better look at Angela. She blushed.

Before she could reply, Lilly said, "No reason to."

"*Sei net so rilpsich*," Chester said to her. I figured a scolding, the way Lilly compressed her lips.

Glenn cleared his throat. "As a matter of fact, there are several gardens in Washington State I'd like to visit. Two on Bainbridge Island."

"Perfect." I briskly rubbed my palms together. "When you come to Seattle, I'll take you there on the ferry." My declaration flew out with too much gusto. I didn't want his parents thinking I was coming on to their son right in their living room.

We spoke of the Pacific Northwest in general terms and then talked about Glenn's nursery. Chester and Lilly didn't sound proud of his accomplishments. Most parents would be. Except my father, who'd consider horticultural jobs beneath him. He'd have a conniption if I married a man who didn't wear a suit to work every day and drive a snazzy new automobile. Come to think about it, he'd never cared for any of my boyfriends. For the first time, his narrowminded attitudes irked me. Why must he act superior to everyone?

"I thank the *gut* Lord every day Glenn's back." Chester gazed at his son.

"We only have one child." Lilly directed the force of her attention to me. "He moved to California, knowing the *Ordnung* forbids us to fly, and taking the bus would keep us away from the farm for too long."

I didn't let on I was aware of Glenn's circumstances and the catastrophe that sent him back to the area. "I'm sure you missed him very much."

"*Ya*, we did," Chester said. "But young people need to make their own decisions."

Lilly folded her arms across her flat chest. "It would have been better if he'd stayed home to begin with. Chester and I would have moved into the *daadi haus*." She pointed to a door that appeared to lead to the extension of their home. "We needed him to run the farm and he knew it."

"How did you manage?" I couldn't help ask.

"We eventually sold all but one dairy cow, and we rent the cornfields to a neighbor on a year-to-year basis." Chester tugged his earlobe. "Our Glenn is generous with supplying us money for our needs."

"But that isn't what we want." Lilly's words bulleted out. "We want him living with us here. He could sell that big fancy nursery—"

"Now, Lilly…" Chester said slowly, sliding his thumbs up and down his suspenders.

Our mother's name was not mentioned again. In fact, no reference to Silvia or our family was made. Lilly might not have been aware Mother was once Chester's girlfriend. If Silvia even had her facts straight. Lilly struck me as the jealous type. Speaking of Mother might start a quarrel.

Before I knew it, we were preparing to leave.

"Thanks for having us." I took a final look around, noting a bookcase filled with hardbound books and board games I envisioned Glenn using as a child. One pot of geraniums on the window ledge.

Angela and I were ushered out like unwanted guests. Lilly marched through the kitchen and back room, and flung the door open.

"Have a safe journey home," she said, all business. We stepped outside, and she directed her attention to Glenn. "Goodbye, *Lieb*."

"*Gut* ta meetcha," Chester said to me, but his serious expression told me otherwise. Phooey, I wanted them to like me.

Glenn, Angela, and I slid into the pickup again—I made sure I sat in the center—and we headed back to the main road.

"Your parents are very nice," I said. In truth a better description of his mother would be aloof and standoffish. But his father seemed okay, although rather distant when he found out who we were. "I wonder if either of us reminded your father of our mother."

"Rose!" Angela knocked her knee against mine. "I don't think we should talk about this."

"Why not?" She didn't answer. I supposed Glenn might not be aware Chester ever knew Mother, but I'd gone this far and decided to wade in deeper. "Silvia showed us a photo of your dad and our mother together when they were teens."

"They were standing with Silvia and our uncle Leo," Angela added, as if trying to deflect my arrow.

"Chester had his arm around her."

"So? That doesn't prove anything."

Intent on his driving, Glenn stared straight ahead at the slow-moving tractor in front of us. He pressed his foot on the gas pedal and aimed his pickup onto the opposite lane. We passed the tractor and then swerved back onto our side just before reaching a bend in the road.

"We should have said something before now," I said. "You might not have wanted to take us over there."

He pulled the transmission into third gear with a swift motion and we cruised around the corner. "I gleaned from Silvia that *Dat* used to be sweet on your mother, but that was back in the Dark Ages." He picked up speed. "Still, I believe *Mamm* was pleased that your mother moved so far away."

The further we got from his parents' house, the more I wished I'd initiated a conversation about Mother no matter how Lilly reacted. She didn't like me anyway. When Silvia died, Chester would be one of the few left who remembered Mother as a girl. That was huge to me.

"By the way," I said to Angela, "Glenn told me all about Silvia."

Blinking, she responded with questioning eyes. Was she going to make me pry the truth out of her?

"Her health." I surveyed her soft and innocent face and realized she had no idea what I was talking about. "I assumed you knew." Losing courage, I forced out the words. "Angie, I wish I didn't have to be the one to tell you. Silvia has a serious heart condition and may not live more than a few more months."

Her jaw slackened and she looked past me to Glenn just as he glanced her way.

"No, it can't be." Moisture rimmed her eyes and her hand moved to her mouth. She looked pitiful, like she was breaking apart. I wish I'd chosen a gentler method of dropping the bomb. But there was no better way to tell her tragedy was set in motion and couldn't be stopped.

As Glenn and I filled her in, I felt a transition in Angela's and my relationship. I was stepping out of my little sister role and becoming her peer.

FIFTEEN

Angela

With Rose and Glenn behind me, I fumbled with the door-knob; my fingers were so rubbery they barely functioned. Rex raced around the side of the house, his tail wagging.

I shouldered Silvia's front door open and spotted our beloved aunt prone on the couch, the cushions consuming her flat silhouette. I thought of Mom, who'd never said, "I'm going to die." And I never spoke the word *death*, even in the last days. I'd mirrored Mom's passive face until the end: dry eyes and no talk of the ominous clouds looming on the horizon. Like clambering up a sand dune, always slipping back further, Mom allowed the tidal wave to wash over her and carry her away. I never said goodbye to her, and I reprimanded myself for my cowardliness. I'd learned my lesson; I wouldn't let Silvia leave this earth without a proper farewell.

Reminding myself the rain falls on the wicked and the just, I tried to bring logic to Silvia's illness. It made no sense why a kind woman who'd never hurt anyone should suffer. Silly as it might seem, I was hoping Silvia would fill the void left by Mom's death and become my surrogate mother.

I moved closer, my eyes fixed upon Silvia's ashen face. Why had she devised this charade? Was she denying her reality or had she submerged into total acceptance? Or was Glenn mistaken? No, he wasn't the type of man to toss words around to dazzle his audience like Frederick did. If Glenn said Silvia was dying, it must be true.

I evaluated her translucent skin. According to Glenn, the disease had spread throughout her body, but I hadn't heard coughing nor did she exhibit shortness of breath. She walked slowly and stopped often to view the scenery, which could be a ploy to cover up fatigue. I felt irritation mingle with my sadness. The truth was, Silvia, who'd seemed genuine, had been lying to Rose and me. And she'd neglected her body. Knowing her sister died prematurely, shouldn't she have demanded better health care? I recalled Rose's mentioning Silvia's lack of mental clarity; maybe our aunt was a hypochondriac and only imagined she was sick. When I'd had chicken pox as an eight-year-old, Rose had feigned illness to gain Mom's attention. I wished Frederick were here to help me sort this out.

No I didn't. He was the worst person to seek advice from when I was stressed. Weakness and fear angered him, like Dad in that regard.

Silvia lay still, and her breathing was so shallow for a moment I thought she wasn't. Then Rex's moist nose brushed her face, and her eyes opened. She pushed her frame to a sitting position and checked the clock. "You weren't gone very long."

"We went over to see my folks," Glenn said. We hadn't given Silvia our itinerary when we left.

"How'd that go?" she asked him without getting an answer, only a quick lift of his eyebrows.

"We had a nice visit." Rose gazed up at Glenn, her stance inclined toward him as if she knew him well—or wanted to. "I liked his parents."

I assumed her statement was for Glenn's benefit. She couldn't have missed the way Lilly scrutinized Rose and me like a security guard at the airport. I wondered why a sweet man like Chester married her, especially with a woman like Silvia close by.

Rose rambled on, declaring she'd appreciated their house and admired Chester for splitting his own wood. How could she speak so glibly, as if our previous conversation never occurred? I wanted to scream out for Rose to shush, but then what?

Minutes later, Glenn left. I experienced a new sensation of loss at the fading sound of his truck's engine.

"I have someone filling orders for me this week, but I need to call home and check in if I can get reception," Rose said. Then she mounted the stairs to use her phone in private.

Silvia started to get up, but I raised my hand to stop her. "You've been waiting on us. What can I do for you? Let me cook dinner tonight. Please."

"I'm going to pop a roast and some potatoes in the oven, but you could toss a salad later if you'd enjoy it."

"Sure, and I'll do the cleanup."

Rex spun in a circle and plopped at her feet. She scratched his hide through his thick fur. "This old fellow has been with me many years."

I wondered who would take him when she died. Phyllis hadn't seemed a dog lover, at least not this one. I was growing fond of Rex, but I knew Frederick would ban him from our house. Rex probably wouldn't adapt to city life anyway.

I scanned the room and saw generations of family history. From what Phyllis said, I doubted she and Hugh would ever move in here; the house would leave the family for good. If I were Silvia I'd be frantically writing lists and making sure everything was smoothed over, tidied up, and taken care of before I took my final breath. Maybe Phyllis was tying those knots, although she seemed somewhat detached from Silvia even as she showed concern for her. "Have Phyllis and Hugh already left on their trip?" I asked.

"Yes, they left today."

Phyllis's fretting made sense to me now. "It must be nice having her live close by."

"Yes, although in the past we didn't see much of each other."

"That's too bad." I couldn't imagine their getting along worse than they did now, but I was overly sensitive, according to Frederick.

"It was my fault." Her slender fingers wove together. "My husband, Frank, and I had a rocky marriage. He'd already moved out and we were headed for divorce when he died. With her older sister and brother off at college, Phyllis got the brunt of it living here with me. There were a couple of years when I wasn't much good to anyone. All I did was mope around feeling sorry for myself. I'd tried everything to keep the marriage together, but Frank had a roving eye. Which I knew from the start."

"But you married him anyway?" I glanced out the window and saw a mattress of clouds obscuring the sun. "How did you meet?"

"He worked for my father at the lumberyard. Frank had the nicest biceps I'd ever seen and long black eyelashes. When he asked me out I was the envy of all my girlfriends. I knew he drank too much and couldn't say no to a beautiful woman. Any woman, really. But that didn't stop me."

She pointed across the room to the built-in bookcase behind the puzzle table. "He's in that family photo, far left."

"You have his picture on display? How can you stand to look at him?" I didn't want to see what the scumbag looked like and averted my eyes. "Why, if Frederick cheated on me I'd burn his pictures." Or had he been unfaithful already?

"When Frank left, I boxed his photos and stuck them in the basement," she said. "But I found Phyllis was hiding one in her closet. I realized pretending we were never married was hurting her, so I sucked in my pride and did my best to forgive him the way the Amish would. I've learned a lot from them."

How could she act so cavalier? My gaze finally landed on the photo: two parents and three teenage kids in front of a Christmas tree. I stood and stepped closer to see the man who'd wrenched his family apart was brown-haired and sported a roguish moustache. I was filled with revulsion, even if he did resemble Frederick with facial hair.

"Forgiveness didn't come easy." Tension gathered in her face. "It was my nature to hang on to things. But after Frank passed away I got tired of living the role of the wronged woman and stopped fueling my bitterness. I even shed a few tears at his funeral. Not that what he did was all right. It stunk, and if he were still alive I might be tempted to kick him in the shins." She gave an elfish grin and swung out her foot to demonstrate. "I forgave him, but I'm no angel."

"I think you are. I can't imagine what I'd do if Frederick had a woman on the side. Would I even want to know?" I tugged at my hair. "I could never leave him. How would I take care of the kids' private school and pay the bills? Frederick could empty our savings account. I don't even know how much money we have or where it's invested."

"Dear, there's no need to worry yourself over nothing. From what you've told me, you have a reliable husband. I shouldn't have gotten us on this dreary subject."

I glanced at my wedding ring; it lay twisted to the side. Straightening it, I noticed the diamond was caked with dried hand cream.

On the night we got engaged, Frederick positioned a small black box between us as we ate pizza at our favorite haunt. "Is this what I think it is?" I'd asked, astounded by my good fortune. He opened the box and slid the ring on my finger. "This baby cost more than some men make in a year," he'd said. "You could buy a car with the money I paid for it." He never declared he loved me or asked for my hand in marriage. Unromantic, but back then I found everything he did for me extraordinary. Dad had been stingy with affection and rarely gave gifts, so I'd nothing to compare Frederick's generosity with.

I hadn't cleaned my ring since arriving here, usually a daily ritual. I was surprised to see a diamond could lose its brilliance in a few days. Just before our wedding, Frederick finally submitted to wearing a gold band, although he provided several logical reasons why men shouldn't. "Marriage is built on trust," he'd stated. He would never cheat on me; he could resist any temptation. Wasn't he the one who gave up smoking cold turkey? "I have more willpower than you."

Rose tromped into the room, her hands fisted. She stood before the puzzle table and plucked up a piece. With rapid motions she moved a four-headed shape across the table, and then she tossed it back on the pile and grabbed another.

"A problem?" I moved closer.

She glowered. "No. Everything's peachy-keeno." Her business must be suffering in her absence, but there was no use asking for details. She'd divulge the source of her frustration when good and ready, and she'd probably place the blame on me for tearing her away from Seattle.

Her head tipped back, Silvia was dozing on the couch again and didn't seem to notice Rose's and my dialogue. I wished I could cat-nap as easily and shut off Rose, instead of soaking in her intensity. To keep myself busy and avoid her ire I leafed through *The Connection* again and found an article on gardening.

The sky had turned gloomy, reminding me of stage lights dimming in a theater. I switched on a lamp and then moved to the window. Outside, the sky festered. Solitary raindrops plunged past the windows, landing hard. Treetops bent and leaves swirled. The first rumbles of thunder sounded soothing, like a caged lion at the far end of the zoo. But then the world turned white, and a crash of brittle thunder sounding like a lion tamer's whip shattered the air, almost knocking me off my feet.

"Don't worry." Silvia was awake again. Or maybe she'd never fallen asleep. "We have storms often. It'll pass."

"We don't get much lightning in Seattle." Rose left the puzzle and stood at my side.

A crash ignited and then another, until I was convinced the house would burst into flames. The hairs on my arms lifted, making me shiver and hug myself. Waiting for another assault, I was both horrified and enthralled by the proximity of danger, unlike timid old Angela. Normally, I didn't even like the kids cranking up the bass on their music.

White pea-sized pellets of hail began pounding down, bouncing off the lawn and bending leaves and small branches, sounding like pebbles beating on a tin roof. Rex rushed to the front door and barked.

"It's all right, boy," Silvia told him, but he growled, his hackles raised. If these storms were commonplace, why was he acting protectively? Rose claimed dogs had a sixth sense.

After a few minutes the hail let up, softening to rain. In a quiet space, after a flash of lightning, the lights flickered and then faded out, leaving us in dusklike darkness.

"A tree must have fallen on the electric lines." Silvia got up. "There goes my roast for dinner."

As Silvia lit the two candelabras on the sideboard by the dining table, Rose stooped before the hearth. Like a pro, she crumpled newspaper, arranged kindling and wood, and put a match to her composition. She squatted before her fire, prodding the flaming paper toward the wood with the poker.

Silvia brought a candelabrum supporting three candles to the side table by the couch. "Did Phyllis tell you about my condition?"

Rose stoked the fire as though she hadn't heard her question, leaving me to answer. My mind juggled through the facts I'd been told. What surfaced was how much I loved our aunt.

"She implied you're ill," I said. "And Glenn told us—"

"I wish they hadn't. What's the point?"

Lightning brightened the room, freezing the three of us like dancers under a strobe light. Crackling thunder rattled the windows.

"It might be better for everyone if I were hit by lightning and died quickly, without a fuss," she said. Rose shot to her feet and spun around to face her.

"Sorry, I don't mean to worry you, girls. I won't go outside and do anything foolish."

"We're glad to hear that," I said. For once, I didn't think Rose minded my speaking for her.

SIXTEEN

Rose

With no electricity, the second floor lay swathed in darkness at 7:00 p.m. Clad in my pj's, I left the bathroom carrying a flickering candle housed on a brass base. Its flame made the world sway and pulse. The ticking clock in my room served as my beacon, guiding me to the bed. I set my candle on the bedside table and climbed between the sheets.

I'd left Silvia on the couch and Angela tidying up from our dinner of tuna sandwiches, this time on untoasted bread. With the electricity out, the world offered little entertainment. The candle didn't provide enough light for me to thumb through Silvia's book *Hummingbird Gardens*. I'd never enjoyed grubbing in the dirt, planting annuals, or deadheading my rhododendrons, but if Silvia and Glenn liked gardening there must be something to it. And wouldn't it be delightful to have hummingbirds visit me?

Raindrops plinked a constant refrain against the roof. As the tempo picked up, I got lost in the sound and was sucked back in time. I was fifteen again, standing in the shower stall sobbing as I attempted to wash Dirk's slime away. The hot water scalded my skin. I scrubbed myself with antibacterial soap, but it didn't remove his filth. I felt dirty inside, making me hate the body that just that morning I'd admired in the mirror. I couldn't tell anyone what he'd done to me. Gossip swarmed through high school halls like wasps. I'd never be able to show my face again. My parents—even Angela—would revoke their love. I'd be an outcast.

Weeks later, my breasts grew tender and waves of nausea took over my body like a serpent, sending me heaving to the toilet. I dropped weight like a bulimic and missed my period for more than a month. All I could think about was freeing myself from this cesspool. Finally I did the only thing I thought I could. It was half Dirk's, the monster I loathed and the product of violence. I figured no child deserved that heritage.

Picture this. During my ordeal, Dirk passed me in the school halls without a glance. To him, I didn't exist. He'd been drunk that night and couldn't remember my unforgettable face. How would any guy view a girl who'd traipsed off to his van after one measly dance? What happened was my fault. Over time, coping with my misery, I began excusing him. I'd intended to remain a virgin until I married. I'd intended to demand respect from the boys I dated. What a laugh. I turned the hatred inward to the source of my pain. Me.

I heard a rap on my door. Angela entered the bedroom holding a flashlight releasing a dim beam, its batteries low on juice. She closed the door quietly as if she were hoping Silvia wouldn't hear. Still dressed and wearing a plaid lap blanket as a shawl, she perched on the edge of the bed. A cool current of air followed her, disturbing the flame and elongating the shadows.

"We need to talk." Her voice was all breathy.

I pulled my knees to my chest and handed her my extra pillow while she scooted in and leaned against the wall.

"Coming here was a mistake." She turned off her flashlight. "We're upsetting Silvia, making her depressed."

"That's ridiculous. We don't have that power. Anyway, she wanted us to come. She enjoys our company." I recalled Silvia's innuendo that death by electrocution would spare her family and friends the worry and bother of her slow decline. I'd wondered if she was kooky enough to venture out into the tempest, hold up a metal-handled rake and dare the lightning to strike. If she'd made a move for the door, I'd been ready to bar it or tackle her if need be.

Maybe Angela was right. Our being here was painful for Silvia. But too late; we were here.

"Sis, look, you wanted to forge a relationship with Aunt Silvia. This may be our last chance."

Yanking her hair back with both hands, she held it so tightly it had to hurt. "What if she dies while we're here?"

"She isn't going to drop over just like that." I snapped my fingers for effect, but Angela seemed unconvinced. In fact she looked more frightened, the way the candlelight illuminated the whites of her eyes.

She let go of her hair. It swung forward to conceal part of her face. "I wish we could speak to her doctor. He might tell us if there's any chance she'll get better."

He? I wanted to remind Angela that some of the nation's top physicians were women, but decided to let it go. Who cared? I'd spent too much energy debating the trivial. I needed to stay on track.

"Mother's doctor told us he couldn't predict her death," I said. "He said she might survive three months or live a year." When he'd made his pronouncement I'd envisioned the Grim Reaper randomly lopping off the doctor's patients' heads. As it turned out our mother passed away in exactly three months, right on schedule, submissive to the very last.

"Glenn said Aunt Silvia will be lucky to make it to spring," Angela said.

I pictured Glenn planting Silvia's bulbs, digging small graves for each tuber. Red was her favorite color. I envisioned scarlet roses, carnations, and holly berries, combined into a bouquet at the foot of a gravestone.

The phone rang twice, and then Silvia's animated voice spoke. I wondered if Glenn or another neighbor was checking up on her or comparing damage from the hail. Curious, I wanted to get up to open the door to eavesdrop, but Angela's weight constrained me to the bed like a straightjacket.

"We promised Phyllis we'd stay until she got back from her trip." I tried to gain a distant perspective. "And that's what we're going to do."

"Okay, you're right." She tugged her hair again. "Did you know I started taking medication for depression when Mom died?"

"Yes, you told me one med zonked you out and the other messed up your libido. I thought you were off of them."

"I am. That's what worries me. Three months ago, when I stopped taking all meds, I almost had a nervous breakdown. I couldn't function."

"No way. The older sister always runs the show." Even if she was ditzy. "You're upset from the storm."

"I was scared, but I found the lightning beautiful. Exciting. Silvia didn't bat an eye." Her thoughts seemed to be darting about. Anxiety? I was revisited by the notion that her hierarchical position had slipped a notch. She'd come to me for advice, not the other way around. I decided not to admit the hair-raising terror I'd experienced with each ice-blue flare of lightning. I'd counted the seconds after to gain control rather than judge distance. One second equaled one mile. The pounding thunder followed the lightning by a heartbeat. "Never admit to fear," Father had told me. "Fear is weakness. Then you have nothing."

But I was tired of holding my pain inside. I was the loneliest person on the planet.

"Brad cheated on me." It felt as if a fissure in my dam had sprung a leak. "I couldn't even be gone a few days and a woman answers his phone while he's in the shower. When he called me back he claimed she was his new cleaning lady, but I refused to buy his story. He finally admitted they used to date and that he ran into her while out shooting pool. One thing led to another. He said he doubts he'll see her again. Whoop de doo."

"That rat." Angela's disapproval fortified me.

"I'm mad at myself for not having the guts to end our relationship then and there. Where's my pride? I should have called him every name in the book and vowed to never speak to him again. He had a girlfriend when I met him—" My words slurred. "He cheated on her, so why am I surprised?" I was splitting open, but it felt good. Freeing.

"I'm sorry." She moved to the dresser, found a box of tissues, and handed me a limp square.

I wiped my nose. "It's my own fault. I have a habit of chasing after men who treat me like dirt. I should have settled for someone boring years ago."

"Like Frederick?"

"I meant reliable. It's time I start looking for a man who behaves like an adult and who's straight with me."

Angela lowered herself onto the foot of the bed again. "Who knows if Frederick is always honest?"

"Are we talking about money or women?" Even if Fred thirsted for a meaningless fling, what female in her right mind would glom onto a know-it-all like him? But I reminded myself there were plenty of female piranhas. Spiffed up in his power suit and tie, Fred probably had women hit on him all the time.

"I don't know. I'm letting my imagination take over." She rearranged the blanket, wrapped it across her chest. "The storm coupled with worrying about Aunt Silvia has me doubting everything tonight. I'll never fall asleep like this."

I reached for levity. I didn't know how else to help. "Do you want me to tell you a bedtime story?"

She nodded, so I started. "Once upon a time, there were two sisters, one named Hannah and the other Greta. Their mother didn't want them anymore, so she left the girls stranded in the deepest of all woods, much like the one above this very house." I described the girls' fruitless attempts to find their way home, how they trekked over a ridge and down a rocky gully, where they smelled chocolate cupcakes baking. They followed the delectable aroma to discover a cottage made of carrot cake and roofed with sour-cream icing. "The door made of Madeleine cookies stood open and the mat said *Welcome, Lost Children*, so the girls ventured inside. As they sampled Licorice Pastels and Junior Mints from a dish on the kitchen table, they heard footsteps outside. A moment later an elderly Amish lady came through the door carrying a basket of cherries."

Angela's features grew tense, so I altered the plot. Instead of a wicked witch returning, the kindly woman embraced the lost girls. She promised to care for them and announced, "We're a family now."

As I concluded my yarn, my mind circled back to this darkened room. The candle burned low and the smell of spent wax filled my nostrils. I wished I could rewrite my life's script to produce a fairy-tale ending. But I was powerless. In the morning, Silvia's disease wouldn't be less tragic. Mother had died, and it mattered a year later as much as ever.

Seventeen

Angela

The electricity had started up around midnight. The lamp by my bed—I'd neglected to turn it off—whitened my room and woke me with a start. I thought of Glenn's parents, who hadn't lost the electricity they didn't have. And Glenn? How had he managed? Growing up Amish, he was probably used to improvising.

This morning I was tempted to luxuriate in bed musing about him, but I pushed back the quilt and bent my knees. As my feet landed on the rug, I vowed to stay focused on Aunt Silvia. I'd do everything in my power to make my last few days here a blessing for her. Oops, Rose would say I sounded like Mother, who often used the word *blessing*, implying all good things came from God. In any case, I was going to devote my every fiber to helping and loving Silvia, even if it meant pasting on a smiley face and coexisting impeccably with Rose. If she'd let me.

I entered the kitchen to find Silvia alone. "Good morning," I said. "Is Rose up?"

"Not yet."

"Great." Knowing I'd risen before Rose filled me with childish euphoria I knew was immature.

"Dear, I forgot to mention my quilting group from church is coming over for lunch today." Silvia poured me a mug of coffee. This scenario was all wrong; I should be waiting on her.

"Thanks." I took the mug. My hunch was Cousin Phyllis knew nothing about it. Should I call her? What if Silvia overtaxed her meager store of energy? "Are you sure you're up to entertaining?"

"I'm just serving cold cuts." She carried a bowl of lettuce to the sink and doused it with tap water. "Nothing special. And one of the women is bringing dessert."

"How about I make a quiche?"

"I couldn't ask you to go to all that trouble."

"No trouble. I can practically make one with my eyes closed, I've done it so many times." I opened and rifled through her refrigerator to find ham, Swiss, mozzarella, and broccoli. "These would be a tasty combination. And you have green onions, half-and-half, and eggs." My chance to shine. "Once I chop the veggies and ham, and grate the cheese, all I'll need is flour and a spot to roll out the dough." I set the oven to 450, and then I placed a cast iron pan on the stovetop. "I want to partially bake the shell, and sauté the onions and broccoli. I hope you don't mind."

"Absolutely not. Make yourself at home."

After a quick breakfast, I located a ceramic mixing bowl and whisked eggs with half-and-half. Oh, cooking in our aunt's kitchen was a pleasure.

Busy mincing onions and garlic, and chopping broccoli on a wooden cutting board, I reviewed the details of Silvia's life I'd wanted to know. I'd pretend I was Rose and bulldoze my way in. "Dad said that years ago you wanted to join the Amish church."

"I feel foolish even admitting it, dear." Her cheeks flushed. "Things didn't work out…"

"But now you're Mennonite?"

"Yes, although about ten years ago I started attending a community church. I enjoy the eclectic mix. Many of the members are either Mennonite or ex-Amish."

"You mean Amish who've been shunned?" Using the side of the knife I added the onion, garlic, and broccoli to the warm skillet atop a dollop of butter.

"A few have been for various reasons. And Glenn attends out of preference. I think I told you that he was never baptized Amish." Silvia drained the lettuce in a colander.

"Glenn goes to your church?" My voice sounded too zealous. I shouldn't be asking about him. "Where's the nearest Amish church?" I started chopping ham and plunked a square in my mouth; I couldn't resist.

"No churches. Amish meet every other Sunday in a member's home, barn, or shop. The other Sundays are days for family, socializing, and building community. Although they may attend a service in another district."

"That sounds fun." I added the ham to my creamy concoction. "Have you ever been to an Amish service?"

"Yes, but it's been years. I could arrange to take you to one if you were staying longer, dear." She placed the wet lettuce into a colander. "I should warn you they last three hours and most likely you wouldn't understand what the preachers were saying. Mostly German or Pennsylvania Dutch. Or the words to their lengthy German hymns. But the songs are breath-taking to hear."

I congratulated myself for learning all kinds of information about the Amish and Glenn in Rose's absence. But I wanted to change the subject before my sister appeared. "I didn't realize you were a quilter," I said.

"Your grandmother made the quilt on your bed. All the rest around the house are mine. But I don't sew much anymore."

Ten minutes later, as I rolled out dough, Rose shambled in. "Wow, you're up early, sis." She looked groggy, her eyes puffy.

"No, you slept in."

She glanced at the clock on the stove. "Ten o'clock? Guess I needed the catch-up." Rose poured herself coffee and splashed in half-and-half. "What's up?"

"Silvia's quilting group is coming at noon," I said.

Her eyes searched mine. "Really?"

"Yes, I just found out about it myself." I tried to let her know I was as bamboozled as she was by raising my brows, but she stared back at me blankly.

"Need help?" she asked.

"No. Everything's under control."

My terse remark must have made her feel inadequate, because her voice came out a sad refrain, like a dirge. "I've never been much use in the kitchen."

I couldn't agree with her more, but no way would I let her lure me into a contentious conversation. Mom had tried to interest Rose in cooking, but my little sister refused, as she did with everything Mom suggested. Not that Rose didn't abound with talents. She did.

I felt bad if I'd hurt her feelings, but if I attempted to soothe her wounded pride I'd bring forth her wrath like taunting a rattlesnake.

Rose leaned against the counter. Her elbow knocked a clove of garlic; it rolled and fell to the floor. "What's wrong with me? I'm usually not such a klutz."

"No matter, dear." Silvia dried her hands on a towel. "You just got up."

"Maybe I slept too much." Rose scooped the garlic off the floor and dropped it back onto the counter. "There must be something I can do to help."

"After breakfast you could set the table for six if you like. Just a small group today. I already draped a red-and-white checked cloth on the table."

"Okay." Rose sipped her coffee.

"I could make you breakfast, Rose." Silvia set the towel aside.

"There's leftover oatmeal on the stove still warm," I said.

Rose frowned as she brought out a bowl and served herself without thanking me.

Eighteen

Rose

I set the table with care so my big sister couldn't straighten up after me. Angela had edged me out of the kitchen. She'd made it clear I was in the way. Subtle motions, like opening the oven door when I stood in front of it.

Although I felt annoyance toward her brewing, the household seemed back on track today. Yet of course it wasn't. Silvia was seriously ill. I needed to reaccept the inevitable. Life was never fair.

Knuckles rapped on the front door and Rex woofed. "There's my first guest," Silvia said. I loped to the door and opened it to save Silvia's stamina. And to beat Angela.

"*Gude mariye*," said a rotund little woman as she shimmied in, carrying a wicker basket. She wore a high-neck, avocado-green longish dress, the fabric awash with daisies.

Silvia greeted her with, "*Wie geht's*, Kay." Earlier, Aunt Silvia had explained many of her church members were either Mennonite or ex-Amish. But I had no idea they'd speak Pennsylvania Dutch at lunch. How would I communicate?

His tail wagging, Rex sniffed at the basket.

"Naughty *hund*." Kay's voice carried a singsongy accent. "There's nothing in there for you. Only the quilt I made for my new grandson. Wait until show-and-tell time." Kay gave her plump shoulders a shrug. "I shouldn't boast, but I can't help myself." She turned to me and said, "Your aunt has helped me with my stitching. I can never thank her enough."

Standing at my side, Silvia chuckled. "Rose, this is Kay. And she was already a proficient quilter when we met."

"A pleasure to meet you, Rose." Kay gave me a spontaneous hug. She stood even shorter than I did.

"Since you and Angela are here we'll speak English," Silvia said.

"Phew. Otherwise I'd be lost. Aunt Silvia, did you learn Pennsylvania Dutch growing up?"

"Yes. I've always felt a kinship to the Amish and Old Order Mennonites. Papa wanted us to be one hundred percent American and disapproved of it, but I learned *Deitsch* when visiting Amish neighbors. Kay got me speaking it again ten years ago when she invited me to her church's quilting club. I ended up joining her church."

"Do you quilt?" Kay asked me.

"No. I've never given quilting a thought, but suddenly I wish I had."

"Someday you must."

"Maybe today she'll get hooked." Silvia gave a sly grin.

"I've never even learned to sew past replacing a button."

"No matter, you're still a young woman." Kay's giggle brought a smile to my face. What a cutie.

The doorbell rang, and two more women arrived. Lucy, clad in a demure gingham dress and white head covering, and Eleanor, the oldest—I guessed eighty something. She wore an eggplant-colored dress and a pleated head covering somewhat different from Lucy's. Like Silvia, none of the women used makeup or painted their fingernails.

"I've known your aunt for more than fifty years," said lavender-clad Lucy. She set down her quilted bag before embracing me. "That makes us family."

How nice was that? Apparently I had a ready-made family, even if only for an afternoon.

When Lucy released me from her arms, Eleanor extended a bony hand to shake mine. Her grasp flaccid, she was tall and slim, her face gaunt.

Kay sniffed the air. "Something smells *appeditlich*."

Lucy nodded. "*Yah*, delicious."

Moments later, Angela carried the quiche to the dining table and Silvia introduced her to everyone. I brought in the salad and a platter mounded with cheeses, olives, and sliced salami.

"Lunch is ready, dear friends," Silvia said. "Please have a seat, everyone."

I claimed the chair next to Silvia, on her left. Angela sat on her right. My sister and I seemed to share the same goal, to remain as close as possible to Silvia before we left. Oh gee, I wasn't ready for that yet.

"Who wants to say grace?" Silvia asked. We all fell silent.

Finally she bowed her head. "Okay, I will."

Before bowing my head, out of deference to Silvia, I noticed everyone but Eleanor closed her eyes. Kay's hands clasped each other under her double chin and Lucy's forehead lowered almost to her plate. But Eleanor stared across the room as if used to entertaining herself while the others indulged in their childlike ritual. She and I must have thought alike when it came to God. But seeing her severe countenance evoked pity for her. Would I eventually look like her? If I made it to her age. Having a mother die prematurely raised my odds of following suit. My genes stunk.

While my thoughts rambled like school kids' at recess, Eleanor noticed my staring. She shut her eyes and bowed her head. I assumed for my benefit.

"Thank you, dear God," Silvia said, "for the freedom to meet with friends and family, and for this meal." I tried to imagine how I'd feel in her place. I'd savor each taste and consider each moment precious, like a unique snowflake begging to be admired before it melted. Often I went through the motions of life on automatic pilot. At the end of my day I collapsed into bed. The next morning I'd rise with my alarm clock and repeat the cycle. I appraised my days by how much I'd accomplished. How I contributed to my business or completed household chores. When I thought about it, my death was also approaching. Even if fifty years in the future. My life would be extinguished, and then what? No one would notice my sales figures or whether I'd repainted my back steps.

Angela cut and served her quiche as if she were the hostess. We passed the salad and platter around.

"Here are the articles I told you about." Eleanor extracted two magazine clippings from her purse to give to Silvia. One title read "Vitamin B Fights Fatigue," which sparked my curiosity. Apparently Eleanor and I shared common interests. But she was my least favorite woman at the table. I don't mean to imply she was a bad person. It's more like she was wearing an invisible suit of armor to keep others at a distance. Maybe the way I did.

Silvia moved the clipping enough to peruse the second article's title: "Lyme Disease: The Silent Predator." What was Eleanor thinking bringing an article of such serious nature to the table? How could we continue our fun now?

Silvia thanked Eleanor as if the subject matter were of no particular significance. Then she folded the papers and set them next to her plate. These women must know Silvia wouldn't be hosting many more quilting club meetings. How could they act so nonchalantly about losing her?

"Rose, you look like your mother," Lucy said.

I didn't realize any of the women knew Mother.

"Yes, the same eyes and nose," Silvia said.

"I've told Rose that, but she won't believe me." Angela spoke as if I were a mute child. Couldn't she keep her yap shut?

Everyone had appreciated Mother's classic good looks, but I'd spent my life trying to be her opposite. Angela must have noticed my cringing, because she changed the subject by asking Lucy if she'd grown up around here.

"Yes and no." Lucy spooned an olive onto her plate. "My family lived in Manhattan, but we spent our summers in the area. When my husband and I retired, we moved here."

"Were you and our mother friends?" Angela asked. I noticed Silvia stopped chewing her food.

"Yes, very good friends," Lucy said. "As a teenager, she rode the train down to visit me several times, but when we went to college we lost touch."

What gives? Mother told me her parents took the family to New York City to see the Christmas store windows when she was nine. And then again at age twelve. But she'd made a point of saying she'd never gone back. Our mother harped about honesty and she had hokey Scripture verses to prove it. Like somewhere in Proverbs where it stated that he who poured out lies will perish. Wow, I heard that one a few times. She'd made it seem as if we were living in a titanic Monopoly game and we'd get sent straight to jail if we lied. Which didn't stop me.

"Are you sure Mother visited you?" I asked.

"Oh, my, yes," Lucy said. "Juliana loved window shopping on Fifth Avenue. She always insisted we walk by Cartier and Harry Winston to look at the jewelry."

Weird, but I told myself Mother would never lie. I must have misunderstood her. Growing up, I didn't listen to half of what she said. On the other hand, maybe she'd fibbed and figured Angela and I would never meet her childhood friends or spend time with Silvia, who wasn't verifying Lucy's statements.

To alter our conversation's path I said, "Your quiche is scrumptious, sis."

She beamed. "You want the recipe?"

"Uh, that's okay."

Later, after coffee and Kay's homemade blackberry pie—I couldn't resist eating seconds—the women offered to clear the table. Angela and I assured them we'd handle everything. Then we straggled into the living area.

Silvia and Kay landed on the couch and the others on chairs.

"Most days we work on a group project," Silvia told Angela and me as we found seats, "but Kay and Lucy have appointments."

"Next week we'll start a new project to be donated to an auction to collect money for orphans in Haiti." Kay set her basket at her feet.

"We still need to choose the pattern and colors," Lucy said, "but spending time getting to know you is more important."

"Today we get to show off." Kay brought out an adorable baby blanket in flamboyant colors for her grandson and held it up. "It's a variation of the Log Cabin. For a granddaughter I would have made Sunbonnet Sue."

"It's as cute as can be." Angela took it from Kay to examine.

Lucy stood and unfolded an elegant queen-size quilt to be given to her future daughter-in-law in a pattern called the Double Wedding Ring. The intricate hand stitching on the ivory background was meticulous. The pattern's palette was a subtle rainbow of teal, burgundy, and pink.

Silvia and Kay congratulated Lucy on her even stitches and care to detail. "Marvelous," Silvia said.

"Did you bring anything?" Lucy asked Eleanor.

"No, I made a slight error. I'll have it fixed by our next meeting."

"You should have brought it anyway. We could help."

"No, I'd rather do it on my own." I figured Eleanor was covering up embarrassment.

"Are you working on a quilt?" I asked Silvia.

"Not right now." She massaged her hands. "My fingers get so stiff."

Kay wrapped an arm around Silvia's shoulder. "You poor thing."

Lucy moved to Silvia's other side and said, "We love you."

"I have an idea." Eleanor pressed her palms together. "Silvia should select our next pattern and choose the colors." Her gaze clung to Silvia's. "Please keep attending our meetings, if only to encourage us. I'll give you a ride if you need it." So she wasn't a cold fish after all.

"You seem fine today," Kay told Silvia.

"Having my nieces here has pumped up my energy."

Minutes later, Silvia, Angela, and I escorted the women to their cars. Kay sidled up next to her spiffy red Volkswagen Jetta. Not the old-lady car I'd expected.

As she hugged Angela, she repeated her advice. "Do learn to quilt. You two are fortunate to have your aunt as an instructor."

"Rose, dear, I'll send you home with a couple of books for beginners," Silvia said. "And I have plenty of scraps to get you started on a nine-patch. Would you like that?"

"Yes, okay."

"Would you give me fabric too?" Angela muscled her way between us. "Rosie and I could practice together."

I figured it would never happen.

Kay also gave me a hug. "I hope we meet again," she said.

"Me too." I meant it. I'd love to be part of these meetings even if they didn't seem to get any quilting done. These women were treasures.

NINETEEN

Angela

"This bed was your great-grandmother's pride." Silvia stroked the wooden headboard, its surface carved into scrolls and flowers. "Once she and Papa got their feet on the ground, she wrote home to report what a grand one they'd purchased—proof they'd done the right thing moving to the New World."

We stood in Silvia's bedroom, the first time I'd more than glanced through her doorway. With Rose nearby, I looked around and made note of Silvia's cotton nightgown and her mandarin-collared bed jacket draped over a chair. The bureau, topped with a doily, was covered with framed photographs and a tortoiseshell comb, hairbrush, and hand mirror. A kerosene hurricane lamp and Bic lighter had probably come in handy last night.

"As I told you, I'm a packrat." Silvia noticed my gaze surveying each item. "Phyllis refuses to look in the storage area, and she's warned me everything her two siblings don't want goes in an estate sale."

How could Phyllis make such a cruel statement? I felt anger settling in my jaw, my molars clenching. Once Phyllis experienced the agony of losing her mother, she wouldn't be so offhand. Or was she like Rose—detached and indifferent? I doubted Rose ever thought about Mom.

Silvia moved to a mirror-fronted door and pulled it open to reveal a long darkened room reminding me of my parents' basement in the old house, where Mom used to stow unwanted furniture, Christmas decorations, and Rose's and my childhood art projects and toys. Dad, who demanded order in his castle, had often prodded her to empty the basement, although he had no plans for the space. I think he sporadically threw things away on the rare occasions Mom went out of town. Why else would my dollhouse, which I'd planned to give to Tiffany, have disappeared? And what happened to Mom's nutcracker collection?

Silvia entered the closet and flipped on a low-wattage lightbulb. "Watch your step," she warned us, but Rose flounced right in and found another light fixture at the far end of the room. It had been Rose's idea to come in here and dig through the trunks—not an activity I thought she'd choose. I assumed Rose, who bragged she gave away or threw out something each time she bought its replacement, and had so recently said she'd thought about getting rid of half her own belongings, planned to help Silvia transport her unwanted possessions to the nearest drop-off spot for charitable donations. Why not as long as we were here looking for quilting material anyway? One of Rose's mottos: If you don't use it, toss it or pass it on.

Following them inside, a musty warmth smelling of mothballs engulfed me. Ahead lay cardboard boxes and steamer trunks— the kind ocean-going travelers once took around the world—and dresses in garment bags. The hodgepodge reminded me of a secondhand store. A brigade of cleaning women would need a week to straighten this mess. Or I could do it; I enjoyed organizing and vacuuming.

To one side of Silvia's bedroom door stood shoes and boots. Above them hung what appeared to be an Amish dress and apron.

"What's this doing here?" I touched the apron's hem.

"Gathering dust." Silvia's said. "I sewed it many years ago and then hid it from my parents."

"You made it to wear yourself?" Rose asked.

"I had this crazy fool notion…"

"I bet it would fit you, Rosie." I expected my sister to tell me I'd gone off the deep end, but instead her hands explored the cobalt-blue dress's cotton fabric.

Silvia opened the nearest carton, pulled out a square of brown fabric, then shoved it back in the box. "I keep meaning to donate these scraps to Kay. She quilts using vintage material." She nudged the box toward the door with her foot.

Rose shuffled through the garment bags hanging on the rack and exhumed a purple velvet dress with the same-color-thread embroidery on the bodice. "This looks your size." She handed it to me.

I held the dress to my body, but the waist hit me three inches above the navel. "The width maybe, not the length." I bet Rose wanted to embarrass me; she'd latch onto any chance to compare her slender figure to mine.

"That was Grandma's," said Silvia. "She saved it for fancy occasions. If you'd like it, it's yours."

"I can't think of one excuse to take it home with me." I rehung it in the bag. "It would wind up in the back of my closet with my wedding dress and never be seen again." Still, I couldn't stand having it discarded or used as a child's Halloween costume.

Above us, at the peak in the roof, a dust-covered spiderweb dangled from the unfinished ceiling. I hated spiders and every other crawly bug.

Rose moved further into the room's shadows. As if on a mission, she zeroed in on a trunk. Her hands moved to raise the lid.

"That's filled with your mother's belongings," Silvia said abruptly, like a warning.

"Mom left a trunk?" I couldn't believe our good fortune. "Dad gave away most of her possessions. I hardly have any mementos. She and I were almost the same size. I'd love to find a couple of personal items—a sweater or shawl."

As I stepped to Silvia's side, the pungent odor of mothballs emanated from the trunk. My hand moved to my nose as I watched Rose lift the lid and pull out a garment made of striped fabric. The sight of the blue-and-white satin stopped my breath.

"Look, sis." She grasped it by the waistband; the fluid material cascaded to the floor. "It's the dress in the photo."

A segment of Mom's life unearthed itself. I was inundated with a jumble of emotions: tenderness, puzzlement, dread. "Concrete evidence," Frederick would call the dress. Proof that Mom indeed posed with Chester.

I set the purple dress aside and peered into the trunk to see flattened clothing. I felt like an archaeologist happening upon a shrine. Or was it a mausoleum? Half of me yearned to examine every article of clothing, but the other half argued not to disturb the past. Mom used to say, "Curiosity killed the cat," when, as a child, I asked too many questions.

Or was this trunk her parting gift to us? Christmas in October?

"When Juliana married your father, she packed the clothes she didn't want in this trunk, which Mama intended to eventually send her. Juliana kept putting her off, saying she'd come back and sort through it. But she never did, not until she visited with you children." Silvia's voice choked, and then she sniffled into her hand, which caused moisture to press at the backs of my eyes.

"I wasn't going to do this." She dabbed her eyes with a handkerchief. "I swore I wouldn't cry during your visit."

My arm glided around her birdlike shoulders.

"Don't pay attention to sentimental old me, dear. You two see if you want any of your mother's things. Please, you'd be doing me a favor."

Instead of taking the next item, a woolen garment, Rose dipped her hand to the center of the trunk and came up brandishing a packet of envelopes tied by a narrow ribbon.

"Look, sis. Letters addressed to Mother. Should we read them?"

"Sure." Again, I was tickled by our good luck. "Maybe Mom had a pen pal. Maybe they're from a relative in the old country."

"No, the stamp looks American," Rose said.

"They could be private." Silvia's voice sounded strained.

"You're right." I was disappointed, but I wanted to act like the woman Mom taught me to be. She was trustworthy; she'd never snoop through my diary. "If Mom had wanted us to see them, she would have brought them home."

Rose held up the letters, the light turning them gold, making me hope she defied me, but for once she obeyed my wishes.

"I guess." She reburied them in the trunk's depths and then snatched them up again. "On the other hand, Mother left these where any family member could read them, so they can't be confidential." She extracted an envelope from the middle of the packet and deposited the others in the trunk. I could see the handwriting was unfamiliar, not Dad's, and there was no return address on the upper left-hand corner.

She lifted the letter's flap.

Wishing to err on the side of caution, I said, "Wait, Rosie, this feels wrong. We should discuss the pros and cons of reading them over tea."

But Rose pulled the letter to her torso, guarding it with her other hand.

"Dear, sometimes people hang on to things because they don't know what else to do with them," Silvia said. "Like that silly dress."

"And my high school yearbooks," I gave as an example. "I wouldn't want anyone reading what my friends wrote in them." Particularly notes from my first sweetheart, Rusty.

"Mother's dead," Rose said, as if we didn't know. "What difference could it make? Maybe they're love letters from Father."

"They aren't," I said. "Look at the handwriting. It's a cursive script. Dad prints with a bold hand." I glanced to Silvia for support, but she stared at the letter. Did she recognize the handwriting? Why didn't she say something?

With haste, Rose unfolded the letter; the paper was crinkled on the corners as if it had been handled many times. What should I do? In a way I appreciated Rose's impudence. If the early American pioneers had been as timid as I was, they never would have crossed the Rocky Mountains and settled on the West Coast. But when did my little sister start making the decisions? A band tightened around my scalp; my temples throbbed. I should plug my ears and refuse to listen.

Rose cleared her throat. " 'Dearest Juliana.' "

Maybe I'd made a mistake about the handwriting. Dad sent the letters. I was touched that at one time he showed Mom affection. I couldn't remember his ever kissing her in front of me. At least Frederick gave me a smooch in front of the kids every so often.

" 'Are you suggesting we remain friends?' " Rose went on, her cadence slowing as if the words were too heavy to carry. " 'I've loved you my whole life and now you expect me to attend your wedding and watch you marry someone else?' "

"Dad wouldn't have written that." I stepped closer. "Maybe the letter was to a Juliana in the generation prior to Mom's."

"No," Rose said. "Mother told me her parents chose her name to honor a family friend, not a relative."

She read ahead silently and then said aloud, " 'Am I supposed to forget I fathered your child? I would have raised it, but you didn't give me the choice.' "

"Hey, wait a minute. I'm our mother's oldest child." I felt a pinching in my stomach, sending ripples of wooziness up to my throat. My hands clasped my midsection. "Who wrote that letter?"

Rose glanced to the bottom of the page. Her face bunched up like she'd been slapped. "Chester."

"Glenn's father?"

Clutching the letter, Rose's hand dropped to her side. She looked Silvia square-on. "What does he mean? Did he get her pregnant?"

I could tell from Silvia's ghostlike expression that she was sickened by the thought of Mom and Chester together. She busied herself refolding the dress. "We should put things back the way they were."

A whirlwind of questions bristled through my mind. Had Mom—my foundation, my biggest fan—been a lying hypocrite? Did I really want to know?

"So Mom had sex," Rose said. "Big deal. I lost my virginity when I was fifteen."

I stared at her for a moment. Silvia didn't say a word.

"I can't believe my ears." My words ricocheted off the ceiling. "I didn't even know you had a boyfriend until you were in college. Are you proud of yourself?"

We three stood like scarecrows with half our stuffing shredded out. Our silence turned the airless room into a vacuum.

"Was Mom pregnant?" I asked Silvia.

"I think so."

"What happened to the baby?" I felt as if I were wandering in a tunnel.

"She said she lost it early." Silvia fastened her gaze on a wizened-up spider lying on the floor by the trunk. "I was two years younger. She didn't tell me everything."

"Spontaneous miscarriages are not uncommon." Rose spoke matter-of-factly. "They often happen in the first trimester."

I supposed she was right. A friend had miscarried three times before bringing her now eight-year-old son to full term.

"Did doctors do abortions back then?" I hoped the answer was no.

"Sure, even if they were performed in back rooms." Rose's words came out like a three-wheeled cart; she was floundering, wobbly.

"She wouldn't have done that," I said, more to assure myself than convince her. "I remembered Mom stating that if a young woman was old enough to engage in sex, she was old enough to bring a child into the world, even if it meant giving it up for adoption. And Chester stated he would have raised it."

"Men say all sorts of things." Rose flipped back to her authoritative voice.

"Girls, there's no use second-guessing what happened in the past." Silvia wrung her hands. "It was so many years ago. It doesn't matter anymore." Easy for her to say; she wasn't the one whose mother was a fraud.

We could ask Chester what happened to the child, I wanted to suggest. I'm sure Rose was contemplating the same thing. She scanned the rest of the letter, then refolded it and stuffed it into the envelope with difficulty, as if the envelope had shrunk or the letter had grown. I thought of Alice in Wonderland, how she suddenly didn't fit in her little world anymore. I wanted to go back to the way things were just minutes ago.

"We might have had an older brother or sister," I said, and Rose winced.

"If Mother had married Chester, she wouldn't have married Father. You and I wouldn't have been born."

"She could have given birth and still married our father. Silvia, are you sure Mom didn't disappear somewhere for six months, let's say to boarding school that was really a home for unwed mothers?" Our grandparents would have preferred that route.

"I don't think so, but I went away to work at a camp for three weeks. When I got home, she'd already left for college, where she met your father."

I tried to envision the moment Mom and Dad had first set eyes on each other, but all I saw was my mother and Chester free-falling together into high grass. Passion, fire, a child—all destroyed so our mother could raise her social status and marry into my father's wealthy family. No, Mom wouldn't do that. Would she? She seemed a stranger to me now.

Silvia moved to the back of the room and pulled a string, extinguishing the lightbulb, darkening her face. She lingered in the shadows; the dim light behind me reflected in her eyes like suffocating candlewicks. Then she retreated toward her bedroom. As she passed Mom's trunk, she closed the lid, concealing the packet of letters.

Maybe she thought she was doing Rose and me a favor by sheltering us from the truth, or perhaps she honestly didn't know what had happened. Well, if she didn't, who did?

I rode in the backseat of Silvia's car behind Rose, who'd insisted on driving to give Silvia time to recoup after a busy day. Leaving the closet thirty minutes ago, Silvia had declared we three needed a spell out of the house. "To get some fresh air. It'll do us good."

It would have taken more than a change of scenery to clear my head. My mind was in rebellion, refusing to wrap itself around the facts. I wished I could blot all memory of Chester's letter from my brain like the clean swipe of an eraser on a chalkboard. Why had Mom left this ugly legacy? I'd heard of criminals planting clues, daring or possibly hoping the authorities would nab them. Did Mom want Rose and me to read the letters? Or did she wish to impart that excruciating luxury on Silvia?

I was beginning to understand why Rose, as a girl, resisted Mom's overtures. My sister wasn't as gullible as I, someone who'd believed everything Mom told us. Our mother sculpted my life; I was an obedient blob of clay. She influenced me more than any one person. Even though I had come to adore him, I might not have married Frederick if she hadn't urged me to. I wasn't looking for a good catch, as she'd described him. More than anything I'd wanted someone to love me forever.

I wondered if Dad knew about Mom's dubious past. He probably thought his treasured bride arrived at the altar unblemished. She'd always acted shocked when he related details from his clients' lives: the man being sued by his live-in mistress of six years and the bored housewife who fooled around with her dentist.

Had Mom been an actress? A sham?

Rose slowed Silvia's car to turn into Glenn's nursery parking lot; the tires caught nuggets of gravel, spitting them under the wheel wells. Rose had suggested we come here. "Strictly business," she'd said when I challenged her reasoning after what we'd just learned. "It may be my last chance to check out his inventory," she'd insisted.

I felt so depleted I'd contemplated staying home to hibernate as I did many afternoons waiting for the kids, but Silvia and Rose wouldn't hear of it.

I supposed I could rest when I returned to Seattle. If I went home.

I stiffened. Where had that preposterous notion come from? Of course I'd go back to Seattle. Eventually. But since I was here, I might stay longer to help Silvia empty Mom's trunk. Why should Silvia be stuck with the burden? Then I could go through the rest of the trunks and the boxes, maybe even hold a garage sale. And learn to quilt. Let Rose get back to her hurry-up life. I wasn't needed at home. The kids had already outgrown me. They were happier under a sitter's supervision or hanging out at their friends'. Frederick didn't miss me, and I didn't really miss him. When my mind was snarled up like a knotted twine, he was the worst person to turn to for support.

Rose stopped the car in front of the store, parking between two others. Glenn must have seen our arrival, because he approached the sedan and opened Silvia's door while I exited the backseat on the other side. He glanced across the roof of the car and our gazes met, neither of us releasing eye contact for a few seconds longer than seemed proper.

He could never love Olivia. Or even Rose. He wanted me.

Again I was dumbfounded by my thoughts. Men in white jackets would be carting me to the funny farm if I kept this up.

Rose said hello, capturing Glenn's attention. As I rounded the car, my gaze took in his muscled shoulders and long legs. I wondered if admiring his physique made me depraved, but I assured

myself it was perfectly normal. When people fantasized about own-
ing a Ferrari, it didn't make their ten-year-old Honda less adequate.
Or did it? Mom once told me daydreams diminished what you had.
Or did they propel you to a higher place?

The truth was, Glenn in a plaid flannel shirt and jeans with a
tear at the knee made Frederick seem like the monarch who ends
up naked in "The Emperor's New Clothes"—a puffed-up rooster
strutting before an eagle. Glenn demonstrated that strength didn't
dwell in a man's billfold or depend on his slick tongue. It was evident Glenn cared more about other people than himself or material
wealth.

"I've decided to enlarge my line of birdfeeders," Rose said.
"Weathervanes too." She reached out to touch his arm in a coquett-
ish manner. "I hope you don't mind if I borrow some ideas."

"Not at all. I'm honored."

I thought she wasn't going to wear makeup all week—that's what
she'd said—but I noticed lipstick embellishing her mouth and rouge
intensifying her cheeks. And she was wearing a clingy knit top. And
jeans with Lycra, one size too small, accentuating her figure.

A young Amish man ambled over to ask Glenn about the recent
vandalism—someone had hacked down a dozen saplings.

"My only Tsuma gaki maples." Glenn spoke to Silvia. "Missy
tried to warn me last night, but I ignored her growls. I thought a
coyote was prowling about."

"How terrible. Who would do such a thing?"

"I have my suspicions but no proof."

Silvia shook her head. "Have you reported it to the police?"

"Not yet."

"If this keeps up you'll have to."

"I s'pose."

Customers wandered by, chatting. Chickadees—one of the few
birds I could identify—landed on a birdfeeder.

"Glenn?" Olivia appeared with a UPS box in her arms. After

we exchanged greetings, Olivia looked up at Glenn. "This is from L.L.Bean. Ya want me to put it in your house?"

"*Nee, denki*. I can do it." He lifted the box from her arms and she retreated to the shop.

Glenn suggested Rose, Silvia, and I follow him to his home while he dropped off the package.

"We'd absolutely love it," Rose said, atwitter. Where was her sense of decorum? She was practically slobbering on him. Had she forgotten our beloved aunt was sick? Had she forgotten Chester's letter? All Rose thought about was Rose.

We followed Glenn across the parking lot and then mounted wide front steps leading to the house's wraparound porch, a luxury most Northwest homes lacked. Rose sashayed ahead and languished herself on the hanging bench suspended by a heavy chain, its green-and-white cushions striped. She set it in motion, lifting her feet and swinging like a trapeze artist.

"This porch is one reason I bought the place." His gaze on Rose, Glenn's mouth widened into a smile. "My intention was to sit here and relax. I keep forgetting to do that."

"You should." Rose glided to her feet. "On hot summer days, this would be the perfect spot to sip lemonade or iced tea."

I used to think I took after Mom in personality and style, but I realized Rose was our mother's daughter, the way she flaunted herself. I recalled the photo of Mom—her Jane Russell lips and sultry gaze—and wondered if Chester was still under her spell, which would explain why Lilly acted standoffish.

Glenn opened the front door, painted brick red. A black cat dashed out, then circled back and massaged itself against Rose's pant leg. She was a magnet for animals, and men.

"You're the cover girl on the catalogue," she said to the feline. A moment later, Glenn's lab pranced out.

"You met Missy the other day," Glenn said. "She's having pups next month."

"Are you sure she's going to wait that long?" Rose stood back to appraise the dog's ample girth. "Now that I look at her closely, I estimate she'll have a litter of ten in three weeks."

"I want one," I said.

Rose's brows raised. "Yeah, right."

"I do," I repeated, even if she was right. Frederick wouldn't let me, making me feel powerless. And resentful. I was tired of other people dictating my life.

"If you're serious, I could send one once it's weaned and old enough to travel," Glenn said. "I'm planning to keep a male, and a friend asked for a female, but if Rose's prediction is correct you'll have plenty to choose from."

"You'd better ask your husband." Rose wagged her finger at me.

"Thank you, little sister."

"We can talk again, after the pups are born," Glenn said, and the corners of Rose's mouth angled down.

"Great." Long after Rose bid farewell to Glenn, he and I would still be in contact. As friends, of course.

He led us into the house and set the UPS box on a wooden bench, next to a Philadelphia Phillies baseball cap. Straight ahead expanded a wooden flight of stairs, and next to it a hallway emitted the aroma of warm dough. To our left lay a living room with a shoulder-high hearth, and a leather couch and a corduroy-covered recliner pulled close, I imagined so Glenn could cozy up to the fire's warmth on wintry evenings. Over the mantel hung a painting of a fisherman wading in a mountain stream, and next to the fireplace stretched a floor-to-ceiling bookcase chock-full of books I'd love to explore.

To the other side of the front door, six cane-backed chairs clustered around a dining table. An arrangement of exotic flowers looking like tropical sea anemones sat on its center. A woman's touch?

"The house looks beautiful." Silvia unbuttoned her jacket.

"Thanks." Glenn turned to her. "I've been meaning to have you over. It's been six months since you've come to dinner."

"Don't worry, dear. I know how busy you are."

We moved through the hallway and entered the kitchen, an airy room stylishly updated with frosted-glass-faced cupboards, granite counters, and brushed aluminum appliances. Above the stove hung a wide assortment of pans, and a Cuisinart and a panini maker resided on the counter. I could have had fun cooking in a space like this.

Glenn introduced Rose and me to his housekeeper, Edna, a silver-haired Amish woman standing before the double-basin sink, drying her hands on her apron. She had maybe ten years on Silvia, making her in her midseventies. She and Silvia greeted each other with familiarity. "How've ya been?" both women asked, and then they chuckled. I decided Edna was the floral arranger and her presence explained why a bachelor's house was so tidy. I hoped. I couldn't imagine Glenn ever moving back to his parents' home and living without electricity and modern conveniences.

"I'm delighted to meet you," Rose said with saccharine sincerity. She rushed over to shake Edna's hand, while I greeted her from across the room.

"The cat and I came with the place." Edna's grin revealed a missing tooth. "I worked for the former owners since I was eighteen. Glenn rents me the cottage next door for a pittance and keeps me on so an *alt maedel* will have a place to live and support herself."

"Not true," Glenn said. "Without Edna I'd be wearing wrinkled clothes and eating frozen dinners every night." He glanced at a cloth-covered bowl on the counter where bread dough must be rising. "I couldn't live without her homemade cinnamon rolls."

Edna gave Glenn another grin, proving that we women didn't outgrow the need for men's compliments. Reminding me that I couldn't recall the last words of approval I'd heard from my husband.

Rose bopped over to the counter and peeked under the cloth like she owned the place. "I have a bread-making machine. But I'd love to learn how to knead dough properly."

"Ya come back again, and I'll give you tips," Edna said. "'Tis not difficult."

"Fabulous." Was Rose turning into a merry homemaker? She'd often complained she hated cooking.

"I'll bet Silvia could show you," I said, and Rose riveted me with her evil eye.

"I'm not really much of a baker," Silvia said, maybe to be polite. Or was she encouraging Rose with her tomfoolery?

Minutes later, Glenn, Silvia, Rose, and I exited the kitchen and descended the back porch steps toward a path leading through an herb garden. Rose stopped midway down the stairs to call over her shoulder, "See ya later, Edna," through the screen door, as if certain they would meet again.

"Goodbye, honey," Edna said. I didn't think she'd much noticed me, which I supposed didn't matter. Still, Rose's carrying on was like a pebble in my shoe.

The scents of sage, rosemary, and lavender swelled in the afternoon sunshine. It felt close to 70 degrees in this sheltered location. Rose oohed and ahhed over the dense plantings, and tore off tips of leaves, rubbing them in her fingertips to inhale their heady perfumes. Then she daintily slipped a basil leaf into her mouth and swallowed it. "I'd do anything to have fresh herbs in my kitchen. The wilty stuff I buy at the grocery store doesn't compare to this."

I found her behavior atrocious. My sister was making a ridiculous spectacle of herself, although Glenn appeared to be enjoying her performance.

"Rosie, you should put in your own herb garden," I said.

"I don't know how."

"You could grow them in tubs and containers outside your back door." I couldn't have sounded more sincere. "That's a nice sunshiny spot."

"I'm so busy—"

"I'd help."

"I'll keep that in mind, big sister."

Leaving the herb garden, we came to a small barn, its door open to reveal bales of hay, several empty stalls, and a buggy.

"You own a buggy?" Rose strode to its side with us following in her wake as if we were Her Highness's entourage. Her hand smoothed its glossy surface. "It looks brand new."

Glenn expelled a sigh. "My folks gave it to me years ago, hoping to entice me back. I wish they hadn't. Buggies are expensive."

Rose traveled its length, as if she hadn't ignored them since we'd been here. "Do you ever drive it?"

"A couple of times a year." He pointed to a roan-colored mare in the pasture next to the garage. "Autumn needs her exercise and I like to know I can still drive one."

"Autumn. What a charming name." Rose's voice climbed in pitch. "I'd love a ride."

"Glenn, why don't you drive Rose back to my house?" Silvia suggested.

"Sure, all right." He turned to Rose. "It'll take me a few minutes to bridle and hitch her."

"I can wait. Autumn is my favorite time of the year."

Seeing Rose's face painted with a blissful grin made me feel like rubbing her expression off with steel wool. Why, only last week Rose said she liked summer best, followed by spring. She'd complained about raking the leaves in her yard, said she was overwhelmed with orders, and lamented that the daylight hours were shrinking.

Whatever possessed me to bring her on this trip?

TWENTY
Rose

Glenn steered his frisky mare and the buggy out of the nursery parking lot and onto the road like a speedboat on a lake. The breeze sent my hair in all directions. I must have looked a sight. But I didn't care. The faster he drove the better. Although nervous being conveyed by a horse, I wanted to be distracted by the zing of adrenalin. And to have Glenn all to myself. I'd savored Angela's sourpuss expression when we'd said farewell to her and Silvia a few minutes ago. Priceless.

Glenn and I passed a farm with a herd of honey-brown Jerseys, their eyes dark and luscious. I recalled that Chester used to own dairy cows. His letter crept into my thoughts again. When reading it to Silvia and Angela, the word *charlatan* came to mind. With disgust, I'd remembered how Mother got on my case about boys. She wouldn't allow them in the house when she wasn't there to chaperone and used to wait up after my dates, as if inspecting my neck for love bites kept me out of trouble.

By the letter's last line, I was all set to hate her forever. But then I pictured her a pregnant teenage girl terrified to tell her parents, like I was. Out of the blue, a wave of compassion passed through my chest, softening me like a sponge. I could see her checking for her menstrual period and experiencing the first signs of pregnancy.

Tender breasts, fatigue, and nausea. Increasing daily until she'd do anything to free herself.

I figured Angela, who liked wrapping messes into neat little packages, thought Mother miscarried in a most convenient manner that went unnoticed by our grandparents. Or that she stole off to a home for unwed mothers where she gave birth to a perfect little baby, who grew up in an ideal household. But my gut told me Lucy, her friend living in New York City, gave Mother the name of a doctor. If he was a real one. A desperate young woman might risk her life and turn to any quack for assistance. I shuddered to think what primitive technique he'd used. A coat hanger? Mother could have died of the subsequent infection. But she saw no other choice.

Yet if that's what happened, I wished she hadn't done it even if she hadn't loved Chester. She might have grown into their marriage the way a dog and cat learn to co-exist in a household. And wouldn't their common love for this wee child have cemented their union? I realized I was pretty much saying it would have been better if Mother had married Chester and not Father, in which case I wouldn't have been born. Truth is, since my mid-teens I'd wondered many times, what was the point of living? I'd resigned myself to trudging through my days like a workhorse slowly plowing a never-ending field. A pessimistic outlook that needed changing. I should learn to accept situations and move on.

And what about Glenn? If Chester hadn't married Lilly, Glenn wouldn't have been born either.

As cool wind circled my ears, I sank down in the bench seat and stabbed my hands into my pockets to keep them warm. Letting my neck relax, I turned my eyes up to catch sight of branches flying by. Mammoth clouds looked like castles, their turrets building to the sun, an apricot-colored orb. The sky was vaster than any ocean.

His arms relaxed, Glenn's hands jiggled the reins. So he'd been Amish. And could be again in the future, for all I knew.

"I can't picture you in LA wearing a power suit." I ratcheted up my volume to be heard above Autumn's clip-clopping hooves and the wheels rumbling on the asphalt.

"I only have two suits left. If it weren't for weddings and funerals, I think I'd have given them away." For an instant, he glanced my way. "You got some sophisticated guy in a suit waiting for you back home?"

My first inclination was to describe Brad, inflating his attributes to make me look desirable. But why bother? "No boyfriend. Just my little dog." Branches dipped over the road. One seemed so low I ducked needlessly.

I supposed I could win Brad back. But the longer I was around Glenn the more I was losing interest in Brad. I'd met him at happy hour in an upscale restaurant's lounge. The kind of place I bet Glenn never patronized. And where Brad probably met my replacement the moment I left town. Which made me want to avoid pick-up joints forever. I didn't even drink alcohol much, because I turned into a goofball and then woke up the next morning feeling as though my head spent the night in a vise. But bars and taverns had been the only venues I could think to meet men. Except for the blind date Angela set me up with. What a fiasco.

"Where can I take a classy lady like you?" Glenn asked.

He thought I was classy? Or was he teasing?

"Wherever you like, kind sir." I lay my cheek on the seatback, watched him drive, and tried to ignore the cars behind us.

"Have you ever seen a covered bridge?" he asked. "In this neck of the woods, that's the best we have for excitement."

"Sounds intriguing." *You're intriguing*, I thought. But he was oblivious to my musings.

We headed into a covered bridge, built in the 1800s according to Glenn. A sign stated No Motorized Vehicles.

The best way to describe the one-hundred-foot-long structure was to say it looked like we were entering an extended garage with an opening at the far end. Inside, I could see the bridge's bare bones, its exposed wooden trusses and planked flooring.

On the other side he said, "We need to get turned the other way." He spoke to Autumn in Pennsylvania Dutch and maneuvered the reins until she'd made a 180.

Rolling slowly through the bridge again, he hooted and the horse whinnied. I laughed out loud, my voice echoing. I hadn't heard myself belt out a boisterous volley of laughter in ages. Glenn was a good influence on me.

In a moment, we emerged into daylight.

"Tell me what you do for fun in Seattle," he said.

My fingers worked through my tangled hair. "My business keeps me pretty busy. I have a five-year plan…" Was work all I thought about? I'd bore him to death. "Let's see, I enjoy walking my dog. And seeing rainbows. And full moons. And watching old black-and-white movies." Now I really sounded lame.

"You could do those things anywhere."

"I guess. But I'm definitely a city girl."

"If you say so."

We slowed at the top of a ridge. Below us spread a chartreuse-green field dotted with grazing Holsteins. Beyond the field, sparkles of sunlight skipped off a pond. We traveled down the hill to the water's edge and then circumvented its shoreline. Most of the buggy drivers approaching from the other direction raised a hand in greeting. Except one, an older bearded man wearing a black hat, whose buggy was open in the front. At the last moment he tipped his head.

"*Ach*, that's the bishop. I hope he doesn't get the wrong idea."

I glanced over my shoulder. "I thought you said you got along well with the bishop."

"With my folks' bishop, yes. But I live in a different district. The bishop in my district is a fair man, but he's putting on the pressure to join the church. He'll no doubt report back to my parents that he saw me."

"Wouldn't they be pleased you're using the buggy?"

"Not with an English girl."

The vermillion-orange sun was already sinking behind the ridge. The tip of my nose grew icy cold. But I didn't want to go back to Aunt Silvia's yet. Glenn reached into the backseat to grab a fleece-lined jacket and gave it to me, when in fact he could have used it himself. A gentleman in every sense.

"Thanks." I draped the jacket across my chest and snuggled underneath it.

"I'd better get you home, young lady."

"That was it? Come on. Show me one more tourist attraction." I figured he was having fun taking his buggy out for a spin even if his horse was probably growing weary.

As he zigzagged back to Silvia's, he fingered the reins. He must have enjoyed the feel of the leather. A couple of miles further he pulled to the side of the road at a wooded area between two farms. He tethered the mare to a fence rail. I zipped on the jacket and followed him through a thicket to a clearing smelling of mushrooms and dank soil. Our appearance scared up a flock of doves, their wings beating the air in a mournful tune. Sunk into plump moss and foot-high grass stood a couple dozen rough stone markers, their fronts chiseled with writing and primitive drawings.

"You've brought me to a graveyard?"

"One of the oldest in the state. Not many people know it exists."

The backs of my knees weakened. After Mother's funeral, I vowed I'd never set foot in a graveyard again. Only last week, I had a nightmare about the rainy afternoon we buried her. In my dream, Mother was alive and roaming the periphery. But only I could see her. "Mommy!" I yelled. Which was baffling because I never—and I mean *never*—called her that. She either couldn't hear me or didn't want to. I tore off after her phantom shape. Until I ran right into the chain-link fence enclosing the graveyard, waking me up.

At my feet a lichen-covered headstone listed at a sixty-degree angle. How I felt, off-kilter. To regain balance, I stooped to inspect its inscription.

"Mother of seven died at age twenty-nine," I read aloud. "Terrible. She must have died from childbirth."

"Or influenza. No antibiotics back in the late 1700s."

The next time I visited a graveyard we might be burying Silvia. I spoke over my shoulder. "Shouldn't Silvia get a second opinion in Philadelphia or New York, where she'd find prominent specialists?"

"She already tried that route and got misdiagnosed. Some well-meaning physicians suggested she had MS, Parkinson's, and one was sure she had lupus, a chronic inflammatory disease. Another said her symptoms—her pain and fatigue—were psychosomatic. He prescribed pain medication and anti-depressants. Then Silvia's heart stopped working right—something to do with her left ventricle—and she ended up in the ER twice."

"She sounds frighteningly like our mother, who went to Seattle's top cardiologist. For all the good it did."

"Silvia has a good cardiologist, but she likes her naturopath best, a Lyme-disease-literate doctor who believes the bacterial infestation is the cause of her problems. But I'm afraid Silvia has given up the battle. She says the cure makes her feel worse than the illness."

I decided to push the gloomy images away. "She wants us to enjoy ourselves, not get depressed bemoaning her fate."

I noticed Glenn's elongated shadow. He stood right behind me. As I rose to my feet, I rotated to him. In an impetuous act, I reached my hands up to his shoulders, then his neck to feel soft wisps of hair between my fingers. His hands moved to my waist. But he didn't draw me closer, or resist. Maybe not a good idea, yet I'd gone this far.

I pushed up on the balls of my feet and lifted my chin. My hands coaxed him down and our lips met. They brushed each other before softening together. As Glenn returned my kiss, a smooth, sweet sensation expanded deep inside my chest, like when caramel melts in your mouth and you can't get enough of it. His arms encircled me until only my toes touched the ground.

I was kissing him because I was sad about Silvia and angry with

Mother. And because Brad hurt me. I needed strong arms around me. Propping me up was more like it. Any man's would do.

No, I liked Glenn. And I couldn't remember enjoying a kiss more.

When we parted, his questioning eyes gazed down at me. I should be beet-faced, as I should have been embarrassed for inviting myself on this ride. Most women would be. But by now he understood I wasn't like other women. I acted before I thought. And I hid my feelings and intentions like an Oscar winner.

"Where did that come from?" One of his hands anchored the small of my back.

"I felt like it."

He still supported part of my weight, telling me he wasn't appalled by my audacity.

To kiss him again was an option. But I reminded myself how many flash-in-the-pan love affairs meant nothing to me now. Years later, those men, some of them now faceless strangers, still sucked my energy like a slow leak in a life raft that you didn't notice until it was too late. I needed to ease into my next relationship slowly and cautiously. Not like this.

"Time for me to take you home." He released me, stepped back. His stare probed mine as if wondering if I'd do something else screwball.

The ground beneath me lay unevenly. One of my feet was lowered in a dip, but I did my best to appear at ease. I said, "My sister and Silvia will think you've kidnapped me."

"Or maybe it's you who have kidnapped me?"

I couldn't produce my usual quick comeback. Let's see, I'd asked him for a ride, begged him to extend it, and then kissed him. He probably did think I was a nutcase. Or worse.

Although the temperature was dropping, I was so toasty warm I unzipped the jacket. Heat rose up my neck and into my cheeks. Guess I was embarrassed after all.

Twenty-One

Angela

I paced Silvia's kitchen like a caged panther. I was ravenous, but nothing in the refrigerator looked appetizing. Not even the left-over lasagna that would emerge from the microwave bubbly warm.

When Silvia and I had returned home two hours ago, she said she needed to run another errand. Why didn't she mention it while we were still on the road? I offered to go with her, but she'd declined my company. I should have insisted. Anything would be better than waiting here by myself, checking the clock every five minutes. Where were Rose and Glenn?

My tortured thoughts steered themselves to the storage room and Chester's letters; I pictured myself creeping up the stairs to read them. No one would ever know. But that would be a Rose-like exploit I wouldn't succumb to. Growing up, she was our family's detective, a regular Sherlock Holmes, her eyes and ears unobtrusively gathering clues. In the name of solving mysteries, a week before Christmas she'd rooted out our hidden presents in Mom's bottom bureau drawer or in her closet and then complained that our parents had purchased me better gifts.

As I headed into the living area, my frazzled mind tried to organize what little I knew about Mom and Chester's affair. I hated the word *affair*, but what else could I label their relationship?

Fact one: They'd made love. Was I a prude for finding their conduct horrendous? Rose would tell me, "Get over it." I supposed I must.

I stared up at the wooden beam supporting the ceiling that seemed ready to crash in on me.

Fact two: Mom told Silvia she had miscarried, no doubt what happened. But then, why was Chester's tone accusatory? He said he would have raised the child, which made me think Mom did something.

I heard a vehicle hauling into the driveway, but Rex didn't bark. I didn't want Rose and Glenn to find me gawking out the window, so I grabbed a book off the side table, situated myself on the couch, and pretended I was reading about Japanese bonsai trees. A moment later, Silvia stepped inside. She tugged off her jacket; it dropped to the floor as if she were shedding a burden. Without noticing me, she collapsed onto the armchair only feet away from the couch, her arms dangling.

Her vacant eyes finally focused on me and they came alive, although the rest of her face remained passive. "Hello, dear. Is Rose back?"

"Not yet. I hope nothing's wrong."

"They're fine. Glenn's a careful driver."

"I'm sure he is." I was concerned about Rose's behavior, not Glenn's driving skills. I imagined he did everything well. "Do you think they'd make a nice couple?" I asked, hoping to sway Silvia against Rose. But Silvia's expression revealed no distaste; instead her mouth stretched into a grin.

"It would be my joy to have two people I love get together. But I retired from the matchmaking business when I lost a close friend trying my hand at it. I introduced her to my husband's best friend. I thought they were a match made in heaven, but they ended up hating each other and blaming me."

"That's too bad. It's for the best if Glenn and Rose don't fall for each other since they live on opposite sides of the country." A twang of uneasiness made me fidgety. I stood, picked up Silvia's jacket, and folded it over the back of the couch.

Silvia's eyelids drooped, showing her true fatigue.

I'd been selfishly thinking about myself. "How are you feeling?" I wondered where she'd been that demanded privacy. She hadn't come home with a shopping bag.

"Better now. I tried squeezing too much into one day. A short nap will fix me up." She exited the room; her footsteps ascended the stairs like a whisper.

Rex bustled to the front door and woofed. So much for Silvia's nap, but she didn't come back downstairs.

Minutes later, Rose paraded through the doorway like a cheerleader celebrating a winning football game. "We're home!" Since when did she consider Silvia's place home? Rose had done nothing but complain about her cramped bedroom, the worn furniture, and the antiquated kitchen since we got here.

Glenn, his hair mussed in the cutest way, filled the doorway as he entered behind her. The sight of his robust face strummed me out of the doldrums and into good spirits. I sent him a smile that he returned.

Rose slithered out of an over-sized jacket I'd never seen before and handed it to Glenn. She was practically rubbing up against him like a feline in heat.

"Glenn drove me all over the county." She caught sight of herself in the mirror above the coat rack. "Ugh, I look horrible. Angela, entertain Glenn until I get back, will you? Go sit in his buggy and tell me if it isn't the most fun in the whole world." Then she spun off, I assume to douse on more makeup and squeeze into something sexy.

Glenn glanced out the window at the pewter-gray clouds advancing up the valley. "It looks like rain. I should bring Autumn into Silvia's garage. Her car's parked in the driveway."

"I'll come with you, if that's okay." Rose asked me to look after him, after all.

How tall was he? Over six feet. Another couple of inches and he'd have to bend his head to get out the door. Rose was much shorter than he was, but a difference in height wouldn't matter. Before I could stop myself, I envisioned them in bed, clasped in each other's arms.

So what? I refused to feel jealous of Rose. I was a happily married woman. Well, the married part was right, even if I wasn't happy. I'd made my choice and was stuck with it.

As I followed Glenn he scanned the sky. The horse's ears bent back. "Those clouds look like they mean business." He opened the garage door, dragged it up like an accordion. I noticed he'd filled a pail of water that was half-empty for the mare.

A raindrop dampened my scalp. "Uh-oh."

"I'd better hurry." He took hold of Autumn's bridle, led her into the garage, and tethered her. Only half of the buggy fit in.

"Should we run back to the house?" I said, not relishing the thought of sloshing through the downpour in my loafers.

"I think I'd better stay out here with Autumn for a few minutes," he said. "It'll probably ease up soon."

Another globule of rain hit my forehead. "I'll wait with you, if that's okay." I opened the buggy's passenger door and climbed aboard. He dove in on the other side.

As if King Kong were tipping a bucket of water, rain splattered from the sky, sounding like a percussion band on the buggy's roof.

"What if it gets worse?" I asked.

He chuckled. "We'll float away?"

"I thought it rained a lot in Seattle, but we have sprinkles compared to this."

"Your sister says you worry too much."

"She was talking about me? I'm sure she had nothing positive to say. If anything, she doesn't worry enough. I could give you an earful about impulsive Rosie. Growing up, she used to leap off the twenty-foot diving tower at our friends' beach club on Lake Washington to prove she was as tough as the boys. Who knew if a sunken log floated just below the water's surface? As an adult she catches spiders in her house and lets them go in the yard, and she even captured a bat trapped in her attic and then set it free."

"She sounds unique," he said.

"She is. One in a million." I wondered if she was ogling out the window; seeing us out here together might bother her. No, she didn't consider me a rival for Glenn's affection. Because I wasn't.

"She's right about one thing." I settled into the bench seat. "This buggy is wonderful. But I have to wonder why you hang on to it."

"Old habits die hard."

"You mean you might eventually return to the Amish community?"

"I don't know. The bishop in my district is a forgiving and reasonable man, but he told me it's time to get off the fence and become baptized, meaning I'd have to run the nursery without electricity. He said he'd gather a crew to help me set it up in accordance to the *Ordnung*—the unwritten set of rules Amish must obey."

Glenn swiped his hand down his chin. "Living as an Amish man requires a multitude of strict parameters, including selling my pickup. But I could hire English—non-Amish—drivers. And keep a phone and fax machine in the office."

"And your home?"

"If I kept the house, all electrical wires would be removed, like Edna's cottage. Nothing I haven't lived without before. The Amish are very ingenious. Using gas and propane you'd hardly know the difference unless you enjoy watching TV and owning a computer."

I thought of my children and how better their lives would be without electronic paraphernalia. Mine too. I wasted too much time watching mindless TV and playing solitaire on the computer when I could just use a deck of cards. Or read a book.

"I've grown used to central heating," he said, "but warmth mainly in the living room and kitchen encourages a family to gather for fellowship."

I pictured my kids dashing to the other end of the house to gain distance from me after supper. And Frederick, if he happened to be home, couldn't wait to leave the dining room table.

"Not that I have much of a family," Glenn said.

"Unless you got married?"

"Or moved home to care for my parents. They'd hoped for ten children, but *Mamm* miscarried several times, and they ended up with one. I've been a terrible disappointment, as you can imagine."

The moist air hung pregnant with negative ions. Raindrops blobbed down, rivering together into a clear sheet across the driveway. If we were on the road, we'd lose vision and be forced to pull onto the shoulder. As I listened to the beating rain, my mind entered forbidden territory. I imagined we'd been somewhere—a picnic up a dirt road no one ever used—just the two of us.

I recalled decades ago the newspapers had a heyday when President Carter admitted he'd lusted in his heart. Mom told me the Bible proclaimed lusting was a sin even if you didn't act on your immoral feelings. But I closed my eyes and allowed my thoughts to wander where they pleased. I envisioned Glenn and me sitting on a blanket by a stream. We laughed like old friends who had catching up to do. In my musings, we noticed the first raindrops and moaned in unison. We stuffed our lunch of turkey sandwiches and my homemade coleslaw into the basket, and carried it to his buggy to finish our meal.

After his last bite, Glenn complimented me on the marvelous food. He took my half-eaten sandwich from me and placed it on a napkin. My senses came alive as I inhaled his breath, smelled his warm skin. The pattering of rain on the roof sounded like a love song. He stroked my cheek and then moved closer, his arm reaching around my shoulder. I didn't resist his strength, but rather sank into his embrace. Our lips barely touched. Then they joined feverishly. I would give him anything he asked.

I opened my eyes and saw the real-live Glenn still on his side of the buggy watching me. Had he and I experienced simultaneous daydreams? He immediately glanced away as if uncomfortable. Making me feel embarrassed.

I tried to blot the fantasy from my mind by forcing myself to remember Frederick and our first kiss. We were sitting on a lumpy couch in the sorority house talking. While I was mid-sentence, he suddenly pressed his lips against mine with too much force, choking off my words. His eyes closed while his hand investigated my knee; I grabbed his hand, pushed it away. I decided to never go out with him again. But later, as my sorority sister and I compared dates, she described Frederick as having future potential. "Once he gets his degree, he'll earn $100k easy," she'd said. Over the years, I'd heard Dad gripe to Mom that he should have had sons. He'd complained he needed someone to take to Mariners games; premium seats costing a bundle were a waste of money on girls. Mom assured Dad Rose and I would marry fine young men someday, so I accepted landing his perfect son-in-law as my mission.

What qualifications did Frederick actually possess? He was taller than I was, in my stocking feet; he was clean-cut and dressed well, like an Ivy-leaguer. He was good-looking—in the right light. He was crazy about sports and spent weekends surfing between stations watching simultaneous games. When not out on the golf course, he still did. Had I taken into account kindness, manliness, or chemistry—the qualities Glenn possessed? Did I consider that perhaps I was settling for second best?

Glenn shifted position. "Sorry I don't have an umbrella."

"Understandable. Most men don't carry them." Although Frederick popped his plaid umbrella up at the first hint of rain to keep his perfectly styled hair dry. And he wore leather driving gloves, even in summer, which embarrassed the kids. And me.

The windows were fogging up. How long had we been out here? Ten minutes? Rose must have thought we'd gone for a drive, or was she watching us from the house, waiting for the rain to lessen so she could separate us?

Glenn's hand rested on the door handle. "Looks like we'll have to make a dash for it after all. Or I could come back with an umbrella." What gallantry. I was touched.

"No, I'll come with you." I didn't want to be separated from him—ever. Which I knew was lunacy. But I realized I didn't love Frederick anymore and probably hadn't for years. I was so entrenched in the ruts of my mundane life I hadn't noticed our marriage deteriorating to a wasteland. Compared to Silvia and her friends, I was still a young woman. I deserved better. I needed more.

Glenn removed his jacket and offered it to me, but I said, "No thanks, I don't care if I get wet." What did a little water matter in the eye of a hurricane? I wanted to share the news with him—that my life was taking a profound turnaround—but reminded myself the fantasy was mine, not his. Or was it? I hadn't imagined the way his eyes locked onto mine every time we met, or the electricity dancing between us. The buggy was alive with it right now.

He draped his jacket over my shoulders and then opened his door. When I hesitated, he extended his hand. I took it. For a moment we held hands gazing into each other's eyes like a couple of lovesick teenagers. Or was I misreading his expression in the faint light?

"Come on." He pulled my arm gently. Still grasping his hand, I followed behind him and jumped to the ground. He reached around me and slammed the door.

We raced for the house. By the time we reached the front door my feet swam in my shoes. Somewhere along the way my hand slipped out of his.

The living area lay empty and silent except the sound of water running upstairs. What was Rose doing up there?

My skin tingled from the warmth of the house; a droplet of water slid down my cheek. Did Glenn want to take a hankie and dry my face? And then kiss me? No, he was an honorable man and wouldn't cross the boundary. I must make the first move.

What was I thinking? I would do no such thing. "I'll get us some towels."

"No, thanks. I'd better take Autumn home." His tousled hair formed curls and his shoulders were dark with moisture.

"Oh, your poor horse." I handed him the drenched jacket.

"Please tell Rose and Silvia goodbye for me." Wearing the jacket, he backed out into the rain, and pulled the door closed behind him.

Listening to his buggy's wheels churning on the driveway minutes later, I leaned against the door and relived the imaginary kiss over and over, each time a wave of delight rushing to my core, until it became real.

TWENTY-TWO

Rose

Silvia's Adirondack chair stood at the end of the grassy lane. I was drawn to its brilliance, its red enamel paint shiny with dew. I removed a tissue from my pocket and swabbed up most of the moisture. I sat low to the ground, my knees higher than my waist.

As I inhaled the morning's clarity, I yawned. Several times last night, my mind ascended through slumber's doorway. I found myself mulling over Glenn. Was he a night owl like Angela or a morning lark like me, up at dawn? Did he read before turning in, watch TV in bed, listen to music, or simply dive under the covers after a day of strenuous work?

Glenn was both physically and mentally stronger than I was. Not how I'd describe most men. He'd remained in control. Even when I kissed him. A brash act that turned to his advantage. I could usually read people's body language. But on the buggy ride I had nary a clue what he was thinking or feeling. Then when we got back I'd asked him to chat with Angela while I spruced myself up. A mistake. Had she said something critical or dismissive? He'd left without saying goodbye and didn't call me later as I thought he would. I was flat-out disappointed. I shouldn't have taken so long. Knowing Angela, she couldn't wait to launch him on his way home. She wanted Silvia and me to herself. And she disapproved of my male friends.

Feeling the chair's chill hardness against my back, I recalled Glenn's lips. Soft but firm. He didn't kiss me like a man who was pining for another. But he hadn't asked me for more, as most single men would. Did Glenn find me unattractive? Or was he playing the gentleman because I was Silvia's niece? No worries. In a few days I'd be home parked in front of my plasma TV with my Minnie at my side, begging for popcorn. "The Dynamic Duo," I called us when leashing her up for a neighborhood walk and no one else could hear me carrying on as if my dog understood every word. When it came down to it, she was my best buddy. I had people-type girlfriends: Jennie, a former coworker at Nordstrom; Shauna, a beagle-owner I met at the off-leash area; and Meagan, whom I'd known since college. But their lives orbited around their husbands and children. Who could blame them? If I had a family, I wouldn't hang around a single woman like me either.

Before I could stop myself, my mind opened its top drawer, hidden from the outside world, and strewed the contents on the grass. The horrible solitude of my life shaped itself into a three-dimensional image. I saw a dark cavern. I bumped against its walls, groping for companionship. A child is what I longed for. Someone who would never leave me. Maybe I really should have accidentally-on-purpose gotten myself pregnant years ago and given up on finding a husband. But I had a father, and distant as he was, I'd needed his presence, his fortitude. To deprive a baby of a dad would be wrong. But my biological clock was running down. This month, another egg would wash away, another chance pass by. I had only so much time.

Mother had taught me a woman's body was her own. But Dirk robbed me of my power. He forced me into a no-win situation. A catch-22. As a teenager, I couldn't have raised a child by myself. If I'd decided to give birth, I would have been forced to live in a home for unwed mothers and then give the baby up for adoption. I would have lost a grade in school and everyone would have known my disgrace. I thought I was making the best decision I could at the time.

But the bottom line was I was childless. Inside, I wept at dying barren. Maybe I was infertile and didn't know it.

A nearby oak tree branch swayed, then a squirrel scampered down its trunk clasping an acorn in its mouth. When it noticed me, it darted among the bushes.

An acorn sprouted from its hard crust, I thought. A green flick on the forest floor. Its arms stretched up, its bark thickened, bulging with life, and leaves pushed their way toward the sunshine. Like October's exotic foliage, I was wearing a maroon sweater. Were my colors about to fade to drab dull? A rainbow without the sun was just drizzle. No pot of gold sitting at the end of anywhere.

Maybe God was punishing me. I didn't put much faith in the higher-power theory. Although I supposed a benevolent super-being could have set the universe in motion and then stepped back to watch us self-absorbed ants milling around on the ground for entertainment. But I did believe in Satan. The devil. The evil force that infused a person like Dirk and allowed him to commit a sick crime. After he brutalized me, I turned unclean, as if a plague had entered my body, changing my DNA. I might as well have contracted AIDS or hepatitis. His vile act took over my world.

I looked up and saw Silvia, her breath clouding from her mouth. "You found my favorite seat, dear." I started to rise, but she stopped me.

"Stay put. There's no one I'd rather see sitting there." She pressed her fingertips to her lips for a moment. "Rose, dear, I owe you and Angela an apology. I should have told you I was ill months ago. But I was afraid you wouldn't come visit me."

She was right. Everything changed the moment Glenn informed me Silvia was terminally ill. I'd thought it peculiar Silvia hadn't attended Mother's funeral and assumed Father had discouraged her from coming. Now I understood. Silvia was wading through her own anguish.

Any irritation I had about her secrecy dissolved. "If I were sick,

I'd act the same way," I said. "I hate people fussing over me. At least, I think I do. Maybe I've deflected others' attention so often they've given up."

"As long as I'm around, I won't give up on you, dear." It was the sweetest thing anyone had ever said to me.

Getting to my feet, I wrapped my arms around her and rested my head on her shoulder. I thought I was going to sneeze, but instead I let out a sob, followed by another. I couldn't contain my grief. It flooded out. I shook to the bones, gasping for air in between the moans.

"Do you want to talk about it?" Silvia asked.

I raised my head and backstepped a couple of feet. "I wouldn't know where to begin." Tears streamed from my eyes. My blubbering turned into hiccups. Silvia handed me a handkerchief and I dabbed my face. I'd never let anyone see me like this. Not since I was five and howling after stepping on a bee. Mother had tried to comfort me. I remembered her soft bosom, her silk nightgown, and her rose-scented perfume, that she claimed she'd started wearing in my honor when I was born. As girls, on weekend mornings, Angela and I would fluff up her pillows and sit in bed with her. She'd read the Sunday paper and sip coffee. Nothing said, just being alive. Together.

"You miss your mother?" she said. I nodded. "Tell me about her, dear. Were you two close?"

"We started out okay. I was never a mama's girl like Angela, but for the first twelve or so years of my life, Mother and I got along fine." I spoke through a clogged nose, my eyelids swollen. "Then one night, while listening to Father berating Mother for something he didn't like again—his voice seemed to boom through the walls— I began to see her as a weakling. Her voice became too faint to be heard. Even now, when the phone rings and I still expect to find her on the other end, I can barely remember what she sounded like. She rarely spoke during the last months." Just murmurs like the sound of distant lapping waves.

I sniffed and dried my runny nose. "On the other hand, Father's voice seemed to grow in volume. Clear across the country, I can hear his stern words as if he's lecturing through a megaphone. Nothing positive, mind you. He grills me about my business's profit and loss. What percent do I dole out for overhead? Have I paid my quarterly taxes? Just once, I wish he'd tell me he was proud of me. Or that I looked nice." Why was I still waiting for his affirmation? "But that's like asking my dog, Minnie, to feed me dinner and scratch my back. It ain't gonna happen."

"Our heavenly Father's ears are always open, dear." Her face was serene. "Shall we pray to him about it?" She closed her eyes and waited. Was I supposed to say something?

To get this awkward situation over with quickly, I gave it a shot. As a gift to her. And what did I have to lose? "Okay, God, if you exist, bring out your magic wand and fix my life, presto chango. And while you're at it, make Silvia's diagnosis a humungous mistake. Her doctor misread the test results and is liable for malpractice. And turn Mother into Saint Juliana, who never lied or hurt Chester."

The corners of Silvia's mouth lifted a tad, but her eyes remained shut. "Help us accept what's gone by and is out of our control," she said. "And answer the questions we don't know how to ask."

Because she was so sincere, the child in me half expected the ground to shake or a bush to catch fire. But nothing happened, as always. Newton's Law of Inertia declared things at rest would remain at rest unless acted on. If God was out there, he was asleep at the switch.

Silvia's eyes opened and she grinned as though the two of us had set an elaborate machine in motion. She believed the myths she'd learned in childhood. In a way, I was envious of her. My world would be more fun living in ignorance.

We returned to the house, our arms linked and our feet falling into synchronized steps. I felt better, like I'd finished a race. Out of breath but invigorated. My river of sadness had crested its banks.

But my crying binge hadn't repaired my brokenness. My tears hadn't extinguished the burning coals smoldering at the bottom of my throat. If only there were a way to alter my life's trajectory.

I wanted to tell Silvia I loved her, but couldn't find the right words. Then it was too late. We were at the kitchen door. I slowed my pace and she entered first.

Once inside, Silvia ascended the stairs to her room. She'd told us at breakfast she didn't feel up to attending church this morning. I headed to the first-floor bathroom to wash my face. There was nothing to be done about my bloodshot eyeballs or the puffy half-moons sagging under them. If Angela asked why I look bedraggled, I'd claim I'd experienced an allergy attack.

Entering the living area, I saw my sister sitting on the couch, thumbing through an old Martha Stewart magazine, *Living*. There was no logical reason as to why I'd always flinched at the sound of Martha's voice. Years ago, while eating a late lunch, I'd watched reruns of her TV show. One day a man brought adorable baby chinchillas. I wanted to run out and buy one, but I managed to control my zeal, which fortunately faded after a few days. As I'd watched, I thought about Angela glued to her TV set at that very moment. For some reason, our sharing a common bond poisoned my attitude toward the television show. Why? Did I feel vulnerable? How many of Angela's favorite activities did I dislike out of mere obstinacy?

She stopped perusing the magazine and was now staring out the window.

"You okay, sis?"

"Yes. I guess I didn't sleep well." She didn't seem to notice I'd been crying.

I peered over her shoulder to see the magazine article was about planning a wedding. I'd always dreamed of an afternoon wedding.

Me in a long white gown. Father escorting me down the aisle. A bridal bouquet of roses, of course. Dancing at the reception.

Fat chance. At my age, I'd settle for an off-white pantsuit and a visit to the justice of the peace.

"Remember how nuts you and Mother went when you got married?" I said. "Matching flowers, matching candles, matching lipstick, matching bridesmaids' dresses. Boy, mine was ugly."

I snorted as I remembered how ghastly I looked in peach. Angela had insisted the color didn't sallow my skin. But I was a winter and stuck to jewel tones or basic black. And my bridesmaid dress lacked a waistline. Its hem hit me at the widest part of my calf, making me look stocky. I was ticked off. But Mother exclaimed it was Angela's big moment so I must cooperate. "The happiest day in a woman's life," Mother had said. So I went along with it, thinking my turn for marital bliss was just around the corner.

"None of that matters now." Angela's facial expression was deadpan serious. "A waste of time and money."

"You're pulling my leg, right? I remember the chaotic weeks before the wedding. I thought you'd go insane if my shoes weren't dyed exactly to match my dress. You loved every anxiety-ridden minute of it."

"I'm not that person anymore."

"Really? When did this transformation occur?"

"I was so stupid. I was more enamored with the ceremony than the man I was marrying." She set the magazine aside. "I knew more about bridal gowns and boutonnieres than I did about Frederick. Only which sports teams he followed and his business aspirations. I didn't even know if he wanted children, and thankfully he let me have two."

"This is news to me. But maybe it's better that way. I ask too many questions and find out my boyfriends' frailties. Then I decide I can't put up with them. I'm too picky." I wouldn't tell her that half of the men had discarded me.

"No you're not, Rosie. You're smart."

"Yeah, so smart I'll die an old maid." The skin on my face tightened, no doubt creating added wrinkles.

"You're darling," she said, "and have an hour-glass figure. The perfect guy will show up one of these days."

"It depends what you mean by perfect. Your preferences in men and mine live on opposite ends of the spectrum." Yet if I was attracted to Glenn, maybe my tastes were sliding down the scale toward mediocrity. No way. Glenn was one if the finest men I'd ever met. Just my luck he resided on the other side of the country. And what if he joined the Amish church?

TWENTY-THREE

Angela

"You're acting like I never do anything for you," Frederick chided me, his voice blaring through the telephone receiver. My asking him for a ride home from the airport had launched a tirade. Nothing I hadn't heard before.

"You live in a palace," he went on—a slight overstatement. "And you drive a new car. I buy you whatever you want. What about the diamond earrings I gave you for your birthday three years ago? Don't they count for anything?"

If I had to thank him for those earrings again I'd scream. Yes, I was thrilled to receive them, even if Frederick was out of town on my birthday and then handed them to me without ceremony three days later. He'd brought up the lavish present and its hefty price tag dozens of times, as if he wanted me to cut him a check plus interest. I recalled the box, concealed neatly in silver paper with a pink bow. I suspected his secretary, Jill, had wrapped it for him. She'd probably picked out the earrings too.

"Frederick, I appreciate the gifts, I really do." My resolve was shrinking; my words came out just above a whisper. "But what I want is you."

"You *have* me, for pity's sake. What's gotten into you? I've never cheated, not even once, and don't think there aren't plenty of opportunities in my line of work. But I've never gone there. No, sir. Why are you so insecure?"

"I'm not. At least I don't think I am." My eardrums started ringing, like someone had let off a firecracker a foot from my head. I pictured Frederick's face flushing and then draining white, the way it did when he was in a rage. My husband was livid, which usually sent me scurrying to my familiar hiding place, apologizing, even if I hadn't done anything I regretted. But this time I stood firm and said, "If you love me so much, then please meet us at the airport so we won't have to take a taxi." I didn't care about saving the cab fare. I wanted his full attention.

His exhale sounded like wind forcing its way through a car's cracked window. "First of all, my clients pay me five hundred dollars an hour. A rather expensive cab ride, don't you think? Second, I have a commitment. A commitment!"

Sweat accumulated on my palm and my heartbeat sped up. I held the phone away from my ear to lessen the volume, but could still hear him clearly.

"Important people are expecting me at a meeting," he said, all pompous. "I can't skip out on a whim."

"I'm not important?" He could reschedule his meeting, and I doubted anyone would view picking me up after more than a week's absence as capricious, but there was no use continuing the conversation if he wouldn't listen.

So I hung up.

"Oh, no. I didn't say goodbye," I told the telephone. "I should call him back and patch things up." But that would be like sticking my hand in a sweltering oven without a mitt. I'd learned over the years to give Frederick space—or rather, to allow myself a buffer zone. In a few minutes he'd busy himself and forget we ever had this conversation. In fact, he'd forget about me. I doubt I entered his mind during the day unless he needed something.

I thought about Glenn, a man who would give a woman his full attention. When his eyes focused on you, it was as if you were the only living, breathing person in the hemisphere. The whole world stopped on its axis. Remembering the feel of my hand in his, I envied the woman he chose for his wife. Would it be Olivia? I imagined her nestled against him in his buggy as he wheeled around a corner, her shoulder snuggling up against his. If only I could spend one afternoon with him. It would be the best day of my life.

Rose marched into the living area. "Why do you let Fred hassle you like that?" She must have been eavesdropping in the hallway. "The way he treats you has bugged me since the day I met him."

Out of habit I defended him. "He's not so bad. And as a matter of fact, I just hung up on him without saying goodbye."

"It's about time. You remind me of Mother, the way she used to grovel at Father's feet." Rose had elevated our father to an unrealistic pedestal, like he was Thomas Jefferson or Abraham Lincoln. I agreed. The way he'd built his thriving law practice and retired at age sixty-two, Dad deserved admiration. But she was insinuating Mom aggravated Dad into hounding her.

Since hearing what Chester wrote in his letter, my feelings about Mom were muddied, like a stirred-up puddle that wouldn't settle. But I said, "If I remind you of Mom, I'm glad, because I loved her."

Rose's jaw unhinged; her teeth bared and her tongue bloated. I didn't have the strength to match words with her, not after Frederick's monologue. I got up, spun away, and made a retreat to my bedroom, but her Frankenstein's monster footsteps followed me. So I swerved to the right and opened the door to the room across the hall from mine. The cluttered area housed two twin beds with a nightstand tucked between them, a black sewing machine out of the fifties set up on a table, and an ironing board. On the wall above the sewing machine, hundreds of spools of thread—a fusion of color—hung suspended on wooden dowels affixed to a board. At the far end of the room stood a bookshelf laden with folded fabric pieces and a bureau, the top drawer partially open to reveal a swatch of mauve-colored cloth.

A layer of dust veneered the nightstand and lampshade, and dust bunnies and bits of thread huddled on the floor in the corners and under the furniture. I noticed a canister vacuum cleaner. As a gift to Silvia and to shut out Rose, I plugged in the vacuum and switched it on. A monstrous whirring sound filled the air, but Rose's coach-at-the-sidelines volume matched it.

"Let me get this straight." She closed in on me. "Because I think Mother should have stood up to Father's bullying, it means I didn't love her?"

I knelt on all fours between the beds, poked the wand under one of them, and sucked up dust balls and loose threads. Rose hopped on the other bed, her foot inches from my shoulder. She'd never had a problem watching me work, unlike me. If I had been watching her, I would have found a rag and can of Pledge and chipped in.

Vacuum wand in hand, I crawled to the other bed. Her feet were in my face, but she made no effort to move them. Did she even know what love was? Growing up, she'd treated Mom like a punching bag that deserved a daily thrashing. No hitting, just words—but Rose's verbal abuse cut deep.

"Have you forgotten everything Mom did for us?" I arched my neck to see her glaring down at me like a vulture. "Remember how she quit her book club so she could take me to dance rehearsals?"

"Big deal. She would have done anything for you."

"Hey, just a minute. Mom drove you to your horseback riding lessons, until you lost interest. And don't forget summer camp."

"She sent me there to get me out of her hair."

"That isn't true. You begged to go." I worked the vacuum around the room's perimeter, prodding it behind a stack of cardboard boxes and under the ironing board, careful not to disturb the iron—turned off but plugged in. No wonder Phyllis worried about Silvia's burning down the house. I bent to unplug the cord and noticed something shiny couched up against the wall under the sewing machine.

Rose switched beds, leaving a rumpled spread in her wake, to get a better view of me, I assumed. As a girl, she rarely picked up after herself or straightened her room. If I'd been her mother, I would have confined her to the house until she'd done her chores. Well, maybe not; I couldn't even get my own two children to obey me. It was impossible when your husband ran interference for them, the way Dad championed Rose.

"Mom gave you your allowance even when you didn't finish your chores." I straightened my spine.

"Okay, I had it made. But you and I haven't lived at home for almost twenty years. Haven't you wondered what Mother did with herself all day after we moved out?"

I wouldn't let her scoff at Mom, but I couldn't come up with anything better than, "She read and went out to lunch with friends." I remembered Mom's Nicole Kidman face, showing few wrinkles— no laugh lines either. "Why put her down now? If you had problems, you should have told her."

"I did once. I said to her, 'How can you let Father treat you like a servant? Why don't you say, "I quit. I don't like golf, so you won't be seeing me at the country club anymore. And since I don't drink martinis, mix your own."'

"'What good would that do?' Mom asked in her quavering voice, and I said that if nothing else, standing up for herself would empower her with dignity. I'd wondered if living like a serf for forty years caused her demise."

I yanked on the wand and the canister hit the edge of the bed. "I highly doubt that."

"Then why is she dead and Father, who smokes cigars and drinks too much, is getting his second wind?"

I turned off the vacuum. "I'm surprised to hear you admit he has any bad habits. You forgot to mention the expletives he belches out when he gets mad." It bothered me that Mom never asked him not to swear in front of us. "They had a system that worked for them. Marriage is like a dance. Our parents stayed married longer than most couples."

"But at what price? And why must the man always lead?"

How would Rose, with her never-ending trail of men, know anything about marriage? I stared her in the eye. Being taller gave me an advantage. "If you ever get married, maybe you'll have more empathy." I could see from her contorted features that my direct barb hit its mark.

"Short-lived relationships are better than crummy ones." She let out a huff. "You're so incredibly passive, as if Frederick is the president."

"I like the man making the decisions. It's the best way to raise children." But Dad's domineering personality had split our family in half. Mom and I were on the second-string team.

"What about when the kids leave?" she asked.

"I'll…I'll move here." The words sprang out of my mouth before my brain could decipher their meaning. Of course, I wouldn't move to Pennsylvania. Not without Frederick and the kids. But I indulged myself, allowing my imagination to explore the possibility. If I never returned to Seattle, Frederick wouldn't beg me to come home, nor would he visit me—out of spite. A man who refused to fetch his wife from the airport would probably think, *Good riddance. She's too high maintenance.* And the kids would be relieved not to hear my harping voice coercing them into finishing homework or going to bed on time. They'd watch TV until midnight, and then the next morning talk Frederick into telling the school they were sick. They'd have the time of their lives.

Wanting to finish my cleaning project, I switched on the vacuum again and concentrated my efforts on the area under the sewing machine table. Watching the loose threads vanish into the wand, I wished I could eliminate my problems as easily.

Driving Silvia's car on my mission back to the town with the antique shop, I felt disengaged from my family in Seattle, unplugged like the iron from the wall. I pulled to a halt at an intersection. Off to the right stood an Amish schoolhouse, no doubt with only one room. I watched the children frolicking in the fenced-in playground surrounding the small and plain structure. Several preteen girls, their skin pink with perspiration, kicked a ball, until a group of boys stole it away, dribbling it further.

I thought of my daughter, Tiffany, and I ached for her. Or maybe I longed for the girl she was before she'd entered her teens and apparently decided I was the enemy. She'd barely hugged me in years and shrank away when I kissed her on the cheek.

As I watched, I wondered if Tiffany were readying herself for school. Not a morning person, she generally started her day grumpy. It was difficult maintaining my perky voice while I drove her to school. I missed the little girl who'd played dress-up in my closet and begged to wear my jewelry and makeup. Now she turned up her nose at my outfits and complained, "Do you have to wear that same pink sweater again?" I pretended to ignore her because I figured she was going through a phase and would eventually step out the other end like Cinderella once her fairy godmother worked her magic. In the meantime, I was a target at a shooting range. Surely Amish girls wouldn't treat their parents with disrespect.

Tiffany metamorphosed into a loquacious butterfly the moment she was with her friends, as if bottling up her pleasant conversations for them. Quite annoying. But of course I loved her desperately. My universe orbited around her and my other two planets, my son, Daniel, and Frederick.

Or rather it used to.

As I sat in the car with the engine idling, two bearded Amish men—one almost as tall and broad shouldered as Glenn—strode across the road; they gave me a thank-you wave. Glenn had become part of my subconscious, a reference point. I wondered what he noticed when driving past this school. He could have attended it or helped maintain the grounds after a winter's storm.

Right now, Glenn might be standing at Silvia's front door greeting Rose, who was infatuated with him. I could tell by the way her face had changed since we'd been here; the serious crease between her eyes was all but gone.

A horn honked. I checked the rearview mirror to see two cars and a horse and buggy had stopped behind me. I was sitting here like a ninny. I sped the car forward and located the antique store Rose and I visited on our second day. I'd come to purchase the music box for Tiffany, even though she'd rather have a new iPod or a gift certificate for iTunes. I might as well slip a twenty-dollar bill into an envelope and put a happy face on the front. No, she hated the way I signed notes with happy faces. I couldn't win.

As I located a parking spot around the back of the building, I decided to buy the music box as a souvenir for myself. I'd place it on my bureau in the center, which meant moving my jewelry box to the left and my photo of the kids to the right. Would it be too ridiculous to find my old ballet slippers I'd saved from *Swan Lake* and display them on a hook on the wall? I'd stored a framed photo of me from the production that I could position next to them.

Was I building a shrine to myself? Why remember the past I couldn't recreate?

Dancing had come easily to me. When I was young, my supple limbs naturally went where I directed them. All consuming, all important, dancing had dominated my life. I ate, slept, and worked toward my goal of developing my future career. No matter what I was doing, half of my focus centered on it. Even when relaxing, I was either thinking about or preparing to dance.

When had I given up my dreams? The day I started college and was barraged with homework and sorority activities? My first date with Frederick? All I knew was, the desire evaporated like a tear on a hot, glass stovetop, which actually happened one night while I was storing Frederick's uneaten dinner when he never showed up.

I strolled around the side of the building and made a beeline to the table where I'd seen the snow-globe music box but couldn't find it. With so many items in the room—Depression-ware, silver-plated tea trays, salt and pepper shakers that held absolutely no appeal to me anymore—my vision groped, my eyes straining to recognize its shape. It was gone. Disappointment hit me hard.

"May I help you?" asked the saleswoman I'd spoken to the other day. She sat at her desk, her shoulders cloaked with one of those loosely crocheted shawls that would make me look like a blimp.

I knew better than to directly inquire after an item; the price would double. But there was no way around asking. I'd come to buy the music box and this was my only chance.

"I might have sold it," she said when I described the pink-clad ballerina inside. "Things come and go so quickly." She scanned the tables. Then moving to a shelf against the wall, she reached up. "This it?"

The snow globe appeared small in the woman's hands; curved glass shone between her long fingers. She turned it upside down and wound the metal knob, and then she placed the globe on the counter. While the snowflakes settled around the pirouetting ballerina, out floated *Swan Lake*'s theme melody, each note clean and compelling.

My usual procedure when buying antiques was to barter. Never pay full price—part of the fun. But I handed over my Visa card and signed my name without reading the total, and then I watched the woman wrap the globe in newspaper and pack it in a small cardboard box.

As I drove back to Silvia's, the snow globe lay on the passenger seat next to me. I checked the rearview mirror and saw a pickup behind me that looked like Glenn's. The road took a curve and I lost sight of the vehicle, but on the next long stretch, it appeared again. If Glenn, he'd recognize Silvia's car and perhaps follow me back to her house. He was the type of man who would go out of his way to say hello to a friend or pick her up at the airport. Yes, unlike

Frederick, he would gladly drive all the way to the airport to fetch me—and Rose.

My face warmed as I recalled Glenn's and my conversation waiting out the storm. Nothing had happened, but it could have. If he'd reached out to me, I might have kissed him. The thought of our lips meeting like satin brushing against velvet sent a thrill through me.

He'd held my hand, his large fingers grasping mine gently but decisively. Just a chivalrous act he'd offer any woman facing a torrential downpour? Or had he been longing to—dreaming of—taking my hand in his? I liked to think the latter. I envisioned him following me up Silvia's driveway, his getting out, and coming to my door to open it. Frederick rarely opened doors for me even when my arms were burdened with bags of groceries. If I complained, he'd remind me women's lib taught him to treat me as an equal, not an invalid. He alleged he was demonstrating respect. I'd never appreciated his sarcastic repartee.

I could see Glenn's wonderful face and experienced a pulsating round of exhilaration. I imagined us standing awkwardly close together, but he didn't step back. He could scoop me into his arms with little effort; he must have been considering that too. But again, he was waiting for me to make the first move. He'd never take advantage of me.

"I didn't think I'd see you again," Glenn might say, implying he would miss me in the coming months the way I'd miss him. Yes, I would recollect his demeanor, his words, and wonder what might have been if only I'd met him earlier in life. Or if Frederick died in an accident, which wasn't so far fetched the way he jockeyed his Audi S8 between semi-trucks on the highway. Or maybe, in spite of Frederick's professions of loyalty, he'd ditch me for Stephanie.

He came home some evenings with a better shave than when he left in the morning. Was that smooth chin for her benefit? He didn't bother cleaning up for me on weekends. If a man and his female assistant shared enough cozy meetings together, sparks were bound to detonate. He and Stephanie were probably already sleeping together. How could I have been so blind to ever think their meetings were strictly business?

At Silvia's driveway I put on the blinker, made my turn, and then waited for the pickup to do the same. But the driver cruised down the road without tapping the brakes. I craned my neck to see the pickup was smaller than Glenn's—maybe a Toyota—and darker blue. I watched it round the bend. The sound of its engine grew faint, and then all I heard were a cow mooing, distant horseshoes clopping, and silence.

I got out of the car and noticed my reflection in the window: a middle-aged woman somersaulting into a make-believe life. Could I distinguish what was real anymore? I must deflate these fantasies before I did something crazy. As soon as I got Silvia alone, I'd ask her what to do.

No, unburdening my problems on her would be selfish. The last thing our aunt needed was added anxiety. Worrying about me might weaken her immune system and invite her Lyme disease to multiply. Leaving me Rose, who was opinionated and honest to a fault, but who had ample experience with men. Beneath her porcupine quills, I liked to think she cared about me. And I had no one else to turn to.

TWENTY-FOUR

Rose

"You make me sick!" I yelled at Angela full force. My vocal cords grated against each other, sending out a bark rivaling Rex's. Did my sister honestly think I'd approve of her shenanigans or encourage her in any way?

Angela and I were in the basement doing laundry. Cellar was a better name for this funky space, with its open back staircase and cement walls and floor. The air smelled humid. I bet all sorts of spiders and beetles were holed up behind the gold '80s Maytag washer and dryer, and shelves stacked with canned peaches, tomatoes, and pickles. I saw a dead centipede in the corner. Perfect. Angela was afraid of creepy-crawlies. I wanted to see her squirm.

A moment ago, with Silvia out of earshot in the garden, Angela notified me Glenn had been making eyes at her since they'd met. Even though nothing would come of it, according to her, they shared a mutual attraction. She might as well have skewered my chest with a pitchfork. I felt betrayed. A lifetime of resentment boiled to the surface, oozing out my pores like diesel oil.

I torqued up my volume another notch. "Are you making this up to hurt me?"

Rather than defend herself, she sucked her lips in and began dragging the recently spun clothes out of the top-loading washer and transferring them to the dryer. Her atypical silence told me she was being truthful. She thought she and Glenn were in love. Or at least had the hots for each other. How disgusting was that? I wished I'd laundered my things separately—or hadn't listened to my sister when she suggested I didn't need to pack enough clothes for the whole trip. "We can do laundry while we're there," she'd said.

At this moment I hated Angela so much the thought of my belongings touching hers nauseated me.

"I don't care." I wanted to regain my dignity, but fury won out. I scooped an errant wet sock off the floor and pitched it at her. But it veered off course, hit the washing machine, and wilted to the ground. "Go ahead and ruin your life." In a sick way, I almost hoped she would so she'd crash and burn. I might even call Fred and fill him in on her escapade.

I stepped closer until her widened blue eyes merged into one hideous Cyclops orb. "What's wrong with you?" I asked. "Does Princess Angela have too much? Everything a woman could want and that's not enough?"

"I should have known better than to confide in you." She bent to retrieve the fallen sock and then reached into the washing machine and grasped one of my knit tops. Her fingers wrung the green fabric. I yanked it from her before she ruined it.

"For almost a week you haven't mentioned a thing." I flung my shirt into the dryer atop the heap of clothing. "You let me fall for Glenn all the while you're making moves on him. Luring him from me, like you always have. Every guy I ever brought home had a crush on you."

"That's not true." But we both knew as teenagers the boys I invited home lusted after her. The blonde goddess with a blemish-free complexion paraded through our family room in her jersey cheerleader uniform. The mini skirt exposed her shapely thighs and calves.

"Everyone's always liked you better. Even Mother." The truth of my words choked off my breath. I recalled at age sixteen realizing

I'd never grow as tall as Angela, even though Mother had assured me I would. It became evident I'd never emerge an elegant swan. I hated it when Mother claimed I possessed my own special beauty. I took Chester's letter as further proof that she was a fibber. "I was a second-class citizen."

Angela let the washer lid slam shut with a resounding bang. She faced me, her features angular and her shoulders squared. "You're the one who's lost her mind. Mom always treated us fairly. She didn't favor me. And even if she had, as adults you and I both have good lives. We should count our blessings instead of griping about what happened when we were children."

"What would you know? You've always gotten what you've wanted. And now you're stealing Glenn." I'd woken up this morning thinking possibly God or some cosmic force had brought me to Lancaster County to meet him. Not that I thought God ran a dating service. But the longer I was here the more I thought it was no accident.

"Rosie, you're being ridiculous." She shut the dryer door with a swipe of her hand. "I'm married. Glenn is all yours."

"He could be if you'd butt out. But you've cast your spell. It's too late now." It felt divine to spew out my malice. An exhilarating relief to use a serpent's tongue.

"For heaven's sake, nothing happened between us." She punched the Start button. The dryer squeaked as it spun. "I said he was staring at me. For all I know, he was wishing he was with someone else, like Olivia." Her eyes brimmed with moisture. I bet thinking about Glenn with another woman caused her grief.

"Were you two out in his buggy alone together?" I asked.

"We were waiting out the storm—"

"Having a cozy heart-to-heart. Don't deny it." I belted out my words.

"We were just hoping the rain would let up. Maybe I imagined everything. He probably doesn't care if he ever sees me again." She fiddled with the control knob, turning it to permanent press. "I wish I'd never brought this up. I don't owe you an explanation. You choose to be single. You must like it. You never do anything you don't want to."

How dare she? All of a sudden I was sitting in the hot seat needing to defend myself. Vulgar phrases belonging in a men's locker room caroused through my brain faster than I could speak.

"That's right." Her voice turned shrill, her volume expanding. "You won't go out with a decent guy. I introduced you to Joel Erickson, but he wasn't exciting enough for my little sister. He was too stable and too much of a gentleman."

"Your dentist? I actually got my teeth bleached just to meet him. He was as boring as unsalted French fries without ketchup. And get this. He's into myrmecology, the study of ants, of all screwy hobbies." I forced a toothy smile for effect. "At least I'm not stuck with a Frederick Strick clone," I said.

What was I doing? I should be elevating Fred. Giving her examples why she should remain faithful to her marriage vows so she'd keep her mitts off Glenn. What if she left Frederick? Her kids would be devastated and Fred might even be heartbroken. Not that he didn't deserve to pay, the way he'd treated Angela. And Glenn? He might fall all over himself trying to be first in line for my sister's attentions.

"Rosie, life is more than thrills." Her foot shoved the plastic laundry hamper against the dryer. "Initial infatuation fades into reality within the first year, or when the wife gets pregnant. It always does. Real life is waking up in the morning and loving your husband with bad breath, and his loving you when you have the flu and look like you've been shipwrecked for a month."

"Spare me," I said. "Who are you to give marital advice, you Jezebel?"

Her hand moved to the nape of her neck. I'd zapped her too hard. I felt a slice of contrition. I wished I could restart the conversation.

"This is the last thing I wanted." Her voice lowered an octave. "Our trip was supposed to bring us closer."

It was? I was about to tell her she'd sabotaged our time together. Nah, that would only drive us further apart. I heard Silvia closing the refrigerator in the kitchen. "Oh no! How long has she been in the house? Has she heard everything we've said?"

Angela aimed her iciest glare at me as if declaring our war-of-the-words was entirely my fault. Then she turned on her heel and tromped up the stairs. I bet she'd avoid me the rest of our trip. I felt utterly alone. I considered hiding down here until Angela went to bed and then packing my bag and hitchhiking a ride to the airport. But I hadn't seen a cab or bus anywhere close to this house.

Wait a doggone minute. I had as much right to be here as she did. Anyway, we were leaving in two days.

I ascended the steps to the first floor. Thankfully, Angela's bedroom door was closed. I entered the kitchen as if I'd nothing to hide. Silvia might have heard me profess my fondness for Glenn. But where was the crime? I was single.

Silvia stood at the counter near the sink, lopping off a dozen radishes' leaves with a knife big enough to split a turkey. Indirect sunlight gaining entrance through the window turned her salt-and-pepper hair into a halo. I cleared my voice so I didn't startle her. She glanced up.

I decided to get the worst over with. "How long have you been in the house?"

"A few minutes." She placed the radishes in a metal bowl. "I tried not to listen, but I couldn't avoid it."

"Sorry. We must have sounded like a couple of alley cats." I wondered what Silvia thought of us now. If Father were here he'd throw the fit of the century. He'd verbally slash Angela with words she'd never forget.

Silvia submerged the radishes in tap water. Her silence and quick movements revealed she was upset. Had she already noticed

Angela's making goo-goo eyes at Glenn? Or worse, had she seen Glenn coveting Angela? If so, Silvia probably regretted inviting him over and promoting their time together. She might not allow Glenn back again. Meaning I wouldn't get to see him. On the other hand, maybe Silvia only heard the tail end of Angela's and my squabble. And she blamed me.

"We usually don't argue like that." I moved closer. "Mostly because we don't spend time together."

"Don't worry, dear. I grew up in a lively household." She started scrubbing the radishes. "Remember, I had an older sister—your mother. We used to tangle something fierce."

"Over Glenn's father?" A rude question, I knew, that hung in the air between us.

She tipped the radishes into a colander, let them drain, and then stowed them in the refrigerator before answering. I didn't mind the wait.

"Chester was my first love, only he didn't know it. He lived strictly for Juliana. She was the sun's radiance, making it impossible for him to notice the lesser stars in the sky." She held the knife under the tap, flushed water across the blade, and then set it in the drying rack. "When Juliana married your father, I thought there might be a chance for me. Chester still came over. We'd sit together and talk. But he never gave me more than a passing one-armed hug, like his kid sister, and then his hands would drop to his sides and off he'd go." She rinsed the cutting board. "Within months Chester started courting Lilly. I didn't get the attraction, but he never asked my opinion. He married her soon after. That was that."

"Did Chester love Lilly?"

"The day they got married? I doubt it, but apparently it didn't matter to her. She recognized a good man when she saw one."

I pictured Glenn and me, strolling arm in arm through his nursery in front of his friends and employees. But the woman I saw with him was tallish and blonde. Like Angela. Which fueled my anger.

"Do you think a man can learn to love a woman?" I asked.

Her lips lifted into a smile, like a crescent. "Sure. You could say I married my husband on the rebound. But I loved him and I think he loved me, although he had odd ways of showing it."

She dried her hands and started us wandering into the living area, maybe to put more distance between Angela and me. Not a bad idea. I headed for the jigsaw puzzle and sat down. Silvia sat down next to me, I chose a violet-colored shape and started looking for other pieces the same color. I should buy a puzzle when I got home. I'd derived great enjoyment from this mindless activity. It calmed my runaway thoughts.

"I wish Juliana had lived long enough for us to resolve our differences," Silvia said. Was she hoping to inspire me to make up with Angela? Since my sister set out to provoke me, she owed me an apology.

Silvia collected amethyst-colored pieces, piling them in the center of the table. "I spent a lifetime comparing myself to Juliana. I need to forgive her for being prettier and for having Chester love her. And, I suppose, for dying."

"I haven't forgiven Mother for dying, myself." The words stampeded out of my mouth. "Or for loving Angela more. I know she did."

Through her glasses, her gray eyes filled with compassion. "Rose, I'm sure your mother loved you equally."

"No, even in her final days when I sat by her bed, I could tell she wanted Angela there instead of me." Mother had said she liked my visits, but I didn't believe her. I needed concrete actions, not words.

Silvia didn't try to persuade me otherwise. Which I appreciated. Or maybe I'd rather she did. I didn't know. A good five minutes of silence elapsed with us sorting through the puzzle pieces. I fit several together.

"I've been meaning to ask you where the puzzle's box top is."

"It was missing when I bought it at a tag sale."

"But it will be impossible to finish. A puzzle with no picture to use as a guide is like setting off on a road trip without a destination or map."

"I know my final destination." She gave my hand a pat. "Where I'll get a chance to see Juliana again."

She planned a rendezvous with Mother in heaven? Fat chance.

I continued moving a four-headed piece around until it linked up with two others. Gee, I loved the sensation of easing into a perfect fit. An image came to mind of my sinking into a bathtub. The water almost too hot, yet when I submerged I found it warm and safe. As Mother's womb must have felt.

Was there a way to recapture that feeling of security?

TWENTY-FIVE

Angela

Rex barked, alerting Silvia, who looked out the window toward the garage. "Chet Yoder's buggy is in the driveway."

"Glenn's father?" I asked. "Is he alone?"

"Yes." Her hand moved to her mouth, muffling her words. "I wonder what he's doing here."

"Maybe he thinks Rose and I already left, and he wants to see how you're feeling." Or was he here to apologize to us for Lilly's less-than-cordial reception? Thank goodness he hadn't arrived earlier, when Rose and I were talking about Glenn. Now I knew how Mom had felt weathering her assaults. Only this was worse. Rose insinuated I'd committed adultery when in fact I'd done nothing wrong. Yes, I was tempted, but temptation itself wasn't evil.

After all, when seeing a double-fudge chocolate-chip cookie fresh from the oven sitting next to a glass of frothy milk, what woman wouldn't be tempted to start dipping and munching? But as long as she didn't act on her desire the calories wouldn't expand her hips or clog her arteries. And who was Rose to cast accusations like splats of hot grease off a frying pan? Why, she'd made me so angry I raised my voice, which I rarely did with my children and certainly not with Frederick.

I'd considered calling him, but he hated complaints about Rose.

His advice was always the same: If you don't like someone, quit spending time with them. Period. That's why he never saw his cousins, who lived across Lake Washington. They bored him.

Maybe that's why he avoided me.

Waiting for Chester to reach the front door—he seemed to be taking his time—I squatted before the hearth to assemble a fire, the first since my Girl Scout days. Rose made fire-building look easy, so I decided to give it a shot. I erected a teepee of kindling over crumpled newspaper and lay three eight-inch split logs on top. I struck a match and nosed it against the newspaper, but the flame blinked out.

Silvia unlatched the front door and opened it.

On my third attempt, the match and newspaper finally ignited, the flames invading and tangling between the kindling. I felt a hint of warmth. Earlier, while reclusing in my room, I remembered when Mom became bedridden. I'd decided to pray for a miracle the rest of the day. After I'd bowed my head I was swathed in serenity, but my mind kept tripping off on tangents.

For one thing, I needed to contact Rose and tell her Mom's doctor wanted to hospitalize her. I wished Mom had called Rose herself, but she sounded so weak I offered. I labored over the right phrasing, but when I reached Rose on the phone she seemed indifferent, even hostile. My mind had flailed about like a bird trapped in a house. We had that happen once: a young robin, its wings unsure, flew through our kitchen's open doorway, and was terrified. It thrashed against the walls and ceiling until, exhausted, it huddled on the floor in a corner, at which time I dropped a towel over it and was able to carry the traumatized creature outside.

I wished someone would drop a cloth over me and gently, lovingly, transport me to a safe haven where no one was sick or brokenhearted.

I turned my head to see lanky Chester entering the house. "*Wie geht's.*"

Glenn would look like his father someday, I thought, and my

heart swelled with tender feelings trenching deeper and turning more complex.

"This is a surprise," Silvia said. "I thought you were going to wait."

He removed his straw hat. "I couldn't take a chance—" Chester must have noticed me and clipped his sentence short.

She took his hat and placed it on a hook. "Come in and make yourself comfy." She guided him into the living area. He sat on the edge of the couch and spoke in quiet spurts about the drop in temperature and the coming winter. Glenn's voice echoed behind his. It had been twenty-four hours since I first contemplated giving up everything to be with Glenn. Which I knew wouldn't happen—unless Frederick left me for another woman, not out of the realm of possibilities.

Silvia said, "What can I do for you, Chet?"

He ran his fingers through his hair. "The letters. I thought I'd better come for them before your nieces left." For such a large man his voice emerged faintly, like he didn't want me hearing. Pretending I couldn't, I turned to the fire and watched the flames nipping at the wood.

"I should have sorted through her things years ago." She wrung her hands. "I'm sorry."

"Not your fault. But I don't want anyone else seeing them." Meaning Glenn and Lilly, I presumed. But if he wanted the letters, he couldn't have them. I planned to slip into Silvia's closet later today to read them. Since hearing the first one, its contents had infested my mind like worms boring into an apple, slowly making their way to my core. I'd tried to dismiss thoughts that Mom was no more virtuous than Rose. But last night images of Mom pregnant and married to Chester had invaded my dreams. Then, an instant later—time races by in nightmares—Mom was cradling a newborn, who turned out to be Glenn! I woke up shivering, the covers plowed back and the quilt off the bed.

I hoped Chester's other letters would redeem Mom. And they

might tell us what happened to their child. Rose and I had a right to know.

I heard my sister trotting down the stairs. She entered the living area. "Hi, Chet. You talking about Mother's letters?"

"Rose." I got to my feet and bulged my eyes at her, but her gaze swept past me, landing on my fire. Her dark brows lowered into a frown.

Not waiting for Chester's answer, she declared, "I'll get them." She darted out of the room and took the stairs two at a time. Miss Smarty wanted to be in control and for Chester to like her. For once couldn't she use her noggin and consider the consequences before acting?

I called out, "Rosie, wait," and started for the stairs. I would wrestle the letters away if that's what it took to gain possession. Before my foot could reach the first step, the floorboards above the living area moaned; she was already in the storage room. When I was halfway up the stairs, a thwacking sounded, which must have been the trunk's lid closing. Then a moment later Rose bounced out of her room, clutching the packet of letters as though she'd found the golden egg Mom used to fill with pennies and hide on our childhood Easter egg hunts. Under the overhead light, I saw a magenta velvet ribbon encircling the envelopes.

"Rose, what are you doing?" I stood in the middle of the top step, one hand on the railing, barring her descent. But slippery Rose dodged by me, just like when we were kids and I'd caught her in my bedroom snooping through my diary. She'd sing her six-note taunt, "Angela loves Rusty," while dashing for the safety of the first floor or yard.

"Rose, wait." Pivoting, I lost balance, grabbed hold of the railing on the other side, and steadied myself. Then I trailed her back to the living area in time to see her give the envelopes to Chester. I could kick myself for not reading them earlier. I was too polite—what Rose called wimpy. But not this time. The letters would not leave this house. When Chester stamped and posted them, he'd transferred ownership to Mom, then her children. Or were they legally Dad's? In any case, in his absence Rose and I were his representatives.

I lowered myself onto the armchair perpendicular to the couch, my knees only feet from Chester's. His hand remained open, like the letters were scalding his palms. I was tempted to snatch them away, but what would Silvia think of me? I told myself to quit worrying about her opinion and take action.

"Chet, we read one," Silvia said, and his shaky hand closed around the letters, creasing them. "I'm sorry, I knew it was wrong," she said. "There's no excuse."

"We don't need an excuse." My voice gushed out like a faucet that wouldn't shut off. "Juliana was our mother. We have a right to know if we have an older brother or sister. Sometimes adopted children look for their birthmothers. I'd love to know our sibling, wouldn't you, Rose?"

I turned to her for support, but she folded her arms across her chest. I wished Glenn were here. He could speak to Chester and Silvia on my behalf. He owned their respect and trust.

As I imagined reasoning with them, a tidal wave of thought hit me: Glenn was the right age to be Rose's and my older brother. His hair was almost the same shade of brown as Rose's, and he loved the outdoors and animals the way she did, and gardening the way Silvia did. And Silvia's extreme fondness for him was like an aunt's toward her nephew.

No, impossible. Lilly was his mother. Wasn't she? Or did she adopt him? I felt panic rising in the back of my throat as my mind wrapped itself around the ugly possibility. If true, the joke was on Rose, who salivated over Glenn like a Great Dane on a dish of tapioca pudding. But if she couldn't have him, neither could I.

In a swift motion Chester bolted to his feet and strode to the hearth. He ripped off the ribbon, and it twirled to the floor. Then he tossed the letters into the fire. A rush of light enclosed and devoured them in a blizzard of flames.

I ran over, my hand swinging out for the poker, but it was too late to salvage the letters. There was nothing to be done but watch the blackened papers rise and fall like dying breaths of air. It took all my strength to keep from screaming.

"I'll be going now," he said, and then he took a step toward the door.

I hurried over to him, grabbed his forearm, and felt hard muscles. He was older, but I didn't have the physical power to keep him here.

"Tell us about the child," I begged.

He stared at me as if I were speaking a foreign language. Finally his lips formed the words, "There was no child. Juliana saw to that."

"Are you sure? Maybe she didn't go to college. Maybe she was put in a home for unwed mothers."

"She went to college in September. I visited her there, and found her with your father."

"But still—"

"She wasn't pregnant. Her waist was as slim as ever. If anything, she'd lost weight. And she made it clear she wanted me to disappear."

Mom had told me she met our father the first week of college. "It never hurts to marry money," she'd said more than once. I imagined Chester, a down-to-earth young Amish man, taking a bus to see her and combing the campus until he found the object of his love. Was she embarrassed by his sudden appearance? Did she tell Dad that Chester meant nothing to her, and later did they chuckle about his shabby appearance?

I'd never know the answers to those questions. But one thing for sure, when she went to school, Mom was not pregnant. That settled that. Like receding waters after a flood, my disappointment was laced with relief. I had no other sibling. Glenn was not my brother, which simplified everything. And also opened a multitude of possibilities.

"I try my best not to think about her." He turned to Silvia and gave her a half-smile. "I must admit, and don't tell Lilly this, I had a dream about Juliana the other night. We were out dancing."

"I remember those late nights," she said, standing. Her eyes came alive and she let out a soft giggle. "I can't even stay up past nine anymore."

"Juliana had enough energy for all of us. And she was always the prettiest girl there."

"She was beautiful," Silvia said, a fact I think still hurt her. Is that how Rose viewed me? Would I forever be her big sister and never her friend?

"All these years and there's still a hole." He placed his hand over his heart and gave it a pat. "A piece is missing. Once it's lost, it's gone for good."

Silvia's hand moved to cover her own heart. It was plain to see she loved him; she felt his loss as her own.

He said, "But I found a good woman who gave me a son I wouldn't trade for anything. Our Glenn . . . well, you know how *wunderbaar* he is." Glancing at me, he added, "I don't want him following in his father's footsteps, longing for someone he'll never have."

What had Glenn told him? My face warmed as Chester's eyes rested on me as though I were in a police lineup.

"Your son is the most levelheaded young man I know." Silvia looked like a flower waiting to be picked as she gazed up at him. "There's no need to worry about Glenn. And as for you, your life has turned out well. None of us gets exactly what we want." She glanced to Rose and then me. "The secret to a happy life is to accept our losses, make the best of them, and trust the Lord to guide us."

Yes, that's what I needed to do. But how did Glenn fit into the picture?

TWENTY-SIX

Rose

*N*either Angela nor I said goodbye to Chester as he left. He seemed older, his shoulders rounded. By the front door he gave Silvia a discreet one-armed hug. Silvia shut the door behind him. Then she let out an audible sigh.

For several minutes Angela and I hovered before the hearth like zombies, staring into the dying embers. Traces of blackened paper lay around the fire's skirt like brittle eggshells, too delicate to be touched. Then in slow motion Angela receded from the room.

Dumb me. I'd been flattered when Chester came calling on Silvia until he dumped the letters in the fireplace. The last thing I imagined he'd do. Giving him the letters proved I was clueless. Why did I assume every man of Father's generation would act like him? Now that I thought about it, our father never would have put in writing anything that could be used as evidence against him later.

As the flames cremated the paper, my jaw dropped open and my mind converted into a battleground. I'd botched things up again. I thought Chester would treasure the letters, not destroy them. Did he still despise Mother despite the nice things he'd just said about her?

At least I'd had the foresight to read all the letters this morning while Angela was out. I took one from the bottom of the stack and stuffed it into my duffel bag. I figured no one would know the difference. But that didn't erase my out-of-control act of giving the rest to Chester. I'd stepped outside the family ring. I'd given Angela every right to be furious. As for Chester, who could blame him for trying to protect the two people he held dearest?

"Rose, dear?" Silvia stepped toward me, opened her purse, and extracted her car key. "Do you want to get out by yourself?"

"I guess." My vocal cords were too rigid to shape a firm reply. "Yes, I need to get away." To hide.

"You could go to the grocery store," she suggested. "We can use another carton of milk, and we're low on eggs."

"Okay."

I didn't remember putting on my jacket or stepping outside. I found myself sitting in her car behind the steering wheel with the engine idling. Specks of light glistened off my lashes. I flipped down the visor to check myself in the mirror and saw a white facial mask with two bloodshot eyes filling with clear liquid. A sob gathered from the bottom of my stomach and heaved out my mouth. Followed by another. My features twisted out of shape. I wept like a woman who'd lost her family in a war.

After five minutes of blubbering, I wiped the tears off my cheeks. What was happening to me? I'd cried more this week than I had in the last twenty years. Releasing the parking brake, I rolled the car onto the road and drove aimlessly. Eventually I spotted a ma-and-pa-type grocery store. I glanced to the passenger seat to see I'd neglected to bring my purse. A wasted trip.

A half mile farther I turned onto a small road. My energy depleted, I pulled onto a strip of packed dirt and killed the engine. I parked next to a six-foot-high wooden fence containing a pasture of clover and grasses. At the opposite side of the field stood a barn and house. Through the slats of the fence, I saw a predominately white, dapple-gray mare that I bet was a standardbred. She was exquisite. If you liked horses. Apparently I did. In spite of my feelings of despondency I got out of the car to admire her.

I inhaled the aroma of moist grasses and soil. "Pretty girl," I said. The mare lifted her head. The breeze caught her flowing mane like a river. Eyeing me, she hesitated. Then she approached me at a trot, her gait so smooth she seemed to float an inch above the ground. She stopped twenty feet away and shook her head. I couldn't decipher her message. There was a time I could understand most animals. Not as well as Dr. Doolittle, my favorite childhood book character. But I would have known if a horse's shaking its head was a playful act or if she was warning me to keep out of her pasture or I'd be sorry.

She shook her arched neck again.

Forcing my trepidation into submission, I climbed the fence and clicked my tongue. She bobbed her nose and then gazed intently over my shoulder. I glanced around and noticed an ancient tree studded with red apples on the other side of the road.

"You hungry?" I jumped down, booked across the pavement, and picked a blemished but edible piece of fruit. Returning, I clicked my tongue again and offered the treat on my flattened palm. But the mare remained at a cautious distance.

Duke had been my favorite horse at summer camp when I was twelve years old. Sometimes, when daydreaming, I could feel his bristly mane between my fingertips and smell the fragrance of his warm back beneath the leather saddle. I recalled the weightless sensation as he moved, his massive legs like pillars of a temple. My hips had swayed with his rhythm. My spine relaxed in a way I'd never felt again, even under the hands of a massage therapist.

The next year, more than anything I'd wanted to take horseback riding lessons, but Father, who called horses stupid animals, said, "The nearest stable is twenty miles away. How are you going to get there? And how are you going to pay for it?" For once, I'd wished Mother had outranked him and stood up for me. Instead she secreted me off to a stable once a week and asked me not to mention it to him.

Childhood fantasies lost forever, I thought.

The mare exhaled a gust of air through her flared nostrils, bringing me back to the present. She stepped closer, snatched the apple, and withdrew a few yards to consume it. Then she stared at me with hopeful eyes.

"I see. You'll only come if I have a treat?" I clucked my tongue, extended a hand again. Finally the mare ambled over and snuffled my empty palm. The hairs on her muzzle tickled my hand. I scratched her forehead and then the ridge running down the front of her head. She showed me her pleasure by working her mouth in a relaxed manner.

I ran my fingers through her magnificent mane. "What's your name?"

"Dee-Dee," a young girl's voice said boldly from inside the fence. Behind her followed another horse, a chestnut swayback. I assumed a gelding.

"She belongs to my *dat*." A scarf covered the girl's sandy hair. She wore a skirt and rubber boots that came up to her knees. She pointed to the tree. "She wants apples."

Was that an order? My usual stubborn reaction was to do the opposite of what people told me. But I said, "Yeah, okay. Just a minute." I crossed the street and fetched two more apples. I served Dee-Dee first, then the gelding, long in tooth, crunched into the other.

"Are you from around here?" The girl's high-pitched voice was as singsongy as Olivia's.

"No, I live in Seattle." I wasn't used to kids I didn't know speaking to me. In the city, they were nervous around strangers. Even when I was walking Minnie in my neighborhood.

"Dee-Dee likes you," the girl said. "She's usually spooky with new people. Ya want to ride her?"

"Bareback and without a bridle? Uh…no thanks. I can't remember how to ride anymore. I'd tumble off." Land on my keister. "I'm sure your parents wouldn't like it."

When Dee-Dee had consumed her apple, she raised her head

and pricked her ears. In a burst, she rotated away from us. Her legs gathering momentum, she initiated a canter toward the barn. She swooped her head and she broke into a gallop. Her tail lifted and her hooves clopped the thick sod.

"She's like that sometimes," the girl said. "*Dat* thinks she hears someone calling her, and then she takes off. That's why he named her Distant Drumbeat. But I call her Dee-Dee for short." Her hands clamped her pint-size hips. She stepped closer. "You ever had a horse run away with you?"

"Is that your game? You wanted to scare me out of my wits?" I grinned at her cheekiness. She reminded me of myself at her age.

"*Nee.*" She smirked, making me think she was pulling my leg. "Dee-Dee likes you or she wouldn't let you pet her. She's always a perfect lady with me." She tittered. "But she bites my big *bruder.* 'Tis *gut* because he chases and teases me. But he won't come anywhere near Dee-Dee."

"I think this gelding, bridled and saddled, is more my speed. Even then, it's been years."

The girl gave the air a small farewell high five. "I'd best go finish my chores. You should ride Dee-Dee next time. Come to our house." Then she strode away with the gelding in tow.

I figured I'd never see her or Dee-Dee again, which shouldn't bother me. But it did, big time. Then a pleasing thought permeated my musings. When I got home, I could take horseback riding lessons. I bet stables owned tame, user-friendly horses for beginners.

Rose, you can't afford lessons, an inner voice sounding like Father rebuked me. And I lived in the city. I'd need to drive to Woodinville, at least thirty minutes from Seattle. An hour round-trip when I should be working. And I'd look ridiculous. Everyone I knew would think I was loopy.

Except Glenn. He struck me as the kind of man who'd admire a woman who accepted new challenges. But he couldn't care less about me.

TWENTY-SEVEN

Angela

I sat in my room, trying to concentrate on my romance novel, but distracting thoughts dive-bombed my mind like mosquitoes, never landing long enough for me to swat them. In Technicolor, I recalled Rose, proudly bounding down the stairs wielding the letters. She'd handed them to Chester as if she and he were part of a tag team—conspirators. I saw Chester thrusting the letters into the fireplace as though they carried a deadly virus. The flames reached up to devour them; the charred papers disintegrated.

Anger grated between my clenched teeth. In some ways I despised my traitorous sister. And I hated myself for choosing today to build my first fire.

I was on the novel's second-to-last chapter, the story escalating to its climax. But my brain hadn't ingested one phrase for the last ten minutes. Where were Amanda and Ramon, anyway? I reset my vision to the top of the page and saw they were trying to escape a uniform-clad gendarme—really a spy. Amanda suspected Ramon was responsible for hoisting a priceless Monet painting from the Musée d'Orsay, and Ramon mistakenly believed Amanda held prejudices against his family, Jews who'd lost everything during the Nazi invasion. Crossing the traffic-filled street, his hand enclosed hers. She didn't yank it away as she had earlier.

My gaze abandoned the page and honed in on my snow globe sitting on the bureau. This wasn't the first time I'd been envious of a novel's heroine. Unfettered Amanda could shed her former identity and step into an exciting new life. If I were in her place, what would happen to the kids? Frederick would rage about getting custody, but in fact he was rarely home and spent little time with them. Did he even know their birthdays or had he ever bought either of them a Christmas present? He'd provided the finances and showed up for meals occasionally, but that was all. Yet I must consider the possibility Daniel and Tiffany would choose to live with their father. In which case I'd see them on occasional weekends and holidays. Maybe that scenario wouldn't be so awful; they might be happy to see me.

A gentle knock rapped on the door and Silvia entered the room. Her footsteps whispered, unlike Rose who stomped around like the FedEx man delivering a package. Thirty minutes ago, when I'd looked out the window and seen Rose leave, the chill in the house warmed ten degrees. The longer she was gone the better. For the rest of the day, I wanted to pretend Chester's letters didn't exist. Well, they didn't anymore.

Silvia wore an anxious expression. "Are you all right, dear?" She sounded like Mom prying when she knew Frederick and I were fighting.

Squirming inside, I got to my feet and set the book on the bureau next to the snow globe. "Sure, I'm fine." I never told Mom the complete truth either. I figured, why worry her when Frederick and I would eventually make up? Or rather, I'd apologized to put an end to the stalemate.

"I couldn't live with myself if I stood by and said nothing," she said.

"If you're worried about me, please don't be." I forced the corners of my mouth into the pseudo-smile I'd donned most of my adult life.

"Dear, I heard you and Rose talking about Glenn."

"I didn't mean it," I said too quickly, my voice tinny. "Really, I never do crazy things."

"None of us thinks we will, but in the right circumstances…"

"Glenn's not the source of my problem." I lifted the snow globe and tipped it back and forth. The iridescent flakes shimmered through the clear liquid, swirling around the dancer. "Now, Frederick is a different story."

Silvia's gaze intensified. "Has he done something to upset you?"

"Just the usual. I shouldn't have brought up his name. I don't want to talk about him." I shook the globe again. The tutu-clad woman held her position, even upside-down. I was like her, trapped in a confining bubble.

"I remember when I was your age, life wasn't a tea party," she said. "I was glued to the house, waiting on everyone, and getting no thanks for it. Not that I didn't encourage my husband and children to treat me like hired help the way I catered to them." She paused until I glanced at her. "I felt like running away sometimes, dear."

"I'd never do that." Yes, I might. But she seemed satisfied with my declaration.

"Good." She tilted her head, her voice taking on a playful tone. "Right now, if you could do anything, what would it be?"

I was glad we were moving to another subject. "Rose and I used to play this game. We'd compare our dreams after the lights went out and we were supposed to be asleep. But she didn't end up the Dr. Doolittle of the animal world, and I didn't become Anna Pavlova."

"Why not start dancing again?"

I deposited the globe back on the dresser. "A dancer has a short window of opportunity, even if she's the most talented person in the world. I mean, when you get too old, you hit a wall. No callboards looking for past-their-prime, unexceptional ballerinas. Painters, writers, and actors keep going for the rest of their lives, but my time has come and gone."

"Not so fast, dear. Several women I know take dance classes. Phyllis took tap dancing and Jazzercise, and had a great time."

I pictured a roomful of round-bellied, cellulite-thighed women—like me. "I wouldn't be caught dead in leotards. I can't even touch my toes anymore, let alone keep up with fast-paced music." I wanted out of the limelight. "Silvia, what did you want to be when you were young?"

"I rarely admit this. Even at my age, it's embarrassing to say out loud." She clasped her hands together, shoulders back, head erect, adding an inch to her stature. "An opera star. A diva."

I tried to maintain my serious expression, but couldn't help smiling.

"That's okay." Her lips formed a crooked grin. "It's hard picturing me and Caruso on stage at the Met. Now, your grandpa, he could sing. He'd burst into Rossini or Verdi while out splitting wood or gardening. Gorgeous. And Mama also had a lovely voice: an alto, dark and rich in timbre, like fine Chianti. I, however, didn't inherit the family vocal cords or the finely tuned ear. 'You have to listen more,' my father used to say. 'Don't sing until you've heard the note in your inner ear.'"

Seeing I didn't understand, she added, "I was tone deaf. Great volume and range, but I couldn't sing on pitch."

"I'm sorry." The enormity of her loss bombarded me; Silvia had dreamed of a career she couldn't experience, not even as a teen.

"Never mind. I learned to play the cello instead. For some reason I can hear pitches not produced in my own body. Maybe not as rewarding as singing *Un Bel Di* from *Madame Butterfly*, but the cello can be beautiful too."

"Yes, absolutely. I have one of Yo-Yo Ma's CDs. I can envision you playing something light and airy like a flute or mandolin, but not an instrument as large as you are. When was the last time you played?"

"Maybe a year." She led me to the hall closet, pulled coats aside, and showed me a four-foot-long black case any gangster would covet.

"Would you play something for me?"

She massaged her fingers. "All right, but keep in mind I'm a little rusty, and the Lyme disease makes my hands feel like they have arthritis."

"Let me carry it." I lugged the case into the living area. My vision moved to the hearth, where the spent fire emitted a feeble ribbon of smoke. Again, I relived snippets of Chester's visit like a newsreel on fast-forward. But I sat down on the couch and directed my full attention to Silvia, who settled on the upright chair by the puzzle table.

As if they were old friends, she extracted a cello and bow from the case and spent a few moments tuning up. I was impressed she could manage; I didn't know we had a musician in the family. Growing up, Mom forced Rose and me to study piano, but Rose refused to practice and I got too busy with my dance lessons.

Silvia sent the bow across the strings, initiating the first note. Pure, like a feather slicing through a cloud, the tone vibrated, saturating the room. One tone melted into the next as "Green Sleeves" unfolded itself.

When the song concluded, she lay the bow aside. "After I got married and had kids, I rarely played. I did what I thought everyone else wanted me to do." She adjusted her glasses; they'd slipped onto the bridge of her nose. "I actually think Frank would have stuck around more if I'd continued playing, joined a string quartet or community symphony, in spite of his complaints that my practicing drowned out the TV."

She set the instrument back in the case. "Now, what are we going to do with you? You're still a young woman. Too young to be giving up, feeling defeated."

I started to protest, but she hushed me. "Yes you are, dear. With a full future ahead of you."

The fact that Silvia, who was seriously ill, was giving me a pep talk made me love her all the more. How could I leave her? If only I hadn't brought Rose along on this trip everything would be different, the path to my staying so much wider. For one thing, I probably wouldn't know about Chester's letters to Mom. Even if Silvia and I had stumbled upon them, we wouldn't have snooped into Mom's personal correspondence out of respect. Eventually I would have met Glenn while he was planting Silvia's spring bulbs, and we could have spent long hours in the garden together. He might have taken me to see the creek and for a ride in his buggy.

I might have stayed here longer, building myself a nest to land should Frederick and I part ways.

TWENTY-EIGHT
Rose

At 8:00 a.m. the next day, the roads clouded with mist, I picked my way back to the pasture, intending to catch a glimpse of Dee-Dee. And maybe the preteen would come speak to me. But the pasture gaped empty.

At the far end of the field, smoke ribboned out of the home's chimney. I imagined an Amish woman my age washing the dishes after feeding her family. I longed to meet her. Nah, I couldn't rap on the door and expect to be invited in.

Feeling the weight of loneliness, I sat in Silvia's car until the windows fogged up. I shouldn't waste my day lolling by the side of the road. I flicked on the defroster and drove away without a destination in mind, but migrated toward Glenn's nursery. Like a homing pigeon. No surprise there. I couldn't keep my thoughts from drifting back to him.

Ten minutes later, I entered his vacant parking lot. I didn't see another soul. The retail shop must not open until nine. It was only eight thirty. I coasted up in front of Glenn's house and waited several minutes. But even the dog and cat must be sleeping in.

I couldn't bring myself to tramp up the porch steps and knock on his front door. I knew how to hide my insecurities, but fear crippled me. Preparing to leave, I released the parking brake and set the car in

reverse. Then it occurred to me Edna might be pruning the herb garden. Trying to ignore an escalating case of the jitters, I got out and
circumnavigated the house with furtive footsteps. The air was coming alive as the sun warmed the earth, emitting steamy perfumes.

Not watching the cement pathway, my foot swung into a metal
watering can. The empty vessel scudded several feet, clanking as it
hit the trunk of a crab apple tree. So much for sneaking up. Still, I
didn't hear Missy barking the way my Minnie would.

I rounded the bend and noticed the cat on the back porch
grooming her paw. Had Glenn or Edna put her out this morning?
Or was she returning from a night of scavenging for mice? She sent
me a plaintiff meow as if she hadn't eaten for weeks. "I'm wise to
you." My neighbor's tabby visited me daily, begging for handouts.
And I couldn't resist rewarding him with a saucer of cream.

"Want to go inside, Miss Kitty?" The cat's waiflike plea gave me
an excuse to climb the steps to the kitchen door. Peering through
the glass, I spotted Glenn at the table studying a dog-eared book as
thick as a dictionary.

A Bible? He was reading it first thing in the morning instead of
the newspaper? I got this funny feeling inside my chest like when
I first saw Silvia's Bible by her bed. She and Glenn belonged to the
same club. I felt like an outsider. I couldn't pretend to believe in God
when I didn't. Mrs. Porter, my Sunday school teacher, said the Bible
had tailor-made messages just for me. Like a fortune teller. She'd
said many times she prayed, read a passage of Scripture, and found
the answer to her problems. Sounded far fetched.

Glenn's Bible was opened near the back. His eyes seemed to be
resting on one phrase, as if pondering its meaning. He looked peace-
ful. He must not know about Chester's letters to Mother. Which
was good. Glenn and I didn't need that logjam separating us. Not
until we'd laid more solid groundwork. Or said our final goodbyes.

With the cat purring and rubbing my calves with her back
and tail, I tapped on the door's windowpane with a shaky hand.

Glenn glanced up, and his lips parted as if I were the last person he expected. Before he could stand, my sweaty palm grabbed hold of the unlocked doorknob and opened it.

The cat darted into the kitchen, skimming past Missy, who hastened to the door. Giving me an excuse to step inside.

"Am I intruding?" I said.

"Not at all. Good morning." Glenn placed a bookmark in the Bible and set it aside. I wondered if his parents had bought it for him or if he purchased it when Mary Ann left him. I'd heard of desperate people turning to God when all else failed.

He pulled out the chair next to him. "May I offer you coffee?" A mug and a carafe sat on the table. "Or I can make tea."

My nostrils embraced the bitter aroma of freshly ground beans. "Coffee sounds good."

He fetched another mug from the cupboard and served me from the carafe. "You may need milk," he said. "I brew a strong pot."

He was right. My lips puckered as I swallowed my first sip. "I'll get the milk." I glided across the room to the refrigerator jam-packed with what looked like tasty fare protected by clear plastic wrap. Coleslaw, potato salad, sliced turkey, and a bowl of jumbo-sized brown eggs that could win a blue ribbon at a state fair.

"You've got enough to feed twenty people," I said. "Planning a party?"

"No. Edna's visiting her niece in Indiana. She was worried I'd starve."

"Little chance of that." I topped off my coffee with organic milk, and then I lowered myself onto the chair next to him, keeping my weight forward. I was anything but relaxed.

He wrapped his mug in his hand. "What brings you out so early?"

I admonished myself for not waiting until later to visit him. But by then he'd be busy or gone.

"I needed time out of the house. To think." I tasted my coffee. "Glenn, I've decided I like you." My hand flew to my blabbermouth.

I took a calming breath and started again. "I mean, all of this." I scanned the room, noting the row of ceramic containers marked bread, flour, all-purpose flour, and sugar, and the copper kettle on the stove. "I like your lifestyle, the way you live."

The sparkle in his eyes showed amusement. "So you thought you'd come by and see how I start my day?"

"Sure, before you got all spruced up. Still in the rough."

"I don't think I've met a more honest woman." He stroked his unshaven chin. "Unless you're funning me."

"I'm not sure what I'm doing." I set my elbows on the table. "I do know I'm not ready to go back to Seattle. Don't get me wrong. It's a marvelous city. But over the last week it stopped being home for me. Maybe because I'm single and my mother's dead. And I could use distance from my father." For the first time I couldn't hear his authoritarian voice in my ears. "And I've grown to love Aunt Silvia." I rolled my eyes to keep them dry. "Apparently I'm going through a mid-life crisis."

I sat up straighter, folded my hands in my lap. "So how about you? What's in your forecast? Olivia?"

He laughed out loud. "You don't pull any punches, do you?"

"I don't have the luxury of time."

"Nothing romantic going on there, although I'd like Olivia to work for me forever. She's a sweetheart and industrious, but the stars in her eyes are definitely for someone else. A low-down good-for-nothing, as far as I'm concerned. Maybe the bishop and ministers can set him straight."

"Are you jealous or overly protective?"

"Protective. I think he's been vandalizing the nursery, but I have no proof." He wrinkled his brow. "She's too young for an old guy like me, don't you think?"

"You're not so old. I'm guessing forty-something?"

"Just turned forty-one."

"Any children?" I could tell I'd touched a raw nerve by the way he averted his gaze.

"Not yet." He took a lingering sip of coffee. "Mary Ann didn't want kids. But as soon as she married Philip they had three. Guess I'll never understand women."

"What about my sister?" I tried to look detached. "Do you understand she's married?"

Rubbing one eye, he remained silent for the longest moment. I steeled myself against the blast of truth. For him to admit he was attracted to her and not to me.

"Yes, I know she's married. Where did that question come from?"

"I thought you two…"

"No. I steer clear of married women. Especially ones with beautiful younger sisters."

He found me beautiful? Or was his lighthearted banter a smokescreen to camouflage amorous feelings for Angela? If he'd stretch the truth about my looks, could I believe anything he said?

I felt as if I were treading water in the ocean and had a choice which direction to swim. Retreating to the safety of what I knew, out of habit, or fording on into uncharted waters. I'd run away from confrontation too many times in my life.

I pressed onward, like Fred would in the courtroom. "Glenn, I hear you've been staring at her. Ogling, is more like it."

"She told you that?" His face blanched pasty white, as if the blood were draining out of his cheeks. Guilty as charged, Fred would tell me.

"Yes, she did." I wanted to say it didn't matter. But there was no reason to lie to Glenn and every reason to be honest. No more pretending to be someone I wasn't.

He poured himself more coffee, filling the mug too close to the rim. "When I first saw Angela, I gave her a double-take. I thought she might be someone I knew from California. And then I saw her ring, which shouted, 'Hands off, buddy.'" He avoided mentioning if he was pining for her from afar. Or if he preferred willowy blondes over short brunettes.

"Are you sure that's all there is to it?"

"Okay, I admit I found her attractive." He hesitated. "But that's as far as it could go."

Instead of slicing me in half, his declaration bounced off like a sword's blade on a rock. I waited until we made eye contact to say, "Here's the sixty-four-thousand-dollar question." I imagined a snare-drum roll. "Are you over her?"

"There's nothing to get over." His hazel eyes returned my stare, telling me he was being truthful. I hoped.

"If I acted out of line, I'd better get over to Silvia's and apologize." Before he could walk his chair away from the table, I reached out and placed my hand on his. How's that for bold?

"Never mind," I said. "That's all in the past. Let's talk about us instead. You and me, and what we're going to eat for breakfast."

I moved to the gas stove, brought down a cast iron fry pan, and turned on the burner. "How do you like your eggs, Glenn? Scrambled, over easy, or sunny-side-up?"

Angela looked ready to pounce on me when I waltzed into Silvia's house singing.

"Where have you been?" she demanded. But I didn't turn defensive. I felt too good. Better than I had in years.

"I was at Glenn Yoder's." I basked in the sound of his last name, which would suit my first. Rose Yoder had a nice lilt to it. Oh, what a beautiful morning!

Hold on there. I'd better not get ahead of myself. Glenn had revealed he was contemplating joining the Amish church, a lifetime commitment, which wouldn't include me unless I did too. A highly unlikely occurrence. According to Glenn, few non-Amish successfully joined. Would I even contemplate the radical lifestyle, not to mention learning the language? And where did God fit in?

"We got busy talking and doing chores," I said. Playing hooky, getting to know each other. "I helped feed his chickens. His favorite Rhode Island Red is named Matilda." The hen had strutted over and cocked her fancy head.

Angela must have been dumbfounded, the way she stared. Again, we'd switched places. I rambled on like I was the talk-a-lot sister. "It was fun looking for eggs. To think the ones you just ate were freshly laid. That's why they tasted so good, their yokes sitting up firmly when I fried them over easy. The way Glenn likes. Plus two slices of eight-grain toast, light on the butter, and homemade raspberry jam, one of Edna's specialties."

She gaped. "You cooked for him?"

"Yeah. You didn't know I could make a mean breakfast, did you? And my gastronomic skills are about to improve. After all, I taught myself how to make birdhouses." I shrugged off my jacket. "Later, Glenn and I stood in the field behind the nursery watching a hawk circling in broad arcs, looking for his next meal. Sis, have you ever wondered how it's possible for a bird to float on something that can't be seen?" His powerful wings had rested on transparent cushions. "There's a creek at the back of the field that swells into a river in the winter. Birds twittered in the trees on the far bank and frogs croaked, and we heard the rustling of dry leaves, maybe a deer."

Her cheeks blotched red. "Sounds fun, for an animal lover like you."

"It was. Just my cup of tea."

Rex lumbered over to us and sniffed my pant legs. "Rex, old fella, I spent the morning with another dog. Can you ever forgive me?" He rubbed his forehead against my knee.

"What else were you doing?" Angela probably thought Glenn and I were cavorting between his sheets. But she couldn't be more wrong.

"Nothing outlandish. We were two single people having a good time." In the course of conversation, Glenn had mentioned the only woman to share his bed would be his future wife, if he ever found one, ruling out casual love affairs. I'd never heard a man say that before. And he'd mentioned he was tired of his bachelor's life. He'd like to spend his evenings and vacations with someone. And he was open for kids, if it wasn't too late.

"Rosie." Angela gathered my attention like the sweep of a broom. "I've been waiting here to apologize, but you're making it difficult."

"If you're apologizing for our verbal tussle yesterday, I was the one doing most of the yelling. You don't owe me a thing. I over-reacted." I doubted Glenn would care for screaming. I needed to start acting like a lady, as Mother would say. She wasn't wrong about everything.

"I should have responded with patience, not anger." Angela sounded like she was reciting a prepared speech. "I was so mad at the way things were turning out. Helpless is a better word."

Like the Grand Coulee Dam cracking open, I thought, and she was trying to stop the deluge with a drinking glass.

"Everything's gone wrong." Her lips formed a grim line. "Maybe discovering Aunt Silvia was sick... No, that's not it. It's my fault. It's me. I'm changing."

"You too?" My mouth widened into a grin.

"Are you making fun of me?"

"Not at all. I can relate. Last month I was walking around like a robot. Today I feel like a million bucks. I really do." I was too happy not to let it show. "It's not only Glenn. Although he's part of it."

Angela's pale face wore a mask of misery. I scolded myself for causing her pain. It wouldn't hurt me to be kinder. From now on, I'd try to emulate Silvia. Why hadn't I thought of that earlier?

But I had to ask, "Do you have the hots for Glenn?"

She coughed a false laugh. "No, don't be silly." As if on stage after final curtain call, she turned away, her loose hair swinging to conceal her features. "This is a ridiculous conversation," she said over her shoulder. "I'm married."

"What does that have to do with anything? That's like closing your eyes and plugging your ears during a storm and then claiming it's a clear day."

"Don't worry about me." Her voice waned as she retreated from the room. "My eyes are wide open."

TWENTY-NINE

Angela

I climbed the stairs and entered the bathroom, looking for dental floss. Rose's clear-plastic cosmetic bag, containing a razor, a travel-sized bottle of mouthwash, and tweezers, perched on the glass shelf above peach-colored hand towels.

When I awoke this morning and found Rose gone, I figured she'd gussied herself up, flounced over to Glenn's house, and charmed her way in like a magazine salesman. She'd claimed she'd cooked and served him breakfast. The idea of Rose and Glenn cozying up filled me with envy, followed by loathing. Why, I could have fixed a much finer meal than Rose: French toast with warmed maple syrup or eggs Benedict with Hollandaise sauce. And I'd clean up after myself, unlike Rose, who'd probably left the mess for Edna.

I picked up Rose's cosmetic bag and scanned the contents on the other side: hairpins, Maybelline mascara, Cover Girl foundation, and powder blush. Nothing out of the ordinary, like birth-control pills. Were they hidden in her suitcase? She'd managed to avoid getting pregnant all these years. But she could accidentally-on-purpose forget to use birth control, entrapping Glenn into fathering a child. A revolting thought.

I heard Rose downstairs singing to herself: a lovely lyric soprano voice any choir director would welcome. She sounded as if she had lots to croon about, as if her future were unfolding, while my life was narrowing into a one-way street.

I pulled on the medicine cabinet's faceted glass handle and peeked inside to see several bottled tinctures I'd never heard of: cat's claw, samento, teasel root, and what looked to be homeopathic remedies. Plastic vials of antibiotics—Doxycycline and Ceftin—crowded next to a cluster of sleep and pain medications. Did Aunt Silvia's aching limbs keep her awake at night, contributing to insomnia and low energy?

I located dental floss, reeled out a couple of feet, and wrapped one end around my finger. My hands performed the mindless task, a sawing motion between my teeth that might tax an older woman with arthritis. I chided myself for not asking Silvia about her illness and treatment. When Mom was sick, I'd accepted her doctor's diagnosis without question; I never suggested Mom seek a second or third opinion. I should have gone to the library or googled articles about MS, lupus, and heart disease, and become the family expert. Mom's symptoms paralleled Silvia's: fatigue, migrating aches and pain, dizziness, brain fog and memory loss, followed by heart blockage.

When Mom left Pennsylvania it seemed she tried to erase all traces of her former life. On one of her rare visits, did she carry Lyme disease with her to Seattle—an ironic legacy that eventually killed her? I wished Silvia had a computer and Internet access so I could spend the rest of the day amassing information about the illness. Not that I was as proficient on the Web as Tiffany and Daniel.

Last night I'd missed my two kids fiercely, but my longing changed to vexation when I called home. Tiffany answered the phone in a chipper voice, and then she turned into a sourpuss when she recognized mine. "Sorry, I'm swamped with homework," she said. "I'm in the middle of an assignment." Without a goodbye, she handed the phone to Daniel, who didn't appreciate my saying, "Tiffany, sweetie, what would you think about a mother-daughter trip sometime? Just the two of us."

He cut me off with, "Uh, Mom? I don't think so." The rest of our conversation was like prying nails from a two-by-four using tweezers. Finally, I gave up and asked for Frederick, but Daniel said he didn't know where his dad was or when he'd be home. Figured.

. After hanging up, I'd wondered how I could garner my family's respect, or at least their attention. What would my ungrateful brood think if I stayed here another six months or a year? Would the dirty clothes mountain at the bottom of the laundry chute, the mold on the uneaten leftovers in the refrigerator putrefy, and the dirty dishes in the kitchen sink pile so high that my husband and children would beg for my return? Unlikely, since Olga, our cleaning lady, had a key to the house and showed up weekly. Frederick preferred the way she folded his boxers better than my method.

Like a banner unfurling itself, a startling decision came to me. I was going to stay here, at least through the winter and into spring. If and when I returned to Seattle I could file for separation. No, I might as well file for divorce and get the inevitable over with. I remembered the name of an attorney my husband hated, probably because the man was as pugnacious as Frederick. With the lawyer's help, I was pretty sure Frederick would be forced to maintain my lifestyle.

In any case, I should go back to school and get a teaching degree. I wasn't stupid; in college I'd earned excellent grades. Or could I be a dancing teacher's assistant? I'd volunteer for a few months to see how it went.

As my outrageous thoughts spread their limbs and made themselves comfortable in my mind, I waited for panic to grab hold of me, for my vision to dim and my legs to weaken. But I felt fine: strong and in control. I scooped in a chest-full of air. I didn't live in fear of losing Frederick anymore.

Returning to the first floor, my bare feet breezed down the stairs. If I didn't know better, I'd say I weighed pounds less. Without effort, I stepped over Rex, lazing at the bottom of the steps. "Good boy." Guess I wasn't fearful of this big fellow anymore either.

The telephone chimed. I crossed the living area to answer it. "Hello?"

"Angela?" Glenn's voice sent a tingling swoosh of excitement from my belly up through my chest, like when an amusement park ride took an unexpected dip. He was no doubt calling Rose or Silvia, but I didn't care. I'd enjoy a brief but meaningful chat with him. We could talk about puppies, a perfectly innocent topic. And who knows where our conversation might lead us?

"Hi, Glenn. You're just the person I wanted to speak to." I was unable to disguise my eagerness. And why should I?

"Who's Glenn?" Frederick's words pinged out the receiver like plastic bullets. I felt caught—guilty. Had my voice revealed I was captivated by another man?

"Angela? Is that you?"

"Yes, Fred. I thought you were someone else." Oops, I'd accidentally abbreviated his name. I was in double trouble, but I wouldn't apologize. He was just Fred to me now.

"Who's this Glenn person?" His words drilled into me like a jackhammer.

"Did you call for a reason, Frederick?"

"Yes. My appointment canceled so I've decided to pick you and your sister up at the airport after all." He always avoided saying Rose's name. Yes, she was ornery, but he should treat her with respect if for no other reason than she was my sibling.

"Give me your flight number," he said, doling out orders. "When you land, call me on my cell phone."

My feet planted themselves; I was rooted here in this room. "That won't be necessary. You don't have to pick us up." I glanced around at the eclectic mix of furniture, the old-fashioned pieces harmonizing like flowers in an Amish garden. "Frederick, I may not be coming home."

After a moment, he said, "What do you want from me?" He switched his tone and spoke blandly, apparently restraining his temper. "I said I'd come to the airport. You win this round, okay?"

"This isn't a contest. And I'm done being the family doormat."

"Huh? You have the easiest life of any person I know. I'm the one who slaves all day." Someone must have walked into his office because he said, "Put them on the desk and close the door when you leave," in a muffled voice. Then he trumpeted, "Angela, you dilly-dally all day long doing nothing."

"Maybe you're right. I'm lazy." I pictured myself in the mall searching for unneeded outfits that went unworn. "If I'm guilty of wasting my life, I have no one to blame but myself. But that's going to change."

"But— I put a bundle in your account every month."

His words made me realize I was too old to be on an allowance. Didn't I legally own part of the law practice? It was once my father's. Which made me Frederick's partner. I should review the monthly profit-and-loss statements, and write my own checks. Someday I'd make an appointment with the accountant and learn how to read the books.

"You're a good provider, but this conversation isn't about money. I'm not going to be invisible anymore," were my final words, before saying goodbye. He didn't comment.

Clunking the phone into its cradle, I felt my heart pounding like a rock in a tin can. Frederick was right. I lived like a queen and had no justification to complain. Would my ranting send him into another woman's arms?

I looked out the window and saw Rose clad in running tights and a zipped hooded sweatshirt, helping Silvia load her wheelbarrow. Rose had sized Frederick up from the start. I wondered if she knew he was cheating on me but didn't let on. Or if he'd ever made a pass at her.

Outside, she lifted the wheelbarrow's handles, pressed her weight forward, and wobbled the three-wheeled cart around the side of the house, out of sight. I'd tossed away my chance for her friendship when I got honest about Glenn. She'd never forgive me. But I needed to stop fretting about Rose and about Frederick. Which left what to think about? Glenn. Silvia.

I wondered when her quilting group met again. In the meantime, I'd ask Silvia to help me start a small sample. She'd taught me that it was okay to remain childlike. Even with death stalking her, she was serene and centered. Where did she find her confidence?

Rex stretched to his feet, wandered over to me, and rested his chin on my knee. "You don't have to worry about anything, do you?" I stroked his head and my pulse relaxed to a steady beat. After a few minutes, Rex seemed sated of attention and returned to the bottom of the steps. I got to my feet and thumbed through Silvia's personal telephone book to find Glenn's home number.

"Glenn," I blurted out before realizing I was speaking to his recorder. His message stated he regretted missing my call. After the beep I said, "It's Angela, Silvia's niece. I'm serious about wanting one of Missy's puppies."

Thirty

Rose

Silvia and I ascended the forested hillside above the house. We inched along, the way she paused every few minutes to admire a wild dogwood, spicebush, or witch hazel. Or pointed out the melodious trilling of a wood thrush. At this rate we'd never make it to the top.

More than an hour ago, I'd steered her wheelbarrow to the lane near the vegetable garden where she gave me my preliminary pruning lesson. When she set aside her loppers, I'd asked about the view from the hilltop. "Can you see down the valley?"

"Yes, on a clear day. It's been five years since I've ventured up there. Want to take a look?"

"Absolutely. This is my last opportunity." Angela and I would return to Seattle midday tomorrow.

Our arms linked, we strolled in tandem across the lawn then cut through the sloping apple orchard. The thick grass stuck to our calves. We scaled a path skirting a stone fence, a three-foot-high structure of granite chunks. Each would take four strong men to lift. When I asked Silvia how the fence got there, she said farmers removed the stones from the rock-infested soil two hundred years ago and constructed it as a boundary.

We crawled along, finally nearing the summit. The fence slanted off at a forty-five degree angle, blocking our progress. On the other side, the deciduous trees were interspersed with pines and other evergreens.

"This is where my property ends. My neighbors don't mind us coming here. At least the old ones didn't. It's been so long, they could have sold their acreage. But since they're Amish, I doubt it."

"Do you want to turn back?" I wondered how she would manage to scale the fence. And I doubted there'd be much of a view through the trees.

"No, we've come this far."

"Then we'll forge ahead." I considered the many favors I could have done for Mother in her last few months. Errands to the drugstore, books from the library, cups of broth or tea.

I picked my way over the fence and then reached back to take Silvia's hand. Her fingers were like a child's. Soft and fragile, allowing themselves to be held as I guided her. Stopping on the apex, she teetered before finding her footing on another rock. She was wearing beige Keds and white socks.

Her full weight came down hard on the ground. But she seemed pleased with her accomplishment. "We used to scramble over these rocks like chipmunks, your mother and I." She surveyed the length of the fence. "Our summer days were spent dashing around playing hide-and-seek and trying to get lost. But we always found our way home when we got hungry."

"I can't imagine Mother playing up here."

"Juliana was as adventuresome as our brother. She'd even hold the snakes and spiders Leo caught. I guess you'd call her a tomboy until her teens."

"She sounds like me. Or is it the other way around? I was like her? Are you sure? I figured you and Mother had the same kind of relationship Angela and I did. My big sister was always a hot-house plant. I loved the out of doors. No matter the weather."

Her grin turned impish. "Actually, around the fifth grade I got caught up in the Nancy Drew mysteries, which kept me inside many an afternoon. People change."

Could they really? Unlikely. But I didn't voice my doubts.

We took several steps up the slope. She stopped to gaze at a cluster of white dapple-barked birch trees, standing like a field of picket fences. Or was she catching her breath?

"Don't expect all your answers in one fell swoop," she declared, apparently commenting on my statement thirty minutes earlier, that my life wasn't turning out as planned. As if only a moment had transpired. "I suggest you let your ball of yarn unwind as it will. Some people spend their energy trying to keep their world from unraveling, attempting to hold on to what they know. But eventually it all falls apart." My eyes followed her gaze up through the canopy of almost-bare branches to see shapes of indigo-blue sky framed like stained-glass windows by the steely brown bark.

She turned to me and said, "You might as well enjoy the ride, make your life a glorious journey instead of trying to play it safe, doing what you've always done." She coughed. The sound registered in my ears like an alarm. Like when you leave a store and the anti-theft device goes off. Even if you haven't done anything wrong, all eyes turn on you and you feel convicted.

"Let's rest for a minute." I noticed a low slab of stone pushed up against the hillside like a bench, several yards away. I led her to it. She maneuvered herself to a sitting position. Her complexion had turned ashen gray. Her gaze set blankly on the forest floor. Then her lids slid shut.

The sun dipped behind the treetops. Now that we were stationary, cool air penetrated my hoodie and tights. It must be after five. The sky's color was draining and the trees blended into one another. I hugged myself for warmth, rubbed my upper arms. I'd been a nitwit for bringing Silvia up here so late in the day, her wearing a cotton blouse and her lightweight denim jacket. No hat or gloves. Soon the temperature would dip to the forties or lower. In the paper this morning, the weatherman had predicted arctic air approaching from the north.

Except for a twig cracking under foot when I shifted my weight, the air fell silent. The birds, once abundant, had stopped their calling. Nocturnal animals like opossums, badgers, and coyotes would soon preside over these woods. What creatures watched us with glowing infrared eyes even now as I scanned the forest? I wasn't usually spooked by wildlife, but I shuddered. They could observe us clearly while we turned blind without sunlight.

Silvia's eyes remain closed. Two slits across a chalky mask. Her mouth opened, the weight of her jaw unhinging and dragging down. I watched her face for signs of life. Her features lay motionless.

She'd stopped breathing. What should I do? I didn't know how to perform CPR.

"Aunt Silvia, wake up!" Her ribs expanded to take a shallow breath. I knelt and wrapped an arm around her shoulder. Hoping to rouse her, I rocked gently. She felt light, but I wasn't strong enough to carry her home. I considered dashing back to the house for help, but how would I find my way back here again? Even if I returned, Silvia could catch pneumonia. Or take her final breath and pass into the next realm to join Mother.

Silvia stirred. Her eyes opened to half-mast. She wasn't wearing her glasses. When and where did they fall off? We'd never find them now.

"Dear, I've heard that the elders of a local Indian tribe used to wander off to the caves in these hills to die. Much better than a hospital bed."

Had we entered the Twilight Zone? "You can't die yet." My voice echoed with throaty vibrato. "I'd never forgive myself." Tears stung the backs of my eyes, but I contained them. This fiasco was my fault. I must not fall apart.

"Sorry. I didn't mean to scare you." She sat up somewhat straighter, for my benefit, I assumed.

"I'll tell you something ironic, dear." I heard a tremor in her voice. "When bad things happened I used to console myself by saying, 'It could be worse.' One of the kids would flunk a math test. 'Could be worse,' I'd tell myself. My husband was fooling around again. 'It could be worse.' Then, my sister, Juliana, called to tell me she was dying. And I could come up with no cliché to comfort myself." Another cough erupted from the bottom of her chest. "I actually felt responsible, as if my jealousy had caused her to get sick. I prayed, 'Please, Lord, forgive me and save Juliana's life. Perform a miracle.'" She paused, and then inhaled through her mouth. "Now I'm the one who needs the miracle."

I didn't want her talking like this. Each word pierced my eardrums. "It isn't fair," I said.

"You're right. Life is sometimes not fair from our perspective. A couple of months ago I was driving into town minding my own business when a cement truck zoomed out of a driveway and nearly rammed into me. He would have if I hadn't swerved. I barely missed a telephone pole and mailbox. I could have died right then and there, way before my doctor's schedule."

"I'm glad you didn't. I wouldn't have gotten to know you." I tightened my embrace.

"We have many choices, Rose, but we can't choose our final breath."

A tear escaped and trickled down my cheek. "I won't let you die tonight." I stroked her back, felt a narrow rib cage. "I'm not done pumping your well, learning your secrets to happiness."

"Rose, only through God can we attain contentment. He loves you."

"Not me. I'm damaged goods."

"He'll make you new if you let him."

Her words were a balm, quieting the perpetual negative voices reverberating in my brain. I felt a new sense of peace and joy.

Her face gathered movement. "I could show you several verses in Psalms that have given me strength. If you wouldn't mind."

"Okay. I remember from Sunday school, 'The Lord is my Shepherd, I shall not want.' And something about walking through the valley of death."

"The Twenty-third Psalm. I'll write it out on a card for you. In fact, I have an extra Bible, if you'd like it."

"All right. Not the memento I'd planned on taking home with me, but I'll keep it by my bed and read a few pages every night."

Darkness surrounded us. An opaque shroud like a black hole. Where were the moon and the stars? A blanket of fog must have rolled in. I stared toward where I thought the house stood. No lights. No cars on the road. No battery-powered buggy headlamps or blinking orange taillights. No horse's metal shoes.

Getting to my feet, my ankles informed me the slope was steep. I leaned into the hill to steady myself. I took her hand and pulled her to a standing position.

"You point us in the right direction and I'll get us there." I felt uncertain. None of the inky silhouettes looked familiar. What if her internal compass had spun around too? Still, as long as we headed downhill, logic assured me we should eventually come to the road.

Her first step wobbled. I slipped my hand under her elbow and then around her waist. As we picked our way to the stone fence, the earth thickened, going spongy. My weight sank into the pillow of leaves. Before I knew what was happening, Silvia fell out of my grasp. She tumbled forward, landing on her hands and knees. I let myself sink down beside her, the ground so soft it swallowed us up.

"Are you all right?" I asked, pleading with the Lord at the same time.

"I think so. I've become a clumsy old woman."

"No. It was my fault. I should have stationed myself downhill below you. Do you think you broke anything?"

Her ghostlike face reminded me of Mother's when she lay on death's bed. An eclipse of the moon. I was as helpless now as I was then. Puny. I was incapable of caring for others. But I picked myself up and then lifted Silvia to her feet. She teetered, but I steadied her. "I won't let you fall again," I vowed.

I made good use of the biceps I'd built working out in the gym and hauling lumber for my birdhouses. Crossing the fence, I grasped her under the armpits and took on half her weight. We stopped several times as Silvia coughed and then gasped for breath. I wouldn't allow her to sit down for fear she wouldn't get up again.

I saw an arc of light bouncing off tree trunks and stretching out. Then my eyes distinguished the shape of a man and two large dogs zigzagging in front of him.

"Glenn!" I hollered. "Is that you?"

Angela opened the front door as we approached the house. She must have been watching for us through the window. She was wearing the same taut expression of the woman I saw last winter on TV whose snowboarding son was missing in avalanche country.

"Where have you been? Is Aunt Silvia all right?" Angela's words burbled out of her mouth like marbles.

"Mostly tired," said Glenn. I'm glad he didn't mention Silvia and I were lost. Or how frightened I was. I was sure he'd picked up on it. I doubted Silvia could have kept going much longer. Her coughing was almost constant. Propelling itself into overdrive. Robbing her of oxygen.

He carried her inside and lowered her onto the couch. When he'd found us, with Rex and Missy's assistance, Silvia had insisted she was capable of walking. But Glenn paid no attention. He scooped her up in his arms and declared she weighed less than a bag of compost. "Let me be a hero," he'd said. Then he handed me the flashlight and pointed me in the right direction.

Finally inside, my fingertips stung as toasty air surrounded them. Angela had the heat cranked up to eighty. Or maybe my body temperature had lowered. I kept my hoodie zipped up and my hands in the pockets. I was grateful for the safety of this room. But I felt exhausted, numb. I could crawl into bed and sleep for twenty-four hours.

My sister draped a lap blanket around Silvia's shoulders. "I was scared to death," Angela said. "I called Glenn. I figured he knew your property. I was about to call the police."

Silvia tugged the blanket up around her neck so only her face showed. "I'm afraid I slowed poor Rose down. We were enjoying ourselves. Right, dear?"

"Yes." I tried to maintain a composed expression. "At least on our way up the hill."

"I'm grateful beyond words you're all right." Angela placed a hand on Silvia's forehead as if checking one of her kids for fever. Then Angela's eyes locked onto mine. "I was worried about both of you," she said. "If anything happened to my little sister, I don't know what I'd do."

In other words, she'd miss me if I never returned? Really? Or would my permanent absence simplify her life?

THIRTY-ONE

Angela

Tucked Aunt Silvia into her bed with a hot water bottle and an extra woolen blanket. Her skin was sallow, as if the blood had receded, wilting her cheeks.

"Make sure she rests," her doctor had told me on the phone minutes ago. He seemed well acquainted with her tendency to take on too much.

The moment I hung up, Silvia apologized for not feeding us dinner and being a better hostess. "I'm not used to all this fuss," she'd said, and then she emitted a cough—I hoped not the first sign of pneumonia. With her vitality compromised, would the Lyme disease gain velocity, spiraling through her body like a forest fire?

I heard Rose's and Glenn's voices out in the hallway, speaking too quietly to be clearly understood. Something was happening between those two, making me miserable.

Silvia stretched her hand toward the lamp.

"I'll get that." I flicked it off, darkening the room. Deprived of light, my senses were dulled. I'd spent every ounce of adrenalin worrying about her and Rose. Thirty minutes after they'd disappeared this afternoon, I coaxed Rex outside to search for them. I thought he would identify Silvia's scent and track her down like Lassie, but he was content to stop at various bushes to sniff and lift his leg. I'd located the wheelbarrow outside the vegetable garden and called their names, and then I moved to the road past Silvia's mailbox, which I found full of envelopes and catalogues, indicating they hadn't gone that way. Then I'd circled around to the driveway and saw Silvia's car. Back in the house, with Rex snoozing again, my mind delved into frightening possibilities. Had Silvia and Rose been kidnapped? No, it was unlikely anyone would abduct them to hold for ransom because we weren't millionaires, and I would have been contacted by now. Another thought: while strolling the road, had one of them been hit by a car or buggy, then whisked off to the hospital? No, I hadn't heard a siren. I'd finally convinced myself Silvia and Rose had moseyed down the road a half-mile to visit a neighbor. But although Rose would forget all about me, Silvia would have called to tell me where they were so I wouldn't worry. Unless the neighbors were Amish and didn't own a phone.

To allay my fears, I brought out my novel and finished the final chapter. Amanda conveniently received a scholarship to continue her studies in Paris; Ramon was exonerated of thievery and offered a job at a prestigious auction house. On July fourteenth, Bastille Day, the two lovers shared a kiss under the Arc de Triomphe. Passions sizzled as the fireworks rainbowed across the sky. A joyous finale— what I'd expected.

But not what I wanted. Today I'd needed a *Casablanca*, Humphrey Bogart and Ingrid Bergman ending: a noble farewell, because a marriage commitment outweighed personal longings. Something to guide me back to Frederick instead of giving me the green light to call the airline to cancel my ticket and stay here.

Silvia's head sank into the down pillow. Her lids shut and her breathing slowed to a shallow rhythm through parted lips. How could I leave her? Sure, Cousin Phyllis lived close by, but Silvia needed constant companionship. And Phyllis seemed to find Silvia exasperating—sort of the way Rose was repelled by Mom.

I stepped toward the open door and saw Rose and Glenn.

Towering over her, he grasped both her hands. Her gaze was lowered and her posture bent; she looked as washed-out as Silvia.

"You'll see," he said, "she'll make it through the night just fine."

Rose hugged him quickly, and then she vanished into her room.

Without noticing me, he turned to leave. He'd already said his farewells to Silvia. There was nothing more to keep him here.

I trailed him down the steps; his shoulders filled the stairwell. Missy lay by the front door, her legs folded under her torso and her chin on the floor. Rex, sacked out by the couch, didn't seem to mind her presence. Missy stretched to her feet, wagged her tail, and then she sniffed under the front door. Her girth had expanded over the last few days.

Glenn went to the sideboard, took up the flashlight he'd brought earlier, and finally glanced at me—the whole of me, not into my face. "Goodbye, Angela," he said from across the room.

This is it, I told myself. No curtain call.

Before I could respond, he opened the door and Missy hurried out, no doubt eager to get home—the nesting instinct I'd once felt before giving birth. That seemed like one million years ago. Someone else's life.

Glenn walked outside and closed the door. The latch clicked.

"Farewell, sweet prince," I whispered under my breath. Glenn was the closest thing to a prince I'd ever met. When I'd telephoned him earlier, I prefaced my request to come over with, "If you're not too busy." He'd replied there was nothing he wouldn't drop to help Silvia, or any friend. His laying everything aside to fly here filled me with elation. Now I wondered what he was doing when I called. I forgot to ask if he missed dinner. And I forgot to thank him. How rude and thoughtless.

In a burst, I dove into my jacket. My hand tore at the knob. As I tried to swing the door open, its corner caught on the area rug. I kicked the mat aside and lumbered after him. Following Missy, he was halfway to his truck.

I felt like I was stepping into a canoe in the middle of a lake. I loped toward him in uneven steps. He was only feet away, but he still hadn't turned around.

"Glenn. Wait. I forgot to thank you."

He pivoted to face me, his somber features illuminated by the porch light. "No need. I was glad to help."

As I stared into his face, I felt a tingle of attraction rekindling itself, welling up in my chest like a breath I couldn't quite catch. Glenn's handsome features were engraved in my mind and carved in my heart. I'd never forget him. And why should I?

I thought of Frederick—he'd be infuriated if he knew what had fueled my desire to stay here. Or maybe he'd be relieved to get me out of his hair. Did I care what he thought?

What happened to me? I'd always viewed Rose as out of control and man crazy, but maybe I was the sister with the problem. Was I falling for Glenn or was I merely obsessed with him?

The night air surrounding us, I found another excuse to continue our conversation. "I should give you my telephone number or email address. For the puppy. I want a girl that looks like Missy. I wish I'd brought paper and pencil with me."

When Missy heard her name, she moved to Glenn's side.

Glenn held the darkened flashlight to his middle. A protective gesture? "I can't guarantee there will be any females, but if there are, I'll let you know through Rose. She's thinking about taking one too."

"What for? She already has a dog." Did Rose decide to buy a puppy just to spite me? Was she planning to blitz Glenn with emails and phone calls that she'd explain as business-related? I felt the horns of sibling rivalry pushing through the top of my skull.

Then, from the depths of my childhood memories, I recalled the morning Rose's piebald guinea pig, Mulligan, died. Devastated, eight-year-old Rose had folded her furry pet in a towel and buried him in the yard next to the birdbath. She solemnly marked the spot with a stone with the letter M painted on top with red nail polish and then lingered by the grave until Dad insisted she come in for dinner. The next day, Mom offered to buy Rose another pet, but she'd refused because she said there'd never be another Mulligan. Which demonstrated her loyalty. More than I possessed.

Struggling for equilibrium, I couldn't help asking Glenn, "Will you miss Rose?" *And me*, I wanted to add. Would he miss me?

His face relaxed into a smile. "She's nothing like the women my mother tries to fix me up with, that's for sure—" He cut himself off, flicking on the flashlight and splashing a cream-colored glow across the bushes. His voice and actions told me he considered Rose a viable candidate in the dating department. He might have been attracted to me when we met, but those feelings were long gone now. I was relieved I'd never shared my fantasies with him. Wouldn't I be embarrassed? It was time to start acting like a real big sister, like Jo in *Little Women*. That is, put Rose's interests ahead of my own.

I moved closer. "Rose might be open to a relationship if the right man came along."

He chuckled, flicking off the flashlight. "Even so, it would be a long drive to pick her up for a movie or dinner."

"True." I could think of multiple reasons why a relationship between them would not work. For one thing, she belonged in Seattle, with our father. She didn't even like Lancaster County—not the way I did. And wouldn't she make Glenn miserable in the end? She'd drop him after a month and swing back to smooth-talking Brad or someone like him. She went for those pretty-face boys.

"Well, goodbye." I put out my hand to shake his—a formal gesture, when in fact I wanted to hug Glenn. To hold on to him and never let go.

For a moment my hand hung in midair, like a hummingbird hovering, and then his hand rose up to take it, his fingers surrounding mine. Even in the shadows I could see his gaze embracing mine. We stood there, grasping each other for a moment. Or was I the one who did all the holding?

Then simultaneously our fingers loosened, and we stepped apart.

Thirty-Two

Rose

On Angela's and my final morning in Lancaster County, we sat at Silvia's bedside. Angela occupied the overstuffed chair, and I was on a straight-back chair borrowed from my room. The rain scattering on the roof above us sounded like children's feet running.

Except for letting her make a trip to the bathroom, Angela and I insisted Silvia remain in bed. Not an easy feat to corral a woman who usually burst into action the moment she woke. But over the length of the night her cough had worsened. I could hear the hacking from across the hall. I brought her a cup of herbal tea, a blend including ginger, around one a.m. and then again at three. The warm liquid seemed to tame her coughing.

Fifteen minutes ago, I brewed coffee. Angela fixed oatmeal, topped with brown sugar and milk. We arranged Silvia's breakfast on a gold Florentine tray. I carried it upstairs and placed it on Silvia's lap.

Angela seemed different today. On the quiet side. And serious. And I didn't feel my usual urge to argue with her or outdo her. I didn't even suggest she sprinkle raisins atop the oatmeal instead of using refined sugar. For once we worked as a team.

Silvia finished her last bite of oatmeal and then blotted her mouth with her napkin. "Thank you, dear ones."

I felt as if I were blindfolded and stepping into thin air. "Aunt Silvia, I've made a monumental decision." I'd rehearsed my opening line, but my mouth seemed clogged with peanut butter. I swallowed and started again. "What I'm trying to say is, I'd like to live here with you. If you'll have me."

Silvia sipped her coffee. Was she buying time? Trying to digest my statement?

Angela jumped in. "You can't be serious, Rosie. What about your business?"

"I don't blame you for being shocked. I was too." In the waning hours of the night, I'd prayed. With God at my side, I wasn't flying solo anymore. I'd measured and weighed my future like a chemist pondering a new formula. I kept coming up with the same solution. "I can make birdhouses and conduct my mail-order business just as easily from here. The main reason I work at home is Walter next door. But he and his wife are moving into a retirement home after Christmas. I'll buy a space heater and set up shop in Silvia's garage."

Angela gaped at me as though I were speaking pig latin. "Is this about a certain person?" She dipped her chin and lifted her brows in a knowing way. Telling me she was referring to Glenn. I had no doubt he would have gathered Amish neighbors and searched all night until they'd found Silvia and me.

"Sis, I've never met a finer man. He strikes me as someone whose sense of right and wrong outweighs momentary pleasure." Those of us who've lived through hell have gleaned a kind of smarts and determination more fortunate people lack. "Even so, I wouldn't move clear across the country with the notion of ensnaring a man. I'm not that kooky or presumptuous. It would be for me. I want to help Silvia. The way I should have served Mother." I removed the tray, set it on the dresser, and then returned to my chair.

"You're sweet, dear, but I can't accept your generosity. You mustn't put your life on hold for me."

My heart swelled with gladness as I straightened her covers.

"Living here won't slow me down." I recalled the decrepit barn I saw our second day, its boards feathered gray like the breast of a turtle-dove. "When Angie and I were out driving, I noticed a barn ready to collapse. I'm planning to track down its owner, and if the wood's for sale, I'll buy the boards to make birdhouses. And a potting table for you, Aunt Silvia. I've been toying with some new design ideas. If Glenn gives me the okay, I'll sell the tables at his nursery. I like Lancaster County, buggies and all. Everything in Seattle is too new. No history there." I pictured myself submerged in freeway traffic, my fingernails drumming the steering wheel. I used to think the city's hubbub energized me. Not anymore.

"Won't you be bored?" Angela tried to communicate through narrowed eyes. I ignored her.

"No, sis, I'll find plenty to keep me busy. I'll finish Silvia's puzzle. Then buy another. And another."

"But you said living here would make you crazy."

My shoulders lifted. "Guess I've made an about-face that will surprise everyone."

"Dad will think you've flipped your lid." Angela's mouth grew small. As if he were listening in on our conversation. About to chastise us.

"I'd be lying if I said I didn't care what Father thought of me. I do. Too much. I can hear him now. He'll lecture me on sound financial choices and call me irresponsible. He's not used to me defying him. He might even cut me out of his will. But he's been wrong about things. And wrong about people. Like about Aunt Silvia."

Silvia coughed, sounding like the breeze rustling dry leaves. "Rose, dear, how about all your friends? Won't you miss them?"

"I have a new one. You. I've made up my mind. There's no chang-ing it. Angie can tell you how stubborn I am." Kindly, Angela didn't agree that often I was a bulldozer stuck in high gear. But this time tenacity would pay off.

"On the practical side, I need to tie up loose strings," I said. "I know a Realtor who can rent out my furnished house or even sell it for me. I'll get my business caught up. Pack my necessities and tools. And return to Pennsylvania within two weeks. I think I can manage all that. The only problem is whether Rex will eat my little dog, Minnie."

"He's a big showoff. You saw how he acted with Missy here last night. He loves other dogs. Even cats." Silvia's face was a treasure map of fine lines. "But I can't believe you'd want to live way out here with an old woman. A sick old woman, to be precise. You realize I'm dying."

"Who says you're going to die? I won't let you."

A grin crept across her face. "Rose, dear, even you can't stop that."

"But I'm not ready to say goodbye." Although eventually I'd have to. I imagined her in heaven, wearing a flowing robe of fabric lighter than chiffon. Lounging on a cloud playing her cello.

"Do you think there really is a heaven?" My voice wavered as I steered our conversation down a blind alley. "That you'll see Mother again?"

"Yes, I look forward to it. Juliana and I will be sporting new perfected bodies, just like God promised."

Did that mean in heaven my emotional scars would be healed? But what about here on earth? How could I rid myself from my assailant, Dirk, the invisible piggyback who still navigated my life? I ached to vocalize my thoughts. I'd bottled my agony inside too long. I couldn't wait to share my story. The whole grotesque tragedy. But now was not the time.

Angela's features tightened as she glanced in my direction. "Do *you* think Mom got into heaven?"

"I don't know." I wondered if she was including me in the discard arena. Where jaded people who weren't invited to God's final fiesta waited out eternity.

"Even in the last moments of life, God is quick to forgive," Silvia assured us.

"I hope you're right." Angela's head gave a slight shake.

"If he's anything like me, he won't." I got this itchy feeling akin to regret. Or maybe sorrow for all the wasted hours I'd fumed and plotted revenge. "I've held on to every wrong committed against me."

"So have I," Silvia said. "If I'd forgiven your mother, we might have enjoyed a true friendship, like I hope you two girls have someday."

"We're getting there," I said.

One corner of Angela's mouth lifted, but her thoughts seemed far away.

THIRTY-THREE

Angela

*R*ose and I lingered in the kitchen cleaning up after Silvia's breakfast. Rose stood at the sink, chiseling burned oatmeal off the bottom of the pot with a spatula. I wondered why she'd insisted on tackling the unpleasant chore even though I made the mess when I turned the stovetop up too high. She must have wanted my hands free to pack my suitcase so we could leave.

I dawdled. I felt as if I were straddling the San Andreas Fault. I'd seen photos of the giant fissure left by earthquakes. I needed to leap to one side or the other before I toppled into the crevice.

I looked around the kitchen and inhaled the trace aroma of decades of cooking: yeast, marinara sauce, garlic, nutmeg. My eyes canvassed the wall, fixing on the framed words *Dopo il bruto viene il bello*, embroidered by Grandma Luisa's hands. Silvia had suggested Rose and I each select a piece of furniture or object as our own. "Put your name on a slip of paper and tape it to the back so Phyllis can send it to you when I don't need it anymore," she'd said.

I chose the embroidery because it would remind me of Silvia's heritage and because Grandma had something in mind when she skillfully stitched each word. Loosely translated it meant *After the storm comes a beautiful day.*

What a lovely thought, if only it were true.

When Rose announced she intended to fly to Seattle and then return to live with Silvia, it was as if my sister had barged into my mind and was speaking my thoughts. Then a moment later Silvia thanked her and talked about heaven, sealing the deal. Ruining everything for me.

Rose turned off the water and tipped the pot over in the drying rack. "You should be packing, sis." Her duffel bag already sat by the front door. She'd left most of her clothes in the upstairs bedroom for when she came back. "Phyllis will be here in an hour to pick us up and then it's off to the airport."

"I'm vacillating." Half of me in a trance. "I could stay longer."

Rose's brows furrowed. "What on earth for?"

I considered several motives, but only one I'd share. "To make up for lost opportunities. I didn't spend enough time with Mom in her last months. I let my children and Frederick and my self-imposed busyness distract me. Even during the school day, I flitted around like a moth circling our porch light, accomplishing the insignificant. Mom needed me at her side, loving her."

My legs weakened as I envisioned Silvia confined to her bed, making Rose's moving across the country all the more painful. "How can I say goodbye to Aunt Silvia when her health is deteriorating so quickly? Just yesterday morning she seemed strong enough to thrive another year, but today she's running a low fever. This afternoon her temperature may spike. I'm used to nursing Daniel and Tiffany when they're sick."

Rose grabbed a hand towel. "Phyllis promised she'll look in on Silvia after she drops us off," she said, as if our cousin's brief visit would solve everything. Phyllis was my age, but I bet she and Rose would fall into a tight friendship that excluded me. If I stayed, I'd be the one to enjoy the relationship with Phyllis, and with Silvia.

"Rosie, I still don't understand why you want to move here."

"Unlike you, I have no one depending on me in Seattle but Minnie. For once being single and childless is a good deal. Silvia might recover with me here to keep her company." She dried her hands, blotting each finger thoroughly. "I'm going on a mission to locate a better Lyme-literate doctor, as Glenn calls them. To get a second opinion."

"But if you stay, you might get Lyme disease too."

"I'll be extra careful. Anyway, Glenn says tick-related diseases have spread all over the country. Even to Washington State." Always, her pendulum swung back to Glenn.

I crossed my arms. "I still don't buy your radical transformation. I remember the day we arrived—your wisecracks about this house, not to mention the Amish."

She folded the towel into a neat rectangle and hung it on the oven door handle. "Yeah, I was acting like a bratty kid tasting her first broccoli. In truth, I have much to learn from them. I might even give studying Pennsylvania Dutch a stab. I'm good at picking up languages."

I didn't dare comment on her ambitious plan. Knowing Rose, if she set her mind on conquering Pennsylvania Dutch, she would.

Leaning against the counter, her elbow and hip supported her. "And I want to learn to drive a buggy. I had so much fun with Glenn."

I opened the catch-all drawer, located a pad of Post-its and a pencil, and wrote my name on the top piece of paper. "Are you sure this move isn't really for him?" My voice cracked, betraying my tumultuous emotions.

"I have lots of reasons to stay." Her chin raised, and she directed her full attention on me. "Although I like him. And so do you?"

Like seemed too banal a verb to capture my feelings for Glenn. Who wouldn't like him? I was sure his customers did. And Olivia was smitten, even if dating someone else. But did I know him well enough to love him? I said I loved chocolate, but mostly I craved it.

"I like Glenn as a friend," I said, "and because he's kind to Silvia." I was trying to convince her, and myself. I envisioned his arriving at the kitchen door on his way to survey the garden. Rose would invite him in for coffee; they'd sit with Silvia at her bedside. The intimate scene made me feel like a misfit.

I stood on tiptoes and affixed the Post-it to the back of the embroidery. Although someone like Rose could crumple up the paper and toss it away, claiming the embroidery for herself, as she'd done with everything else. Nothing was under my control. Even if Glenn didn't fall for her, he would never be mine. Because I'd either be a married woman or a divorcée with two kids living on the other side of the country. I couldn't win. And if I went home, Frederick might continue ignoring me, no matter what I did. I was enveloped with a comatose sense of letdown, like at Mom's funeral, grief and loss crowding in on me, closing off my throat.

I searched for ways to lift my spirits and recalled the counsel I gave my kids when they were down-in-the-dumps disappointed, like the soccer game when Daniel kicked his team's ball into his own goal and the day Tiffany's classmate didn't invite her to the girl's birthday party. Both seemed like terminal disasters at the time. I'd encouraged my kids to focus on the positives in their lives, which is what I should do now.

What did I have to be thankful for? For one thing, I hadn't shop-lifted for six days, a small but sturdy victory. But I pictured myself wandering the mall next week, surrounded by crowds—bored and isolated. What would stop me from falling into my bad habit again?

Okay, shoplifting was more than a habit, this impulse to amass pos-sessions, my need for an adrenaline high to conceal my pain. I could use a friend. Someone to watch over me day and night. Like a dad, only better, because he wouldn't put me down or wish I were a son or be more like Rose. Leaving God. I recalled Mom's reading to me from the Bible: "For He Himself has said, I will never leave or forsake you."

"How will you feel if Glenn and I get together?" Rose snagged me back to the present. "He said he's tired of being a bachelor." Her cheeks blushed. "He wants to spend more time with me. If it's okay with you."

"You don't need my permission."

"Yes, I do. Whoever said blood is thicker than water was right." She stood taller, her feet together. "You're more important than any man."

"I am? Thank you. I'm touched." And amazed. "I'll be fine with it. I love Frederick despite all his faults." When I said the words, something inside me loosened, giving way. "If I didn't, I guess my feelings for him would have faded to apathy. And I know he loves me too."

She kept her thoughts to herself, encouraging me to be honest.

"Rosie, I think he might be flirting with the enemy."

Her hands moved to her hips. "Anyone I know?"

"His paralegal, Stephanie." Her name filled my mouth with a sour taste, like rancid milk. "She's a twentysomething who could model for the *Sports Illustrated* swimsuit issue."

"Any proof?"

"Incontrovertible evidence, as Frederick would say? No. Just womanly intuition." Should I continue? Her open face revealed genuine concern, so I offered more data. "He stays out late and turns off his cell phone so I can't reach him." I noticed the framed embroidery hung at a tilt; I reached up to straighten it. "Not long ago I walked in his office and found them together."

Rose's mouth puckered. "Were they kissing?"

"No. He was at his desk and she was standing behind him reading his computer screen. She backstepped away so quickly when I opened the door, I'm not sure anymore." Revisiting the incident made me queasy. "Maybe it was nothing. Maybe I overreacted. But the bottom line is Frederick can't stand looking at me. He only comes to bed after the lights are out."

"Then he's nuts, sis. You're beautiful."

"That's sweet of you to say. I guess I don't blame him for losing interest." I patted my belly and grimaced. "I've let myself go."

"Because you're a few pounds overweight? If Fred doesn't recognize how phenomenal you are, he's a fool. When you get home, tell him how you feel."

"What if he doesn't care anymore?"

"You need to try."

"I should confront him, even if he roars with laughter?"

"He'd better not." Her words blasted. "He'll have to answer to me."

I followed Rose into the bedroom where my empty suitcase yawned open on the floor.

"I have an idea," Rose said. "Why don't you sign up for one of those couple's weekends? Where they teach you how to communicate. A woman told me she and her husband were on the brink of divorce when they went."

I scooped a sweater from the bureau drawer and lobbed it into the suitcase. "Roping Frederick into anything is like lassoing a bull." I collected my dirty socks and lodged them in a plastic bag. "Even if he went, he might make everyone miserable."

"But you got him to take Lamaze classes and he seemed proud he'd helped you through delivery."

"Both times he looked away at the last minute. A nurse had to prop him up so he wouldn't faint."

"So? At least he was there. Our father never would have gone to the hospital with Mother." She wedged my cosmetic bag into the suitcase between two pairs of heels I'd never worn because my dressy outfits didn't fit this casual lifestyle.

"You should fight for your marriage," she said.

My first reaction was to ask what she knew about marriage, but I wouldn't speak that way to a girlfriend. I'd rather have Rose as a friend than win another senseless argument. But going home seemed the equivalent of defeat. A mongrel with its tail between its legs; a sparrow with a broken wing.

Yet I missed Frederick. My love for him ran deep as an underground river, miles beneath the earth's surface. But somehow I'd let him—caused him?—to think too little of me.

"All logic says I should hold my marriage together for everyone's sake." I'd speak my mind to him even if my boldness opened the escape hatch for him to distance himself even further, into another woman's arms. "But when I get home, my husband may find me changed." I imagined his piqued expression when I announced my new dinner policy. "From now on, if you don't confirm you'll be home for dinner, I won't cook. No more hours of preparing meals, hoping you'll show up and then storing the leftovers in the refrigerator. Instead, I'll take the kids out somewhere fun. I need to work on my relationships with Daniel and Tiffany."

Thinking about my beloved children filled me with such intense longings I wondered how I'd managed to stay away from them so long. "Yes, I know they're spoiled, but no matter what kind of attitude they hand me, I adore them and need to find ways to reconnect."

"Good for you." She laid my folded slacks and a jacket into the lid of my suitcase, zipped the meshed lid closed, and then straightened up to face me. "I was like Tiffany at her age." Her eyes turned into deserts of sadness. "Even though I pushed Mother away, I needed her."

"And she needed you, Rosie. So do I. I need my sister." Hearing a volley of thunder rumble across the hill above the house, I recalled waiting while Glenn searched the woods the night before. "I was scared for you last night," I said. "I don't think I've ever been more frightened."

"Me too." Her face was transparent, like a child's. "Aunt Silvia was so weak. I thought she might die. If I'd let her down, I'd just as soon be dead myself."

I imagined autumn leaves shriveling and spinning in the wind, floating to the ground, landing upon the leaves from last year and the year before. Layers and layers, new upon old, from the beginning of time. Our lives were fleeting, each day precious, never to be seen again.

"I thought about you out there." Rose bent her head, her gaze not meeting mine. "It's time to forgive you," she said. "It's not your fault you were older and cuter. You never asked me to walk in your footsteps."

"Yes, I did. I assumed you should live your life exactly the way I did. And I was wrong. In hindsight, you're smarter and have accomplished more with your life than I have."

"Not true." She raked her fingers through her bangs. "You're the one who came up with the idea for my business. I've never thanked you. I owe my success to you."

Again, I was touched beyond description. She was still my feisty little sister, but her crustacean shell was softening. "You took the idea and ran with it," I said. "You deserve all the credit."

I checked my watch. It was time for us to bid farewell to Silvia. "Phyllis should be here any minute." I guessed I was leaving after all. I couldn't send my little sister off on the plane alone. But when I closed my suitcase and stood it on end, Rose blocked my exit.

"I'm sorry I gave the letters to Chester." She mashed her lips together for a moment. "Why am I so lamebrained?"

I wished she wouldn't bring up that hideous scene just when we were having a civil conversation. If we started fighting, I might stay here to avoid sitting next to her on the jet. "Let's not talk about it."

"Sis, early that morning, I sneaked into the storage room and read them all." She chewed on the side of her thumbnail.

"You read them without telling me? How could you?" My hands balled into fists as I envisioned her removing the sheets of paper from the envelopes, her gaze greedily devouring the words, the thrill of secrecy. For a lifetime I'd turned the other cheek and pretended I wasn't offended by her shocking actions, but not this time. It was my chance to vent, to crush her. Like I said to Frederick, I was done being a complacent doormat. But if I lit into her, I wouldn't find out what Chester's letters to Mom said. Rose would clam up and never tell me. I waited for her to answer, but she stared at my suitcase.

"Well?" I said. "What did the letters say?"

"In the last few, it sounded as if she'd apologized." Her voice came out like a sliver of light through Venetian blinds. "From what I could tell, she hated herself, but it was too late to fix her mistakes. Her only option was to move as far away as she could."

I wanted to believe Mom felt remorse. That she was young and foolish and didn't intentionally hurt Chester. I wanted my love for Mom to ease back into its former velvet-lined spot in my heart.

Rose cleared her voice. "One more thing I should tell you. I kept one of the letters. The last one he wrote."

Again, outrage pummeled into me. "You have a letter hidden somewhere?" My words hissed out like air from a punctured tire. "Are you keeping it as a souvenir? Planning to show it to Dad? To blackmail Chester?"

She wore a turtleneck and jeans, the pockets flat, so she must have the letter stashed in her purse or bag.

"Am I going to see this letter?" I restrained myself from slapping her.

"Sure. In fact, you can have it." The corners of her mouth dragged down. "I had no idea Chester would destroy the others. Sometimes I do the stupidest things. I make Mother look like an angel." She shook her head as though I couldn't possibly understand all she'd been through.

When I saw her bathed in weakness and regret, my hands unclenched. Her vulnerability dwelled just beneath her tough-guy facade.

"Someday I'd like to hear your life story from your side of the fence." I wished I could read her childhood diary to find out what had damaged her spirit.

"There is something… Maybe I'll tell you about it later." She glanced outside. Rain rattled the house as the wind kicked up, pressing against the windowpanes; shiny drops rolled down the steamy glass.

"You know those bulbs Glenn planted?" Her eyes got teary.

"They'll lie in the frozen ground all winter. Like they're dead. Waiting for the sun to warm the earth and give them life. That's me. I've waited all my life for something or someone to give me meaning." She blinked. "To fill me. To love me."

"I love you, Rosie." She didn't say she loved me in return, but that was okay, because I knew she did. I inched closer, into her forbidden zone, the three-foot perimeter she usually wouldn't allow me to enter. But she didn't move away.

Cleansing tears filled my eyes. My arms stretched out to enfold her. I'd never hugged another woman other than Mom. Not a real hug. But I grasped onto Rose with all my might.

At first her arms hung limply at her sides, then I felt them lift to embrace me. We clung to each other like siblings separated since birth.

EPILOGUE

*S*ilvia and Chester wandered behind the house to admire the flamboyant sea of red tulips—far more festive than she'd envisioned them last fall when death's hands gripped her. But steadfast Rose had nursed her through the frigid winter with the help of a doctor savvy about Lyme disease.

In her mind, Silvia thanked the Lord for her plentiful blessings.

Silvia was grateful Chester had attended Rose and Glenn's late April wedding the day before, as had several of Glenn's Amish employees. Of course, Chester was disappointed Glenn hadn't joined the Amish church. But before the ceremony, sitting next to her in a pew, Chester turned to Silvia and loosely quoted from the Bible. "In Genesis, God said it is not good that a man should be alone." Silvia wondered if Chester was speaking of himself. She'd stolen a quick peek at him, now a widower since Lilly's unexpected death late last fall after a stroke. He would be in mourning for a year, but he had often been Silvia's dinner or supper guest ever since, including coming to her home with Glenn on Christmas Day.

Rose and Glenn's wedding had been full of surprises, including Angela's arriving with her husband—not such a bad guy after all—and their two children, who immediately became enamored with Lancaster County. The four were already making plans to visit the newlyweds next year.

Angela and Frederick had held hands as they entered the church and cozied up next to each other. Since her return to Seattle, Angela had called Rose and Silvia several times. She'd been honest with Frederick about her unhappiness and fears for their family. To her delight, he'd been willing to go to counseling to rescue their marriage. Her relationships with Tiffany and Daniel were improving as well.

The girls' father had flown in to escort Rose down the aisle. He'd even given Silvia a peck on the cheek when he arrived.

Wearing a flowing white floor-length gown and a demure veil of delicate lace, Rose strolled down the aisle on her father's arm. As they reached the altar, her radiant eyes locked onto Glenn's.

The minister had asked the elated couple to repeat their vows after him.

"I, Glenn, take thee Rose, to be my wife from this day forward…" Glenn's voice was steady and sure. "To love and to cherish…"

In a blink, it was Rose's turn. "I, Rose, take thee Glenn…until death do us part."

Had there been a dry eye in the house? Silvia had dabbed tears of happiness from her cheeks.

At the reception, when Rose tossed her bridal bouquet, Olivia leaped up to snag the pale pink roses. Rose had clapped and cheered along with Angela and the other guests.

After all, Glenn had just promised to love Rose for a lifetime.

Discussion Questions

1. Which character did you identify with the most? What part of their personality and behavior did you relate to?

2. Did your feelings for this person change throughout the book? Have you ever found yourself changing your opinion about someone?

3. If you and a sibling or other family member were estranged or at odds, would your first response be to try to mend the relationship or to avoid seeing them? What might you do to rebuild the relationship?

4. Rose and Angela see themselves as opposites to the other sister. What characteristics do you think they have in common, and what obstacles do they share?

5. Past experiences often shape the contours of a person's life. Do you believe there's a way to move beyond a horrendous experience, such as Rose's, and find contentment and confidence?

6. Harboring unforgiveness can adversely affect relationships. Do you feel maintaining a grudge hurts you more than the other person?

7. In light of question 6 above, what do you think are some of the best ways to rid oneself of the burden of holding on to resentment and bitterness?

8. Both Rose and Angela are contemplating changing the course of her life. Have you ever considered making a radical transformation?

9. In Matthew 18:21-22, Peter asks Jesus how often he had to forgive his brother, and Jesus instructed Peter to forgive seventy times seven. Does this sound unrealistic and impossible?

10. This book is about connecting with family—those close by and those far off. Do you stay current with those you love?

Acknowledgments

With heartfelt sincerity, I wish to thank each of you for reading *A Letter from Lancaster County*. Thank you! I am indebted to those who have written short but sweet reviews on Amazon and other online book vendors. Your reviews are like gold to this author.

I'm thrilled that Kim Moore and the folks at Harvest House Publishers have welcomed me aboard. Many thanks to my fabulous editor, Jean Kavich Bloom.

Much appreciation for Sam and Susie Lapp, Old Order Amish author Linda Byler, Old Order Amish quilter Emma Stoltzfus of E.S. Quilts, and many generous Amish friends who prefer not to be mentioned by name, for their encouragement and for verifying facts. Thank you to the staff of the Lancaster Mennonite Historical Society, the Lancaster Italian Cultural Society's president, Rudy DeLaurentis, and to PA Lyme (http://www.palyme.org). Thanks to friend Herb Scribner, owner of Zook's Fabrics, and to Karla Hanns, for answering my many quilting questions.

Mega-gratitude to my faithful writing group, including authors Judy Bodmer, Roberta Kehle, Kathleen Kohler, Thornton Ford, Paul Malm, Peyton Burkhart, and Marty Nystrom.

And a round of applause to Chip MacGregor, my literary agent extraordinaire!

ONE

Mamm peered out my bedroom window as buggy wheels crunched to a halt in the barnyard.

"*Ach*, Evie." She spoke over her shoulder. "Rueben and Marta are here. Two days early."

I wasn't packed yet, but I plastered on a smile and said, "*Wunderbaar*," as if my whole world weren't being turned upside down. I flew to the window to see my brother's boisterous family of five gathering boxes from their buggy and making their way up the stairs to the back stoop.

Minutes later, Marta, my tall and angular sister-in-law, marched into my bedroom and gave me an unenthusiastic one-armed embrace. "Almost finished packing?"

"Uh…not quite yet. I thought you were coming the day after tomorrow." I'd hoped to leave with dignity and leisure—not be booted out of the house like a stray mutt. Although I'd known this day would come. My brother now owned the house and would run the farm so *Dat* could retire.

She straightened my *kapp* and tied the strings under my chin. "I wanted to be here to help ya." Marta's gaze landed on my unmade bed. "Where's your suitcase?" She called to her twin daughters. "*Kumm rei*, Nancy and Mary Lou. Help your *aenti* move out."

"I'm the one who needs help," *Mamm* said, I figured for my

317

benefit. "Want to see the *daadi haus*, girls?" My prudent mother had already thoroughly cleaned and moved my father's and her belongings into the small house attached to a corner of the larger home, where my grandparents had once resided.

"Ya best be packing, Eva." Marta's voice sounded domineering, as if she'd already claimed her role as matriarch of the household. "Our daughters will need to sleep in here tonight."

"They could sleep with me." I straightened my sheets, blanket, and the quilt my grandmother had made me as a girl. "We can have a slumber party."

"Why must everything be a party with you?" Her eyes squinted above her beaky nose. "If you'd stayed on the straight and narrow and found yourself a *gut* husband, you wouldn't be in this awkward predicament."

Her words harpooned into my chest, but I refused to look away. "You may be right." Although I wasn't guilty of the rumors spread about me, I recalled the words the minister expounded in church last Sunday: Turn the other cheek. "Okay. I'll get ready right now."

Marta called down the stairway to the kitchen to my *bruder*. "Rueben, will ya please bring up an empty suitcase for your sister?" Then she strode over to my solid-colored dresses and black aprons hanging on hooks on the wall. Her long arms scooped the clothing up like sheaths of harvested wheat. Before I could open my mouth to ask her to stop, she tossed them on the bed atop the quilt. I hoped my new bed would be big enough to accommodate it—if the place even had a bed. I'd neglected to inquire if it was furnished. I should have asked a myriad of questions before accepting the job.

As I gathered my toiletries, my mind spun like a windmill during a tempest. I'd planned to first drive over to the nursery and survey my new home, described as a cottage by my cousin Olivia. At this point, I'd be happy with the storage shed. Yet Olivia had told me the place was cute and recently vacated by the housekeeper who'd lived there most of her life. The cottage would be strictly Amish, meaning no electrical wires or telephone. Apparently, propane lights illumi-nated the interior, and a small refrigerator and gas stove provided cooking options. I'd also forgotten to ask her if it had a bathroom.

Reuben lumbered up the stairs and opened a suitcase on my bed. Marta gave him a look of appreciation—an outward show of affection was *verboten* in our Amish community. I figured she never showed affection. Yet they had three children, so who was I to look down on them? She and my brother had a happy marriage, while I was doomed to be single the rest of my life.

My task was swiftly accomplished with both of us working at it. After we had placed my belongings in the case, I sat on the lid while Marta fastened the metal latches with gusto.

"There. Now you're all packed." She grabbed hold of the han-dle and lugged the suitcase down the stairs. Following her into the kitchen, I scanned the only home I'd ever known. I recalled an abun-dance of fond memories of sitting at the kitchen table with my par-ents and siblings, of helping *Mamm* wash the dishes after meals. I hadn't wanted to live here forever, but I felt the weight of defeat. I'd expected to be married by now with children of my own.

"Darling daughter, ya don't have to leave us." *Dat* stepped toward me from the utility room. "We could move you into the sewing room." My father and I had always shared a special bond.

I wouldn't mention how difficult living with my sister-in-law would be if she kept reminding me of my past. Yet I had no right to complain after the embarrassment I'd caused the family by pining away for Jake Miller these many years. Not to mention the rumors about my birthing a child out of wedlock in Ohio. Even though innocent, at times I'd been tempted to confess my guilt before the whole congregation just to put an end to the whispers.

"I'd better follow through as planned, *Dat*. I don't want to be labeled a quitter before I even start." Besides not wanting to live with Marta, I couldn't imagine myself in the cramped room housing the treadle sewing machine and piles and piles of fabric. I'd amassed most of it while working at the fabric store in Intercourse. "You know it's full of material. Though that's my own fault for not resisting sales plus my employee discount at Zook's. I'd assumed someday I'd need all of that fabric to sew clothes for my own family."

He stared at the oval rug on the floor at his feet. "Did you have to quit that job for some reason? Your boss was *Englisch*, but he's a fine man."

"I loved that job, but only women shop there. I'm hoping to meet someone. Someday."

Dat winked. "*Yah*, I suppose not many single men come in for quilting fabric. But you could go to singings."

"At age twenty-nine, I'd be the oldest girl there." And not yet baptized.

"If only you hadn't gotten mixed up with that miscreant Jake Miller."

My jaw clenched at the sound of his name. "That's ancient history. And he didn't do it."

"How do ya know for sure? Were you there?" He wagged his calloused finger. "Few acts are worse than burning down a farmer's barn."

"But I'm sure Jake is innocent."

"Because he told you so? If he's so upstanding, where is he now?"

"I have no idea."

"Maybe it's for the best."

"*Yah*." I might go looking for him if I knew where he was. A scandalous mistake.

Half an hour later, while *Dat* hitched up our mare, *Mamm* left the *daadi haus* and moved to my side. She took my hand.

"I noticed you left your hope chest, Evie. Does this mean you've given up on finding a husband?"

"*Mamm*..." I couldn't bear to have this conversation again.

She must have sensed my discomfort. "No matter. We'll keep it here."

With *Mamm* on my heels, I dragged my bulky suitcase down the back porch stairs. *Dat* had already loaded the buggy with several cardboard boxes filled with a cornucopia of items I might need: a pot, a pan, mismatched plates, and a coffee mug I'd picked up at rummage sales, and my boots. He lifted my suitcase and wedged it in. *Mamm* placed a wicker basket of food items on the front seat. I noticed a tear at the corner of her eye and guessed her sadness stemmed from the fact that she'd missed the opportunity to see me wed. She'd dreamed of hosting a big wedding in our home as was customary. Her guest list and menu had been planned for years, including planting copious amounts of celery. I'd let her and the whole family down.

"Wait!" Marta charged down the back stairs carrying my quilt. "Ya forgot this." She shoved it in the back.

Moments later, *Dat* steered the buggy out of the barnyard. The mare transported us past familiar farms, outbuildings, and fields dotted with baby corn bursting through the spring soil. I spotted an Amish woman collecting her laundry, the rainbow of garments sorted by size and colors. Her youngsters danced around her, playing keep-away with clothespins. The woman looked about my age. I felt like an over-the-hill has-been.

My throat tightened with envy. I recalled something else the minister said about overcoming this emotion—it did nothing except to embitter a person and anger the Lord.

An hour later, I spied the "Yoder's Nursery" sign inscribed in tall letters from way down the road. I'd driven by the plant nursery many times, but I had never entered it because my parents insisted we shop locally at an uncle's small establishment. As we drove past the barn just this side of Yoder's that my Jake had been accused of burning, I couldn't bear to look at it even though it had been promptly rebuilt. I was thankful *Dat* made no further mention of the scandalous incident that still haunted me. It was the beginning of the end of my world.

As we neared the nursery's front driveway, I sat forward and gawked out the window. *Dat* piloted the buggy onto the gravel parking lot large enough to accommodate fifty or more automobiles, although only a half dozen were present today. Several horse and buggies were stationed at a railing. I canvassed a retail shop's exterior—a smallish structure made of gray stone—and four large-scale greenhouses. Behind them were acres of deciduous and evergreen trees planted in neat rows.

My stomach clenched. I felt like a child might on her first day of school in a different district where she knew no one.

Dat slowed us to a halt. "Look at all those fine Amish men working here." He stroked his graying beard. "Most are single."

"*Yah*, I see they're clean shaven. But they are too young for me."

"You look youthful for your age, Evie."

"*Denki*, but you know age is not my only problem."

"I thought that whole misunderstanding was cleared up. If either the deacon or bishop had thought you were guilty of any indiscretion, he would have stopped by to speak to us years ago." He patted my knee. "Your *mamm* and I prayed for you many a time that you wouldn't run off and do something foolish."

"*Yah*, I know, but—"

"Now, now. Most everyone in the county has forgotten all about the incident."

"I wish that were true, *Dat*, but just last month in the fabric store I noticed two women staring and whispering about me."

"Is it possible you overreacted? Were they one of us or *Englisch* tourists?"

"Probably tourists, but—"

"There's your answer. Are you not used to *Englischers* gawking at you by now?"

"*Denki, Dat.*" My father was the kindest man on earth.

"The Lord abhors a malicious gossip." He jiggled the reins and steered the mare away from the greenhouses and toward the far end of the parking lot. A three-story white house with black shutters framing the windows grabbed my attention. Even under the gray-ish sky, the structure's brightness made me stare. Next to the house, a colossal maple tree spread mammoth limbs baring unfurling leaves.

"Is that the owner's house?"

"Sure is. He did a fine job fixing up that old place. It was dilapidated when he purchased it."

"*Yah*, it's a beautiful home now. But where will I live?"

"Hold on. The cottage is around back." He clucked to the mare, and she rolled us forward, skirting the house. *Dat* seemed to know where he was going.

"Have you been here before?"

He fingered the reins. "A few years ago I stopped and looked around."

A fair distance from the house stood a sturdy cream-colored structure with a forest-green door. A rocking chair rested on its narrow porch. In a couple of windows, green shades were rolled partway down.

Dat hauled back on the reins and jumped out of the buggy. He tied the mare to a hitching post, mounted the three stairs, and strode over to the front door.

I sat, paralyzed. I couldn't recall ever being so anxious.

"Evie, ya look like you saw a ghost. You okay?"

"Guess I'm a little *naerfich*." To put it mildly.

"No need to be nervous." He turned the knob and swung the door open. "Guess they don't keep it locked."

I climbed out, landing hard. The earth beneath my feet seemed to undulate, but I steadied myself as I grabbed the handle of the wicker basket.

I clambered up the wooden steps. "Maybe you'd better go in first."

I motioned to *Dat*. "What if the previous occupant's still there?" Or a rat? I liked to think of myself as fearless, but I felt barely strong enough to carry the basket.

Dat chuckled as he stepped inside. "Come on, *dochder*. It's nice in here."

I peeked around him to see a tidy room with a single bed against the far wall and a recliner near the fireplace. I could tell a woman or two had spent hours cleaning this cottage. The white porcelain sink under the window and the counters were spotless. On either side of the counters stood a gas stove and a propane gas refrigerator. And there was a bathroom—a white-tiled cubicle with a shower, a sink, and a mirror above it.

The walls were painted buttermilk white, and the varnished solid wood kitchen cabinets, trim, and bathroom door were honey colored. The beige linoleum floor begged for some colorful throw rugs, but all in good time. If I stayed here.

Dat hauled my suitcase inside, and then he brought in the rest of my things. I strolled over to the bed and pulled back the blanket to see clean white sheets. "My quilt will fit perfectly here."

"You're all set." He kissed my cheek. "I'd best be getting back to see how your *bruder* and his family are doing, not to mention helping your mother get settled in the *daadi haus*."

"You're leaving already?" I had a panicky feeling in the back of my throat. "If only Olivia still worked here."

"Your cousin will no doubt come visit."

"Wait. Did she tell you whom I was to speak to?" My voice came out with a quiver, sounding timid.

"Glenn Yoder. He's a fine man, even if he broke his parents' hearts by not joining the Amish church. He married an *Englisch* woman older than you are. She gave birth to their first child several months ago."

"Really?" Maybe there was still hope for me.

Two

As I listened to *Dat*'s buggy roll away, I second-guessed my decision to move here. If I hurried, I could catch up with him and return home.

Hold on. That was downright silly, immature thinking. I was a grown woman and needed to take care of myself.

First things first. I stowed *Mamm*'s food in the pint-sized refrigerator. I'd never seen an empty one before, and so clean inside too. Our refrigerator at home was always jam-packed with meats, cheeses, and yummy leftovers. Well, I doubted I'd starve working near a café, which apparently stood behind the greenhouses. I supposed it depended on what they served. I knew Olivia's baked goods would be available if employees were allowed to eat meals there. Still, after laboring in the soil all day, they might not be welcome to dine with the café's patrons.

I unclasped and opened the suitcase, and then I spread an armload of clothes across the bed. A tall bureau stood ready and welcoming. Above it hung an oval wood-framed mirror with a bedraggled old woman gawking in it.

Ach, my heart-shaped *kapp* had collapsed like a failed soufflé. Clumps of my sandy hair straggled out from under it. I untied my *kapp*'s strings and then decided I would fix my hair later. My wrinkled beige dress and black apron did nothing to improve my appearance. Fortunately, no one would see me for the rest of the day.

I knelt down and pulled out the bottom drawer. I was pleased to see plenty of room for my socks, which I placed inside. On my knees, I arranged them neatly. I imagined moving into my future husband's home someday. Always his face looked like blond and handsome Zach's, my first love. Silly musings. I was determined to replace his face with another man's. Soon, I hoped.

Without warning, the door blew open. I let out a surprised yelp.

"Sorry I startled you." A tall man dressed in jeans and a yellow collared work shirt stepped into the room carrying an LED lamp. Not Amish, judging by his clothing and *Englisch* haircut. "Are you the new employee?"

I got to my feet and put out my hand to shake his. "Yes. Hello, I'm Eva Lapp." I scanned the bed and felt heat flushing my face when I saw my nightgown draped across it. I swiftly bundled it up and stuffed it in another bureau drawer.

"That's odd." He tilted his head. "We weren't expecting you for a couple days."

"I'm sorry. I should have called ahead of time to warn you I was coming early." I'd spare him the details of my humiliating mad dash to get packed and leave home.

"No matter. I'm Stephen Troyer. I'm in charge of the nursery while the boss is out of town for the week. I just stopped by to make sure everything is okay." He set the lantern on the small table next to the recliner. "We're happy to have you, Eva. The café has been practically running on its own for a few days, ever since Olivia left."

"Café? I thought I'd be working in the nursery with plants. And perhaps maintaining a vegetable garden." Gardening was my passion.

"No, we have plenty of staff in the nursery. Although the little herb garden might need some tending now that Edna's gone. She's the Amish woman who used to live here, and she was my boss's housekeeper for many years. But she had a stroke, and her family moved her to Indiana to live with one of her nieces.

My mind spun with the impossibility of the situation. "But…I know nothing of running a restaurant." Or even cooking.

The corners of his mouth dragged down. "Can you manage a cash register and credit cards?"

"*Yah*. I did that at a fabric store, my last place of employment."

"And can you brew a decent pot of coffee?"

"I'm used to making it for large crowds after church service and such. Nobody has ever complained."

"Anything will taste better than the coffee made by the two girls we have now." He raked a hand through his nutmeg-brown hair. "Olivia said you could accomplish anything if we give you the directions. We were so relieved when she suggested you and said you needed a place to live."

"I'm afraid my cousin might have stretched the truth a little." I scanned the cottage and reminded myself she was doing me a favor. "I don't possess half of Olivia's culinary skills. Only what I've done at home. I always favored the garden and helping *Dat* with the milking when he needed me."

"No cows to be milked around here. But we do have chickens and fresh eggs you're welcome to gather and eat for breakfast." He stood before me, his chocolate-brown eyes probing mine. "Look, Eva, should I find someone else for the job?"

I canvassed my cozy new abode again. "*Nee*. I'm sure I can learn what's needed."

"We hope to get busy. The goal is to have the café cover its overhead and make a profit. My boss was determined to build the place. It was his dream and design, so there you go. The nursery is a bustling place spring through autumn. In winter, we sell Christmas trees. So we plan to have the café open all year."

"I'm used to waiting on impatient customers. *Ach*, we would get buried at the fabric store during a sale. And I'm here now." It must be God's will, wasn't it?

"Come on. Let me walk you over there right now before you

settle in." I understood him to mean, *Before you make yourself at home in case I have to kick you out in favor of someone else more suitable for the job.*

He glanced down at me. "I feel as if I know you, Eva. Have we met before? Wait. Didn't you used to date my old friend Jake Miller?"

I cringed. "Many years ago."

"I heard he still lives up in New York." Again, he gave me an inquisitive look, waiting for my response.

"So I've heard." Jake had sent me only two letters—both without a return address—and left one voice message on the phone shanty recorder during the first year…unless *Mamm* had intercepted others and erased them. And tossed further letters in the trash. No, she wouldn't do that—would she?

"The last I heard, Jake was working for a construction company." Stephen's tone was somber.

"Is he…is he married?"

"I don't know. Possibly, after all this time."

I expelled an audible sigh and felt my shoulders droop. Well, of course he'd be married by now and probably had several children.

"You know about that barn fire?" Stephen's mouth grew hard.

"*Yah*, I'll never forget as long as I live. Praise the Lord no people were killed. Still, I felt sorry for the calves." I snuck a peek into his solemn face. "Still an unsolved mystery?"

"Yes, but this I do know. Jake wasn't guilty. He was with me that night, not that he was following the *Ordnung*. I was and still am Mennonite, and not under the same restrictions. But I was acting like a knucklehead."

"I've always wondered why Jake didn't defend himself." Finally, I might get a straight answer to the questions that had plagued me.

"Well, like I said, he was running around, as you call it, and we were both up to no good. On a lamebrain lark, Jake bought a wreck of a Toyota sedan and hid it from his folks. You know, he was in *rumspringa* and young and thought he was invincible. Fact is, he and I and some buddies were in that old ramshackle barn that very evening, drinking beer, playing cards, and joking around, but nothing more. We were using a battery-power lantern and knew better than to smoke in there. When we left the barn, it was standing. None of us would've been foolish enough to do anything to start a fire. We knew the value of barns. Someone must have seen the car and reported it."

"Why didn't you tell all of that to the police?" Better question would have been why hadn't Jake defended himself?

"The barn's owner was Amish and didn't press charges. Our heads hanging low, we all helped rebuild that barn better than new. Tongues were wagging the whole time, but no one came out and accused us."

I fiddled with my *kapp* strings. "But still, you could have spoken up. You both should've come out and confessed to being in the barn."

"You're right, but that would have meant telling everyone Jake owned a car. He sold that ill-fated Toyota a week later. I still feel as if it were my fault. I was a year older and should have set a better example for him."

Stephen must have seen an expression of worry in my face. "Soon after that, Jake went away for the summer up to New York and has only returned a couple times that I know of."

"And you never hear from him?" What was I doing speaking of a subject so personal with a stranger? Yet for years I'd ached to have this conversation with someone who'd known Jake. It was as if a gravitational pull still drew me to him.

"A couple of calls to my cell phone." Stephen shifted his weight. "He asked about you."

I held my breath and waited for him to continue.

"Jake said he'd heard you had a new boyfriend out of state."

"Did you tell him that I didn't?" My mouth was so dry I could barely get the words out.

"I'm sorry, Eva, but I had no way of knowing that. I'd heard you were seeing someone in Ohio."

"None of those stories were true." I shuddered to think of what Jake and Stephen had heard. Rumors that I'd run off to Ohio to give birth to another man's child out of wedlock had swirled like a flock of starlings throughout the county. But I was there taking care of premature newborn twins for a cousin.

Scratching his chin, Stephen appeared uncomfortable. "Shall I show you the café now?"

"*Yah*, sure."

He moved toward the door just as an Amish woman carrying towels glided onto the porch. I had a multitude of questions I still wanted to ask Stephen, but our conversation would have to wait.

"Oh." Her eyes widened. I was glad the door was open. The last thing I needed was to be seen as loose, something I wasn't and never had been. But shaking a bad reputation was like pulling your foot out of a wasp's nest without getting stung.

"Eva, this is Susie."

"Nice ta meetcha," we said in unison. Then we chuckled.

Susie seemed around seventeen. Maybe younger. "I brought you some clean towels."

"*Denki*. I wasn't expecting to be waited on, but I'm delighted. In my haste I neglected to bring towels and a washcloth."

"Edna left them, so they're nice and soft." Susie stepped into the bathroom and spoke to us through the open door. "I have to do several loads of laundry every day anyway, so it's no trouble, really." She hung the pink towels on a rack.

"Thank you very much."

"My brother Mark works here too."

"He's quite popular with the young ladies," Stephen said, a corner of his mouth lifting.

"*Yah*, he is." Susie sent me a grin.

"But no time to chitchat right now," Stephen informed her in a no-nonsense manner, as if he wanted her to get back to work. "We're off to the café."

I followed Stephen down the steps. A black cat streaked across our path. I increased my speed to keep up with his long legs. We strode by the main house and then the enormous glass greenhouses, which I was dying to explore.

We passed several young, clean-shaven Amish men wearing straw hats on the slate walkway who spoke to Stephen, asking questions and listening to his instructions. I was surprised to hear him speaking to them in fluent Pennsylvania Dutch.

One of the young men tipped his hat at me and sent me a goofy grin that seemed flirtatious. But he was too young for me.

About the Author

Kate Lloyd is a novelist, a mother of two sons, and a passionate observer of human relationships. A native of Baltimore, she often spends time with family and friends in Lancaster County, Pennsylvania, the inspiration for her bestselling books in the Legacy of Lancaster Trilogy. She has Mennonite relatives in Lancaster County and is a member of the Lancaster County Mennonite Historical Society. Kate and her husband live in the Pacific Northwest.

Kate loves connecting with her readers. Please feel free to visit her at:

Website: www.katelloyd.com

Facebook: https://www.facebook.com/katelloydbooks

Twitter: @KateLloydAuthor,
https://twitter.com/KateLloydAuthor

Pinterest: Kate Lloyd,
https://www.pinterest.com/katelloydauthor

To learn more about Harvest House books and
to read sample chapters, log on to our website:

www.harvesthousepublishers.com

HARVEST HOUSE PUBLISHERS
EUGENE, OREGON